Also by Alejo Carpentier

REASONS OF STATE

REASONS OF STATE

Alejo Carpentier

Translated from the Spanish by Frances Partridge

ALFRED A. KNOPF   *New York · 1976*

THIS IS A BORZOI BOOK
PUBLISHED BY ALFRED A. KNOPF, INC.

English translation copyright © 1976 by Victor Gollancz Ltd.
All rights reserved under International and Pan-American Copyright Conventions.
Published in the United States by Alfred A. Knopf, Inc., New York.
Distributed by Random House, Inc., New York.
Originally published in Mexico, Spain, and Argentina as *El Recurso del Método*
by Siglo Veintiuno Editores, S.A., Mexico City, Madrid, and Buenos Aires.
Copyright © 1974 by Siglo XXI Editores, S.A.,
© 1974 by Siglo XXI Argentina Editores, S.A.

Library of Congress Catalog Card Number: 75-36816
ISBN: 0-394-49909-3

Manufactured in the United States of America

First American Edition

To Lilia

REASONS OF STATE

ONE

*. . . it is not my design to teach the method that
everyone must follow in order to use his reason
properly, but only to show the way in which I have
tried to use my own.*

DESCARTES. *Discourse on Method*

1

. . . But I've only just gone to bed. And the alarm has gone off already. Half past six. It's impossible. Quarter past seven, perhaps. More likely. Quarter past eight. This alarm clock would be a marvel of Swiss watchmaking, but its hands are so slim that one can hardly see them. Quarter past nine. That's not right, either. My spectacles. Quarter past ten. That's it. Besides, daylight is already shining through the yellow curtains with morning brilliance. And it's always the same when I come back to this house: I open my eyes with the feeling of being *there*, because this same hammock accompanies me everywhere—house, hotel, English castle, our Palace—because I've never been able to sleep in a rigid bed with a mattress and bolster. I have to curl up inside a rocking hammock, to be cradled in its corded network. Another swing and a yawn, and with another swing I get my legs out and hunt about with my feet for my slippers which I have lost in the pattern of the Persian carpet. (*There*, always thoughtful for my moments of waking, the Mayorala Elmira, my housekeeper, would already have put on my shoes for me; she must be asleep in her camp-bed—she has her fads too—with her breasts uncovered and petticoats over her thighs, in the darkness of the other hemisphere.)

A few steps towards the light. Pull the cord on the right, and with a rattle of curtain-rings above, the scenario of the window is revealed. But instead of a volcano—the snow-covered majestic, remote, ancient Home of the Gods—in front of me stands the Arc de Triomphe, and behind it the house of my great friend Limantour, who was Don Porfirio's minister, and with whom I have such profitable talks about economics and our problems. A slight sound at the door. And in comes Sylvestre in his striped jacket, carrying aloft the silver tray—thick, beautiful silver from my mines: "*Le café de Monsieur. Bien fort comme il l'aime. A la façon de là-bas . . . Monsieur a bien dormi?*"

The three brocade curtains have been pulled back, one after the other, showing a fine sunny day for the races, and Rude's sculptures. The boy-hero with his little balls exposed to view, being carried off to war by a tough, dishevelled chieftain, one of those—make no mistake—who utters yells of victory but will hurry from the van to the rear if things turn out badly. Now *Le Journal*. The *Excelsior*, with so many photos in its pages that it's practically a cinema of real life. *L'Action Française* with Pampille's gastronomic recipes, which my daughter outlines in red pencil every day for the attention of our excellent cook, and Léon Daudet's abusive editorial, whose inspired and apocalyptic insults—supreme expression of the liberty of the press—could promote duels, kidnapping, assassinations and shooting daily in our countries. *Le Petit Parisien*: the rebellion in Ulster is still going on, with its concerto for machine-guns and Irish harps; universal indignation has been aroused by the second round-up of dogs from Constantinople, condemned to eat one another on a desert island; more rioting in the Balkans, that eternal wasps' nest and powder-magazine, but very like our provinces in the Andes. I still remember—on my last journey—the ceremonious reception of the King of Bulgaria. He came on a visit here with President Fallières, exhibiting his plumed and braided majesty (for a moment he looked to me like Colonel Hoffmann) in a superb state-coach, while the band of the Republican Guard, stationed at the foot of Napoleon's monument, played *Platcha Divitza*, *Chuma Maritza*, with a profusion of trumpets, clarinets and tubas, enhanced by a zarzuela-like combination of flute and triangle. *"Vive le Roi! Vive le Roi!"* shouted the republican crowd, pining at heart for thrones, crowns, sceptres and maces, very inadequately replaced as a spectacle by presidents in frock-coats with red ribbons across their waistcoats, who moved their top-hats from head to knee in a gesture of salutation very like that of blind men asking for alms after trying to extract the sing-song tune of *La jambe en bois* from the black depths of an ocarina. Twenty to eleven.

Happiness due to an empty agenda-tray, on the night-table beside the hammock, instead of a whole time-table of interviews, official visits, presentation of credentials, or ostentatious entry of soldiers, suddenly bursting in on one without warning, to the rhythm of boots and spurs. But I've slept longer than usual and that's because last night, yes, last night—and very late—I fucked a nun of Saint Vincent de Paul, dressed in indigo blue, with a starched, winged headdress, a scapular between her tits and a whip made of Russian leather at her belt. The cell was perfect, with its cardboard missal made to look like calf, lying on the rough wooden table beside the plated candlestick and the too-grey skull—the truth is I never touched it—which was probably made of wax or perhaps rubber. The bed, however, in spite of its conventual and penitentiary appearance, was extremely comfortable, with its pillows of false serge (down-filled slips looking as if made of austere sackcloth) and that bedstead whose elastic springs collaborated so obligingly with the movements of the elbows and knees working away on them. The bed was as comfortable as the divan in the caliph's room or the velvet seat of the Wagons-Lits-Cook sleeping-compartment (Paris-Lyon-Méditerranée) eternally at a standstill, with two wheels and a little ladder leading up to it, in a passage that always smelled— I don't know by means of what ingenious device—of the breath of locomotives. I didn't have time to try all the possible combinations of cushions and mats in the Japanese House; nor the cabin on the *Titanic*, realistically reconstructed from documents, and seeming as if branded with the imminence of the drama. (*Vas-y vite, mon chéri, avant que n'arrive l'ice-berg . . . Le voilà . . . Le voilà . . . Vite, mon chéri . . . C'est le naufrage . . . Nous*

coulons. Nous coulons . . . Vas-y. . . .) The rustic attic of a Norman
farm, smelling of apples, with bottles of cider within reach; and
the Bridal Suite, where Gaby, dressed in white and crowned
with orange-blossom, was deflowered four or five times a night
if she wasn't on day-shift—"on duty" it was called—because
one or two friends of the house, in spite of their grey hairs and
the Legion of Honour, still enjoyed from time to time the glory
of Victor Hugo's triumphant awakenings. As for the Palace of
Mirrors, it had so often subjected my image to lengthenings and
foreshortenings, distortions and grimaces, that all my physical
proportions were imprinted on my memory, just as an album
of family photographs catalogues the gestures, attitudes and
clothes of the best days of one's life. I understood very well why
King Edward VII had kept a private bath for himself there,
and even an armchair—today a historic object, put in a place
of honour—made by a skilful and discreet cabinetmaker, so
that it allowed him to submit to delicate caresses which might
be hindered by his capacious abdomen. Last night's spree had
been very good fun. However—because of the amount I'd
drunk—I was left with a sort of fear lest my sacrilegious
amusements with the little Sister of Saint Vincent de Paul
(another time, Paulette had presented herself to me as an
English schoolgirl, armed with tennis-rackets and riding-whips;
yet another time, very much made up like a sailor's whore, in
black stockings, red garters and high leather boots) might have
brought me bad luck. (Besides, that skull, now I came to think
about it, was pretty sinister, whether it was made of rubber or
wax . . .) The Divine Shepherdess of Nueva Córdoba, Miraculous Protectress of my own country, might have known of my
deviations from the mountain fastness where her ancient
sanctuary stood, between crags and quarries. But I calmed
myself by reflecting that they hadn't gone so far in their zeal
for authenticity as to provide a crucifix in the false convent of
my guilty adventure. The truth was that Madame Yvonne,
dressed in black with a string of pearls, exquisite manners and
a way of speaking which passed from Port Royal to the argot
of Bruant, according to circumstances and the condition of the
client—much like my French which was part Montesquieu,

part *Nini-peau-de-chien*—understood each person's whims perfectly, and yet always knew exactly where to stop. There was no portrait of Queen Victoria in the Room of the English Schoolboy, any more than there was an icon in the Room of the Great Boyar, nor a too-ostentatious Priapus in the Room of the Pompeian Fantasies. And when certain clients visited her she took care that *"ces dames"* should take up their position, as actors say: that they should concentrate on interpreting their parts—whether that of impatient girl-friend, satanic nun, provincial girl full of perverse curiosity, aristocrat concealing her identity, grand lady come down in the world, foreigner-passing-through-and-avid-for-new-sensations, etc., etc.; in short that they should behave like well-trained actresses, and they were forbidden to snatch coins off the corner of the table with their sexual labia, as other girls of a very different style did in the Salon of Performances down below—*"au choix, Mesdames"*—wearing nothing at all exept a bolero made of Spanish sequins, a Tahitian necklace, or the hint of a Scottish kilt with a fox's tail in the belt-buckle.

Now Sylvestre brings in the barber. While he shaves me he tells me news of the latest exploits of the apaches, who are now using motor-cars and guns. Just as he is powdering my cheeks he shows me a recent photograph of his son, looking very martial—as I tell him—with cassowary plumes in his shako. I praise the organization and discipline of a nation where a young man of modest origins can by his own virtue and industry rise to the same military rank as soldiers who, before they ever fire a gun, have to know by calculus and logarithms what will be the trajectory and distance of a shell. (My artillery, for the most part, decide on the sighting and angle of a gun by the empirical method—although marvellously effective in a few cases, one must admit—of: "Three hands up and two to the right, with a finger and a half of rectification, towards that house with the red roof. . . . Fire!" And the best of it is that they hit the target.) From beneath the portrait of the cadet from Saint-Cyr the barber brings out a recent photo of a young woman swathed in transparent veils, who is so tremendously excited by the interest at 6·4 per cent on the new Russian Loan, that it seems she would be ready—very discreetly of course—to acquire shares and so restore a fortune once supported by escutcheons covered in gules and ermine, which was now on the point of shipwreck; this young woman—and it was easy to see that her "know-how", as they say, was not to be sneezed at—in short, this young woman . . . (I must first send for Peralta to have a look at me, palpate me, and say . . .)

Through the window-panes summer announces its presence, as if new, just arrived, in the splendid foliage of the chestnut-trees. Now the tailor comes and measures and re-measures me, covering me with segments of sports coats, jackets, frock-coats, adjusting, tightening, joining together, drawing theoretical figures in white chalk on pieces of a dark woollen garment. I turn around, like a mannequin, stopping at angles where my figure appears in a favourable light. And according to the orientation thus imposed on my eyes, I look at the pictures or sculptures surrounding me, which seem to be reborn as I turn, since I've seen them so often that I hardly ever look at them now. Here, as always, is Jean-Paul Laurens' Saint Radegonde, Merovingian and ecstatic, receiving the relic brought from Jerusalem, a piece of the Cross of Our Lord, and offered her in a beautiful marble casket by hooded emissaries. Over there, a spirited sculpture of some gladiators by Gérome, with the retiarius defeated, tangled in his own net, and twisting his body under the victorious foot of a he-man in a helmet and mask, who seems to be awaiting Caesar's verdict, with his sword ready. ("*Macte*" I always say when I look at this work, turning down my right thumb . . .) A quarter turn on my own axis, and I am looking at Elstir's fine seascape, exposing its restless blues between a confusion of foam and clouds, with sailing-boats in the foreground, not far from the pink marble of a *Little Faun*, winner of the Gold Medal in the latest Salon of French artists.

"A little more to the right," says the tailor. And now it is the voluptuous nudity of a *Sleeping Nymph* by Gervex.

"Now the sleeve," says the tailor. And here I am in front of Luc-Olivier Merson's *Wolf of Gubbio*, in which the wild beast is tamed by Poverello's ineffable preaching, has become holy and good, and is playing with some mischievous children who are

pulling its ears. A quarter turn more and it's Dumont's *Cardinals
at Supper* (and what expressions of enjoyment they all have,
and how lifelike! You can even see the veins on the forehead of
that one on the left!), next to which is *The Little Chimney-Sweep*
by Chocarne-Moreau and Béraud's *Fashionable Reception*, where
the red background marvellously sets off the pale low-necked
dresses of the women amongst black tail-coats, green palms and
glittering glass.

And now, almost facing the light, my eyes rest on the *View of
Nueva Córdoba*, a work by one of our own painters, obviously
influenced by some Toledan landscape by Ignacio Zuloaga—
the same orange-yellows, the houses similarly terraced, with the
Puente del Mapuche transformed into the Puente de Alcántara.
And now I am facing the window, and the tailor is telling me
about some of his clients whose names add to his professional
prestige—just as happens in England when a biscuit or jam
manufacturer labels his goods "By appointment to His
Majesty". Thus he informed me that Gabriele D'Annunzio,
who was extravagant and grand in his ideas but always absent-
minded and slow about paying, ordered twelve fancy waistcoats
and other garments to the details of which I hardly listened,
because the mere name of Gabriele D'Annunzio immediately
called up to my mind that mysterious paved and aristocratic
courtyard, hidden behind the façade of a wretched-looking
house in the Rue Geoffroy L'Asnier, where, at the end of a
passage smelling of leek soup, there appeared like some incredible opera set the pavilion with its classical façade, masks
and grilles, in which I had more than once had the honour to
dine alone with the great poet. That luxurious yet secret hiding-
place had its own legends and mythology; it was said that when
Gabriele was alone he was served by beautiful waitresses with
fantastic names, and while his numerous creditors were kept at
bay by a concierge hardened in such duties, inside that mansion
filled with alabasters and ancient marbles, mediaeval parchments and chasubles, amongst steaming censers, the fresh
voices of a choir of child acolytes, alternating antiphonally with
plainsong, could be heard through curtains concealing the
naked bodies of women, a lot of women—and some of them

great, famous and aristocratic—who were submitting to the mood of the Archangel of the Annunciation. ("I don't know what they see in him," Peralta used to say: "he's ugly, bald and squat." "Go and see," I said, reflecting that, for the great man in question, it was probably a good deal more interesting than frequenting the de Chabanais brothel, however haunted that might be by the shade of Edward VII.)

And at this very moment in came Peralta himself, carrying a pile of books on top of which was a yellow copy of *L'enfant de volupté*—the French version of *Il piacere*—wherein my secretary had certainly not found, to his disappointment, the ribaldries promised by the title.

"They were in my room, half read." And he puts them down on the library table, while the tailor carries off his materials, after stripping me of expensive coatings, shapeless evening dress, and trousers badly cut in the fork.

"Give me a drink." Doctor Peralta opens my little boule writing-desk and takes out a bottle of Santa Inés rum, with its label of gothic letters on a canefield.

"This is a life-saver."

"Especially after last night."

"You seemed to have taken a shine to nuns."

"And you to negresses."

"You know, my friend, I'm an incendiary."

"All of us from *over there* are incendiaries," I said laughing, but just then Ofelia, hearing I was awake, began playing *Für Elise* upstairs.

"She gets better every day," said my secretary, with his glass in mid-air.

"Such smoothness and feeling . . ."

Today *Für Elise*, coming so sweetly from my daughter's rooms, although she always made a mistake in the same bar, reminded me of how it had always been played by Doña Hermenegilda, her unselfish and devoted mother—who always made the same mistake in the same bar—and how, *over there,* in those days at Surgidero de la Verónica—days of youthful hopes and torment, sturm und drang, escapades and brawls— after treating me to some waltz by Juventino Rosas or Lerdo de

Tejada, she would move on to her classical repertory by the Deaf Master (*Für Elise*, and the beginning—she never got past the beginning—of the *Moonlight Sonata*), Theodore Lack's *Idilio* and various pieces by Godard and Chaminade included in the album called *Music for the Home*. I sighed to think that it was now three years ago that we had given her a queen's funeral, with her urn under a canopy, and a procession of ministers, generals, ambassadors and grandees, with a military band reinforced by three others brought from the provinces—a hundred and forty performers in all—playing the Funeral March from the *Eroica* Symphony, and—inevitably—Chopin's. Our archbishop had delivered a funeral oration (considerably inspired, at my suggestion, by what Bossuet said in memory of Henriette de France: "She who reigns in heaven...", etc., etc.), adding that the merits of the dead woman were so exceptional and outstanding that her canonization could well be contemplated. Doña Hermenegilda was married and the mother of children, of course—Ofelia, Ariel, Marcus Antonius and Radames—but the Archbishop reminded his listeners of the blessed conjugal virtues of Saint Elizabeth, mother of John the Baptist, and of Monica, mother of Augustine. Naturally, the appropriate words having been said, I didn't think it vital to send up any prayers to the high authority of the Vatican, especially since my wife and I had lived in concubinage for many years before the unforeseeable and agitating vagaries of politics led me to where I now am. The important thing was that my Hermenegilda's portrait, made at Dresden in full colour by the initiative of our Minister of Education, was an object of worship throughout the length and breadth of the land. It was said that the flesh of the dead woman had defied the onslaught of worms, and that her face had retained the serene and kindly smile of her last moments. Women used to say that her portrait miraculously cured the colic and the pains of child-birth, and that promises made to her by girls who wanted a husband were more effective than the hitherto common practice of putting the bust of Saint Anthony upside-down in a well.

I have just finished putting a gardenia in my button-hole when Sylvestre announces that the Distinguished Academician has come to see me—a recently-elected academician, nor do I know how he got himself received under the Dome, since a few years ago he decribed the Forty Immortals as "green-clad mummies in cocked hats, the anachronistic midwives of a Dictionary intended to increase our understanding of the evolution of the language—a sort of *Petit Larousse* for domestic use". (Once elected, however—"*J'ai accepté pour m'amuser*"—he took the trouble to have the hilt of his sword designed by his famous friend Maxence, who had abandoned pictorial creation for silversmith's work, and succeeded in incorporating the spirit of the Bible and mediaeval legends with a style combining the aesthetics of the scenic railway at the Magic City with a subtle flavour of Pre-Raphaelitism—too much for my taste.)

Peralta hid the bottle of Santa Inés and we greeted this witty and polished man, who is now sitting in a ray of sunlight, full of ascending motes of dust, which picks out the red ribbon of his Legion of Honour. Upstairs, Ofelia is trying hard to remove those inconvenient flats from the passage of *Für Elise* which she always gets wrong.

"Beethoven," says the Distinguished Academician, pointing upwards as if giving us an important piece of news. Then, with the indiscreet hand of someone who always treats my house as his own, he turns over the books my secretary brought back a little while ago. *Atheism* by Le Dantec. Good. Solid reading. Bourget's *The Disciple*. Not bad, but don't let's imitate the German *emmerdeurs* with their mania for mixing philosophy into their novels. Anatole France: undoubted talent, but over-estimated outside France. Besides, his systematic scepticism doesn't lead anywhere. *Chanticleer*: a strange thing. A success and a failure. Audacity that is both brilliant and unsuccessful but the only attempt of its kind in theatrical history. And he declaims:

O Soleil! toi sans qui les choses
Ne seraient pas ce qu'elles sont . . .

(The Academician is unaware that for some years past ten thousand bars and whorehouses in America have been called *Chanticleer*.) He grunts ironically but acquiescently at the sight of an anticlerical pamphlet by Leo Taxil, but makes a face of disgust, of open disapproval, over *Monsieur de Phocas* by Jean Lorrain, without perhaps knowing that his own publisher, Ollendorf, has swamped the bookshops of our continent with a Spanish translation of this novel, presented as an incomparable example of French genius, with a coloured frontispiece of a naked Astarte by Géo Dupuy, which at least gives our schoolboys dreams. Now he's laughing, slyly, indulgently, as he comes across *Les cent milles verges*, *The sexual life of Robinson Crusoe* and *Les fastes de Lesbos*, by unknown authors (three asterisks), profusely illustrated and bought by me yesterday in a specialist shop in the Rue de la Lune.

"Ce sont des lectures de Monsieur Peralta," I say, coward that I am.

But our friend suddenly becomes serious and starts talking about literature in the deliberate and magisterial way Peralta and I know so well, trying to prove to us that the true, the best, the greatest literature *from here* is unknown in our countries. We all agree in admiring Baudelaire—sadly buried under a sad stone in the cemetery of Montparnasse—but we ought also to read Léon Dierx, Albert Samain, Henri de Régnier, Maurice Rollinat, Renée Vivien. And we must read Moréas, above all Moréas. (I remain silent rather than tell him how, when I was introduced to Moréas some years ago in the Café Vachetti, he accused me of having shot Maximilian, although I tried to prove that on grounds of age alone, it would have been impossible for me to be in the Cerro de las Campanas on that day. *"Vous êtes tous des sauvages!"* the poet had replied with the fire of absinthe in his voice.) Our friend laments the fact that Hugo, old Hugo, still enjoys enormous popularity in our countries. It's known that *over there* workers in cigar factories— who subscribe to public readings to relieve the monotony of their work—are specially fond of *Les Misérables* and *Notre Dame de Paris*, while *Oration pour tous* (*"naïve connerie"* he says) is still often recited at poetical soirées. And, according to him, this is through our lack of the Cartesian spirit (that's true: no carnivorous plants grow, no toucans fly, nor do you find cyclones in *The Discourse on Method*); we are too partial to unbridled eloquence, pathos, platform pomposity, resounding with romantic braggadocio.

Feeling slightly irritated—though he couldn't have guessed the fact—by an evaluation which directly wounded my concept of what oratory should be (to be more effective among us it must be luxuriant, sonorous, baroque, Ciceronian, original in imagery, implacable in epithets, sweeping in its crescendos), I try to change the subject by laying my hand on an extremely rare edition-de-luxe of Renan's *Prayer on the Acropolis*, illustrated by Cabanel.

"Quelle horreur!" exclaims the Distinguished Academician with a gesture of condemnation. I point out to him that this fragment figures in many manuals of literature for students of French.

"An abomination, due to secular education," says our visitor, qualifying the prose as amphigoric—pretentious, vocative, blown-up with erudition and pedantic hellenisms. No. The people of our countries ought to look for the genius of the French language in other books, in other texts. Then they would discover the elegance of style, the distinction, the sovereign intelligence with which in *L'ennemi des lois* Maurice Barrès can show us in three lucid pages the fallacies and errors of Marxism—which are centred in the cult of the stomach—or give us a marvellous picture of Ludwig of Bavaria's castles, in the phraseology of a true artist, very different from the professorial logomachy of a Renan. Or if we want to go back to the past century, let us read and reread Gobineau, that aristocrat of expression, master of the carefully-constructed and unique phrase, who had exalted in his work the Super-Man, the Men of the Pléiade, sovereign spirits (according to him there were about three thousand in all Europe), proclaiming his inability to be interested in "the mass of those who are called men", whom he saw as a swarm of despicable, irresponsible and destructive insects, without Souls.

At this point I decide to remain silent and not join in the discussion, because the question would bring to light an explanation that would be better avoided: during the fiestas for the Centenary of Mexican Independence, the authorities made arrangements for the wearers of sandals and shawls (*rebozos*), native musicians and cripples, to be kept away from the places

where the main ceremonies took place, because it was better
that foreign tourists and guests of the Government shouldn't
see the individuals our friend Yves Limantour called "the
Kaffirs". But in my country, where there are many—too many!
—Indians, negroes, half-breeds and mulattos, it would be
difficult to hide away our "Kaffirs". And I couldn't see the
Kaffirs belonging to our intelligentsia—who are extremely
numerous—being exactly pleased by reading *The Essay on the
Inequality of Human Races* by Count Gobineau. It would be a
good moment to change the conversation.

Luckily, *Für Elise* starts up again upstairs. And the Academician pounces on this fact to deplore the extravagances of
modern music—or what is called "modern"—a cerebral,
dehumanized art, an algebra of notes, alien to any form of
feeling (just listen to the Schola Cantorum group in the Rue
Saint-Jacques) which betrays the eternal principles of *melos*.
There are exceptions, however: Saint-Saëns, Fauré, Vinteuil,
and above all our beloved Reynaldo Hahn—born in Puerto
Cabello, Venezuela, which is not unlike Surgidero de la
Verónica. I know that my *"paisano"* (he always calls me
"paisano" in his smooth creole Spanish, when we meet anywhere), before writing his sublime choruses for Racine's *Esther*,
had begun work many years ago on a very beautiful opera full
of nostalgia for his native tropics, the action taking place in
picturesque surroundings in every way reminiscent of the
Venezuelan coast he knew as a child, although the programme
described it as a "Polynesian idyll": *L'île du rêve*, inspired by
Le mariage de Loti—and *"Loti, Loti, voici ton nom"*, sang Rarahú
in this history of an exotic love affair, whose plot, according to
certain mischievous critics fond of demolishing everything, was
too much like that of *Lakmé*. But, come to that, one could say
the same of *Madame Butterfly*, a later work then Reynaldo's.
And just as in the old days his *Chansons Grises* were heard at one
of the regular musical evenings of the Quai Conti, we used to
talk about people like the Belgian chargé d'affaires, the Comte
d'Argencourt, who surrounded himself with sodomites although
he wasn't one, because he didn't want to expose his too youthful
mistress to the desires of manly men; or about Legrandin, who

had the brilliant idea of endowing himself with the non-existent
title of "Comte de Mes Eglises" or something of the sort—("If
he had been born in Cholula he could have called himself
Count of the 365 churches," broke in Peralta)—and was
beginning to boast of being a snob in a world where snobbishness was taken as a sign of being enthusiastic for the "latest" in
everything.

Paris, so the Distinguished Academician went on to say, was
getting like the Rome of Heliogabalus, opening its doors to
everything strange, out of joint, exotic, barbarous, primitive.
Modern sculptors, instead of being inspired by the great
periods of the past, marvelled at Mycenaean, pre-Hellenic,
Scythian art, the art of the steppes. There were people these
days who collected horrible African masks, figures bristling
with votive nails, zoomorphic idols—the work of cannibals.
Negro musicians were arriving from the United States. A
scandalous Italian poet had gone so far as to publish a manifesto
declaring that it was necessary to destroy Venice and burn
down the Louvre. That way could only lead us to exalting
Attila, Erostratus, the Iconoclasts, the cake-walk, English
cooking, anarchist outrages, and the reign of new Circes
calling themselves Lyane de Pougy, Emilienne d'Alençon or
Cleo de Mérode.

("I'd willingly be transformed into a swine for them,"
murmured Peralta.)

But now, to cheer up our visitor, I said that every big city
suffered from temporary fevers, foolish enthusiasms, fashions,
affectations and extravagances, which lasted only one day and
made no impact on the genius of a nation. Juvenal was already
complaining of the habits of dress, perfumes, cults and superstitions of a Roman society fascinated by everything that came
from outside. Snobbishness was nothing new. After all, Molière's
Précieuses were merely snobs *"avant la lettre"*. You either have
a great capital or you don't have a great capital. And in spite
of so many novelties, Paris was still the Holy of Holies of good
taste, moderation, order and proportion, and dictated the rules
of polite behaviour, elegance and savoir vivre to the whole
world. And, as for cosmopolitanism, which was also a feature

of Athens, it in no way harmed the authentic French genius. *"Ce qui n'est pas clair n'est pas français,"* I say, proud of still being able to quote a certain Rivarol whom the Marist Brothers of Surgidero de la Verónica made me read in my schooldays.

"Certainly," agreed the Academician: but our politics, our abject politics, with its rioting, and conflict between parties and fierce parliamentary battles, was introducing confusion and disorder into this essentially rational country. The Panama scandal or the Dreyfus Affair would have been inconceivable in the time of Louis XIV. Not to mention the "socialist mire" which, as our friend Gabriele D'Annunzio said, "is invading everything", befouling all that was beautiful and pleasant in our ancient civilizations. Socialism (he sighed, looking at the toes of his patent-leather shoes). Forty kings had made France great. Look at England. Look at the Scandinavian countries, models of order and progress, where stevedores wear waistcoats at work and every bricklayer has a watch and chain under his overall. Brazil was great when it had an Emperor, like Pedro II, who was the friend, fellow-diner and admirer of that same Victor Hugo you all think so well of. Mexico was great when it had Porfirio Díaz as its almost permanent president. And if my country enjoyed peace and prosperity, it was because my fellow-countrymen, more intelligent perhaps than others on the Continent, had re-elected me three, four—how many times? Knowing that the continuity of power is a guarantee of material well-being and political equilibrium. Thanks to my Government.

I interrupted him with a gesture of defence against the expected encomium which would have relegated our countries of volcanoes, earthquakes and hurricanes to the peaceful latitude of Flemish lace-makers or the aurora borealis.

"Il me reste beaucoup à faire," I said. Nevertheless I was proud— very proud—of the fact that, after a whole century of tumult and uprisings, my own country had brought the cycle of revolutions to an end—revolutions that in America were counted merely as adolescent crises, the scarlatinas and measles of young, impetuous, passionate hot-blooded races, who had to be subjected to discipline sometimes. *Dura lex, sed lex . . .*

There were cases when severity was necessary, the Academician thought. Besides, as Descartes put it so well: "Sovereigns have the right to modify customs to some extent."

Ofelia had finished her very long session with *Für Elise*—we hadn't noticed that the piano had been silent for some while—and she now came into the library, looking dazzling but strange, dressed in light-coloured muslin, a feather boa round her neck, a hat wreathed in flowers and with a humming-bird nesting among its roses, embroidered gloves and a parasol whose handle was made of finely-carved ivory; perfumed, and with a suggestion of hidden lingerie wafting through her clothes, her hair waved, her figure enhanced by bows and tight-lacing. She advanced with a lively air, like a ship before the wind, a fully-rigged model of Boldini's.

"It's the day of the Drags," she said, reminding me that while I was talking to the Distinguished Academician a few moments before, I had in fact seen crossing the Place de la Concorde some of those old-fashioned English carriages with double doors and high box seats, drawn by four horses, which would shortly drive off amid a great turmoil of sunshades, whip-cracking and postillions' bugles, to where the President of the Society of Steeplechasers was awaiting them, flanked by two huntsmen in scarlet livery.

"*Jamais je ne vous avais vu si belle,*" said the Distinguished Academician, weaving thereupon an elaborate compliment comparing my daughter to some sort of beautiful Gauguin rising from the foamy waves of a summer dawn.

"We *are* having fun," murmured Peralta.

My face became serious: all this about Gauguin stressed our being foreigners—but Ofelia took it all in good part. "*Oh! Tout au plus la Noa-Noa du XVIe Arrondissement!*"

The truth is that her smooth complexion, derived from her Indian ancestry, was a feature of my daughter's beauty. She had inherited none of the roundness of face, thickness of thighs and width of hips of her sainted mother, who was much more of a peasant in complexion and figure. Ofelia was long-legged with small breasts, and slenderly built—a woman of the new race springing up *over there*—nor did her straight hair, artificially waved to suit the fashion, possess any of the natural fuzziness that many of our countrywomen counteracted by using the famous Walker Lotion, invented by a chemist of New Orleans.

Covering me in exaggerated caresses, Ofelia asked my permission to go away that same night, after the dinner at the Polo de Bagatelle to which she was invited. She wanted to be present at the Wagner Festival at Bayreuth, which was opening on the following Tuesday with *Tristan und Isolde.*

"Œuvre sublime!" exclaimed the Academician, starting to hum the theme of the Vorspiel with the gestures of someone conducting an invisible orchestra. Then he spoke of the superhuman voluptuousness of the second act, of the great solo for cor anglais in the third, of the paroxysmal chromatic progression, almost cruel in its intensity, of the *Liebestod,* and went on to ask my daughter whether she would enjoy visiting the Villa Wahnfried. Gratified by Ofelia's dramatic emotion, as she declared that the mere thought of the Famous Mansion was to her so moving and sacred that she would never dare to enter it, the Academician went to the little boule Santa Inés writing-table and took a sheet of paper. Would she take these lines of introduction to his friend Siegfried, a noted composer, although his works were seldom performed? But . . . how could one compose music if one was the son of Richard Wagner? And now his pen stopped its calligraphic career, adorned with Greek "e"s and tall "l"s: *"Voici, Mademoiselle."* Would she greet Cosima affectionately from him? He warned her that the seats in the Festspielhaus were rather uncomfortable. But the pilgrimage to Bayreuth was something that every cultivated person must experience, even if only once in a lifetime—just as the Mohammedans went to Mecca or the Japanese climbed Fujiyama.

Taking the letter he had embellished with a Renaissance flourish composed of very carefully drawn capital letters, Ofelia left us, with renewed demonstrations of affection for such a kind father, who indulged her in everything—although to tell the truth I hadn't given the smallest signs of pleasure at the idea of this sudden journey, which in fact thwarted my plan for her to act as hostess to a reception shortly to be given here in honour of the editor of the *Revue des Deux Mondes*, who was very much interested in publishing a long article on the splendid prosperity and stability of my country. Her kisses on my forehead had been pure humbug and play-acting for the benefit of our visitor, because in fact she never needed my advice or consent to do whatever she fancied. She used and abused the terror inspired in me by her appalling rages, sudden losses of control whenever I tried to oppose her wishes—rages expressed in frantic stamping, obscene gestures and such foul and insulting language that it seemed to come from a brothel or low night-club. At such moments the "cunts" and "pricks" of the Infanta—as my secretary called her—reached as high as the allegoric figures on the Arc de Triomphe. But when the storm had passed, and she had got what she wanted, Ofelia used to return to her usual delicate language full of such subtle nuances that sometimes, after listening to her, I had to go to the dictionary to discover the exact significance of some adjective or adverb, possibly destined in the future to fill the sails of my own oratory.

When we were alone again, the Academician suddenly seemed depressed, remembering the years of poverty Richard Wagner had gone through, and the contempt that was felt for true artists in this horrible epoch. There was no Maecenas, no Lorenzo the Magnificent, no cultured Borgias, no Louis XIV, no Ludwig of Bavaria. Perhaps some Louis of the card-table? He himself, in spite of his successful literary career, was not immune from want—so very far from immune in fact—that under pressure from emissaries of the Law in cocked hats who might be knocking on the door of his house tomorrow with their symbolic ivory sticks (would such a thing have been conceivable in the Grand Siècle?) he had sorrowfully made up his mind to sell the manuscripts of two plays: *Robert Guiscard* (a historical pageant, whose chief characters were the Norman condottiere, his brother Rogerio and the unfortunate Judith d'Evreux, which in spite of a masterly interpretation by Le Bargy, was a resounding flop) and *L'absent* (a drama of conscience: David and Bathsheba, whose nights of love were poisoned by the ghost of Uriah, etc.) which had been performed more than two hundred times at the Théâtre de la Porte Saint-Martin, to the great fury of that swine of a Jew Bernstein, who had thought of writing a piece on the same theme. . . . But the bookshop round here hadn't any funds available, and lawsuits couldn't be postponed: tomorrow those men in cocked hats with their ivory-handled sticks . . . But perhaps the National Library of my country. . .?

He had no need to say more. I quickly wrote him out a cheque which he received with the distrait air of a nobleman, without even looking to see what sum was written on it, although I suspect he knew from having watched the way my hand moved as I traced the numerals.

"*Ils sont très beaux*," he said: large pages of art paper, enclosed in leather cases stamped with his ex-libris. "*Vous verrez.*"

The package, left downstairs, was brought up by Sylvestre. I untied the string, fondled the covers with their calligraphy in two different inks and drawings illustrating the text; I turned the pages with respectful slowness and felt grateful to the distinguished friend who had thought of the Library of my country to save these invaluable writings—a Library which, modest though it was, possessed some extremely valuable incunables, Florentine maps and a few codices from the Conquest. And noticing that his movements were being orchestrated into an ambiguous ceremony of departure, I stood up, as though to look towards the Arc de Triomphe, declaiming:

Toi dont la courbe au loin
s'emplit d'azur, arche démesurée . . .

Feeling obliged to show me some gratitude, the Distinguished Academician picked up his top-hat and his white gloves and— knowing that it would please me—said that Hugo wasn't such a bad poet after all, and it was understandable that we, who were so generous with our admiration for French culture, should continue to appreciate his great virtues as a lyric poet. But we must also get to know Gobineau; we *must* read Gobineau.

I went with him down the red-carpeted stairs as far as the front door. And I was just going to suggest to Doctor Peralta that we should go to the Rue des Acacias and visit Monsieur

Musard's *Bois-Charbons*, when a taxi drew up in front of us and out got the Cholo* Mendoza in a remarkably agitated state. Something serious had happened to my ambassador, because he was sweating—he always looked sweaty, but not so much as this—his parting was crooked, his tie carelessly knotted and his grey felt boot-tops badly laced. I was about to make a joke about his disappearances of several days—whether to Passy, Auteuil, or who could say where?—with the blonde of the moment, when with an agonized expression he handed me a deciphered cablegram of several pages: it was from Colonel Walter Hoffmann, President of my Cabinet:

"Read it .... Read it."

IT IS MY DUTY TO INFORM YOU THAT GENERAL ATAÚLFO GALVÁN HAS REBELLED SAN FELIPE DEL PALMAR WITH INFANTRY BATTALIONS 4.7.9.11.13 (FOREMOST IN THE COUNTRY) AND THREE CAVALRY REGIMENTS INCLUDING "INDEPENDENCE OR DEATH" SQUADRON, AND FIVE ARTILLERY UNITS, TO CRIES OF "LONG LIVE THE CONSTITUTION, LONG LIVE THE LAW".

"The cunt! The son of a bitch!" yelled the Head of State hurling the cables to the ground. "I've not finished reading it," said the Cholo Mendoza, picking up the papers. The movement had spread to three provinces of the North and threatened the Pacific zone. But the garrisons and officials of the Centre remained faithful to the Government, so Hoffmann assured me. Nueva Córdoba was unaffected. Troops were patrolling the streets of Puerto Araguato. Curfew had been imposed, presumably pending guarantees of constitutional behaviour. The newspaper *Progreso* had been suppressed. The morale of government troops was good, but there was a shortage of armaments, especially light artillery and Maxim machine-guns. His Excellency knew how loyal to him the capital was. They awaited instructions. "The cunt! The son of a bitch!" repeated the Head of State, as if his vocabulary was limited to these sordid phrases when thinking of the treachery of the man whom he had dragged from the squalor of a provincial barracks,

* In Latin America a "Cholo" is usually an educated and civilized Indian. It can also mean a cross between an Indian and a European.

the rubbishy, third-rate soldier whom he had helped, made rich, taught to use a fork and pull the lavatory chain, and converted into a gentleman, giving him braid and epaulettes, and finally appointing him Minister for War, and who now took advantage of his absence to . . . The man who, when in his cups at receptions at the Palace, had so often called him his benefactor, providence, more than a father, a friend, godfather to my children, flesh of my flesh, to be rebelling thus, in the Bolivian style or that of the sudden risings of a past era, clamouring for respect for a Constitution that had never been observed by any government since the Wars of Independence, because as we say *over there*: "theory is always buggered by practice", and "a leader with any spunk pays no attention to documents".

"The cunt! The son of a bitch!" repeated the Head of State, who had now returned to the large drawing-room and was pouring himself great swigs of Santa Inés rum—a rum that no longer seemed merely the nostalgic breath of patriotic feelings in *laissez-vivre* Paris, but had suddenly become the wine of battle, hot and strong, foretelling hard, rough marches and counter-marches in the near future, the smell of horses, soldiers' armpits and gunpowder. And all at once, blotting out Jean-Paul Laurens' blessed Radegonde, Elstir's seascape and Gérome's gladiators, they were in the middle of a Council of War. Forgotten was the adolescent hero of the Arc de Triomphe, although it was true that on its walls was inscribed the name of Miranda, precursor of American independence, who had refused to imitate the treachery of the infamous Dumouriez— another version of Ataúlfo Galván; forgotten was Monsieur Musard's *Bois-Charbons*, where the Prime Minister and Doctor Peralta were so fond of taking a glass of Muscadet in the mornings, an aperitif at noon and a Pernod in the evening, because that establishment with its aroma of charcoal, its modest counter set parallel to a wall covered with out-of-date almanacks, its allegorical picture of the Ascent and Descent of the Ages, its advertisements for Géraudel pastilles and Vino Mariani, reminded them of the bars and taverns of *over there*— with the same ambience, and decorative posters, and the

cheerful sallies of clients fuddled on red wine, but always ready
to discuss questions to do with cycling, recent films, women,
politics, boxing, the passing of a comet, the conquest of the
South Pole, or whatever they liked. . . .

Council of War. Three silhouettes thrown on the walls and
pictures by the lamp on the writing-desk: as in a cinema, the
Cholo Mendoza's restlessly-revolving shadow, the slender form
of Doctor Peralta, busy with papers and ink; the thickset,
broad-shouldered, slow and choleric figure of the Head of
State, gesticulating as he sat in his armchair dictating letters
and plans. To Peralta: cable to his son Ariel, Ambassador in
Washington, ordering the immediate purchase of armaments,
gun-emplacements, logistic supplies and observation balloons
like those recently adopted by the French Army (they would
have a tremendous effect over there, where they had never been
seen before); proceeding, since all wars cost money and the
National Treasury was in a bad way, to hand over the banana
zone on the Pacific to the United Fruit Co.—a transaction
which had been too long delayed because of the doubts,
arguments and objections of professors and intellectuals who
talked a lot of foolishness and denounced the greed—inevitable,
good God, inevitable, fated, whether we like it or not, for
geographical reasons and historical necessities—of Yankee
imperialism. To the Cholo Mendoza: cable to Hoffmann,
ordering him to defend the communications between Puerto
Araguato and the Capital at all costs. Shoot whoever must be
shot. To Peralta, again: cable a Message-to-the-Nation
declaring our insuperable determination to defend Liberty
following the example of the Founders of our Country, that
("well, you know the sort of thing . . .").

And the Cholo Mendoza had already telephoned Cook's
agency: a fairly fast ship, the *Yorktown*, would leave Saint-
Nazaire at midnight. They would have to take the five o'clock
train. Another cable to Ariel, announcing their arrival-time so
that he should find means of getting them *there* as early as
possible: cargo-boat, tanker, whatever was available.

"Tell Sylvestre to pack my bags." He swallowed a large
drink, already mounted on the horse of great decisions.

"Tell Ofelia not to worry. We've plenty of money in Switzerland. Let her go to Bayreuth as if nothing had happened and have a good time with her Niebelungen. For me it's a question of a few weeks. I've thrashed people with more guts than that shit of a General."

And when Sylvestre began carrying down the luggage the Prime Minister thought that probably that affair last night with the little nun of Saint Vincent de Paul had brought him bad luck after all. That starched headdress. And the scapulary. And that rubber skull, certainly bought in the shop called *Farces et Attrapes* in the Boulevard des Capucines—another unfortunate coincidence—that couldn't have helped. But, once again, the Divine Shepherdess of Nueva Córdoba would accept his sincere repentance. He would add a few emeralds to her crown; a lot of silver to her cloak. And there would be ceremonies. Candles. A great many candles. The Flag of her Divinity between wax tapers and the ambos. The cadets on their knees. The ceremony of the accolades. The Cathedral would be lit up and freshly decorated. . . .

Outside, Rude's Marseillaise kept up her imaginary noise—sounding soundlessly—from a deep stone mouth which was only one hole more in the monument where the names of six hundred and fifty-two generals of the Empire, consecrated by Glory, were inscribed.

"Only six hundred and fifty-two Generals?" murmured the Dictator, reviewing his army in his imagination. "Baedeker must have made a mistake."

TWO

*. . . each man is so fixed in his own judgement that we
could find as many reformers as there are heads.*

DESCARTES

2

Two hours after the travellers had arrived in their suite at
the Waldorf Astoria, they were proceeding to sign the final
papers of their negotiations with the United Fruit Company,
rapidly carried through by Ariel while his father and Doctor
Peralta were on the high seas. The documents were incontrovertible, provided that the signatory was by act and right—
and he would continue to be so for a long time according to
forecasters specializing in the politics of this Hemisphere—the
Constitutional President of the Republic. Besides, the Company
ran no risk, whatever happened, because at the start of his
rebellion General Ataúlfo Galván had the intelligence and
forethought to tell the agencies of the press that now as always,
today and tomorrow, *hic et nunc*, both during the progress of
the armed struggle and after the "certain victory"—what a
nerve, brother!—of the movement to seize the leadership, all
the wealth, property, concessions and monopolies of North
American businesses would be safeguarded. It was known by
cablegram that the revolutionaries had consolidated their
positions on the Atlantic coast—up till now they held four
provinces out of nine, that was the dramatic fact—but a
stubborn resistance was frustrating their present attempts to
advance towards Puerto Araguato and cut the communications
between the Capital and the ocean. One squadron of warships
was awaiting the Head of State off a little Caribbean island,
at which a Dutch cargo-ship would drop anchor next day on

her way to Recife. As for arms, bought from an agent of Sir Basil Zaharoff, they were to be despatched from Florida on board a boat registered in Greece, by a freebooter accustomed to hoisting a Panama or Salvador flag once outside the United States' three-mile limit when it returned to its usual business—transporting men, arms, slave-labour, anything that was wanted in South America, whose creeks, inlets and bays he knew as well as did the most travelled of local coastal steamers.

And since there was nothing urgently needing to be done that night, the Head of State, who was a great opera fan, wanted to hear *Pelléas et Mélisande* which was on at the Metropolitan Opera House, with the famous Mary Garden in the leading rôle. His friend the Academician had talked a lot about this score, which was said to be very good and although much discussed at first, had fanatical admirers in Paris, whom that eccentric homosexual Jean Lorrain described as "Pelléasts".

They seated themselves in the front row, the conductor raised his baton and the huge orchestra spread at his feet began to play, soundlessly. It made no sound, but it emitted a murmur, a quivering, a whispering of a note here and a note there which didn't amount to music. . . .

"And is there no Overture?" asked the Head of State.

"It's coming, it's coming," said Peralta, hoping that the sound would grow, rise, become definite and swell into a fortissimo. "*Faust* and *Aida* begin like this, almost in silence (I think they call it *a la sordina*), so as to prepare one all the more for what is to come next." But now the curtain was going up and it was still the same. The musicians were all there, numbers of them, intent, with their eyes on their music—yet they had achieved nothing. They were testing their reeds, shaking the saliva from their horns, giving a half-turn to their instruments, making a string vibrate, sweeping their harps with their finger-tips without succeeding in producing anything like a definite melody. A little stress here, an imperceptible plaint there, themes sketched, impulses still-born, and on the stage two characters gassing away but unable to make up their minds to sing. And now—a change of scene—here is a mediaeval lady reading a letter aloud in an accent from Kansas City. An old man is listening. Shaking his head like someone who didn't want to hear, who was bored; and then came the interval.

The sight of the galleries and corridors now aroused some amusing and pungent reflections in the President's mind, about the artificiality of the aristocracy of New York, and how pompously they showed off, compared to that of Paris. However well-cut a tail-coat might be, on the back of a Yankee it made him look like a conjurer. When he bowed in his white tie and shirtfront one expected a rabbit or a pigeon to emerge from his top-hat. The matrons of the Four Hundred wore too much ermine, too many tiaras, too many of Tiffany's wares. Behind them one glimpsed luxurious houses, with gothic fireplaces bought in Flanders, columns from Cluniac monasteries transhipped in the holds of transatlantic liners, pictures by Rubens or Rosa Bonheur and some authentic Tanagras, whose dancing movements were out of rhythm with the beat of Alexander's Rag-Time Band pouring in through the renaissance windows. Although some surnames from the former Dutch or British ascendancy went back to the seventeenth century, when they were heard in proximity to Central Park they absorbed an indefinable quality of being imported products—at the same time false and exotic, like those vague titles of Marqueses de la Real Proclamacion or del Merito or del Premio Real that we have in Latin America. That aristocracy was as fictitious as the atmosphere of the opera they were putting on this evening, with its floating Mediaevalism, its ogival arches all over the place, its vaguely dynastic furniture, its battlements of no special date emerging from a perpetual mist to suit the taste of the designer.

The curtain went up again and other scenes and another interval followed; the curtain went up yet again and more scenes followed, all submerged in evanescent pearly haze, with caves, shadows, serenades, an invisible chorus, doves which didn't fly, three dead beggars, distant flocks of sheep, things seen by others but not visible to us. . . . And when at last the

final interval was reached the Head of State broke out:
"No one is really singing here; there is no baritone, tenor or
bass ... there are no arias ... no ballet ... not a single
ensemble ... and what a little squit that fat-arsed American
girl is, dressed as a boy, looking through the window to see
what's going on in the room where, needless to say, the
handsome young man and the long-haired blonde are hard at it.
And the cuckold in despair downstairs. And that old man with
a face like Charles Darwin, who says that if he was God he
would be sorry for human heartache. The fact is that although
our friend the Academician, and that other chap, D'Annunzio,
tell me that this is a masterpiece, I'd rather have *Manon*,
Traviata and *Carmen*. And talking of whores, take me to a
brothel."

And, in no time, the three of them found themselves in an
apartment on 42nd Street where some blondes, with faces
made-up and hair combed to look like cinema stars, served
them with mixed drinks—it was the fashion at this time to
mix drinks—after which they amused themselves by comparing
what was provided here with the Veracruzan *minyules* of the
Hotel Diligencias, pink punches of the Antilles and Cuban
mojos with their iced mint leaves, *rocios de gallo* (made of gin
and angostura) and *zamuritas* of cress or lemon, pineapple or
agave juice with salt, from our Torrid Zone. The women were
amazed that in spite of his obvious age the Head of State could
swallow so many drinks—always with a regal and deliberate
gesture—without getting tangled up in stories which never
ended, or losing his aristocratic air. It was unusual for his son
Ariel to see him drink like this—"It's a special occasion,"
said Peralta—because when the Dictator was moving in
Palace circles he was—with his famous drinking of healths
in mineral water, and his praise of Peregrino, whose bottling
establishment he had bought—a model of sobriety. At fiestas
and celebrations he never exceeded one or two glasses of
champagne, and his tone became emphatic and his brow
furrowed when he broached the serious theme of the constant
proliferation of bars and taverns, one of the great social
problems of the nation, a defect we owed to the vicious nature

of the Indians and the Spanish colony's ancient monopoly of aguardiente. But people didn't know that inside a case invariably carried by Doctor Peralta—which looked as if it contained papers of transcendental importance—there were in fact ten flasks, very flat and curved to slip easily into a pocket, such as are made in England, which, being covered in pigskin— and bought at the smart Parisian shop *Hermès*—never clinked when they were thrown together. So it was that in the Presidential study, in the dressing-room attached to the Council Chamber, in his bedroom—and of course the Mayorala Elmira was in the secret—in the train, in the pauses of any journey by road, it was enough for the Head of State to put a thumb to his left ear for one of the flasks instantly to appear out of the secretary's bureaucratic briefcase. In other respects, the always serious, frowning drinker—a "before-breakfast man" for whom the good Elmira prepared lots of tamarind juice quite early to refresh "his livers" (she always used the plural) —took the greatest possible care to hide a longstanding addiction to Santa Inés rum, which—it must be admitted—in no way affected the rhythm of his movements, nor the balance of his judgement when faced with some unexpected predicament, nor the almost natural flow of his perspiration: he always, talked to people—his head slightly on one side so that his breath would be diverted—across a table, or keeping a definite distance, thus increasing the respect due to his patriarchal figure. To these precautions he added constant use of tooth-paste, peppermint lozenges, cachous, and a suspicion of liquorice, flavouring the halo of Eau de Cologne or lavender water that always clung to his under-garments and stiff shirts, all most suitable to the dignity of the Head of the State.

Seeing his father drinking that night, Ariel was amazed to find he had a power of absorption greater than his own.

"It's because he has a virgin organism," said Doctor Peralta. "He's not like us, who carry the 'mother-liquor' about inside us and can never get rid of it."

Next day, after purchasing from Brentano's an exquisite edition of Sarmiento's *Facundo*—which gave rise to some bitter thoughts about the dramatic fate of Latin American peoples,

always engaged in a Manichaean struggle between civilization
and barbarism, between progress and dictatorship—the Head
of State went on board the Dutch cargo-ship which was to
make a short call at Havana. And the sea was becoming less
grey, and the broad yellow Caribbean moons were shining on a
recurring baroque pattern of sargasso and flying fish.

"The air already smells different," said the Head of State,
absorbing a breeze laden with the unmistakable scent of
mangroves.

Arrived in Havana, the Consul told them that, in spite of his
present lack of light arms, Colonel Hoffmann was maintaining his defensive position, although the revolutionaries
had made no futher progress. Everything was the same as
when the cable was sent to Paris. As the news was good and
carnival was in progress, the Head of State watched the fancy-
dress procession and masquerades, and threw paper streamers
down on them from above. Then he hired a black domino and
went to the Shoemakers' Ball, where a mulatto girl dressed as a
Marquise of the period of Louis XV or XVI—in a red
crinoline, with powdered hair, a beauty-spot on her rouged
cheek, a red and green fan and a tortoise-shell lorgnette—
taught him how to dance without dancing, all on one tile;
to jig up and down, almost without moving, in smaller and
smaller, slower circles, ending up in mutual immobility,
breathing the perfume of satin so drenched with sweat that it
was more like skin than skin itself—all this in a din of cornets,
clarinets and kettle drums, produced by Valenzuela and
Corbacho's orchestra. When the masqueraders began to
disperse, the lights of the theatre to go out, tier by tier, the
mulatto invited the Head of State to sleep with her in a room
she had near the Arco de Belén, in a "modest but respectable
house"—so she said—with a patio planted with pomegranates,
basil and ferns. They took a cab, drawn by a scraggy horse
whose driver urged it forward—it was practically asleep—with
a spur fastened to the end of a stick, and passed between tall
sleeping houses smelling of dried beef, molasses and the steam
of roasting, blown this way and that, as they entered the
orbit of the breeze from the port, the effluvium of brown sugar,

hot furnaces and green coffee, within a widespread reek of stables, saddlers and mildewed old walls still cool with night dew, saltpetre and mosses.

"Watch while I sleep, my friend," said the Head of State to me.

"Don't worry, my friend, I've got the needful here," I said, taking my Browning out of my breast pocket. And while the Head of State and the mulatto disappeared for I don't know how long behind a blue door, I installed myself on a cowhide stool, with my weapon across my thighs. However, no one knew that my President was in the city. He had disembarked with a false passport, to avoid the news of his journey reaching the place where he wanted to arrive entirely unexpectedly.

The cocks crowed, the awnings were brought down, and in a few minutes the normal everyday noises increased; lorries and vans went by, with their crescendo and decrescendo of bells; blinds were pulled; shutters creaked; trays and buckets fell over: "Flooo-wers, flowers; brooo-brooms; lottery-tickets; a lucky number?" Hawkers of fruit, avocados and tamales cried their wares with a sound like Gregorian chant; others offered to exchange bottles for toffee-apples, and the morning news was shouted by paper-sellers: a Cuban airman, Rosillo, had beaten the Frenchman, Pegoud, at looping the loop on the Bien Aparecida airfield yesterday; a suicide by fire; cattle-rustlers captured in Camagüey; a cold spell—13 degrees according to the Observatory—on the heights of Placetas; confused situation in Mexico—where there actually was a revolution going on, as we know by the terrifying accounts of Don Porfirio; and in our own country, yes, in our own country, the crier's voice had named it, there had been a victory for Ataúlfo Galván (yes, "a victory", I think he said) in the region of Nueva Córdoba.

The shock of this awoke the Head of State who had been asleep with one huge thick thigh thrown over the just as fleshy but longer thigh of the mulatto, and composed and dignified, we now walked together to San Francisco quay, where the cargo-boat was waiting to weigh anchor. A barrel-organ decked out in tassels and portraits of La Chelito and La Bella Camelia suddenly struck up the piercing din of a bull-fighting pasodoble.

"What a noisy town!" remarked the President. "Our capital is a monastery in comparison."

And here we are now, in Puerto Araguato, where Colonel Hoffmann is waiting for us, standing stiffly to attention, wearing his best monocle, and with the good news that nothing has changed. The rebellion has only been supported in the Northern provinces, whose population has a long tradition of hostility to the Central Power, believing themselves slighted, belittled, treated like a poor relation, although they possess the richest and most productive land in the country. Of the fifty-three risings in the last century, more than forty were led by caudillos from the north. Nobody yet knew, except the Ministers and highest officers of the Army, that the Chief of State was to arrive today. This should make the most of the surprise. (Feeling sadder now than before at the treachery of the man I had most trusted, I had been gazing at the view of the port from the deck of the cutter which was conveying me and was suddenly moved to sentimental but irrepressible tears by the sight of the rows of cottages and farms heaped up against the hill, like fragile cards in a house of cards. With my anger dissolving at this reunion with my own country, I noticed from the quivering of the lamplight, that this air was the air of my air; that some water brought me to quench my thirst, though it was water like any other, suddenly reminded me of forgotten tastes, linked to faces from the past, to things seen by my eyes and stored away in my mind. Breathe deeply. Drink slowly. Go back. Paramnesia. And now that the train is going up and up, in endless curves and tunnels, making short stops now and again between cliffs and the scrubby woods of the Torrid Zone, I see, with the eyes of smell, the outline of leaves growing inside chapels of shadow; I depict for myself the architecture of a tree by the plaintive creaking of a bough; and know what funguses grow on the bark of the amaranth by the permanence of its remembered aroma.

As though naked and unarmed, mollified, disposed to indulgence, settlement, possible accommodation—things derived from an *over there* which from hour to hour was being left further behind at the foot of its Arc de Triomphe—as I climbed towards the seat of the Presidency and regained an aggressiveness possibly due to the surrounding vegetation and its uninterrupted battle to reconquer the open space of the railway-line along which our locomotive was winding, I considered recent events with greater animosity and passion. Every two hundred metres climbed by the engine added to my authority and stature, strengthened also by the thin air from the high peaks. I must be hard, implacable; this was demanded by the implacable, pitiless Powers that still made up the dark and all-powerful reason of existence—the visceral peristalsis— of the world in gestation, though problematic as to shapes, desires, impulses and limits. Because *over there*—now the over there of *over there*—the seaport of Basilia still continued to exist and carry on its Rhenish occupations of the year 1000, and the Seine with its bâteau-mouches was still cut up by the changeless cross-bars of the Pont Neuf with its booths and pseudo-renaissance tabarins; while here and now, jungle scrambled over jungle, estuaries twisted and turned, rivers changed course and left their beds between night and morning, so that twenty towns built in a single day out of anything from plastered dung to marble, from pigsties to castles, from gaucho guitar music to the voice of Enrico Caruso, suddenly fell into ruins, disreputable and abandoned, until even the saltpetre had ceased being of interest to the world, even the sea-birds' excrement—the guano, such as covers the rocks with milky slime—was no longer quoted on the Stock Exchange, with shouting and scribbling on slates, bidding and overbidding, now that its place had been taken by some chemical substance manufactured in German test-tubes. As I filled my lungs with the breath of my native air, I became more and more a President.) And I really was the President, standing erect and stiff on the platform of the train, my expression hard, whip in hand, my attitude grim, when we arrived at the Capital through the familiar landscape of the suburbs; here was the soap factory, the sawmill, the power-house; on the right the rambling country house with caryatids and telamons, and its ruined mosaic-covered minaret; on the left, the huge advertisement for Scott's Emulsion and the other for Pompeian Lotion. Sloan's Liniment, useful for everything; Lydia Pinkham's Vegetable Mixture—a portrait with bare throat and cameos— sovereign cure for all menstrual disorders. And above all— above all—Aunt Jemima's Flour—be sure to remember the brand—a universal favourite in suburbs, tenements and small-holdings because the label had on it the figure of a negress from the South, with a check handkerchief on her head such as is worn by the people of the lowlands hereabouts. ("She's almost exactly like the grandmother of that Prussian, Hoff-mann," people used to say jokingly, remembering that the old woman had been relegated to the furthest outbuildings of his house, and was never present at the Colonel's dinners and parties; she was only seen in the street when going to six o'clock communion, or she would take to haggling at the top of her voice over the price of marjoram or lettuces at the stalls of market-gardeners, who used to drive their heavily-burdened donkeys from the surrounding mountains in the early mornings, before the daily awakening in sunlight of the Tutelary Volcano.)

Railway-lines crossing, signals rushing to meet us, and at two o'clock in the morning we entered the deserted station of the Great Eastern Railway, all made of iron and frosted glass— much of it broken—built some time ago by the Frenchman Baltard. The United States military attaché was waiting for us on the platform, along with members of the Cabinet. And in several motor-cars we crossed the silent town, as silent as if uninhabited, because of the curfew which had been put forward from eight o'clock in the evening to six, and (starting today) to half-past four. Grey, ochre and yellow houses with doors and windows closed and rusty pipes spouting water from their roofs slept on raised side-walks. The equestrian statue of the Founder of the Nation loomed in melancholy solitude, in spite of the presence of the bronze heroes standing beneath him in the Plaza Municipal. The Grand Theatre, with its classical columns, looked like some sumptuous cenotaph in the absence of any human figures. All the lights of the Government Palace were lit, in honour of the Extraordinary Council which had lasted ever since breakfast time. And at ten o'clock, in response to a very sensational special edition of the morning newspaper, an enormous crowd had assembled in front of the façade of tiles and volcanic stone built in the days of the Conquest by an inspired Jewish architect, a fugitive from the Holy Inquisition, to whom we owe the most beautiful colonial churches in the country—the finest of all being the National Sanctuary of the Divine Shepherdess in Nueva Córdoba.

When the Head of State appeared on the balcony of honour, he was greeted with acclamations which sent a great cloud of pigeons over the roofs and terraces that chequered the valley with red and white, between thirty-two more or less aspiring belfries. After the cheering had died down, the President slowly and with marked pauses, as was his custom, began to make a clearly articulated speech in his resonant tenor voice, exact in its purpose, though embellished, so thought some, with too many expressions like "nomadic", "myrobalantic", "rocambolesque", "eristic", "apodeictic"; before this he had already elevated the tone by a glittering mobilization of "acting against the grain", "swords of Damocles", "crossing the Rubicon", trumpets of Jericho, Cyranos, Tartarins and Clavileños, all mixed up together with lofty palm-trees, solitary condors and white pelicans; he then set about reproaching the "janissaries of nepotism", the "imitative demagogues", the "condottieri of fastidiousness", who were always ready to break their swords in some wild undertaking: creators of discord, whereas industry and a patriarchal view of life should make us all members of one great family—but of a Great Family which although reasonable and united was always severe and inexorable to its Prodigal Sons—who, instead of repenting of their errors as in the biblical parable, tried to set fire to and destroy the Homestead where they had grown to Man's estate and been heaped with honours and degrees. The Head of State was often a good deal jeered at for the affected turns and twists of his oratory. But—or so Peralta believed—he didn't use them out of love of pure verbal baroque; he knew that such artificial language had created a style which was part of his image, and that the use of words, adjectives and unusual epithets seldom understood by his hearers, far from being prejudicial, flattered some atavistic taste of theirs for what was precious and flowery, and thus gained him fame as a master of language, whose tone was in strong contrast to the monotonous, badly-constructed, military pronouncements of his adversary.

The speech ended with an emotional call to all citizens of good will to be calm, peaceful and united, worthy heirs of the Founders of the Nation and Fathers of the Country, whose revered tombs were lined up in the aisles of the pantheon close by (". . . turn your heads and contemplate with the eyes of your mind the tall Babylonian tower that . . .", etc., etc.).

Hearing an end to the cheering the orator retired into the Council Chamber, where several maps were spread out on a large mahogany table. With little flags on pins—one sort for the nationalists, another for the reds—Colonel Walter Hoffmann, President of the Council and now Minister for War, traced a compact and clear picture of the military situation. On this line were the bastards and sons of bitches; here, here and here, the defenders of the national honour. The bastards and sons of bitches had been joined by other bastards and sons of bitches during the last few weeks: this was obvious. But now that the Pacific zone had been handed over to the United Fruit, the possibility of their landing munitions in the Bay of the Negro had been nullified. The loyalists had contained the advance of the revolutionaries to the North East.

"But if we had had more arms we could have done more."

"Within a week we shall have everything we need," said the Head of State, checking the invoices of the cargo put on board in Florida. Meanwhile he must strengthen the morale and combativeness of the constitutional troops. He would set off himself that same night for the zone of operations. The general aspect of the situation, although serious, could be considered optimistically.

"And Nueva Córdoba?" he asked, however, thinking of that extraordinary city of ruined palaces, so rich in mines, possibly too Indian, always leaving a disconcerting aftertaste, alarmingly prone to produce unexpected surprises, which had been such a centre of tough resistance in former revolutions.

"Nothing," replied Hoffmann. "Ataúlfo isn't popular there. So he's left it untouched. Besides, he promised to respect English and North American interests, and there are a lot there, and he wants to show he's as good as his word by keeping the war away from that region."

The Head of State was sleepy. He asked the Mayorala Elmira to get his battle uniform ready, polish his boots, and shammy-leather his peaked hat; then, moved by a sudden caprice, he seized her without warning, pulled up her skirts while she stood with her elbows on a marble sideboard, amazed at the "good condition" the Señor had arrived in from Paris—that stupendous Paris, where men lose their very souls . . . after which he curled up in his hammock and slept for a few hours.

When he awoke he was confronted by the face of Doctor Peralta, but frowning and preoccupied this time. The students of the ancient University of San Lucas had had the temerity to circulate an insolent, inadmissible manifesto, which the President read with growing rage. They remembered that he had gained power by a coup d'état; that he had been confirmed in it by fraudulent elections; that his powers had been extended during an arbitrary reform of the Constitution; that his re-elections . . . in other words, it had been as usual in such matters. The time had come to put an end to an Authority without trend or doctrine, expressed in ukases and edicts by a President Proconsul guided in governmental affairs by messages in cypher from his son Ariel. But the gravity of the present situation—and its new feature—lay in the fact that the students had proclaimed that at the present time there was no difference between a uniform and a frock-coat, and that the Government cause was every bit as uninteresting as that of the so-called "revolutionaries". The players had changed places round the same board, but an interminable game, begun more than a hundred years ago, was still going on.

And to aid the return to a constitutional and democratic order, the figure of Doctor Luis Leoncio Martínez had come forward, an austere professor of philosophy and translator of

Plotinus, well-known to Peralta who had been a pupil of his. He was a man with a high, narrow, balding forehead with prominent veins, dry and short in speech, abstemious and an early riser, a militant vegetarian, father of nine, admirer of Proudhon, Bakunin and Kropotkin, who had corresponded with Francisco Ferrer, the great Barcelonese anarchist, and started a demonstration in the city when the news was received that he had been shot at Monjuich. The Head of State winked at this demonstration because indignation was universal, and because in fact, now that Ferrer was done for and couldn't rouse any rebels, a procession starting at dusk and ending in the nine o'clock evening breeze (three hours of shouting which had nothing to do with opposing the Government) would show our respect for liberty, our tolerance of ideas, etc., etc. Doctor Luis Leoncio Martínez combined his libertarian convictions with a form of theosophy, nurtured on the *Upanishads*, the *Bhagavad Gita*, Annie Besant, Madame Blavtsky and Camille Flammarion, was interested in metaphysical phenomena, and attended very intimate seances for table-turning, hypnotism, knocks and levitation, demonstrating the presence of the spirits of Swedenborg, the Comte de Saint Germain and Katie King, or of the still-alive but far distant Eusapia Paladino.

And now this dreamer, this pale utopian, had appeared unexpectedly in Nueva Córdoba, and was inciting the workers in the copper and tin mines to rebel, with the help of half a dozen student leaders. It seemed a bold undertaking, all the more so when one reflected that he was an academic from the university, admired by some local inhabitants but without political following in the rest of the country. The President's calm was restored by a drink served him most opportunely, and analysing the situation from the tactical point of view, he decided that in fact an attack by a common enemy on General Ataúlfo Galván's rear was in his favour, because it limited rebel action to two provinces of the North East. And if this affair of Nueva Córdoba really came to something, he could in the last resort count on the help of the United States, since the White House was now more opposed than ever to the smallest germ of an anarchistic or socialistic movement in that other America, which was already so revolutionary and Latin. And now the Head of State was beginning to discuss the situation with Colonel Hoffmann when a second news-sheet, written in a satirical and mocking tone, was brought in and revived his subsiding anger—and this time to a more violent degree than before. It made fun of his oratory in markedly creole prose, describing him mockingly as a "Musical Comedy Tiberius", "the Satrap of the Torrid Zone", "Moloch of the Public Treasure", and "Upstart Monte-Cristo", who always travelled about Europe with a million in his wallet. His ascent to power had been the "Gangsters' 18th Brumaire". His Ministry was a "Gold Rush", "Court of Miracles" and "Council of Buddies". No one was spared: Colonel Hoffmann was "a Prussian with a black grandmother in the back yard"; General Ataúlfo Galván a "jabbering street-hawker, an Ostrogoth with sword and buckler", just as a great many functionaries and police chiefs were cast in the mould either of the Inquisition or farce, according to whether they were assumed to be tragic or grotesque. But the worst of all was that his daughter Ofelia was dubbed the "Infanta of King Midas", as a reminder that, while the barefoot women of this country had no hospital to give birth in, the favoured creole, collector of antique cameos, exquisite musical-boxes and race-horses, had given thousands of the national pesos (at an exchange of 2.27 against the dollar) to enterprises and organizations such as "Missionary work in China", the "Society for the Protection of Gothic Art", and the "Drop of Milk Foundation", this last having a European duchess for president. So they passed from joke to joke and the President didn't care for jokes. Moreover, Colonel Hoffmann now arrived with the news that the students had shut themselves inside the University and were holding a meeting to oppose the Government.

"Send the mounted police into the building," said the President.

"But ... what about their ancient privileges? Their self-government charter?"

"I can't be bothered with such swine. They've caused quite

enough trouble with that bloody self-government of theirs. We're in a state of emergency."

"And what if they resist, if they throw tiles from the roofs, if they hamstring the horses as they did in 1908?"

"In that case ... shoot them! I repeat: we're in a state of emergency and this disorderly behaviour can't be tolerated."

Half an hour later shooting was going on in the courtyards of the University of San Lucas. "And if some are killed," said the Head of State, as he buttoned his tunic, "none of those solemn funerals, with coffins carried on shoulders and speeches in the cemetery, which are merely demonstrations sheltering under the guise of mourning. Just give the stiff to the family and let them bury it without weeping and wailing, because if they do otherwise the whole family, mother, grandparents and their brats too will go to prison."

Outside, the firing went on. Eight killed and more than twenty wounded.

"Much good their education has done them," said the Head of State, getting into the long black Renault which was to take him to the railway station. "Have any soldiers been killed?"

"Two, because one student and a janitor were armed."

"See that they have national funerals with gun carriages, funeral marches, and places in the Pantheon of Heroes, since they fell in the performance of their duty."

And the armed forces gathered on the pavements with a great display of helmets, leather belts, chin-straps and spurs, binoculars and riding-whips, and with much going to and fro of sergeants looking like German *feldwebels* and piling the troops into coaches, cattle-trucks and luggage-vans. They began with the élite: the chasseurs and hussars, with shining boots and soldierly spit and polish; they were to go in the presidential convoy. Then, in other trains, came shabbier infantry, in stained tunics and unpolished boots, and after that third-class infantry, with machetes, cartridge-belts, old rifles and odd pairs of shoes. And slipping in everywhere among the groups of soldiers, sneaking through the carriage windows, climbing on to the roofs, were the camp followers carrying stores and kitchen utensils, wrapped up in bedding and bags. Two Krupp cannons had been set up on platform-wagons on a turntable, with its complicated machinery of cog-wheels, levers and handle-bars.

"And is all this going to be needed?" asked the Head of State.

"It's been proved by experience," said Hoffmann, "that water-conduits and four yoke of oxen can be carried in railway wagons."

"Very practical for quick action," said the President, who had been put in a good humour by all these preparations.

In the end, after a delay of three hours spent intercalating trucks, moving trucks, interpolating trucks, extrapolating trucks, finding this wouldn't do but that would do, that the one further up was blocking the brakes, that the cistern-wagon was full of putrid water, and that the cement-mixer didn't work, and after two more hours occupied in pulling up bogies from disused lines, breaking up strings of trucks to make others, moving forwards, backing, while locomotives whistled and the bugles of the military bands sounded, the army started off, to the accompaniment of the indispensable song:

Goodbye, goodbye.
Light of my life,
Said a soldier,
Underneath a window.

The Head of State withdrew early with Peralta into his comfortable presidential compartment, to drink what had been brought in the Hermes case, out of sight of the captains and colonels who were celebrating their departure to the front in the Pullman car around bottles bearing good labels. Sitting on the edge of his bed, he gazed gloomily at the toes of his shining boots, his Sam Browne belt hanging from a peg, his pistol in its holster—heavier and of larger bore than the light Browning for his own personal use.

"General" . . . "My General" . . . "Señor General" . . .

And the sleepers under the railway lines repeated with obsessional regularity as the wheels passed over them: "Gen-ral

... Gen-ral ... Gen-ral ... Gen-ral ... Gen-ral." Possibly he was the only General in the whole world to whom the title of General gave no pleasure, and he only accepted it when he was with soldiers, or when he had, as now, to direct some operation. Because the truth was that he had conferred that title on himself a great many years ago, in an early incarnation of his political life, when he had placed himself at the head of an armed contingent back in Surgidero de la Verónica, and led about seventy men to attack a small fort occupied by some rebels against the Government to which at that time he was loyal—though he was to overthrow it later on (but then with the help of real generals) and instal himself in the Presidential Palace. Now, for a while—as long as the operations lasted—he would once again become "General", "My General", "Señor General". And again he looked at the toes of his boots, his spurs and belt. And he thought mockingly of himself as being like the character in Molière's comedy who was a cook when he wore a cap and a coachman when he put on livery.

"Give me a drink," he said to Peralta, "and reach me that book."

And while waiting for sleep to come, he turned the pages till he came to a certain Sixth Volume which he had been interrupted when reading weeks before. *Chapter XI:* "Since I have arrived at this point, it would seem to be not inappropriate to set forth the customs of Gaul and of Germany and the difference between these nations. In Gaul, not only in every state, and every canton and district, but almost in each several household, there are parties ... *There are parties ...*" "That's why they were able to blast them to blazes as they did blast them," commented the Head of State between two yawns. ... Outside, the singing went on:

The night they killed Rosita,
Oh what luck she had!
Out of the six that hit her
Just one shot left her dead.

3

When General Ataúlfo Galván had been beaten in the first pitched battle and crossed the Rio Verde behind his wretched, broken troops, leaving on the bank his two camp-followers, Misia Olalla and Jacinta the Negress—who had stayed behind to load up with parcels of blouses, worn blankets and ribbons stolen from the shops of a recently sacked village—the first of the lightning flashes that seemed to crack the sky from top to bottom was seen and two endless claps of thunder resounded, forming the overture to months of hard, inexorable, exasperating rain; persistent, sustained rain such as is only seen in these forests. The forested lands lay on the flanks of mountains that were always haze-covered, veiled in mists which cleared in one place only to thicken in another, letting the sun filter through a gap of sky—a few minutes here, a few minutes there—to illuminate the unknown splendour of nameless flowers, scrambling over the tops of hidden trees, or to magnify uselessly, since there was no one to see them, some superb efflorescence of orchids on the roof of the jungle; these were the rain forests, where the mahogany trees, júcaros, cedars and quebrachos, and species so numerous and so rare as to confound traditional classifications—they had even confounded Humboldt himself—were bathed in rains so profuse that when men realized their proximity by smelling them from afar, they had the impression of embarking on a year seven months long occupying its special place within the twelve-month year, or of abandoning the four seasons to keep to only two: one short, moss-covered, a time for hard work, and the other long and wet, of interminable boredom. When the storms had died away a new life began—a new stage, a new stride forwards—surrounded by vegetation so damp and so entangled in its own dampness that it seemed to have been engendered by the lagoons and marshes below, always croaking with frogs, covered with toads, iridescent with wandering bubbles arising from submerged decay. . . .

The army commanders had ordered a number of tents to be set up. The President's was in the middle, its ropes attached to posts supporting a tall canvas pediment crowned by the Republican flag. After supper of sardines, corned beef, baked bananas, *dulce de leche* and Rhine wine, the victor of the day's expedition, thinking his officers might be exhausted after this fierce battle, invited them to take a well-deserved rest until the meeting of the General Staff next day. Colonel Hoffmann, Doctor Peralta and the Head of State were left alone, playing a half-hearted game of dominoes by the yellow kerosene glow of the street lamps. But at that point five, ten, twenty streaks of lightning plunged into the forest, followed by thunderclaps, each echoing for so long that they were blended one with another, bringing in their train the wind that heralded the downpour—the *"gira-gira"* as the locals called it—which in the twinkling of an eye had carried away the whole encampment. While the soldiers did their best to deal with the situation, Colonel Hoffmann and the Head of State, guided by Doctor Peralta, made for a hill, where they had that morning glimpsed the dark opening of a cave. And there they arrived, slipping, stumbling, soaked, shivering with cold, by the light of lanterns. There was a fluttering of terrified bats, which quickly subsided, and then the solid shelter of damp walls, beneath an argillaceous vault festooned with stalactites, under which the rain only made its presence felt like the sound of a distant waterfall. But it was cold; the cold of clay in shadow, on to which water from the deep fissures of the mountain was ceaselessly dripping. The Head of State, sitting on his military cloak, had an unappeasable craving for a drink. (A need that clutched his stomach and his entrails, that made his body seem empty, without viscera, contracted by an urgent obsession which rose towards his throat and his mouth, which concentrated memory in his lips and sense of smell. . . .) Doctor Peralta understood what was happening, and with a sly expression produced the Hermes case, and announced that as a precaution against possible chills during the campaign he had loaded it with brandy, to which—why deny it?—he was a confirmed addict.

"Everyone knows you were the Prior of Santa Inés," said Colonel Hoffmann, suddenly cheering up and unbuttoning his overcoat. And joining his entreaties to the secretary's, he persuaded the Head of State to take some alcohol to preserve his health—more vital now than ever before—from harm from the stormy weather.

"Just this once," said the Head of State, raising the first flask, the smell of whose thick and porous pigskin cover at once brought back the Parisian shop where Ofelia used to buy picador's saddles, reins, bits and bridles.

"Don't hesitate, Señor President; go right ahead; this is a special occasion. A glorious day, too."

"A glorious day, indeed," echoed Doctor Peralta. They were answered by a peal of thunder, which increased their pleasant sense of safety here within. The sweet yet vegetable aroma of the strong liquor drunk in the cave harmonized with the moisture of mud and mosses to call up a remote image of the classical vintners' bodegas where new wine sleeps under deep vaults. His spirits revived, the Head of State remembered a text he had humorously quoted in the Cabinet Council—where he often boastfully referred to books read, quoted poems, appropriate phrases and proverbs suiting the case—during some passing political squabble wrapped up in military jargon. "Blow, winds, and crack your cheeks . . . And you thought-executing fires, vaunt-couriers of oak-cleaving thunderbolts, singe my white head . . ." To which Doctor Peralta, who was more of a Zorrillean than a Shakespearean, replied with some sparks from *Puñal del Godo,* so often launched in our National Theatre by the Spanish tragedian Ricardo Calvo, whose too-pure diction he imitated in a comic manner:

Oh what a threatening storm!
What a night; may heaven preserve us!
Is the terrible voice blind,
and the light that flashes
when the wind blows and rages
and lightning strikes the zenith?

Once more the case of flasks was opened, to celebrate the

"terrible voice" of the poem, and the owner of the "terrible voice" that was roaring. And now that they were sufficiently warmed-up, with their uniform tunics somewhat unbuttoned, Colonel Hoffmann began to describe the campaign: until yesterday there had only been slight armed clashes, skirmishes, sharp-shooting by guerrillas, collision between patrols; on our side the worst had been the blowing-up of a train at the exit of the Roquero tunnel, with a loss of horses and equipment, seventeen men killed and fifty-two put out of action with more or less serious wounds. But the enemy—and he directed the light of his lantern on to a map spread on the undulant surface of bats' guano covering the ground—had steadily retreated towards the Rio Verde, without ever taking the initiative. Today, on the other hand, we had met them in a pitched battle, such as had not been seen since the Wars of Independence. Of course thorough preparations had been necessary. The enemy had got too much help from the partisans, mounts, cattle, sacks of maize, information passed from village to village with incredible speed by these filthy mountaineers, always sympathetic with rioters and pronunciamentos. It was not a modern battle. Half a century ago these Andeans had come, driving us all crazy with their marches on the capital and their caudillos, and (on arriving at the Presidential Palace) had been amazed to find kitchens worked by gas, sanitation, taps running hot water and telephones from room to room. This was why it had been necessary to carry out a huge "mopping-up" operation before the battle: burning of houses and villages, summary execution of all suspects, shooting at random into groups of dancers, birthday or baptism parties, which were merely pretexts for whispered propaganda, passing on of information and revolutionary plotting—not to mention certain wakes when, strange to say, there was no corpse in the coffin.

"But in Santo Tomás del Ancón you had no choice," said the Head of State. Sad, very sad of course, but one couldn't make war with kid gloves on. You had always to follow Von Moltke's two incontrovertible principles: "The best thing that can happen in a war is a quick ending. . . . But to end it

quickly all means are good, not excepting the most iniquitous."
A text of basic importance published by the German General
Staff in 1902 stated: "If a war is waged energetically it cannot
be directed solely against the combatant enemy; it must also
aim at destroying his material and moral resources. Humanitarian considerations can only be taken into account if they
do not affect the result of the war itself." Besides which,
Von Schlieffen had said . . .

"Stop buggering about with your German classics," said
the Head of State. Von Schlieffen wanted battles to be fought
on the chess-boards of maps, from a distance, with communications by telephone, cars and motor-cycles. But in this
damned country without proper roads, and with so many
forests, swamps and mountain ranges, communications had
to be maintained on the back of a mule or donkey—even
horses were no use in some densely-wooded mountains—or by
messengers who could run till they dropped like the Indians of
Atahualpa. Those theoretical battles fought by telescopes and
field-glasses, with squared maps and precision instruments,
made one think at once of certain generals with moustaches
like the Kaiser and a bottle of cognac within reach, not at all
disposed—although there were a few exceptions—to rely on
shooting and hanging. Our battles, on the other hand, had to
be fought with our guts—like today's—forgetting all the
theories taught in Military Academies. And here the old
gunners with their "three hands higher and two to the right,
and a finger and a half of rectification", who could wedge a
gun with a millstone, were much more use than these raw
lieutenants, stuffed with algebraic and ballistic gibberish
which their subordinates didn't understand, and who had to
make calculations in an exercise-book before letting off a
shell, which in the end generally missed the target on one side
or another. "In Latin America," went on the Head of State,
"in spite of artillery, machine-guns and all modern iron-
mongery bought from the Yankees, nature makes us go on
fighting as in the times of the Punic Wars. If we had elephants,
we'd make them cross the Andes."

"All the same, Von Schlieffen . . ."

"Your Von Schlieffen based his entire strategy of war on the battle of Cannae, won by Hannibal." And the President, who had directed the day's operations, surprised the others by revealing—or perhaps wanting to make them believe—that he had been guided in his conduct of the action by Julius Caesar's Commentaries. Three ranks of infantry in the centre; two to attack; the third entrenched as reserve. Two troops of cavalry: on the right, under Hoffmann; on the left, his own. Objective: to break up the enemy's wings, agglomerating and concentrating him in such a way that his rearguard was useless, and to cut off his retreat to the river. Realizing that he was practically surrounded, Ataúlfo Galván had taken refuge on the further bank, leaving on this side his two sleeping companions, Misia Olalla and Jacinta the Negress, who by this time must have submitted to the lust of half a battalion of the Nation's Hussars, taking turns between their thighs, one after another. The battle had in fact been like Caesar's against Ariovistus, beginning by the infantry harassing the ill-armed Indians and negroes who had joined the revolutionaries—in Caesar's case they were Veneti, Marcomani, Heruli; to us they are Guahibos, Guachinangos and Mandingos—until the leader, finding his men virtually surrounded, put the Rio Verde between them. So Ataúlfo Galván became our Ariovistus, who fled abandoning his two camp followers, the Suevian and the Norican. And don't let us forget that Caesar too had to fight against certain *Andes*, who seem to me, I don't know why, rather like our damned Andeans.

"Bravo, my President!" exclaimed Doctor Peralta, full of admiration for his knowledge of the wars of antiquity.

"What I do know is that we gave Ariovistus Galván a thorough thrashing today," said Hoffmann, somewhat pained by the Head of State's lack of admiration for Von Moltke and Von Schlieffen.

They began passing the flasks round again. Now and again, the flash from a streak of lightning came in at the mouth of the cave. The President thought of that boring opera they had seen in New York, where one scene had taken place in a mysterious underground grotto, with its vaulted roof covered in a greenish phosphorescence. Colonel Hoffmann, who had a powerful voice and considered himself something of a *helden-tenor*, was reminded of the caverns of Mime and Alberich, and tried to sing a few bars from Wagner, emphasizing the libretto in hoarse German, without finding the exact words that in fact accompany Siegfried's leitmotiv. Vexed by this failure of memory, which he put down to drink, he picked up a large stone and threw it into the depths of the cave. But the response he received was not the sound of stone on stone, nor yet of a stone falling into mud or water, but the breaking of a large earthen jar, struck in the belly and shattered to pieces. The soldier raised his lantern. On top of fragments of clay a horrible piece of human architecture was sitting erect—yet it was barely human now, consisting of bones wrapped in torn pieces of stuff, of dried worm-eaten skin full of holes, supporting a skull bound by an embroidered fillet; a skull whose hollow eyes were endowed with a terrifying expression, whose hollow nose looked angry in spite of its absence, and with an enormous mouth battlemented with yellow teeth, as if immobilized for ever in a silent howl, at the pain in its dislocated joints and crossed shin-bones, to which there still adhered fragments of rope-soled shoes a thousand years old—yet seeming new because of the permanence of their red, black and yellow threads. It was like some gigantic fleshless foetus, that had gone through all the stages of growth, maturity, decrepitude and death—and returned to its foetal state in the course of time— sitting there, beyond and yet closer to its own death, a thing that hardly was a thing, a ruined skeleton looking out through two hollow sockets beneath a repulsive mass of dark hair that fell in dusty locks on either side of the dried-up cheeks. And this king, judge, priest or general, was gazing angrily from across countless centuries at the men who had broken his former earthenware covering. On the right, on the left, stood six more great jars, close to the walls, glistening with water that had filtered through the mountain. Snatching up several large stones, Hoffmann broke them, one by one. And now six mummies came into view, squatting with crossed arms— more or less flayed, their femurs and joints more or less shattered, with more or less accusing expressions in their blackened faces—making up a terrifying conclave of violation, a Tribunal of Desecration.

"The devil! The devil! Keep away!" all three shouted, disturbing a cloud of bats which went whirling overhead. And still pursued by the vision they had left behind them, they went out into the night, into the rain, making for the camp where the ruined canvas of their tents was floating in muddy water. Wrapping themselves in these, sodden as they were, they sat down at the foot of a large tree to await the first light of dawn. And as it grew colder, the last flasks in the Hermes case were emptied. Regaining that surprising serenity that heavy drinking gave him, the Head of State told his secretary to draw up a report to the National College of Science describing the discovery of the mummies, with indications of the position of the cave and the orientation of its entrance in relation to the rising sun, exact arrangement of the funeral jars, etc., as archaeologists do nowadays. Besides which, the chief mummy in the centre was to be presented to the Museum of the Trocadero Palace in Paris, where it would make a splendid show in a glass case, on a wooden plinth, with a brass plate: *Precolumbian Civilization. Culture of the Rio Verde*, etc., etc. As for dating it, their experts could see to that—they were more cautious in this respect than ours, but eager to prove, every time they came across the handle of some ancient pitcher or clay amulet, that this was an earlier example of the techniques of pottery than the oldest Egyptian or Sumerian specimens.

In any case, the more centuries ago the brass plate was dated the greater the prestige of his country, which would thus possess remains comparable in antiquity to finds in Mexico and Peru, whose pyramids, temples and necropolises represented as it were the heraldry of our civilizations and proved that we were in no sense a new world, nor the New World, since our emperors wore magnificent gold crowns, jewels and quetzal feathers when Colonel Hoffmann's presumed ancestors were wandering in dark jungles dressed in bearskins with cows' horns on their heads, and when the Gateway of the Sun

of Tihahuanacu was already old, the French had not got any
further than erecting a few menhirs—piles of stones without
art or charm—on the coasts of Brittany.

4

By a body I understand everything that can fill a space,
in such a way that any other body is excluded from it.

DESCARTES

Although, after the victory, the Head of State would have
liked to give the troops a rest, proceeding meanwhile to
evacuate the many casualties wounded by bullets, bayonets,
machetes or peasants' knives, he realized that the Rio Verde
must be crossed today, because last night's rain—and it was
still falling—was raising its level hour by hour. It was still
possible for the cavalry to take advantage of a ford nearby;
but the infantry had to use barges, scows and any boats
available, such as a mould-covered ferry-boat, abandoned
among the rushes, which was speedily repaired and used to
take across impedimenta—some Krupp cannon, six pieces of
light artillery, the artillery park, blacksmith's equipment,
tinned foods and cases of gin and brandy for the officers, as
well as pots and pans and portable stoves for the troops—to
which, to the great joy of the Head of State, General Hoffmann
gave the pompous inclusive name of "logistics", when according
to Doctor Peralta it only deserved the title of "swill, kettles and
aguardiente".

But now operations were going ahead with speed, though
there was no enemy to fight, because the rebel forces were
retreating towards the sea with the obvious intention of
entrenching themselves among the low hills surrounding
Surgidero de la Verónica, base of the Atlantic Fleet, with its
two small cruisers of old-fashioned design, and cannons of
limited range, as well as several coastguard vessels of a more

modern type now laid up for careening behind the Naval
Arsenal. Although all villages and hamlets had been despoiled
in their retreat by Ataúlfo Galván's men, the sutlers and
camp-followers always managed to find pigs, young bulls and
hens hidden in caves, cellars and even the vaults of cemeteries,
or bottles of rum, flasks and earthenware jars of strong cane-
liquor and plum spirit buried in domestic patios, sacristy
gardens and even in the dust of graveyards. And so there
followed carousing, uproar and revelry throughout the night
watch, quarrels and music from guitars, gourd-rattles, drums
and maracas, while mulattos and half-breeds of all descriptions
stamped their feet with a will to the rhythm of the *bamba*,
jarabe and *marinera*, before leaving the campfire and going with
their men into some thicket nearby to give them bodily
pleasure.

In April the first attacks were made on the advance positions
of Surgidero de la Verónica, obliging the enemy forces to dig
themselves in, in the city suburbs.

"Foch's wise remark is relevant now," said the Head of
State, quoting a French authority in order to pique Hoffmann:
"When one of two adversaries gives up an offensive, he digs
trenches and buries himself underground." And from the
summit of one of the three hills dominating the town, he
studied its domes and cupolas, its baroque bell-towers, its old
walls built in the Colonial period, with tender emotion. There
he had been born and given his first lessons by the Marista
Brothers (in that two-storied building with ogival windows
between cement pilasters), from charming illustrated books
which told him about the Nile floods, the breaking-in of
Bucephalus, Androcles' lion, the invention of printing, how Fray
Bartolomé de las Casas was lawyer to the Indians, how the
Eskimoes made igloos out of ice, and how the monk Alcuin,
creator of Carlovingian colleges, used to prefer studious boys,
even of humble birth, to the lazy and careless sons of the
nobility. Later on he had received an intelligent education in
History and French combined, using texts in which more space
was occupied—naturally enough—by the Soissons Vase than
the Battle of Ayacucho, and by Cardinal Balue's cage than the

Conquest of Peru, and which necessarily laid more stress on Saint Louis of the Crusades than on Simón Bolivar of Carabobo —although they informed us of the interesting fact that his name had been used to designate a tall hat favoured by Parisian dandies of the last century . . .

So the boy grew up on lesson-books—he understood little mathematics but remembered some classics—and the Head of State was reminded of his adolescent escapades in the streets round the port, noisy with sailors, fishermen, hawkers and tarts, with their lively taverns called such names as "The Triumphs of the Venus de Milo", "Wise Men without Learning", "The Staggering Monkeys", "The Ship on Land", or "My Work-shop"; with its trade in fish-hooks, baskets and nets, its rope-makers, its trucks carrying oysters, octopuses and jurels along pavements where the smell of tar, brine and troughs full of anchovies mingled with the jasmine and tuberose scents worn by prostitutes.

There at his feet lay the town of la Verónica, still so like the copperplate engraving made of it by an English artist a hundred years ago, with the figures of slaves and their masters on horseback in the foreground; there it was, with the massive bulk of its Palace of the Inquisition, on whose terrace some Indians and negroes accused of witchcraft had been flogged, mocked by the crowd and covered with excrement and filth a long while ago.

There was the town of la Verónica, with that big house and its three wings and two roofs—lightning-conductor, sky-blue dovecote and squeaking weathercock—where his children had been born, while he was still leading the miserable existence of a provincial journalist and could only provide them with cane-syrup one day and brown sugar the next, to sweeten the stew of bananas and crusts which was their invariable supper dish. There, in that white-washed patio, he and his family had taken the first jump in that game of hop-scotch which, following in his father's bold political footsteps, had taken them jump by jump, from square to square, from number to number, up the spiral path in the game of royal goose. From Surgidero they had gone to the Capital, always ascending from the tiny area of our port life to the great world outside, the old world, for them the New World, although there was to be sadness among the pleasures and bright lights of that climax of good fortune. Ofelia was who she was—*sum qui sum* ever since a child—and would never be otherwise; she still had the character and appearance of the tempestuous, determined little girl, both stubborn and unstable, who had discovered the universe through blind man's buff, *Frère Jacques*, Ring-a-ring-a-roses, skittles, forfeits and *Malbrough s'en va-t-en guerre*. Nothing could be said against Ariel: a born diplomat, he tricked the priests as a small boy, answered questions with other questions, lied when he wanted to, kept in with both parties, wore a row of decorations, and (when under pressure to explain some awkward incident) had instant recourse to a manual of ambiguities, just as Chateaubriand would have done with ministries in a similar predicament. Radames, amongst many successes, had been struck by cruel and sudden disaster and the evidence could still be seen in newspapers all over the world: having entered himself in a motor race against Ralph De Palma at Indianapolis, he shot to heaven from the burning hot asphalt of the sixth mile, as a result of adding too much ether to his petrol so as to make it lighter, more explosive and dynamic. He had tried to forget the blow of being ploughed in an exam at West Point Military Academy in the intoxication of speed. . . .

And there, limping among the hopscotch squares, he saw his youngest son, Marcus Antonius, in short pants, the most evasive and invisible of the clan, lost among the branches of trees which did not belong to this earth, but to some genealogical forest where he had taken refuge—perhaps because he was the least precocious of the family and the most exotic-looking, both as to profile and eyes. Much given to fantasizing—mad, we should say now—carried away by the impulse of the moment, he had experienced an adolescent mystical crisis, on discovering one day as he stood before the looking-glass on his cupboard that his penis had become twisted into a corkscrew by the clap. Absurdly enough, he decided to go to Rome and kiss the Pope's sandal, and cure himself with cardinal's

permanganate; but he had got no further than the cardinal's
antechambers, where, happening to run into a dealer in
armorial bearings, he convinced himself that he was descended,
by a rather crooked, collateral, indirect and tangled line from
the Byzantine emperors, the last of whom, Palaeologus, died
in Barbados leaving descendants who came to our country.
His mystical aspirations forgotten, he spent a great many
pesos on acquiring the title of *Limitrophe* (*sic*: see Justinian's
Code), Count of Dalmatia as it happened; he paraded his
brand-new nobility throughout Europe, a Title among Titles,
jealous of other Titles, expert in Titles, going to bed with
women of Title, and many comments on his virility went the
rounds among those who had experienced the virtues, well-
known among us, of a "stallion liana" often used by our
ardent old men. With such talents, his life took him from
Andalusian estates to the farms of Peñaranda, from antique
Venetian palaces to Scottish grouse moors, from the hunting
parties of Kolodje to the Alfonsine regattas of San Sebastian,
travelling according to a map of somewhat tarnished nobility
that had seen better days, among whom credit and prestige
was given to the North American coats of arms of Armour and
Swift, the ketchup aristocracy of Libby, who promoted their
advance to grandeur by studying, learning and annotating the
Almanack de Gotha (the entry of their names was always
postponed to the next edition) with the close attention of a
rabbi interpreting the Talmud, or a Saint-Cyran translating
the Bible three times, the better to master the subtleties of its
vocabulary, and the complications of its hermeneutics. Marcus
Antonius was both brilliant and useless; excitable and ambitious
like his father, whose anxieties, however, were unknown to him;
flesh of a flesh to which he felt alien, he declared himself to be
a luxury product, the herald of our culture, a necessary factor
in our international prestige, a lunatic, dandy, collector of
gloves and sticks, refusing to put on shirts which hadn't been
ironed in London, a harsh critic of famous artists, pursuer of
Woolworth heiresses (he dreamed about Anna Gould who had
presented Boni de Castellane with a pink marble palace),
five times divorced, occasional aviator, friend of Santos-

Dumont, champion polo-player, skier at Chamonix, critic of
duelling along with Athos de San-Malato and the Cuban
Laberdesque, brilliant *rejoneador** in the making, believer in
miracles at roulette and baccarat, although somewhat absent-
minded and Hamlet-like at times and given to signing dud
cheques which found their way by way of legal proceedings to
our discreet embassies.

And there lay, at the feet of the Head of State, that same
Surgidero de la Verónica where a plaque set up by one of the
doors was engraved with the date of his birth, and where
Doña Hermenegilda had groaned as she gave birth to her
four children under a mosquito-net as blue as the dovecote
outside.

And that was the town that fell into the hands of the
Government troops, intact and undamaged by shells, because
almost all the disloyal officers surrendered, on a historic
April 14.

Finding himself abandoned by his most trusted men, and
with no one owning a boat or schooner ready to take him on
board, General Ataúlfo Galván shut himself into the old
castle of San Lorenzo, built by order of Philip II on a pinnacle
of rock which narrowed the entrance to the port. And there,
in the middle of the afternoon of the day of surrender, the
Head of State disembarked, followed by Colonel Hoffmann,
Doctor Peralta and a dozen soldiers. The defeated man was
waiting in silence in the main courtyard. His lips moved
strangely, without any accompaniment from his voice, as if
wanting to emit words which refused to be uttered. He was
trying, with a checked handkerchief, to mop the sweat coming
from under his kepi so copiously that it was making dark
drops on the cloth of his military tunic. The President stood
still, and gazed at him for a long time as if measuring his
height. Then suddenly, in a sharp, cutting tone: "Shoot him!"

Ataúlfo Galván fell on his knees: "No, no . . . Not that.
Not a bullet . . . For your dear mother's sake, no . . . For the
sake of that sainted Doña Hermenegilda, who loved me so

---

* A bullfighter on horseback with the *rejón*, a form of spear.

much . . . you can't do that to me . . . you were like a father
to me . . . More than a father . . . Let me explain . . . You'll
understand . . . I was misled . . . Listen to me . . . For the sake
of your dear mother . . ."

"Shoot him!" He was dragged, groaning, weeping and
imploring, towards the further wall. Hoffmann arranged the
firing-squad. Unable to stand upright, the defeated man fell
against the wall, his spine slipping slowly down the stonework
till he was sitting with his boots in front of him, the toes turned
in. The barrels of the rifles followed his descent and stopped at
the correct angle.

"Aim!" The order reaffirmed the position they had already
taken up.

"No . . . No . . . A priest . . . Confession. I'm a Christian . . ."

"Fire!" Rifle-butts on the ground. Coup de grâce, because
that was the drill. Crying of sea-gulls. A very short silence.

"Throw him into the sea," said the Head of State. "The
sharks will finish the job."

This business was finished and done with. But there was still
another, perhaps more serious: Doctor Luis Leoncio Martínez,
whose potential as a leader and fighter had been scorned and
disregarded by us during the urgent emergency of military
action, was free and active in Nueva Córdoba, from whose
town hall he was sending out manifesto after manifesto attacking
the Government. He had built up a strong, a very strong
position in the city, where he had gathered round him students,
journalists, ex-politicians, provincial lawyers, those with
socialist views, besides a few young officers, fresh from the
School of Cavalry at Saumur, who constituted the army's
intelligentsia—an intelligentsia opposed to such men as
Walter Hoffmann, but who—like him—had been formed by
German instructors and were devotees of the pointed helmet.
United there in permanent session, sleepless and with shirts
undone, smoking cigarettes by the gross, drunk on black coffee
and bad cigars, arguing, discussing, rounding on each other,
cursing, their purity of aims worthy of a Committee of Public
Safety, the rebels were drawing up a Plan of Reform which
became ever more radical as the hours passed, and which

having settled the matter of trials to investigate peculation and illicit gains, embarked on the risky project of reducing large estates and dividing them up as common land. The Head of State had learned from letters received that same morning that events which at first he had viewed with a certain irony were really happening: "Utopian vegetarian notions," he had said. Yet now, in Nueva Córdoba—between meetings, rallies, proclamations and factions—intensive military instruction for students and workers was going on, under the leadership of an obscure Captain Becerra—a spare-time entomologist—who had been named Military Chief of the town. And, observing that the movement was gaining strength, with signs of syndicalism inspired by foreign, antipatriotic doctrines, inadmissible in our country, the United States Ambassador offered a speedy intervention by North American troops, to safeguard democratic institutions. Some battleships happened to be manœuvring in the Caribbean.

"It would be humiliating for our sovereignty," observed the Head of State. "This operation won't be difficult. And we must show these filthy gringos that we can manage our own problems by ourselves. Besides which, they are the sort who come for three weeks and stay two years, carrying out huge business deals. They arrive dressed in khaki and go away laden with gold. Look what General Wood did in Cuba."

Three days passed in inspecting and preparing the East Railway, and after a grand campaigning Mass, at which they begged the Divine Shepherdess to grant triumph to the national forces, several convoys set off towards the new front, with a great noise of cheering and laughter under their regimental flags. It was almost midnight when the last train left, with a whistle and hiss of escaping steam. On the roofs of wagons and trucks men in ponchos and women in rebozos were singing hymns and songs together, while bottles of white rum circulated by the light of lanterns, from the coaltender at the front to the rear lights on the guard's van: "If Adelita sleeps with another, I'll follow her by land and sea, by sea in a war-ship, by land in a troop train."

Night lay behind them, and frogs croaked in the black

marshes of Surgidero, now restored to the peace of its slow provincial activities, with gatherings in the barbers' shops, a huddle of old women in the doorways, and—for the young— lotteries and games of forfeits, after telling their beads among the family with their minds focused on the fifteen mysteries of the Virgin Mary.

5

Sovereigns have the right to modify customs

to some extent.

DESCARTES

Founded in 1544 by Governor Sancho de Almeyda, the city of Nueva Córdoba stood out against the surrounding waste land—saffron-coloured deserts, anaemic patches of grass, cactuses, thorn bushes and sponge-trees smelling of the sweat of illness—as blindingly white as a Moroccan settlement, on the banks of a river (dry ten months of the year) whose sinuous course was hollowed out between stony tracts bristling with the bones, antlers, skulls and claws of animals dead from thirst. Under the cloudless sky, from the rapid sunrise to crimson dusk, vultures and turkey-buzzards flew over the hills at the mouths of mines, which were so divided up, and cut into steps with picks, shovels and sledge-hammers, that their original rotundities had been transformed into geometric shapes by the men who had for the last two centuries been extracting the slag hidden in their entrails. Like giants' chairs and sofas, they were sculptures created by the rough, calloused, blackened hands of the peons of the Du Pont Mining Co., who had made of these euclidean shapes resulting from their labours a formless panorama of scree, ridges and hills of rubbish, mineral waste, gravel and pebbles, all adding their desolation to the sterility of the desert. And there, in the most barren region of the country, hedged round by prickly pears, stood the rebellious,

tendentious, combative city of Nueva Córdoba, defying the
Head of State's troops, already victorious in the East.
Thousands of enemies of the regime had surrounded a dry
university professor and made themselves into a Sacred Legion.
And to defend the immediate neighbourhood of the city, the
troops of General Becerra (as he now was) had had more than
enough time to organize a strong line of defence, with a whole
network of trenches and blockhouses surrounded by walls
and palisades made from wooden sleepers destined for railway-
lines. Studying these military preparations through his field-
glasses, the Head of State murmured in a joking tone which ill-
concealed his annoyance: "Just as I've always said. In these
countries strategy is the only thing that works—either Julius
Caesar's or Buffalo Bill's." And in a Grand Meeting of the
General Staff, it was decided that the most adequate way of
dealing with the present situation was to prepare for a classical
siege, cutting off all lines of communication with the small
towns of the north—also disaffected—which were providing
them with food and ammunition: "Even their drinking water
has to be brought from elsewhere! The climate is on our side
here. . . ."

And, having pitched their tents at a reasonable distance
from the defence lines, from which few shots were coming
since the enemy couldn't afford to waste ammunition on
useless firing, they settled to wait. For lack of any other reading
matter the Head of State had begun leafing through some of the
classical works on military tactics which Colonel Hoffmann
always carried in his luggage. And, to mortify the "Prussian
with a black grandmother in the back yard", as the wits of
the opposition used to call him, he quoted the most glaring
idiocies he came across with significant shouts of laughter.

"Listen to this, listen!" he said. And in a portentously deep
voice: "Victory resulted from the fact that the battle had been
won" (Scharnhorst). "He who is on the defensive can pass
to the offensive" (Lassau). "A battle is the only thing that can
produce a result" (Lassau). "It's essential for the head to be
in command, because it controls the reason" (Clausewitz).
"A leader must understand war and its hazards" (Von Moltke).

"It is necessary for the leader to know what he wants and have a firm wish to conquer" (Von Schlieffen). "The general theatre of operations contains only three zones: one, on the right; one, on the left; one, in the centre" (Jomini).

"Where there is no centre there is neither left nor right," observed the Head of State exploding with laughter. "And was this rubbish what they taught you in the Military School?"

The days passed in an inactivity made exasperating by heat and flies, until one morning, dressed in an explorer's pith-helmet with a gauze veil over the neck, and shorts—in the style of Stanley in search of Livingstone—the United States Ambassador appeared in the camp. The news was serious. Several armed bands, under orders from agents of the so-called Caudillo of Nueva Córdoba, had violated the banana zone on the Pacific, and taken possession of 200,000 dollars kept in one of the offices of the United Fruit Company. All work at the Dupont Mining Company had been paralysed, with disastrous immobilization of ships in Puerto Negro. It had become necessary to put an end to the socialist mysticism of Doctor Luis Leoncio Martínez. We couldn't tolerate the encumbrance of a second Madero in South America. If the country didn't quickly return to a regime of calm and respect for foreign property, North American intervention would be inevitable. Under this pressure, the Head of State gave a definite undertaking that decisive operations would begin within the next forty-eight hours. And next day, employing all desirable guarantees for a military parley, he invited young General Becerra to come to the camp, where, without any noise or action that might cast a slight on his honour, he bombarded him with 100,000 pesos, and a little something too—a bonus with several noughts—for the two lieutenants accompanying him. And, as dusk fell, white flags were hoisted over the trenches and block-houses, to proclaim to the inhabitants of Nueva Córdoba that their capitulation had been accepted—in consideration of the superiority of government troops, with the humanitarian aim of avoiding unnecessary bloodshed.

But at this moment there suddenly appeared the gigantic,

frightening, vociferous figure of Miguel Estatua, so-called because he worked and moved impassively, was strong and enormously tall, with broad shoulders widening sharply above a waist so slender that he always had to make extra holes in his leather belts to ensure that the silver buckle decorated with initials—his sole piece of finery—should stay firmly fastened in the centre of his stomach. A master driller and borer, thoroughly understanding the use of dynamite, and nearly always carrying cartridges of it in his mouth when he was going to blow up part of a quarry, the negro had made a name for himself throughout the country by his discovery that he could carve animals out of stone. Yes. That was how it was. He knew of course that the mountain trees are living creatures, to whom one can talk, and that when one says the appropriate words they answer by the creaking and movements of their branches. But one day, up there on that ridge, he came across a great stone which apparently had two eyes and indications of nostrils as well as the outline of a mouth.

"Get me out of here," it seemed to be saying. And Miguel seized his drill and his hammer and began to lower the level here and smooth the surface there, freeing front feet, and then back feet, a spine slightly convex in the middle, eventually finding himself confronted by an enormous frog, the result of his handiwork, which appeared to be thanking him. Excited by his discovery, Miguel began looking at loose rocks and schist, the hard substances surrounding him, with fresh eyes. That fallen rock over there contained a bat; he could see the tips of its wings. Over there was a pelican with its beak gloomily sunk on its breast. From that outcrop of rock a deer was trying to escape, having lain there for eternity, hoping for freedom.

"The mountain is a prison confining the animals," said Miguel. "The animals are inside it; the thing is that they can't get out until someone opens the door for them." And so he began to use all his drills—he had them ending in points, blades, screws and bits—to extract enormous doves, owls, wild boars, pregnant she-goats, and even a tapir, which stood in front of him in lifelike proportions. And Miguel looked at all this, the dove, the owl, the wild boar, the she-goat and the tapir, and saw that it was good, and as he was tired with so much work, on the seventh day he rested.

He lined up all his pieces in an abandoned shed belonging to the Nueva Córdoba Railroad Company, which was no longer any use for mending coaches and trucks, and here people came on Sunday to see the exhibition of animals. His fame spread. One of the capital's newspapers published an article on him, describing him as a "spontaneous genius". But when members of the Spanish Chamber of Commerce came to him with a proposal that he should make a statue of the Head of State, Miguel had replied: "He doesn't inspire me. I don't do portraits of people like him." Ever since, he was without further reason assumed to be against the regime. But others—members of the Literary Club—defended him: "It's because he doesn't dare attack a human figure. It's nothing to do with politics, just fear of failure." And any priests who came near him were commissioned to ask him to do the Four Evangelists, to be set up round the extension of the garden of the canons of the Divine Shepherdess.

"I can't make men out of stone," Miguel had answered. But when he learned that Marcos was starting on a lion (he had recently seen one in the circus which was giving performances in the villages near-by), that Lucas was working on a bull (a bull is a bull everywhere) and Juan on an eagle (there are no eagles here but everyone knows what eagles are like), he accepted the work and began by sculpting the symbolical animals attributed to the Survivors of the Apocalypse, leaving for later on a Matthew whose youthful face he couldn't succeed in imagining. However, he worked, worked and worked, digging out of the stone for the first time some human faces crowned with haloes, putting the finishing touches not with drills, but with chisels as thin as knives, brought from the capital.

And he was busy on this task when he heard the news of the base capitulation. He instantly threw down his tools and rushed into the street. All at once the dreamer, reinventor of animals and people, the absent-minded eccentric, raised his voice at the crossroads, drew himself up to his full height and created himself tribune, leader and caudillo of the people. Such was his authority that he was listened to and obeyed. He ordered the white flags to be hauled down and the white flags were hauled down, and Miguel Estatua saw that it was good to haul down the white flags, and also good to resume the battle. With a cartridge of dynamite in each hand and blazing tinder on his shoulder, he declared that it was necessary to resist until they had by fighting converted daily bread into Daily Bread, earned today and eaten today, and not owed to the stores run by Yankee, national or "associated" companies, who ruled the mines, and paid wages in vouchers for goods. There and then, calling on everyone who would listen, he organized one company of dynamiters and another of sappers. And, roused by a speech couched in sincere if crude and ill-expressed terms—eloquence from the heart, clamorous and rough, but more convincing than an elaborate harangue—the students, members of the intelligentsia, workers in mines and olive-fields, makers of rope-soled shoes and sandals (who had lost faith in the cowardly Luis Leoncio Martínez, although he was still issuing proclamations to the country, asking help from people barely aware of his existence and declaring that he counted on aid from provinces which had never been involved in the movement) announced their decision to fight as long as their means lasted.

However, it was not enough for adolescents, young women and brave boys to mobilize themselves, while old women made lint bandages and old men worked in the forges transforming belaying-pins into spears: all this in an open city, with no old walls—such as some other towns possessed—nor buildings which could be used as defences, and with streets ending in scattered adobe houses encroaching on the surrounding desert. And in spite of mined roads, sending shattered bodies flying into the air, shedding arms and legs in the roar of an explosion; in spite of a bloody battle from patio to patio, from roof-top to roof-top, waged by the defenders with old Winchesters, sporting rifles, blunderbusses from the armoury, Colt pistols, guns with ramrods, and three or four Maxim machine-guns which had to be cooled by urine for lack of water, the government troops captured the plaza round the cathedral, inside which some hundred desperate men had shut themselves with what was left of the ammunition, and were shooting out of windows, loopholes and gateways. Most danger came from the bell-ringers who took aim at everyone advancing along the streets that debouched into the Plaza Mayor. So the hours passed and there they still were, eating a snack and taking a drink now and again; but not succeeding in occupying the now deserted municipal buildings, whose façades and galleries were in the line of fire from that handful of buggers who must still have enough bullets or food for a short while longer. Hoffmann kept his Krupp cannon in readiness; he had brought them in bullock-carts to a point whence they could be trained on the tower. A number of these animals, conspicuously coloured and slow in their movements, had been wounded from above; but even so, bleeding, with the second of the third yoke fallen and the first of the second yoke vomiting spittle, they had dragged their burdens to their destinations. Yet the Head of State for once appeared to hesitate: this was the National Sanctuary of the Divine Shepherdess, patron saint of the country and the army. An object of devotion, the goal of pilgrimages, a jewel of colonial architecture.

"Hell and damnation!" said Colonel Hoffmann, who was a Lutheran. "One can't make war with sacred images." When all was said and done, every building could be restored. And every restoration involved improvements in solidity and permanence for the future.

"And what if the Holy Image should be damaged?" enquired the Head of State.

"They sell some very pretty ones in Saint Sulpice in Paris," remarked Doctor Peralta.

"What are you waiting for, to finish off those sons of bitches?" asked the North American military attaché. "Our marines would have liquidated them by now. They aren't sentimental like you."

"I see there's no help for it," said the Head of State at last. "If Pilate washed his hands, I shall stop my ears."

"A strategic necessity," said Hoffmann. The Krupp guns were tilted to the firing angle. The Old Artillerymen aimed it by "three hands up, two to the right, and a finger and a half of rectification", etc., and the first shot was fired. Hit in the centre, the tower loosed its bells over the roof of the Sanctuary, with a thunder of falling stones and statues. A second shot was fired—by calculation and logarithms this time—and sneaked in at the main door and across the altar without touching the statue of the Divine Shepherdess, who remained there, intact, indifferent, standing on her pedestal without even wobbling—a portent which was thenceforth recorded as "The Miracle of Nueva Córdoba".

"The Virgin was on our side!" shouted the victors.

"The Virgin," said the Head of State, much relieved, "couldn't possibly be on the side of an atheist, a believer in talking tables and gods with six arms . . ."

And then all hell was let loose; free and uncontrollable, the troops abandoned themselves to hunting men and women, with bayonet, machete or knife, throwing corpses into the streets, pierced through, cut open, beheaded and mutilated, to warn the rest. And the last to put up a fight—some thirty or forty of them—were carried off to the Municipal Slaughter-house, where, among hides of oxen, animals' viscera and tripes, or pools of coagulated blood, they were battered and kicked, and hanged from hooks and beams, by the armpits, the knees, round the ribs, or by the chin.

"Who wants a skewerful of meat? Who wants a skewerful of meat?" shouted the executioners, imitating the town crier and giving another jab with a bayonet to a dying man, before posing in front of the camera of a French photographer, Monsieur Garcin, who had been living in the town for some time (scandal-mongers said he had escaped from Cayenne), taking family groups and photographs of weddings, christenings, first communions and "little angels" lying in their small white coffins.

"Look pleasant!" he said to the soldiers, changing a plate, and about to press the rubber bulb. "Two pesos fifty for half a dozen, postcard size, with one hand-coloured enlargement as a souvenir . . . Don't move. That's it . . . Now another . . . With the four strung up over there . . . Another with these danglers . . . Pull down the woman's skirt so as not to show her cunt . . . Another, with that chap with a trident in his guts . . . There's a reduction for anyone taking a dozen."

Already the turkey-buzzards and vultures were flying over the patios of the Municipal Slaughterhouse. From the post office, from the poplars in the park, from the balconies of the Town Hall, hanged men were suspended in clusters. A few who tried to escape were lassoed like young steers in a rodeo, and dragged by horsemen over paving-stones and bare pebbly ground. Some fifty miners, standing with their hands up, were run through in the baseball stadium, opened only a few months before by the Du Pont Mining Co. At the feet of the Divine Shepherdess, standing erect on her scorched altar in the ruins of her sacred dwelling, there was a confused heap of human bodies, from which emerged like things broken off and out of context a leg, a hand, a head frozen in its last grimace. Rifle fire was still to be heard from the miners' quarter, where soldiers carrying drums of paraffin were setting fire to houses full of cries and entreaties.

And at midnight there was a huge explosion in the forgotten hangar of the Nueva Córdoba Railroad Co. Miguel Estatua had just destroyed himself and all his stone creatures with dynamite. A few fragments of the Evangelists flew over the crowd, killing three soldiers by slicing them with haloes filed as sharp as an axe by the chisel of the inspired driller and borer.

Now that the chief focus of resistance had been destroyed, the Head of State returned to the Capital, entrusting to Hoffmann (raised to the rank of General for services rendered) the now easy task of punishing those surrounding villages which had helped the rebels. Doctor Luis Leoncio Martínez had fled towards the northern frontier by way of a dry ravine that lost itself in the inhospitable sierras of Yatitlán. Here and there he proclaimed himself Leader of a Government in Exile or of the National Legalist Party, etc., etc., building up an inefficient nucleus of political exiles, soon to be destroyed—the

President knew all about this—by rivalry, defections, schisms, mutual accusations and litigation, fed by periodicals printing three hundred copies, tracts, and news-sheets with fifty readers. And the Apostle of Nueva Córdoba, deep in theories and wool-gathering, ended up, like so many others, a forgotten man in some Los Angeles boarding-house or squalid hotel in the Caribbean, writing letters and pamphlets quite without interest for those who knew only too well that what counts in politics is success.

When he returned to the seat of Government, the Head of State was received with flags, triumphal arches, fireworks and the march *Sambre-et-Meuse*, which he liked particularly. But in his first press conference he looked sad and frowning, and declared that he felt overcome with grief at the thought—no doubt based on recent events—that the nation didn't trust his honesty, and disinterested patriotism. For this reason he had decided to relinquish the power and entrust his responsibilities to the President of the Senate, in the hope that elections would be held and some outstanding man, some good citizen, more capable than he was of controlling the fate of the Nation, might be raised to the presidency, unless—unless, I say—a plebiscite should produce a contrary result. So the plebiscite was quickly organized, while the Head of State carried on his ordinary business with the noble and serene melancholy— not to mention pain endured with dignity—of someone who believes in nothing and nobody, and who has been wounded to the quick after having done everything possible for the good of other people. The misery of power! The classical drama of crown and purple! Bitter old age of Princes!

As forty per cent of the population could neither read nor write, coloured cards were prepared—white for "yes" and black for "no"—with a view to simplifying the mechanism of voting. But mysterious voices, sly voices, insidious voices began whispering in towns and countryside, in mountains and plains, from north to south and from east to west, that every vote, although secret, would be known to the rural or municipal authorities. There were new techniques today to make this possible. Cameras concealed in the curtains of the pollingbooths and functioning every time a citizen stretched out his hand to a ballot-box. Where this arrangement didn't exist, there were men hidden behind those same curtains. Then— without any doubt—they would examine the fingerprints left on the cards, not forgetting that in small villages everyone knows his neighbour's political views, and twenty negative votes in such places would mean twenty individuals identified without possibility of error. A growing sense of alarm was taking hold of public servants—of whom there were many. On the other hand the mysterious voices were now insinuating, more openly, in taverns, food stores and bars, that the great mining and banana companies, manufacturers, etc., would sack anyone who opposed the Head of State's remaining in power. The disaffected peasants had to look out for the machetes of the rural police. The schoolmasters would be thrown out of their classrooms. The tax returns of some traders—it was understood—would be severely checked since they always managed to trick the tax collectors. It was remembered in time that any recently naturalized foreigner could have his card of citizenship taken away and be sent back to his own country, if he fell into the ugly category of undesirable or anarchist.

As a result of all this, the plebiscite produced an enormous and massive "yes", so enormous and massive that the Head of State felt obliged to accept 4,781 negative votes—a figure arrived at by dice thrown by Doctor Peralta—to show the complete impartiality with which the inspectors of return had worked.

There were more speeches, triumphal marches, fireworks and Bengal lights. But the President was tired. Besides which, his right arm remained out of action day after day, because of some strange and unpleasant sluggishness, heaviness or dis- obedience of the muscles, and he had a sharp pain in the shoulder which neither massage nor medicine relieved, nor even the herbs prepared by the Mayorala Elmira who, as the daughter of a herbalist, knew a lot about plants and roots, nearly always more effective than some of the concoctions of eminent chemists, advertised in the press by beautiful illustrations of

Convalescence and Recovered Health. A North American doctor came specially from Boston and diagnosed arthritis—or something of the sort with one of the new names proliferating on the covers of medical magazines, causing great panic and confusion among the sick—indicating that this country didn't possess certain electric apparatus which was the only means of curing the trouble. The Government unanimously begged the Head of State to go to the United States and recover his very important health. During his absence the President of the Cabinet would be responsible for governing, with the close collaboration of General Hoffmann, in charge of National Defence, and the President of the Senate.

So it was that the Head of State embarked on a voyage in a luxury ship of the Cunard Line. But once arrived in New York, he was aware of sudden, irrational, almost childish fear— perhaps he was tired; his nerves had been affected by recent events—when confronted by Yankee doctors, who spoke a foreign language, were cold in their manner, too ready to use a scalpel, to cut without great cause, addicted to rough, new methods whose consequences weren't fully understood, very different from the gentle, bearable and intelligent therapeutics of the French or Swiss specialists, who were undoubtedly—he was thinking of Doyen, of Roux, of Vincent—at the top of the tree over there. To the aseptic, white, impersonal surgeries full of forceps, probes, saw-edged scissors and other cruel objects on view in glass cases of these Yankee doctors, the President much preferred the consulting-rooms hung with pictures by Harpignies or Carolus-Durand—the Persian carpets, antique furniture, books with eighteenth-century bindings, an almost imperceptible smell of ether or iodine—of the doctors with imperials, frock-coats and the Legion of Honour, who officiated, paternally and elegantly, in the Avenue Victor Hugo or the Boulevard Malherbes.

"Very well," said Peralta. "But . . . do you think it's wise to go so far away? And supposing there's another coup, my President?"

"Ah, my friend . . . Everything is possible in our countries. But I don't think it's likely. We'll only be away a few weeks.

And my health comes first. I wasn't born to be a cripple. And to become a cripple without having ever been to Lepanto would be stupid. Besides, with no right hand I can't depend on my best friend. Because even when I'm in my country, where so many people love me, I only feel calm, firm, and in control of myself during audiences and visits, when I know that's with me." And he pointed with his chin at the place where he kept his Browning, there, under his left armpit, praising the lightness of its trigger and the style of its butt, with the tender accents in which a man boasts of the beauty of the woman he loves: it was faithful, docile, safe, beautifully shaped, of perfect proportions, pleasant to touch, slim and elegant right up to the mouth, well bored though invisibly, and with the National Arms engraved on the back of the butt. It was looked after with maternal affection by the Mayorala Elmira who cleaned it every day when he removed it before he took a long bath, returning it to him recharged and ready for use, just as he was drying himself with a large plushy towel, one of those Ofelia bought for her father in *La Maison de Blanc*.

And so, leaving behind the electric apparatus, progressive inventions, and torture tables of North American clinics, which seemed to him like huge prisons, the Head of State embarked one morning on *La France* to take refuge, after so many trials and tribulations, in the charms of a Parisian summer—so sunny and warm that year, the newspapers reported, that nothing like it had been seen since the middle of the last century.

THREE

*All truths can be perceived distinctly, but not by
everyone, because of their prejudices.*

DESCARTES

6

The travellers were met at the Gare de Nord by the
Cholo Mendoza—yellow gloves, gardenia in button-hole and
grey spats as usual, although it was summer; he had been
notified by aerogram sent off on the high seas, and had hastily
returned from Vichy, where he was combining the water cure
in the day-time with nocturnal cures in the bar, and this
intelligent alternation of spring water with Bourbon had given
him the appearance of a twenty-year-old. The other embassy
officials were on holiday with their children, at Trouville or
Arcachon. And Ofelia was in Salzburg, where the Mozart
festival was opening that very day with *Così fan Tutte*. The
diplomat's expression showed his alarm when he saw that the
Head of State had his inert right arm in a sling made from a
cashmere shawl. A tiresome affliction, but not serious, Doctor
Peralta explained. The doctors over here would put it right
with their up-to-date scientific methods. Besides, the atmosphere, the movement, gaiety and civilized way of life. . . .

Merely by breathing the air here—thus: breathe in, breathe
out, expand the chest—one felt better. And it was well-known
that morale affected the physical state, since pain gets so much
worse when we concentrate on the idea of pain, because, in
fact, modern psychologists had agreed with Epicurus that, etc.,
etc.; but one couldn't talk in all this noise from trains, whistling engines, bustling porters, and perhaps you'd better go on
ahead with the luggage, Cholo, while Peralta and I take

a little walk, as our legs are numb with sitting for so long.

And the Head of State, followed by his Secretary, entered a well-known bistro, rather Flemish in style, with a dart-board and a statuette of Manneken-Pis, where one could drink Hoegaarde bitter, or another beer the colour of cherry-juice, or strong Lambic—"branded" with a red-hot nail dipped in the froth—all of them good to start off a day which should be full of health-giving savour. Everything seemed pleasant today—people sitting outside cafés, soldiers' red trousers, the zouaves' skull-caps, the burning carrot advertising *Le Brazza*, the 'buses with their placards advertising the Opéra, République, Bastille, Parc Monceau and tours of the Napoleonic sights. The returned travellers renewed their old habits of taking idle strolls according to whim, from the *Chope du Panthéon* to the tulip bulbs of the Quai de la Mégisserie; from Chaponac's occult and Rosicrucian bookshop (fortune-telling cards, initiatory leaflets, the works of Estanislao de Guaite) to a gymnasium where they still practised the noble art of all-in wrestling; from the sky-blue shop selling religious objects close to Notre-Dame-des-Victoires to *Aux glaces*, at 25 Rue Sainte-Apolline, where in the mornings an ample blonde was often on duty who was particularly skilled at manipulation à la Duc d'Aumale—which gave an air of somewhat aristocratic raffishness to the cavalry barracks near-by. Everything above and behind the zinc bar-counters spoke the language of smells and taste: brioches in their paper cases; madeleines, fluted like scallop-shells from Compostela, in square glass containers; Dubonnet's cat, the bersagliere on the Cinzano bottles, the gleaming pottery of the flasks of Dutch gin, the wooden ladders enclosed in bottles of marc brandy; the aroma of Amer Picón— something between orange-peel and tar.

"We're better off here than in the Mummies' Cave," murmured the Head of State. And finally they hailed an open car and were driven to the Rue de Tilsitt.

"Paris will always be Paris," opined the Secretary, when, between the horses of Marly, the Arc de Triomphe appeared in the distance, useless and magnificent.

And now, installing himself, sinking into his leather armchair, the Head of State felt something approaching an organic need to re-establish relations with the city. He put through a telephone call to the house on the Quai Conti where delightful concerts often took place: Madame was not at home. He rang up the violinist Morel, who congratulated him on his return in the hasty and evasive tone of someone who wants to end the conversation quickly. Next he telephoned Louisa de Mornand, whose housekeeper kept him waiting longer than she should and then told him that the beautiful lady was away for a few days. He rang Brichot, professor at the Sorbonne.

"I'm almost blind," he answered, *"but I have the newspapers read aloud to me."* And he hung up. "As irritable as ever," thought the Head of State, rather surprised by this strange response and looking up another number in his diary. He rang, rang, rang, first one friend then another, always—except when it was his tailor or hairdresser—being answered by voices that had apparently changed their tone and style. Then he thought of D'Annunzio; perhaps he would be in Paris. After a maid had told him that her master had just left for Italy, he heard the poet's own voice giving the lie to what she said, and launching a terrific invective against the creditors who were literally besieging him in his house. Yes, *besieging* was the word: suggesting a tribe of Erinyes, of Eumenides, of Furies; of Hecate's hellhounds, there at all hours, stationed in the bistro opposite, in the *tabac* at the corner, in the neighbouring bakeries, with their eyes on his door, waiting for him to go out so that they could hurl themselves on him, destroy and tear him with their savage demands for money.

"Ah, what wouldn't I do to have the power of a Latin American tyrant, and be able to cleanse the Rue Geoffroy l'Asnier of rogues and scoundrels as our brave friend who was talking just now did in Nueva Córdoba."

Realizing that the blow was about to fall—and it wouldn't be the first—the Head of State struck the mouthpiece with his fountain-pen, saying: *"Ne coupez-pas, Mademoiselle! ... Ne coupez-pas,"* and then hung up the receiver in the middle of a sentence from his interlocutor, to make him think they had been cut off. But he felt uneasy and disconcerted. He didn't

know how to take this talk of a "tyrant" even though the poet
habitually used "imaginific" and ambiguous language, but as
to Nueva Córdoba, he wasn't aware that D'Annunzio even
knew the name of the town. Something was up. Perhaps it
would be a good idea to ring up Reynaldo Hahn, his amiable
and pleasant "compatriot" from Puerto Cabello. The composer
came to the telephone, speaking in his agreeable Spanish with
a Venezuelan accent, curiously interspersed—a habit he
couldn't explain himself—with occasional turns of speech
obviously coming from the River Plate. After the usual greet-
ings, Reynaldo informed him, in his characteristically mild, slow
and rather lazy tones, as if he were talking about something
different, that *Le Matin* had published a series of savage
reports on the events *over there* in which his "compatriot" was
described as the "Butcher of Nueva Córdoba". All Monsieur
Garcin's photographs had appeared, occupying three or four
columns, and showing corpses lying in the streets, mutilated
corpses, corpses being dragged along, corpses hanging by their
armpits, by their chins, by their ribs, from the meat-hooks in
the Municipal Slaughterhouse, and pierced with pikes, tridents
and knives. And female defenders of the town being forced to
run naked through the streets of the town with bayonets in their
backs. And others raped after taking refuge in the church. And
other women thrown into cattle-pens. And the miners shot
down with machine-guns *en masse* in front of the cemetery wall
with military bands and cheerful bugles playing. All this,
accompanied by portraits of the Head of State in battle-dress,
in profile, half-face, or sometimes back view, but always identi-
fiable by his corpulent frame giving the order for the artillery
to fire on the National Sanctuary of the Divine Shepherdess ("It
wasn't me, it was Hoffmann," he protested), that marvel of
baroque architecture—*la Notre-Dame de Nouveau Monde* as the
newspaper called it. And the unkindest cut of all perhaps was
that when his son Marcus Antonius was questioned by a reporter
two days ago on the beach at the Lido, where he was staying
with an Arsinoe from the Comédie Française, instead of defending his father, he declared: "*Je n'ai que faire de ces embrouille-
ments sudamericains.*"

At last, the appalled listener understood the reason for so many excuses and ancillary rebuffs; now Louisa de Mornand's fictitious absence and Brichot's strange reply were explained.

"I know there's a lot of exaggeration in it all, compatriot. They do extraordinary things nowadays in the way of trick photography . . . You wouldn't be capable . . . Of course it's all false." But he couldn't dine with him at Larue that night. Nor tomorrow, as he had a date with Gabriel Fauré. A lot of work on hand, also: a project for an opera on Moratín's *El si las niñas*, a concerto for piano and orchestra. He was extremely sorry . . .

Overwhelmed, the Head of State fell into the hammock swinging diagonally from the rings which he had ordered to be fixed to two corners of his bedroom, months ago. He wasn't even cross with the Cholo Mendoza, who could well have warned him. But he knew very well that the only French papers his diplomats read were *Le Rire*, *Fantasio* and *La Vie Parisienne*, and they were always the last to know what was being written about their country. He gazed at the moulded plaster on the ceiling with the bitterest feelings he had perhaps ever known. It would have upset him very little to be treated as a "butcher", a barbarian, a savage or whatever else, in places he had never been attached to, and which he had for that reason spoken about slightingly. In his view, Berlin was a city that had every right to its primitive name of "place of bears", with the architectonic heaviness of the Brandenburg Gate, like some granite locomotive, its walled-in temple of Pergamum and Unter-den-Linden: Vienna, in spite of its reputation for elegance and voluptuousness derived from its operetta and waltzes, was really terribly provincial, with its little officials from the dye-works, its ten or twelve restaurants anxious to be like those of this city, besides its café-au-lait-coloured Danube, which only looked blue on an occasional February 29 of leap year; Berne was a boring town with its heraldic statues in the middle of streets that were one vast shop-window of watches and barometers; in Rome, every square, every street-corner was the scene from an opera, and whatever the passers-by wore or talked about they always had the air of the chorus in *La forza del destino* or *Un ballo in maschera*, whereas there was a certain smallness about Madrid, with its kiosks selling mineral water, sweets and aguardiente, its night watchmen with key-rings at their belts, and its social gatherings in the café where the dawn rose on a provincial panorama of last night's cups of chocolate and yesterday's toast, some people just going off to bed while others were starting the day early with fritters and tobacco. On the other hand Paris was an Earthly Paradise, the Promised Land, the Shrine of Intelligence, the Metropolis of *Savoir-vivre*, the Source of all Culture, and anyone fortunate enough to live *here* found that its dailies, weeklies, reviews and books, year after year, praised Rubén Dario, Gómez Carrillo, Amado Nervo and many other Latin American writers who had, each in his own way, contributed to make the Great City into a City of the Gods.

Slowly, overcoming reserve, observing strict rules of polite behaviour, always carefully dressed according to hours, days and seasons, giving valuable but never ostentatious presents, sending flowers at odd times, showing generosity to charity sales and tombolas for good causes, befriending artists and writers who were not eccentric bohemians, and attending important concerts, fashionable meetings and theatrical and musical first nights—thereby showing that our countries *also* knew how to live—he had opened a way for himself, which without elevating him to the peaks of Gotha had nevertheless three times admitted him to Madame Verdurin's musical evenings—not such a bad beginning. When he was tired of all the agitations and crowds of *over there*, he intended to retire and await death in the house that every journey made more pleasant to him. But now everything had collapsed. For ever shut against him would be the doors of the great houses he had dreamed of entering when as a provincial journalist he had walked the steep streets of Surgidero de la Verónica, reciting poems in which Rubén Dario sang of "the times of King Louis of France, a sun with a court of stars on a blue field, when the splendid and majestic Pompadour filled his palaces with fragrance". Or when, sitting in some tavern in the port, in the steam of prawns on the grill, his nose buried in reviews from *over there*, he used to come across works by the most famous painters in the world, showing him the gold and crimson of the foyer of the Opéra, the whiteness of sylphides and willyes, the aristocratic confidence of horsewomen at a gymkhana, the greyness of cathedrals in the rain (*"il pleure dans mon coeur / comme il pleut sur la ville"*), and the iridescence of women whose portraits showed them as birds of paradise, symphonies of jewels, unimaginable beings, suddenly blazing out from the pages of *L'Illustration*—as he sat there, between the siren of a Danish cargo-boat and the squeaking of the crane as it loosed a torrent of coal on to a dirty quay close by.

Now he thought he read scorn and mute accusation in the eyes of everyone who looked at him: his man-servant Sylvestre was rather evasive; the cook, whose gesture of wiping her hands on her apron when she saw him could have various different interpretations; the concierge, reserved and cold, seemingly uninterested in his arm in its sling—or else not thinking it discreet to allude to it; the familiar old *Bois-Charbons*, where he had the half-fearful curiosity to go that same evening to drink a bottle of Beaujolais with Doctor Peralta. Monsieur Musard seemed to be in a bad mood. His wife didn't come out to greet him. And, to judge by their glances, those two men in caps at the other end of the bar were talking about him. In all the cafés the waiters had strange expressions on their faces. In the end, in order to soothe his nerves and after taking Peralta's advice, he turned up without warning at the house of the Distinguished Academician, who owed him so many favours. There, in an apartment full of shadows and with views over the Seine, surrounded by old books, Hokusai prints, portraits of Sainte-Beuve, Verlaine, Leconte-de-L'Isle and Léon Dierx, the President received an affectionate welcome, understanding and lucidity which touched him. Power entailed terrible obligations, his friend declared. "When kings carry out their promises it is terrible, and when they don't carry them out it's just as terrible," he said, perhaps quoting Oscar Wilde. No leader of men, no great monarch or Captain, had had clean hands. Dramatic and comforting pictures passed before the President's eyes, pictures of the destruction of Carthage, of the siege of

Numantia, of the fall of Byzantium. Sudden images arose, confusedly shuffled at random by his memory, of Philip and the Duke of Alba, the Saladin, and Peter the Great obliged by reasons of state to exterminate the Naryshkins in a courtyard of the Kremlin. Besides . . . who had ever been able to control the frenzied excesses and cruelties—lamentable but repeated throughout history—of a brutal soldiery, drunk with victory? And worse still when a rebellion of Indians and negroes had to be crushed. In fact, to speak frankly, that affair had been the result of a mob of Indians and negroes running amok.

His strength of mind restored, and his mood made more aggressive by the conversation, the Head of State suddenly discarded his rather careful French, with its attention to pronunciation and choice of the right word, and impetuously triggered-off a deluge of creole insults, which his astonished friend received like a verbal invasion of ideograms outside the scope of his understanding. Indians and negroes, yes; but "*zambos, cholos, pelados, atorrantes, rotos, guajiros, léperos, jijos de la chingada, chusma* and *morralla*" (Doctor Peralta tried to translate this into a language learnt at Monsieur Musard's *Bois-Charbons*, as *propres-à-rien, pignoufs, galvadeux, jean-foutre, salopards, poivrots, caves, voyous, escarpes, racaille, pègre, merde*) and above all—now the President returned to French—*socialists*, socialists affiliated to the Second International, anarchists, men who foretold an impossible levelling of classes, who fomented hatred in the illiterate masses, who exploited for their own advantage the conceit of uneducated people who had refused the schooling offered them, people crazed by practising witchcraft and unimaginable superstitions, and devoted to saints somewhat like our saints but who were not our saints, since these illiterate people, hostile to the three R's, called the Beautiful God of Amiens Elegná, Velásquez' Crucified Christ Obatalá, and Michelangelo's Pietá Ochum. They didn't understand that *over here*.

"More than you think," observed the Distinguished Academician, growing more indulgent and convinced all the time. Everything could be explained (and he returned to Philip II and the Duke of Alba, passing on to the America of Cortés and Pizarro) by Spanish blood, the inheritance of the Spanish temperament, the Spanish Inquisition, bull-fights, banderillas, cape and sword, horses being disembowelled among sequins and pasodobles. *"L'Afrique commence aux Pyrénées."* We had been born with that blood in our veins; it was fate. Men of *over there* were not like those *over here*, although of course they didn't lack certain qualities, because there had been after all Cervantes, El Greco—who had, by the way, been revealed to the world by the genius of Théophile Gautier.

At this moment, that school-teacher Doctor Peralta sprang up from his chair in a rage and shouted: *"Je vous emmerde avec le sang espagnol."* And, in an irreverent outburst, he paraded before the amazed eyes of the Distinguished Academician, as in the pictures from a magic lantern, Simon de Montfort's crimes and the Crusade against the Albigenses; Robert Guiscard (the hero of his own play, the manuscript of which, bought by our National Library, told how the Norman condottiere had gone through the middle of Rome knife in hand); the massacre of Saint Bartholomew, that universal synonym of horror; the pursuit of the camisards, the massacres of Lyons, the *noyades* of Nantes, the White Terror after Thermidor, and above all, above all (by skilful handling of analogies) the last days of the Commune. Then, the most intelligent and civilized men in the world hadn't hesitated to conquer revolutionary resistance by exterminating more than 16,000 men. The ambulance of the Seminary of Saint-Sulpice—*"Oh! fuyez, douce image!'*—had become a scaffold in the hands of the people of Versailles. And Monsieur Thiers, after his first walk through Paris in the days of punitive measures, had said, in the most ordinary way: "The streets are full of corpses; this horrible spectacle will be a lesson." The periodicals of that time—those of Versailles of course—were preaching the holy bourgeois crusade of murder and extermination. And recently . . . what about the victims of the Fourmies strike? And more recently still? Did the great Clemenceau show any mercy to the strikers of Draveil or of Villeneuve-Saint-Georges? Eh?

Under this frontal attack the Academician turned to look at the Head of State: *"Tout cela est vrai. Tristement vrai. Mais il y a un nuance, Messieurs."*

And then, after a rather solemn introductory pause, raising his voice with each name, he reminded his listeners that France had given the world Montaigne, Descartes, Louis XIV, Molière, Rousseau and Pasteur. The President had a mind to reply that though it had had a shorter history, his own Continent had already produced great men and saints, heroes and martyrs, thinkers and even poets, who had transformed the literary language of Spain, but he reflected that the names he wanted to mention would fall into the void of a culture that knew nothing of them. Meanwhile Peralta was encircling the Academician with awkward questions: just because it was here that Racine's alexandrines were first heard and the *Discourse on Method* was so famous, certain barbarities were all the more inexcusable. It was deplorable that Monsieur Thiers, first President of the Third Republic, illustrious historian of the Revolution, Consulate and Empire, should have given orders for the massacres of the Commune, the shootings at Père Lachaise and the deportations to New Caledonia; it was less grievous that Walter Hoffmann, grandson of a halfbreed and an emigrant from Hamburg, a bogus Prussian and tenor of military mess-rooms, should have carried out—since he had been responsible for the whole thing—the repressive action at Nueva Córdoba.

"La culture oblige, autant que la noblesse, Monsieur l'Académicien."

Seeing that his eminent friend's forehead was dark and frowning, the President silenced his Secretary with an expression of fatigue, and buried himself between the arms of his chair in an attitude of mute despair. He looked at objects in the room without seeing them—the portraits, the old books, an engraving by Granville. The Academician, on the other hand, behaved as if unaware of Peralta's presence, blundering into him as he passed—"Pardon!" (treading on one of his feet) "I didn't hurt you, I hope?" and walked from one end of the room to the other with the expression of someone reflecting deeply.

"On peut essayer! Peut-être?"

He put through a telephone call to the Editor-in-Chief of *Le Matin*. Monsieur Garcin's photos—that damned Frenchman of Nueva Córdoba—had been carried off by some students, refugees from *over there*, who were now in Paris, talking and

agitating in the cafés of the Latin Quarter—all of them followers
of Doctor Luis Leoncio Martínez. The newspaper couldn't
recant, nor yet cancel publication of forthcoming articles
already announced. People would say that it had sold itself to
someone known to possess enormous wealth. The best it could
do was suppress from tomorrow's issue a photo of the Head of
State standing beside a corpse placed on a bodega counter,
under a calendar advertising Phosphatine Fallière, whereon the
date of the massacre could be clearly read. "That's completely
buggered us," said the President, overwhelmed. And if only
there had been—goodness knows what—something to distract
the attention of the public: a big liner sunk like the *Titanic*, the
appearance of Halley's Comet announcing the End of the
World, another eruption of Mont-Pelée, an earthquake in San
Francisco, some lovely murder like that of Gaston Calmette by
Madame Caillaux. . . . But there was nothing. In this bastard of
a summer nothing happened. And in the sole place in the
Universe where other people's opinion had some importance
to him, everyone was giving him the cold shoulder. Seeing him
sunk into a state of despair expressed by his hunched back and
vacant gaze, the Distinguished Academician offered him the
warmth of his friendship with a long pressure of his left hand,
and began talking in a low and as it were confidential voice
about a possible counter-offensive. The French press—sad
though he felt to have to admit it—was tremendously venial.
Of course he wasn't referring to *Le Temps*, connected as it was
with the Quai d'Orsay, nor was its editor, Adrien Hébrard, a
man who would entertain a certain sort of transaction. No
more could one think of *L'Echo de Paris*, to which his friend
Maurice Barrès contributed, nor that splenetic Arthur Meyer's
Le Gaulois. But behind these leading papers were others, which
on condition there were funds available (the Head of State
nodded) would—well, you understand. Everything depended
on doing things diplomatically.

So it was that, three days later, *Le Journal* published the first
of a series of articles under the general title of *L'Amérique Latine,
cette inconnue*, wherein, passing from the universal to the local,
from general to particular, from Christopher Columbus to

Porfirio Díaz (and showing, *en passant*, how a great country like Mexico had been overtaken by the most atrocious anarchy through not having suppressed a revolution in time) it then turned to our own country, praising its cataracts and volcanoes, its flutes and guitars, the clothes and huts of the Indians, its typical dishes such as tamales and chili stews, with references to the great moments in its history—a history that necessarily led to the period of progress, agricultural development, public works, encouragement of education, good relations with France, etc., etc., due to the Head of State's wise conduct of affairs. While other young nations of the Continent were shipwrecked in disorder, that little country was setting an example, etc., etc., not forgetting that, having to deal with populations that were often uncivilized and rebellious and easily seduced by destructive and subversive ideologies (here came opportune references to Ravachol, to Caserio, who killed President Carnot, to Czolgosz, assassin of McKinley, and Mateo Moral who threw a bomb at the wedding coach of Victoria of Battenberg and Alphonso XIII); having to deal with an infiltration of libertarian and anarchist ideas, an energetic government was obliged to take energetic decisions, without always being able to prevent the much provoked, angry and sorely tried soldiery giving way on occasion to deplorable excesses, but, however, nevertheless, as soon as . . .

"You see? my President!" exclaimed Doctor Peralta, reading and re-reading the articles. "That ought to settle the hash of those filthy students who kick up rows in the Latin Quarter with their meetings without any audience and their leaflets that no one reads."

Just then a cable arrived telling the Head of State that a case, a prodigiously large case, a magic case, a providential case had been dispatched a short while ago from Puerto Araguato: a case which contained, with all his ornaments, bits of cloth and bones, the Mummy—the Mummy of *that night*—destined for the Trocadero Museum. Skilfully strengthened with glue and invisible wires, sitting in a new funeral jar open in front—just enough for one to see the whole skeleton—invisibly restored by a Swiss taxidermist, more of a specialist in reptiles and birds, but who had done a masterly job in this case, the Mummy was on its way, was crossing the ocean, and arriving, actually arriving in time to give material to a certain element of the press whose greed and absence of scruples were revealing themselves, and astonishing the President, day by day. For the house in the Rue de Tilsitt was now subjected to a perfect invasion from early morning to night. There were journalists, gossip-columnists, editors of periodicals never seen on stalls or kiosks, reporters, *échotiers*, men in frock-coats, in shabby suits, in bowler hats, in caps, with sword-sticks and monocles— would-be specialists in foreign politics, who knew nothing about America except the condor of General Grant's sons, the last of the Mohicans, La Perichole, and an Argentine tango called *El Choclo* that was the rage of the moment. They came at all hours "in search of information", vaguely menacing, declaring that they were still receiving terrible news from *over there*, that it was known that students and journalists were being ruthlessly persecuted, many European interests threatened, and above all, above all, there was the extraordinary suicide of Monsieur Garcin—a former inmate of Cayenne it was true, but a Frenchman after all—whose body had been found a little while ago, hanging from a disused excavating machine a few kilometres from Nueva Córdoba. Behind *Le Petit Journal*, whose sales were diminishing seriously at that time, there loomed representatives of *L'Excelsior*, insidiously suggesting that pictorial matter was reproduced in its pages unusually clearly; behind *Le Cri de Paris* stood *La Libre Parole*, and so from greater to less, from blackmailing dailies to scandal-mongering reviews, finally reaching the provincial papers—*Basses Pyrénées*, *Alpes Maritimes*, Echoes of the North, Armorican beacons, Marseillaise lampoons —forming a daily procession of treacherous cadgers, who had to be kept quiet by the language of figures, with the splendid help of the Mummy. There it was, photographed from every angle; there was the Ancestor of America, two, three or four thousand years old, according to the whim of the writer, but in any case the most ancient exhibit from the Continent, whose history had been sent rocketing vertiginously backwards by the discovery. There was promise for our scientific institutions, and for the

Head of State, author of this sensational find; thanks for having made such a valuable present to a Parisian museum. But the Mummy didn't arrive. Put on board a Swedish cargo-boat, to be unloaded at Cherbourg, by some mistake it had got to Gothenburg whither the Cholo Mendoza had been sent to look for it.

And meanwhile, ever insatiable, ever threatening reporters kept on arriving at the Rue de Tilsitt "in search of news".

"I can't take any more; I can't take any more," the Head of State groaned, after receiving a visit from a woman journalist on *Lisez-moi Bleu*. "These shits will fleece me utterly! They may say what they like, I won't give them a centime more!" However, he went on handing out and handing out, although now that the Mummy had been photographed, described and compared to other mummies—in the Louvre and the British Museum—it provided no material for any more articles. Searching for a new approach, Peralta studied cases of the Virgin's appearance on earth, in order to relate them to our cult of the Divine Shepherdess—perhaps this theme might interest readers of Catholic papers.

And in the middle of all this confusion the pistol-shot at Sarajevo rang out, followed by the shots that killed Jaurès in the *Café du Croissant*.

"Thank God something has happened at last on this bloody continent!" said the Head of State. On August 2 there was general mobilization, and on August 4 the War began.

"Don't let another journalist into this house," said the President to Sylvestre. And to Doctor Peralta, "Now we can have a rest!"

That same night the Head of State began going his former rounds. He and his Secretary went to Monsieur Musard's *Bois-Charbons*, to *Aux glaces* at 25 Rue Sainte-Apolline; to the house of the English schoolgirls and the little Sisters of Saint Vincent de Paul. Everywhere the talk was the same. Some said that the war would be short and French armies would soon arrive in Berlin: others said it would be a long, agonizing, dreadful war.

"Nonsense," said the President. "The last war, because it

was the last classical war, was the Franco-Prussian in '70." An eminent English economist had recently shown ("and you can find his book in Nelson's Edition") that no civilized nation was in a position to stand the expense of a prolonged conflict. Modern arms were too dear, no country could face the cost of maintaining armies which now add up to millions of men. Moreover, as the French General Staff had already proclaimed: "Three months, three battles, three victories."

At this moment Ofelia arrived from Salzburg by way of Switzerland, pregnant by the Papageno in *The Magic Flute*. They had foolishly embraced one night, when she had drunk so much that she had forgotten to use the diaphragm she always carried in her bag for unforeseen circumstances—and idiotically let herself be fucked in a little house surrounded by pines on the Kapuzinnersberg. She arrived in a fury; furious at having to get rid of *it* elsewhere, because the stupid doctors here wouldn't undertake this form of intervention, whatever one paid them; furious at the article in *Le Matin*, which had been echoed in Germany and Austria, and at a caricature in Munich's *Simplississimus* showing the Head of State in a wide Mexican hat, cartridge-belt across his chest, a millionaire's paunch and a cigar between his fangs, shooting a kneeling peasant woman.

"You've ballsed-up everything as usual!" cried the Infanta. "The monkey's frock-coat doesn't hide its tail! If you killed so many people you might at least have included the photographer!"

"They've seen to that already!"

"Fine goings-on! When everything was past praying for! They did better when they shot that Archduke! Perhaps as things are now they'll forget your imbecilities! Because everyone is giving us the cold shoulder. We're sunk. Up to here in shit" (putting a finger on her forehead).

The Head of State took his right arm out of its silk sling. The power to move it was coming back; already the elbow-joint had stopped hurting. He could almost feel the butt of his pistol. Leaving Ofelia shouting and stamping (she must have had a few more whiskies than usual in the dining-car) he went out to dinner with Doctor Peralta in a basement near the Gare

Saint-Lazare where, sitting at a table covered with pitchers of wine, one could taste eighty varieties of cheese—among them a goat cheese marbled with aromatic herbs whose strong flavour reminded him of the cream cheese of the Andes.

7

. . . when we are particularly pleased with ourselves
our injuries seem to us all the greater.

DESCARTES

That summer was the most beautiful and the sunniest recorded by European meteorologists. The monks in all the German hygroscopes had their hoods permanently thrown back on their necks; the peasant with the umbrella of Swiss hygroscopes remained hidden in his rustic alpine chalet, while that personification of fine weather, the girl with a red apron, was out all the time. The chestnuts bloomed gaily and the birds sang often among the statues in the gardens of the Tuileries and Luxembourg, ignoring the perpetual warlike preparations invading the life of the capital; but there was considerable dismay at a succession of events which took many people by surprise, notwithstanding a succession of dramatically premonitory signs, and reminded those who had experienced it in a disquieting way of the chaotic epic of '70. The Head of State assumed that the very costly campaign of praise of his country and government in the newspapers could now come to an end, since the public were only interested in news of the furies unleashed upon Europe. His campaign had been doubly useless, because of what was now happening and because (to tell the truth) it had not re-established his prestige in quarters where he had been most anxious to have it restored. Or, anyway, he could see no signs that it had. No one had rung him on the telephone to make favourable comments about any article—except his tailor and his barber, of course. The people he was interested in were all on holiday—holidays that had been wisely prolonged in expectation of developments. Reynaldo Hahn, whose opinion he had been brave enough to ask, gave a short, inconsistent and slippery reply: "Yes, I saw . . . Yes, I saw . . . All very good . . . I congratulate you, compatriot." It was obvious that at the end of the year, when he was *over there* again, he wouldn't receive all those cards covered in bells and mistletoe from Paris, those cards on filigree paper, with signatures (far more soothing to his spirit than the praise handed out to him daily by the local press) written by highly esteemed and admired hands in response to his own carefully thought-out Christmas wishes, always accompanied by some charming object made by our country's craftsmen. He had therefore to give up cultivating those persons whose company and friendship he counted on for the days when, having resigned from Office—out of boredom, fatigue or anything else—he could pass the last days of his life in this always agreeable and comfortable mansion in the Rue de Tilsitt. He had no intention of leaving Paris at the moment—and in fact there wasn't much danger here—provided that the treatment of his arm was soon completed; it had already nearly been cured by the skill of Doctor Fournier. obliged by his duties as a house surgeon to remain in the city, Accompanied by his Secretary, the President took long aimless walks, waiting for the evening papers; sometimes, when he felt a desire for fresh verdure, getting as far as the Bois de Boulogne, whose *Sentier de la Vertu* was now deserted, while the swans on the lake stretched their necks interrogatively, vainly hoping for pieces of biscuit which passers-by and children would have thrown them, even a few days ago. They sat together in front of the Pré-Catalan, feeling nostalgic for the charming frivolities of other days, although the Head of State, passing from intimate monologue to semi-confession, suddenly began considering this war from the viewpoint of a somewhat bitter and stern moralist, to Peralta's increasing surprise. Nations given over to luxury and indolence—he said—grew soft and lost their fundamental virtues. Aestheticism was all very well, but to recover the use of muscles grown feeble in the contemplation of Beauty, man felt a need—after his long period of dreaming—

for hand-to-hand fighting, *agon*. The romantic figure of Ludwig of Bavaria, celebrated by our Rubén Dario and even by Verlaine, was all very fine, but for the unity and greatness of a divided and dormant Germany, a solid, rough character like Bismarck, always ready for war, could do much more than the musical prince, builder of castles as poetic as they were remote from all reality. This contest would not last long ("three months, three battles, three victories", said the generals themselves) nor would it be so bloody as the war of '70, because people had learned from the remembered experience and wouldn't allow it to be prolonged as it was in the horrors of the Commune. And France would soon be subjected to a jolt, a therapeutic emergency, a shock to shake her out of her self-sufficient lethargy. She was too stuck up, she needed a lesson. She still believed she ruled the world, whereas in fact her great resources were exhausted, she had entered on a phase of obvious decadence. The Reign of the Giants—Hugo, Balzac, Renan, Michelet, Zola—was over. Minds of such universal brilliance were no longer being produced here, and that was why France was beginning to pay for the grave sin of proudly under-estimating, in this multiform century, what lay outside her frontiers. Nothing foreign to his own country interested a Frenchman, convinced as he was that he was born to delight humanity. But today he was confronted by a new man, thunderously declaring what he wanted, a man who might make himself master of this age: Nietzschean man, motivated by an implacable Will to Power, the tragic and aggressive protagonist of an everlasting reward, repeated today in actions that disturbed the world.

Peralta was well aware of the modest standard of his friend's powers of thought; he was convinced that the Head of State had never read Nietzsche, and that if he was quoting him so authoritatively today it was because in some article read yesterday he had come across some of his views, duly placed between inverted commas. Besides, he was accustomed to follow the ups and downs of his character, and understood that behind these general reflections the President concealed a bitter spite against the people who had humiliated and offended him, closing the road to his chosen abode. When he uttered the names of Bismarck or Nietzsche, he was aiming the mental batteries of his resentment at Brichot the Sorbonne professor, the insolent Couvoisier, the Forchevilles and the Comte d'Argencourt, the unsuccessful diplomat who, on meeting him casually in a bookshop where they were both buying pornography disguised as *Compendium of Hindu Erotism* or *The Licentious Writers of the Eighteenth Century* but illustrated with actual photographs, had ignored him with haughty disdain, leaving his outstretched hand in the air. And Peralta, maliciously observing him, stirred the fire of this growing aggressiveness by trying to find weighty arguments in his casual and unmethodical reading of the previous days about miraculous appearances of the Virgin all over the world, to support articles about "The miracle of Nueva Córdoba", though they hadn't yet been published—or paid for.

One morning he gave the Head of State enormous pleasure by showing him an essay by a famous Catholic writer, celebrated for his irascibility, the outcries and imprecations of an ungrateful beggar ("ungrateful beggar" was his own name for himself), wherein he stated that after the Chosen People of Israel, France was the nation most beloved by God. Without France "God would not be entirely God," he said. Besides, everything went to prove it: the *considerate lilia agri* of the Scriptures announced the Fleur de Lys of French Royalty, the *Gallo* of the Last Supper was a plain allusion to the *Coq Gaulois*. France of the Lily, France of the Cock, France of the Good Bread and Good Wine of the Communion Service, whose position as home of the Chosen Race had been confirmed in modern times—added the writer—by three appearances of the Virgin in thirty-three years; at Pontmain, Lourdes and La Salette.

These prodigies can never have aroused such hearty laughter: "So France is the land of the Paraclete? And what place does this gentleman allow to Spain, which spread the Catholic faith through a portion of the planet stretching from the Rio Grande in Mexico to the snows of the South Pole? And as for Virgins!" The radiant Virgin of Guadalupe, on her sacred rock of

Tepeyac; the Virgin of Cobré in Cuba, whose image appeared floating miraculously, robed in sargasso beside the boat manned by Juan Odio, Juan the Indian and Juan the Slave; the Virgin of Regla, patron saint of sailors and fishermen everywhere, standing in her star-spangled cloak on the Globe of the World; the Virgin of the Valley in Costa Rica; our own Divine Shepherdess; the Virgin of Chiquinquirá, with her proud bearing and beautiful breasts, very much the woman and the lady too, with her castellated crown; the Virgin of Coromotos, who had left her portrait—after an ineffable appearance—in an Indian's hut; the Virgin of the Amazon fighters of la Fe, clad in fiery armour beneath her protective cloak; the Virgin of Quinche, who led the Army of Ecuador; and the Virgin of Indulgences, patron of the army, and military leader of Peru, always accompanied by Saint Pedro Claver, patron of slaves, and the negro Saint Benito—"as black as the nails in the Cross" —and Saint Rose of Lima, dazzling Queen of the Continent, who owned the greatest forests, the longest mountain ranges, the Greatest River in the World. These Virgins advanced in a formidable Squadron of splendour, Our Lady of Regla somewhat blackened, the Virgin of Coromotos with almond eyes; strong and full of pity, beautiful and gentle, carrying the Seven Dolours of their Seven Swords, prodigies, succour, good fortune and miracles, ready to come to the aid of anyone who called them, seen a hundred times, heard a hundred times, diligent and magnificent, omnipresent and ubiquitous, able to appear—like God to Saint Teresa—in the depths of a stewpot or on the summit of an Ivory Tower; mothers, above all, the Mothers of a prodigious Offspring wounded in the side, who one day (seated on the right hand of Our Lord) would distribute punishment and rewards and submit us all to a judgement against which there was no appeal.

"Let that ungrateful beggar, or whatever he calls himself, come here and talk to me about his three French Virgins; the authenticity of one of them, Our Lady of La Salette, has been questioned by the Vatican itself!" We had Virgins, real Virgins, and it was high time to rid these people here of their conceit and suicidal ignorance of everything that didn't belong to them.

They would soon realize what was meant by a strong, well-organized, disciplined, progressive race.

And Germany, where he had spent very little time, suddenly appeared to him as an illuminated tapestry of Black Forests, Master Singers, Soldier Kings, and cathedrals from whose Gothic windows apostles and trumpeters emerged on the stroke of twelve, beside the Rhine—that great Rhine with its incredible castles, sung about and sketched by Victor Hugo—and its water-nymphs who caught young men in the nets of their hair, and its beer festivals attended by cheerful men with solid calves to their legs, who combined yodelling and playing the accordion with a taste for philosophy of the contorted Heidelberg variety, a genius for mathematics, a cult of obedience and love of marching ten abreast—to sum up: everything that those dirty Latins of the Second Decadence lacked. But now they would see who was best, when Generals Moltke, Kluck, Bülow and Falkenhayn paraded through the Arc de Triomphe (he would be watching the spectacle, standing stiffly erect at his window, although perhaps moved by what others might be suffering, but resolved in the Cartesian manner to take as proved everything whose truth was evident to him), mounted on magnificent sorrel horses, escorting the Crown Prince at the head of an impressive procession, with the black dolmans of hussars, frogged Brandenburgs and helmets with a point, to the rhythm of the great march from *Tannhäuser*, taken at a military tempo, faster than is usual at the opera. On that day Germany would finally carry out the role of "regenerative ferment" prophetically assigned to her by Fichte in a historic manifesto—a manifesto that had not been read by the Head of State either, thought Peralta, although he had to recognize his infallible instinct for acquiring information at second hand.

Agitated by the threat creeping towards Paris (though in the streets people went on shouting, "À Berlin! À Berlin! À Berlin!") and asking themselves if it wouldn't be advisable to move their offices to Bordeaux, Marseilles or Lyons, the consuls and high officials of Latin American embassies used to meet together at the times of the morning aperitif, the evening aperitif and a great many late-night drinks in a café in the

Champs-Elysées, and discuss the day's events. Ever attentive to what was said at these gatherings, noting the opinions of each of them, the Cholo Mendoza carried back information that confirmed the Head of State's intuitions. The President had received from his friend Juan Vicente Gómez, one of those generals much addicted to a Kaiser moustache and a monocle wedged in one eye (by confidential word of mouth, because the Venezuelan dictator was afraid they would jeer at his handwriting), the wise advice to remain on the margin of the whole affair (because "the little fellow who gets into a row between big chaps always gets crushed"). Although nearly all these Latin Americans sympathized with France for cultural or sentimental reasons—some loved her literature, others her women, and their duties involved very little work and amounted to long and pleasant holidays while their governments lasted, in the place it was most enjoyable to spend them—there were quite a few who agreed that the war was already lost to this side. One only had to observe the confusion, the fruitless agitation, the *pagaille* they were living in, although it was not reflected in the newspapers, which confined themselves to half-truths or disguised news items, as even Doctor Fournier admitted in the daily sessions of massage and ray treatment he gave to the Head of State's arm, which was every day becoming freer and more mobile. In the streets very different opinions were expressed from those filling the articles of Barrès, Déroulède and other writers who were, like Tyrtaeus, stimulating the national energy: they spoke of whole regiments left without officers, or taken to sectors where nothing was happening and not knowing whether to stay there, advance or retreat. In some units only half the men had proper uniforms, kepis alternated with police helmets, and puttees were supplanted by bandages from the chemist or waxed paper. Later came dramatic tales of rifles without bullets, shells without guns, ambulances losing their way, and field hospitals without surgical instruments. And next came rumours spread by romancers and alarmists and generally accepted in small cafés, porters' lodges and among groups of street-corner strategists: about Uhlans seen only a few kilometres from Paris; a highly secret German plan of penetrating the city through the tunnels of the Metro; the activity of spies, who were everywhere, looking, listening, transmitting messages by a system of curtains shut or drawn at night in attic rooms, according to a code of lights invented by a Prussian crypto-grapher.

Already the first papers referring to the "European War" were arriving from our countries—a fresh, good and exciting subject in these monotonous times—full of sensationalism and emotion. Once again people were confronted by huge headlines, or "Stop press telegrams" printed in twelve point type, as they had been in more interesting times—with some important "news-flash" enclosed in a frame of its own. Many people, accustomed to suppress their thoughts about local happenings for fear of persecution, felt free, elevated and relieved, as it were cathartically, by these great but far-away events, suddenly brought into the forefront of reality. At last they could discuss, argue, conjecture, protest (insult Von Tirpitz, censure Italian neutrality, laugh at the Turks) in accordance with similar tendencies in all the countries of the Continent. *Over there* the clergy were pro-German, because impious France promoted lay education and had separated Church from State, while the Spanish bankers, the many descendants of German emigrants, and the relations and friends of the little clan of officials who were jokingly called "Little Fredericks" were already applauding the Kaiser's certain victory. But all the intelligentsia, writers, academics, readers of Rubén Dario or Gomez Carrillo were pro-Allies (no one understood about the *Entente*), as were all those who had been, or dreamed of one day becoming, school-teachers, along with free-thinkers, doctors trained in Paris and a large section of the middle-classes—above all those who, at social gatherings, sometimes talked French as affectedly and badly as the characters in *War and Peace*. Generally speaking, this was true of the whole nation, because the French came to our countries more for commercial than other reasons, and had never gone in for tiresome competition with the natives, but treated everyone alike amiably, often allied themselves with zambas* and cholas, in this respect being very different from

* Zambo (m.) and Zamba (f.) is the offspring of a negro and an Indian.

those who shut themselves up in "German Clubs", or "German Cafés", which admitted only those of pure white blood, and where the appearance of a negro or Indian would have been greeted by a Fafner-like baring of teeth.

And now they were entering the month of September, amid doubts and anxieties, although the Head of State surveyed the daily prospect with almost enjoyable expectation. To judge from the speed of their operations, Von Moltke's armies would soon reach the Arc de Triomphe without much difficulty, since France now possessed no generals of the stature of those whose names were inscribed on Napoleon's monument. And this proud, perverted metropolis was to experience a purification by fire which more than one French Catholic writer would have compared to Sodom and Gomorrah—or even to the whore of Babylon, after the erection (a word that should only be used in reference to statues or architectural works, according to Flaubert) of its Eiffel Tower, Tower of Babel, modern ziggurat, lighthouse of cosmopolitanism, symbol of the Confusion of Tongues, happily balanced by other pinnacles such as the white cupolas—though its architect had wanted them to be gold—of Sacré-Coeur. But the Head of State, who was a dispenser of indulgences when other people's actions didn't force him to be Distributor of Punishments, was not thinking about fire in terms of conflagrations and collapsing ceilings, but about a psychological fire, a moral chastisement which would force the Arrogant and Self-sufficient to humble themselves and ask for peace. That fire must not of course damage the frescoes of the Panthéon, the pink stone of the Place des Vosges, the windows of Notre-Dame, nor yet the chastity-belts in the Abbaye de Cluny, the wax figures and illusions in the Musée Grévin, or the leafy chestnut trees of the avenue where the Comtesse de Noailles lived (although she was one of those who were cutting him) and still less the Trocadero, where as soon as the war was over our Mummy (now being fetched from Gothenburg by the Cholo Mendoza) would be displayed in a glass case. And it could only need a few days, surely, for the War to be over. Doctor Fournier, as he discharged his patient—whose hand now went to his pistol easily and quickly, without his forefinger going numb on the trigger—broke into lamentations about the lack of preparation on the part of the Supreme Command, the improvidence, negligence, muddle—*c'est encore la débâcle*—that were carrying us towards inevitable defeat.

"*Vous faites bien de repartir chez vous, cher Monsieur. Au moins, là-bas, c'est le soleil, c'est le rhum, c'est les mulâtresses.*"

But on the afternoon of September 7 the Battle of the Marne began. ("A war is not won by taxi-drivers," the Head of State had remarked ironically.) It was soon apparent that in opposition to Jomini's tactics and strategy, the French front line had no centre, this being occupied solely by a weak contingent of cavalry. On the 8th it looked as if they had lost. But on the afternoon of the 9th victory was theirs. That evening, the Latin-American diplomats gathered together in their café in the Champs-Elysées and celebrated this triumph by inviting every prostitute who passed to have a drink, while the Head of State—who had joined them for once—looked imposing in his frock-coat, and with a patriarchal wisdom recognized by all, muttered: "Certainly . . . certainly. . . . However, this doesn't settle anything."

Next day he got up very early, in an embittered frame of mind, and stood contemplating the Arc de Triomphe, whose size seemed to increase or dwindle according to whether his defeatist desires were satisfied or frustrated. Now that his arm was cured, he must think about returning *over there*—he had no reason to stay on here—moreover, he must renounce for the present his hopes of a triumphal procession with deafening yet comic military bands marching like automatons, trombones and trumpets with blown-out cheeks, and all the musicians conducted by an enormous Drum-Major. He was just going to telephone Peralta to suggest a stroll to Monsieur Musard's *Bois-Charbons* when the Secretary came into the room, looking disturbed and holding a long message on blue paper:

"Read this . . . read this."

The cable was from Roque García, President of the Senate:

HAVE TO INFORM YOU GENERAL WALTER HOFFMANN REBELLED IN CIUDAD MORENO WITH INFANTRY BATTALIONS 3, 8, 9, 11. ALSO FOUR REGIMENTS INCLUDING HUSSARS, ALSO FOUR UNITS ARTILLERY

TO CRY OF LONG LIVE THE CONSTITUTION, LONG LIVE LIBERTY.
"The cunt! The son of a bitch!" yelled the Head of State.
But this was not all: three of the "Little Fredericks"—Breker,
the blond "good chap", always favoured by notes and instructions from above; González, who had trained as a soldier in
Germany; and Martorell, a Catalan artilleryman become a
creole out of hatred of the Spanish monarchy—these three
young soldiers, flattered, privileged and rapidly advancing in
the hierarchy, were all taking part in the coup.

"Sons of bitches! Sons of bitches!"

And suddenly giving way to paroxysms of rage, the Head of
State shouted, raged and stormed, and then sank into the
depths of despair, groaning, wounded, seeming as if pierced to
the heart, and stammering out the most damaging adjectives he
could find to describe treachery, felony, ingratitude, deceit and
fraud. His monologue reached a climax of exasperation, only
to relapse once more into lamentations near to tears, as if he
were unable to find words to express his disillusion; then,
quickly recovering himself and again growing excited, he
exploded into a fresh outburst of oaths and terrible threats.

("I've heard that Mounet-Sully is a great tragedian,"
thought Peralta, "but there can't be another like my
President. . . .")

And the Head of State was still shouting and raging, over-
turning furniture, throwing books on the floor, aiming at
Gérome's gladiators with his Belgian pistol, and making such a
furious commotion that Sylvestre came hurrying from the
pantry in alarm.

"*Monsieur est malade? . . . Un médecin peut-être?*"

Suddenly controlling himself—or pretending to do so—the
enraged man turned to his servant: "*Ce n'est rien, Sylvestre . . .
Rien . . . Un mouvement d'humeur . . . Merci.*"

And unfastening his tie, still red in the face, sweating and
with words of reproof ringing in his ears, the President began to
walk from end to end of the room, giving orders and instructions
to Doctor Peralta. Go to the nearest travel agency—the one
near the Opéra would still be open—and do everything
necessary to get them *there* as soon as possible. Ask Roque

García for details of garrisons loyal to the Government. Cable to Ariel; cable to our newspapers with a proclamation to go on the front page ("Once again, the blind ambition of a man unworthy of the rank he possesses, etc., etc. Good: you know what is wanted . . ."); cable to him, cable to the other, cables and more cables. . . .

Just then the cries of the newspaper boys announced a midday edition, with the latest war news.

"As if I cared a damn for all that!"

And out of pure rage he kicked over a picture brought him a few hours before by a pupil of Jean-Paul Laurens, and a protégé of Ofelia's, which was standing on the floor in front of him, waiting to be hung up: *The execution of Ganelon.*

"The cunt! Son of a bitch!" repeated the Head of State stamping on the canvas as if in the figure of the most famous traitor of mediaeval times he saw some similarity to the renegade, infamous, obscene soul of General Walter Hoffmann.

8

*It is better to modify our desires
than the organization of the world.*

DESCARTES

So next morning they would catch the train to Saint-Nazaire, whence a ship was leaving for New York, full of Americans who, having seen the Germans approach too close to the Seine and knowing that the war was by no means over, with its inconveniences and rationing, preferred to return to the opposite side of the Ocean. After the crossing, there would be several days of enforced idleness—as before, at the Waldorf Astoria. There was a possibility of seeing a performance of Umberto Giordano's *Madame Sans-Gêne*, sung by Geraldine Farrar (for the Metropolitan Opera House had announced its world première) and although his daughter took him for an ignoramus where music was concerned, merely because he had on occasion been so bewildered and bored by the telluric entanglements of *Rhinegold* with its confusion of dwarfs, giants and water-nymphs as to fall asleep in his box, the President was very appreciative of Maria Barrientos' coloratura, Titta Ruffo's significant lyrical energy, the pure timbre of Caruso's long, incredibly sustained high notes and his magic voice, so prodigiously enclosed in the body of a Neapolitan innkeeper.

After having got rid of *it* somewhere in Switzerland, Ofelia had left for London, to escape from this tiresome war, now making itself felt according to her in the lack of Russian ballets, tango orchestras and elegant parties in full evening-dress. In England, on the other hand, recruitment was voluntary, and life was fairly normal: so she would go to Stratford-on-Avon with a view to completing her Shakespearian education.

"I wonder if some Fortinbras or Rosenkranz will make her pregnant?" thought her father, well knowing that nothing that happened *over there* in their native land mattered to his daughter, who had decided some time ago to live for ever in Europe, far away—as she said—from "that country of filth and sweat", with no amusements except municipal concerts, family parties where everyone danced the polka, mazurka and redowa, and Palace soirées where the wives of ministers and generals clustered together at the further end of the room from a group of men telling dirty stories, to talk about births and miscarriages, children, illnesses, deceitful servants and deaths of grand-mothers, interspersed with exchanging receipts for crème caramel, egg-flip, babas, marzipan and cream cake.

That night the Head of State and Doctor Peralta paid a farewell visit to Monsieur Musard at the *Bois-Charbons*, and drank heavily. Afterwards they took two girls picked up on the street to a luxury brothel in the Rue Sainte-Beuve, whose entrance hall, decorated with ceramics by Léon-Paul Fargue's father, led to a rickety lift, worked by a piston-rod and got up in traditional style so that it looked rather like the corner of a Norman dining-room moving vertically. It was late when he got back to the Rue de Tilsitt, to find the corridors and rooms heaped with suitcases and trunks packed by Sylvestre. Doctor Peralta showed him some stereoscopic pornographic photographs—the *Verascope Richard*—he had bought the evening before, and which with their double images gave a surprisingly three-dimensional effect.

"Look. Do look at this. You'd think that man was alive. And you can see every hair on those two women. And what do you think of that combination of five in a row?"

In spite of having drunk so much, the Head of State, though intoxicated, was lucid and sad. He was invaded by a feeling of enormous fatigue when he thought of the efforts he had had to exert four times since he took on the Government. Now there would be his arrival in Puerto Araguato. The train of old coaches climbing up to the capital through forests whose trees mingled —it was impossible to know which branches grew from the trunks and which had been cut by machetes—with those that roofed the huts in villages so melancholy and overshadowed by the universal vegetation that a laugh in one of them would have sounded like some obscene explosion of animality. Afterwards, the obligatory speech from the balcony of the Palace. His battledress, probably smelling of camphor, ironed by the Mayorala Elmira, his irreplaceable housekeeper, a woman of excellent judgement, and (when he felt like it) a docile and complacent source of consolation; the journey to the battle front would be towards the south this time—a few months ago it was to the north, on other occasions it had been to the east or west. Now it led to the region of the Quaking Bogs, with their purplish lagoons constantly bubbling and pullulating with the animals and reptiles hidden beneath the deceptive peace of Victoria water-lilies. Marching along flooded paths, with one's face plastered with revolting ointment which for barely an hour kept off the stings of a hundred species of mosquito. It was a world of sweating hibiscus, false carnations—traps for insects—scum which tangled and disentangled its convolutions from sunset to sunrise, funguses smelling of vinegar, oily flowers growing from rotten trunks, greenish dust and tendrils, collapsed ant-hills, deceptive turf that ate into boot-leather. And it was through such country that he must pursue

General Hoffmann, find him, surround him, corner him, and finally put him up against the wall of a convent, church or cemetery and shoot him. "Fire!" There was nothing else to be done. Those were the rules of the game. Recourse to Method.

But something else was perturbing the Head of State this time. And it was a problem of words. When he returned *over there*, before he again put on the General's uniform which everyone knew was phoney—that was the truth—since he himself had assumed it, gold braid and all, on a day of youthful ragging, and kept it afterwards because one general more or one general less in his country . . . now, before increasing his stature by getting on horseback, before girding on the cowboy spurs he usually wore during a campaign, he would have to make a speech, to utter words. And those words refused to come to mind, because the classical, fluent, serviceable words he had always used on former and similar occasions had been so often rehashed in different registers with corresponding pantomimic gestures as to have become worn-out, old and ineffective in the present contingency. Contradicted innumerable times by his actions, these words had passed from the market-place to the dictionary, from fiery tirade to rhetorical repertory, from useful eloquence to an attic full of rubbish—devoid of meaning, dry, arid, useless. For years the pillars supporting his political speeches had been such expressions as *Liberty, Loyalty, Independence, Sovereignty, National Honour, Sacred Principles, Legitimate Rights, Civic Conscience, Fidelity to our Traditions, Historic Mission, Duty to the Country*, etc., etc. But now these words (he was always a severe self-critic) had acquired such a ring of false money, of lead dipped in gold, that he felt tired of the twists and turns of his own verbal labyrinth, and began wondering how he would fill the audible gaps, the written spaces in the proclamations and admonitions inevitably involved in a military—and primitive—operation, such as the one he must shortly embark on. Accepted formerly by most of his compatriots as a man of action, able to direct the fate of the country at a time of crisis or lawlessness, he had seen his prestige diminish and an alarming deterioration in his authority, in spite of every device he had invented to remain in power. He knew that he was hated, abhorred by the mass of the people, and this knowledge made him react against the external world, and at the same time increased the satisfaction and pleasure he found in the servility, solicitude and adulation of his dependants, who had consolidated his interests and prosperity and extended to the utmost a sovereignty quite unsupported by legality and Constitution. But he couldn't fail to know that his enemies were in the right when they accused him of giving more and more concessions to the gringos, and it would have been foolish to deny that the gringos were universally detested on the Continent. We all knew that they called us "Latins" and that to them, this was as good as saying rabble, small fry and negro rebels. (They had even invented the euphemism "Latin colour" to justify the admission of important persons whose complexion was a trifle exotic into New York and Washington hotels.)

And the Head of State went on thinking about the speech he had to make, without being able to imagine it in a favourable light. Words, words, words. Always the same words. But above all, nothing about *Liberty*—with the jails full of political prisoners.... Nothing about *National Honour* or *Duty to the Country*—because these were the concepts always used by top-ranking military men. No *Historic Mission* nor *Heroes' Ashes* for the same reason. No *Independence*, which in his case rhymed with *dependence*. No *Virtues*—when he was known to be the owner of the richest businesses in the country. No *Legitimate Rights*—since he ignored them whenever they conflicted with his own personal jurisprudence. His vocabulary was decidedly narrowing. And he had a formidable adversary: a regiment of the rebellious Army; he would have to speak, yet the exasperated orator felt aphonic, without a language, as if he no longer had useful, dynamic, stimulating words at his disposal, because he had squandered them, blunted their edge, prostituted them in despicable skirmishes unworthy of such extravagance. As our countrymen would say: "He had wasted gun-powder on vultures."

"I'm getting old," he thought. But he had to make up something. Something.

He emptied one of the leather-covered flasks in a series of

short but continuous gulps, and to pass the time of waiting for
ideas that didn't come he picked up one of the morning papers
—*Le Figaro*—which lay folded on his writing-table. There, in
the first column of the front page, and printed in a special
frame, was an article by the Distinguished Academician.
Drawing conclusions from the Battle of the Marne, our friend
affirmed that that military miracle—more than a victory of
arms: a victory for intelligence—signified, above all, the triumph
of the Latin over the German spirit. Heirs to the Great
Mediterranean Culture, descendants of Plato, Virgil,
Montaigne, Racine and the magnificent sansculottes of
Valmy—appropriate to the present situation although their
memory was detested by the whole Faubourg Saint Germain—
they had opposed the Genius of their Race, made up of sanity,
balance and moderation, to the pathological aggressiveness of
the Teutons. The Gallic Cock against dragons, cave-dwelling
blacksmiths and Niebelungen. The nervous, active, thorough-
bred charger of the already almost sainted Maid of Orleans—
she was in fact about to be canonized—against Brünnhilde's
fierce steed. Olympus against Valhalla. Apollo against Hagen.
Versailles against Potsdam. Pascal's essential wisdom against
Hegel's philosophical gigantism—expressed in that obscure
Heidelberg jargon which our minds, addicted to lucidity and
transparency in argument, have instinctively rejected. The
battle of the marshes of Saint-Gond had been a victory for
Descartes, rather than for the '75 cannon. And the writer
closed with a forcible, implacable, unanswerable denunciation
of German culture—or *Kultur*, as he called it—of Wagner's
music, the bad taste of Berliners, the pedantic scientism of
Haeckel, and the ideas of petulant dwarfs who (believing
themselves to be superhuman and disguising themselves as
Zarathustra, with swords at their belts and skulls on their
shakos) had unleashed the present catastrophe, like modern
sorcerers' apprentices. It was war, more than war, it was a Holy
Crusade against Prussian Neo-barbarism.

   When he had finished reading the article, the Head of State
began to walk up and down his room. He suddenly understood
his mistake: the pro-German attitude of a resentful "metic",

an alien in a foreign land—and he remembered that the Greeks didn't use the word in a denigratory sense—was neither useful nor profitable to him. In these crucial moments in his political career, Von Kluck's Uhlans and Von Tirpitz's submarines could not help him. The Valkyrie's cause was a bad cause for him—a cause that "didn't pay". He was forced to admit that in Latin America everyone sided with France—better to say: with Paris. And *over there*, to transfer the problem to our own country, pro-Germans were often Jesuits, pastors of a chosen flock, confessors to rich women and not very friendly to the humble French Maristas who had educated them; pro-Germans were found among rich Spaniards, gentlemen of the *Import-Export*—when they weren't grocers or pawn-brokers—with large balances in banks in Catalonia or Bilbao, antipathetic to the creole by tradition and custom; and also—but this was a special case—among the population of the colony of Olmedo, descendants of Bavarian or Pomeranian workmen who had no importance in public life. Moreover—Good God! I've just realized!—all the Virgins of our countries were Latins. Because Christ's Mother was a Latin, doubly Latin, now that those disgusting Lutherans—like Hoffmann and the "Little Fredericks", who sided with him—have thrown her out of their chapels. The Divine Shepherdess of Nueva Córdoba, the Virgins of Chiquinquirá, Coromotos, Guadalupe, La Caridad del Cobre, and all those who made up the Ineffable Legion of Intercessors, were the ubiquitous manifestations of the one and eternal Presence enthroned in the nave of Notre-Dame by Louis XIII, when he consecrated his reign to the worship of the Virgin Mary. The Virgins must therefore be reckoned on our side—on mine in this conflict, and her image erected on the labarum—since it was the duty of a Ruler confronted by hostile forces to make use of anything that might advance his cause. A Leader of his People, a Director of Men, must be adaptable and never obstinate, although he might have to renounce his most personal desires at any given moment, in order to remain in power. The ideological basis—tactics—of his immediate struggle with the traitor Hoffmann thus became clear. One only had to consider his name; remember his German training;

his eagerness to proclaim his pure Aryan blood, although he had relegated his somewhat negroid grandmother to the remotest buildings in his huge colonial domain. Suddenly Aunt Jemima— as the foolish people *over there* called her—would have to be converted into a symbol of Latinity. (Worried and depressed a few moments before, the Dictator recovered his spirits, drew himself up, banged on tables and began to behave like an orator again.) After all, being a Latin did not mean having "pure blood" or "clean blood"—as the out-of-date phraseology of the Inquisition used to put it. All races of the ancient world had been mixed together in the great Mediterranean basin, mother of our culture. In that tremendous round bed Romans had lain with Egyptian women, Trojans with Carthaginians, the famous Helen with people of dull complexion. The wolf who suckled Romulus and Remus had several teats—and it was known that Italy would one of these days attack the Central Powers—and any cholo or zamba might have fed from them. To say *Latinity* was to say mixed blood, and in Latin America we are all mestizos; all of us have some negro or Indian, Phoenician, Moorish, Celtiberian blood, or the blood of Cádiz—and there's always Walker lotion, or something of the sort, to smooth our hair, hidden away in the family medicine chest. We are all mestizos, and should be honoured that it is so!

And now the Head of State's mind began producing ideas; words returned to him and he was suddenly in command of a new vocabulary. Resplendent words, high-sounding, pleasant to the ear, which must be well received *over there* by those half-hearted, undecided, potential enemies, more or less dedicated to a pro-Ally oulook, who had all become strategists and showed their predilections by moving little tricolor flags on maps spread on café tables, far beyond the point where the army's advance had been halted by the General Staff itself. People felt passionately, and it was intelligent to capitalize their passion for his own advantage. *Alea jacta est.* His mind was made up: he would be a modern Knight Templar joining the Holy Crusade of Latinity. A victory for Walter Hoffmann and his party would mean the Germanization of our culture. It would be easy to ridicule him in the eyes of the public. With his personality, the books he read: the portraits of Frederick II, Bismarck and Von Moltke which adorned his study; the fact that he treated the poor old woman to whom he owed his existence as a far from decorative ancestress—although she was a true incarnation of our race, flesh of our flesh—concealing her under the tamarind-trees, close to the yard where the pig was being fattened for Christmas Eve. The rebel was a living mirror of the Prussian barbarism which had not only been loosed over Europe, but would also soon be threatening these Lands of the Future, since the Germans believed they were predestined to govern the whole globe in virtue of a mystique about being a *superior race*, clearly expressed recently in an arrogant and xenophobe "Manifesto for intellectuals" that had already appeared in our press. So he must raise the Crown of Saint Rose of Lima against the Shield of the Valkyries. Cuauhtémoc against Alaric. The Redeemer's Cross against Wotan's spear. The sword of all the liberators of the Continent against the Technological Vandals of the Twentieth Century.

"Come here, Peralta."

And for the next two hours, always finding striking adjectives and illuminating images—although this time his style was not too ornate—he dictated articles for his country's newspapers, sketching the broad outline of the campaign as he believed it would develop before his arrival.

"Hurry along and take all this to Western Union."

And now, his energies spent, perhaps tired by so much dictation, and with a delayed feeling of sadness, he gazed round the room, at the friendly furniture, pictures, sculptures. Within a few hours he would have to leave this peaceful maternal lap, this period of repose among silks, satins and velvets, and plunge his horse's hoofs for days, weeks, months maybe, in the mire of the southern Torrid Zone—lianas, mangrove swamps with their stagnant waters, murky streams, and tendrils lashing one's face—far from everything that made him happy. He thought about his country *over there*, and felt in advance the boredom of returning to the point of departure after constantly moving forwards with passing years. It would soon be November—our November with All Saints' Day, when the cemeteries were transformed into fairgrounds, with lanterns strung from tomb to tomb, barrel-organs making a deafening din, guitars playing among the graves, maracas and clarinets close to the chapels of the dead, and girls being deflowered between the faded wreaths of a recent burial. Skulls made of sugar candy or pink icing, skulls made of toffee, marzipan, sesame-flavoured paste, amongst the sextons' spades and straps, coffins, urns, a fine show of bronzes and portraits of grandfathers, soldiers, and children in their Sunday best seen through oval glass dimmed by dew and rain. And then would come the vendors of little skeletons wearing crowns, mitres, top hats, kepis, dancing their Dance of Death from cenotaph to cross, with their cries of: "A skeleton for your little boy", which on this day of all days was a summons to gaiety, aguardiente and molasses. And what conversations were embarked on, what jokes and what quarrels flew between cross and cross, angel and angel, epitaph and epitaph!

"Ah, my friend! You're happy with your little dead son!"

"Ah, my friend, and what a bastard and rogue yours was!"

"So they say, my friend! Yours wasn't such a saint either!"

"That's because he took after his grandmother, my friend!"

"Come now, my friend, how can one say who takes after whom?"

Remembering all this, the Head of State saw himself as someone who had been enclosed in a magic circle made by the sword of the Prince of Darkness. History, which was his because he played a part in it, was something that repeated itself, swallowed its own tail, and never moved forwards—it made very little difference whether the pages of the calendar were printed with 185(?), 189(?), 190(?) or 190(6?): it was the same procession of uniforms and frock-coats, high English top-hats alternating with plumed Bolivian helmets, as one saw in second-rate theatres, where triumphal marches of thirty men passed and re-passed in front of the same drop curtain, running when they were behind it, so as to be in time to re-enter the stage shouting for the fifth time: "Victory! Victory! Long live the Regime! Long live Liberty!" It was the classic example of the knife given a new handle when the old one wears out, and a new blade when that wears out in its turn, so that after many years it is still the same knife—immobilized in time—although handle and blade have so often been changed that their mutations can't be counted. Time at a standstill, curfew, suspension of constitutional guarantees, restoration of normality, and words, words, words, to be or not to be, to go up or not to go up, stand up or not stand up, fall or not fall, just as a watch returns to the time it indicated yesterday when yesterday it told today's time. . . .

He looked at the silks, satins and velvets, the defeated gladiator, the sleeping nymph, the Wolf of Gubbio, Saint Radegonde. He longed to stay here, to get out of the magic circle, but just as if it really enclosed him he could not. His will-power was held firm by the roots of instinct, of what he perceived and understood when he opened his eyes on to the world. He knew there were many *over there* who detested him; he knew there were many, very many, too many who were hoping that someone, sometime would be brave enough to assassinate him (if his death could be caused by pressing the mythical button of the Mandarin in the story, thousands of men and women would press that button). All the same, he *would go back*. To show that even though he stood on the threshold of old age, although his body's architecture was in decline, he was still tough, strong and energetic, full of masculinity, very much a man. He would go on destroying his enemies while strength remained to him. He wouldn't copy the sad end of the tyrant Rosas, who died in obscurity at Swaythling, forgotten by everyone—even his daughter Manuelita. Nor did he want to be like Porfirio Díaz in Mexico, pursuing a living death, promenading his corpse in frock-coat, gloves and solemn hat through the avenues of the Bois de Boulogne, sitting sunk in the mournful black leather seats of a phaeton drawn by horses whose slow ambling pace already heralded his funeral. . . .

And now he remembered a certain Holy Week when the people of his home town had organized a great display of the Mystery of the Passion, from a seventeenth-century manuscript preserved in the archives of the parish church. For months and months women and children had saved the silver paper from their sweets and toffees to cover the helmets and shields of centurions, and collected hair from horses, mules and donkeys to make them into crests. A purple velvet curtain had served for the Redeemer's tunic; his belt was a sisal cord soaked in an infusion of acacia flowers; his crown of thorns came from the branch of a shrub known as "snake-bite", which grew on a hill nearby. The Judgement scene had taken place in the patio of the Town Hall, where the Head of State (he was Chief of Police at the time) had consented to take the part of Pilate, sitting in a red armchair in the Chapter House. He had handed the Son of God over to the Pharisees and washed his hands in a Japanese basin lent by the Suárez brothers' china shop. And the ascent to Calvary had begun amid the tears and lamentations of the crowd. A young and simple-minded beggar-woman, who believed she was witnessing the real events she had seen in twenty altarpieces in village churches, had gone up to Miguel the shoe-maker, who was playing the Son of God, and tried to take on her own shoulders the heavy wooden cross he was carrying, stumbling as he went, staggering, falling and getting up again, covered in sweat, half-dead, and uttering desperate groans—an amazingly theatrical martyr—as he advanced towards the hill where he was to pretend to be crucified. Pushing away the intruder who was threatening to spoil his splendid performance, Christ pointed his left hand at her and said:

"And if you take this from me, what shall I be? What will remain to me?" And then went on his way up the hill by the Way of the Cross, while the crowd sang an old tune whose origins had been forgotten, with the slow inflexions of plainsong:

And if I have to die to tomorrow
Let them kill me outright.

Just at this moment Peralta returned from the Western Union office, and finding me still up and somewhat pensive, asked me:

"Why not let all this go to the devil, and stay here, enjoying what you've got? You're not short of cash. What a lot of bottles we could drink! What a lot of women we could fuck!"

"And suppose I did get rid of *all that*, what should I be? What would remain to me?" I said. Yes, I remember saying it and thinking about the people who had turned against me because of that business at Nueva Córdoba, so that my personality had dwindled and become too small and helpless to play a part in this Apocalyptic world. I was taking on the Crusade for Latinity in order to reinstate my image. And if it pleased the Ineffable One to whom my requests were addressed to grant me victory within the next few weeks, I pledged myself, yes, I promised that immediately after my triumph I would bow my head and go as a pilgrim to her Sanctuary as Divine Shepherdess, mixing with the people (but also with those pretending to belong to "the people"), as an act of gratitude and rejoicing for favours received, and sorrow for many sins committed. I would go with those who dragged along their wounded legs, or wept in the night with eyes rolled upwards or with noses eaten away and stumps of their arms joined in an impossible attitude of prayer; among women with closed wombs and breasts of gravel; among those long past adolescence, who could only cry like babies and sidle rather than walk, with withered arms and twisted hands; among those whose voices were for ever dead inside their deformed throats; with the purulent and the paralysed. I would cross the wide tiled floor on my knees, and rejecting the red carpet laid down for the priests, I would drag myself over the stones to the feet of the Mother of God, to express my gratitude in the prose of the liturgy—I don't remember whether I learnt it from Renan or the Marist Brothers: Mystical Rose, Ivory Tower, Golden Mansion, Morning Star, *Ave Maris Stella*.

I look at my watch. Now I must rest a little. I'll have to leave early tomorrow. Already in my nightshirt, for a joke, I put on my English cap with earflaps, and the check Inverness cape I have bought for the journey.

"I look like Sherlock Holmes," I say, admiring myself in the Empire looking-glass mounted on gilt sphinxes.

"You only need a magnifying-glass," says Peralta, slipping into my pocket one of the brandy flasks encased in pig-skin.

. . . and the alarm already. Quarter past ten. It's impossible. Quarter past nine. More likely. Quarter past eight. This alarm clock would be a marvel of Swiss watch-making, but its hands are so slim that one can hardly see them. Quarter past seven. My spectacles. Quarter past six. That's it. Daylight is beginning to show clearly through the yellow curtains. My foot can't find the other slipper which always gets lost among the colours of the Persian carpet. And in comes Sylvestre in his striped jacket carrying aloft the silver tray—made of silver from my mines:

"*Le Café de Monsieur. Bien fort comme il l'aime. Monsieur a bien dormi?*"

"*Mal, très mal,*" I reply. "*J'ai bien de soucis, mon bon Sylvestre.*"

"*Les revers attristent / les grands de ce monde,*" he murmurs, in an alexandrine whose classical scansion brings an echo of the Comédie Française into this house where, in an atmosphere of confusion, far from the scenes to which destiny was taking me, a new chapter in my History was opening early this morning.

FOUR

*What do I see from this window except hats and coats
which might be worn by spectres or well-made
imitations of men, moving by means of springs?*

DESCARTES

9

It wasn't necessary to shoot Walter Hoffmann. Every
conflict has a way of developing in unforeseen ways, and the
treacherous general came to an end which could be seen as
having a certain Wagnerian dramatic power: like the death
throes of Fafner in a considerably more dangerous forest than
Siegfried's, which was almost municipal, a Tiergarten or
Unter-den-Linden compared to the terrifying forest covering
the region of Las Tembladeras—the Quagmires. We had
pursued the rebel into a region of quicksand, where he was
forced to withdraw, all the time being deserted by his men, who
were so oppressed by defeat that they ignored all speeches and
admonitions, proclamations and brandy rations, and admitted
—with anxiety that increased from day to day—that they had
played a rotten card, and that we were the ones who held the
royal flush. It was useless for General Hoffmann, having
discovered the remains of an Indian pyramid in the densest
part of a thicket, to shout to his men:

"Soldiers . . . fifty centuries are looking down at you from
the top of this pyramid" (adding ten to the Napoleonic speech,
out of patriotism).

"It could be seventy-five for all I care," thought the soldiers,
whose "old women"—the rebel camp-followers—declared that
a lot of stones piled up like that, and full of holes, were useless

for anything except a breeding-ground for the most deadly snakes in the world, centipedes, tarantulas, spiders and scorpions "about as long as this" (not bothering to illustrate how long). . . . And after the "Little Fredericks" had fled in the direction of the Southern frontier, mass desertion and fraternizations began, to an occasional shout of "they deceived us, they made us believe, we were sent", until the General and his few remaining faithful followers decided to cross one of the dreaded plains—the only means of reaching the sea—which by the abundance of its quaking bogs had given the region its name. As their advance grew more and more difficult and dangerous, and men kept deserting (first two artillerymen and a lieutenant, then fifteen private soldiers and a corporal, and sixty or so men with a captain), the rebel at last found himself practically alone with his few remaining supporters—and it's easy to imagine what was going on in their minds—on the brink of a yellowish waste, streaked with creeping plants, and dotted with ponds—or rather large pot-holes—of viscid slush, perhaps clay, looking like a thin coating of stagnant mud on top of firmer ground. General Hoffmann landed in one of these holes, as a result of inopportunely urging on his horse with a sharp tug on the reins, so as to avoid a thorny branch that crossed his path. And without warning the horse, feeling its feet sink more and more deeply into the deceptive clay, as if drawn in by some implacable suction from the entrails of the earth, began to neigh desperately for help, exhausting itself in useless rearing, while its frantic struggles and plunges did nothing to free it from slow but inevitable submergence. With the terrible mud now up to his knees, trying to get out of his boots which were becoming heavy as lead, tugging again and again on the reins without response, and seeing that the floundering movements of his horse only hastened his inevitable submersion, the General shouted:

"A rope . . . a strap . . . a belt . . . Get me out of here . . . Quickly . . . A rope . . . a strap."

But the men standing round the pool in frowning silence calmly watched their leader slowly, terribly slowly, drowning.

"Die, you bastard!" muttered a corporal whom Hoffmann

had struck, years before, to punish him for a disrespectful reply.

"Die, you bastard!" said in a louder voice a sergeant whom Hoffmann had refused to promote some time back.

"Die, you bastard!" said a lieutenant, fortissimo, who had begged without success for the Silver Star.

"No, God damn you, no! You can't let me die like this!" yelled their leader, clutching the ears of his horse whose teeth were now just above the quagmire.

"Die, you bastard!" replied the Greek chorus.

The quicksand had risen to the General's neck, chin and mouth, though he still emitted confused cries from a throat choking with mud—bubbling death-rattles, inaudible shouts, last efforts at agonizing cries. . . .

When only his kepi remained floating, one of the spectators threw a small crucifix on to it, but it was soon sucked in by the quagmire, now once more green and placid.

Delivered of his enemy, the Head of State returned to the capital, entered it under triumphal arches put up the day before and decorated with flags and garlands, and received the titles of "Peacemaker" and "National Hero" from both Chambers, the representatives of Industry and Commerce, the Metropolitan Bishop in his pulpit, lesser dignitaries in lower pulpits, and the Press, whose pages described the details of a military campaign conducted in a masterly manner, illustrated with maps covered in black arrows showing the phases of offence and defence, penetration, encirclement and breaking of the enemy lines in the decisive Battle of Four Roads—a drawn-out, bloody, difficult battle, finally won for the government forces by tactical judgement and occasional improvisation. This diagrammatic technique had been popularized by *L'Illustration* to explain the action of the Battle of the Marne.

In a speech full of elevated ideas, the President modestly declared that he didn't deserve the praise so generously heaped on him by his compatriots, since God himself, so great in mercy but terrible in anger, had been responsible for punishing the traitor. Properly considered, Hoffmann's death had been a sort of trial by ordeal, wherein a superior will whose designs were beyond our understanding had spared the victor the pain of shedding the blood of an old companion in arms, blinded by senseless ambition.

This was no time for Shakespeare's cry of "My kingdom for a horse", seeing that the guilty man, perhaps burdened by his own remorse and pursued by the Furies of our arms, actually entered the Kingdom of Shadows on his galloping steed. But the important thing was not that the Enemy of Order had been swallowed up in the quagmire of Las Tembladeras. The important thing was that by so doing he had fortified our Consciousness of Latinity in the face of the conflict now terrifying the world; because we *were* Latin, profoundly Latin, intimately Latin, trustees of the great tradition of the Roman pandects, foundation of our Law, and of Virgil, Dante, Don Quixote, Michelangelo, Copernicus, etc., etc. (a long paragraph, ended off by a long ovation). Aunt Jemima, who had exchanged her usual check cotton handkerchief for a black one in token of mourning, climbed painfully up to the platform to give the Head of State a message of regret from the Hoffmann family, whispering in his ear at the same time that the General's wife deplored her husband's misdeeds, and begged the favour of receiving the pension due to her as the widow of a soldier with more than twenty years' service, in accordance with the Law of June 18, 1901.

Tired out by a war that had taken him to the most unhealthy jungles in the country, the President went for a holiday to his house at Marbella. There was a beautiful long beach, although its black sands were too often invaded by an abundance of bladdery dead jelly-fish lying amongst patches of tar and oil washed up from the port close by. The sharks and giant rays were kept at bay by a quadruple barbed-wire fence, festooned with ragged seaweed. And if there were still a few morays in the hollows of a little rocky promontory, it was a great many years since a man had been emasculated by a barracuda in this resort. When the winds blew from the North—"yelitos" they were called—the sea darkened to shades of deep blue, while gentle waves moved in slow majestic rhythm to cast their foam at the very feet of the coconut and sour-sop trees. But there were mornings too—in summer—when the water

appeared singularly smooth and transparent, without any of
its usual light turbulence; a bather diving into it at once had
the strange sensation of falling into a lake of gelatine. And
then he would find that he wasn't swimming, but *gliding* in a
mass of transparent and almost invisible molluscs, as big and
as round as coins, which had arrived on the beach during the
night at the end of some long and mysterious migration. To
make the resort more attractive, the municipality had constructed a cement pier with a casino at the end supported on
piles, the whole affair copied from Nice—metal framework,
orange tiles, iron dome, green with saltpetre. Roulette,
baccarat and chemin-de-fer were played there, and the few
croupiers in dinner-jackets, counting in *louis* and *centens*—out-
of-date gamblers' coins—had given up saying, "Don't be
afraid to stake", and "Not another cent", as at creole gaming-
tables, and taken to *"Faites vos jeux"* and *"Rein ne va plus"*,
carefully if always peculiarly pronounced.

The Head of State's "Residencia Hermenegilda" dominated
the beach from a neighbouring hill. It was built in a style
somewhere between Balkan and the Rue de la Faisanderie,
with caryatids reminiscent of 1900, dressed like Sarah Bernhardt
and magically supporting on their plumed hats—better indeed
than the Atlases of some Berlin palaces—a wide terrace-
balcony, enclosed by banisters shaped like sea-horses. A tower-
belvedere-lighthouse overtopped the roofs, and displayed the
eternal brilliance of variegated majolica. The vast, cool, high
rooms were furnished with rocking-chairs of New Córdoban
make, hammocks suspended from rings and a few red lacquer
chairs, a gift from the old Empress of China in gratitude for a
consignment of toys—a cable-railway, some kaleidoscopes,
whistling spinning-tops, a musical-box full of Bernese bears,
and a battleship the size of a water-lily for the pond at the
Winter Palace—which the Head of State had sent her years
before, knowing her tastes. In the dining-room was a copy—
reduced in size, of course—of *The Raft of Medusa*, opposite
two charming seascapes by Elstir, which were somewhat over-
powered, truth to tell, by the dramatic weight of the Géricault.
The house was surrounded by a vast garden tended by Japanese

gardeners, where among the box hedges stood a white marble Venus, disfigured by a greenish herpes of funguses hanging from her stomach. A little further on under the pines one could see the chapel consecrated to the Divine Shepherdess by the devout Doña Hermenegilda—a chapel the sight of which now caused the President increasing remorse, as he remembered that the promise he had made her at an extremely painful moment in Paris, of ascending the steps of her basilica with a candle in each hand, still remained unfulfilled. (But at the same time he reflected that the Virgin was as intelligent in matters of policy as in everything; the Virgin, who had just given him eloquent proof of her Divine Protection with Trumpets of victory, would understand that at such a moment the fulfilment of his promise in the sight of everyone, an ostentatious proof of Catholic fervour, would bring down on him—who already had so many enemies—a whole world of freemasons, Rosicrucians, spiritualists, theosophists and those who clamoured against the clergy, not to mention many atheists and free-thinkers—a blaspheming legion of priest-haters, all of them devotees of France, where the clergy were not allowed to teach in schools, theological students were subject to military service, and where the only religion possible in this portentous twentieth century had germinated and grown: *The Religion of Science.*)

Behind the house a little grove of pomegranates shaded the discreet path along which, when night fell, Doctor Peralta used to lead some cloaked woman to the Head of State's bedroom. ("Don't go and die as President Félix Faure did," the Secretary used invariably to remark as he left his charge with his master. "Attila and Félix Faure were the two men who most enjoyed their deaths," the Head of State replied, also invariably.)

Early every morning the locomotive of the Little German Train used to whistle. And the President would go out on to the balcony with a cup of coffee in his hand, to watch it pass. The little engine shone like polished enamel in those green mornings, with its gleaming copper connecting-rods and rivets, climbing the mountain by its narrow track with a cheerful funicular snorting, as it dragged its small red awning-covered carriages behind it up to the Olmedo Colony; it was, in every way, like the cable-railway the Head of State had sent to the old Empress of China to enrich her collection of automatic and mechanical devices. As soon as the little convoy left Puerto Araguato, everything it passed through seemed to diminish in size—intermediate stations, bridges over torrents, level-crossings and their gates, signals—yet it was with a great clamour that it entered the minuscule terminal above, with its load of ten passengers, a few parcels, several barrels, the post, the newspapers and a calf poking its head out of the window of the only cattle-truck. As if it had just come out of a Nuremberg toy-shop, gleaming, repainted and varnished, the little train rested at the end of its journey in a strange exotic world, quite different from that below, with its Black Forest houses built between palms and coffee-trees, its beer-shop displaying the sign of King Stag, its women in Tyrolese dress, its men in leather breeches, braces, and hats with a feather in the band. In spite of being excellent citizens of the Republic for more than a century, they could hardly speak Spanish. Ever since they had been brought here by a certain Count Olmedo, a rich man of creole ancestry, a landowner obsessed by the idea of "keeping the race white", the immigrants had been careful not to mix with women from *here*, who were all suspected of being zambas, cholas or quadroons—one, because her hair was frizzy; another because her eyes were blacker than usual; another because her nose was rather flattened, even though her complexion was pale. So, from father to son, they wrote to Bavaria or Pomerania to ask for women, and generation by generation they had increased and multiplied, singing the Lutheran chorale, playing on the accordion, growing rhubarb, making beer soup and dancing an old-fashioned ländler, and now plump shepherdesses with Aryan pubic hair were to be seen bathing in the mountain streams, and their names might be Woglinde. Wellgunde or Flosshilde. The Head of State had bothered very little about these peaceable, law-abiding folk, who never got involved in politics, and when elections came along always voted for the Government, on condition that their customs weren't interfered with. But now, his daily reading of the French papers made him regard these people with some irritation. Although their houses were traditionally adorned with coloured plates of snow-covered landscapes, the banks of the Elbe, the Festival of Wartburg, or the mythical maiden in a winged helmet who carried the bodies of young athletes killed in battle up to heaven, there hung beside these pictures a portrait of Wilhelm II. And Wilhelm II was materializing in the Press as Antichrist. His armies, his gang of supporters, his terrifying Uhlans had penetrated into harmless little Belgium, into the Flanders of Velazquez' lances—the forerunners of our own plainsmen's pikes—razing everything to the ground. They had advanced as conquerors between ruined cathedrals, stately homes laid low and scattered, and after burning the Library of Louvain had marched sacrilegiously over a pavement of incunables hurled on the ground. *Eins . . . Zwei . . . Eins . . . Zwei.* And with barbarian tread, trampling on unique bindings, priceless manuscripts, parchments with rich capitals and superb lettering, they had marched on, not attacking men so much as the distinguished figures in the Testaments, displayed for centuries, like the pages of open books, on the tympana and over the porticos of cathedrals. *Eins . . . Zwei . . . Eins . . . Zwei.* German cannon had thundered against Isaiah and Jeremiah, Ezekiel and Esdras, against Solomon and the Shulamite, and David who, with Bathsheba—this was the theme of the manuscript play we had bought from our friend the Distinguished Academician—plotted the destruction of the old cuckolded general (every general in a campaign was probably a cuckold, reflected the President, and especially if he was old), before relentlessly hurling themselves against the Beau Dieu at Amiens, or the ineffable figure—now broken and pulverized in an irreversible twilight—of the most beautiful of the Smiling Angels. But perhaps even this was less horrible than the appalling chronicle of rape. *L'Illustration* included some grey pages, not to be read by children, describing how when the German troops took a village or town, they dragged innocent girls, school-children and adolescents to the back of a shoemaker's shop or undertaker's, and violated them—there were nine, ten, eleven such cases, said *L'Illustration*; probably fifteen, said Louis Dumur, who specialized in these atrocities— an operation carried out with servile German discipline, while the *feldwebels*, who controlled proceedings, said: "Now it's your turn . . . Get ready, next man." But all this, the destruction of cathedrals, ruin of hagiography, altarpieces split in half, decapitated sibyls, burning, dynamite, rape, crime, were as nothing before the unprecedented tragedy of *the children without hands*. A German soldier had found them wandering among the ruins searching for their lost or dead mother, and hearing them weeping had gone closer as if to help them, but instead with an unexpected blow of his sabre (did the infantry really carry sabres? asked Peralta) cut off two soft little hands: "So that they can never hold weapons against us." On the title-page of a supplement to *L'Illustration* there was a sketched portrait of one of the victims of this atrocious ablation, holding up his stumps against an apocalyptic background of the ruins of Ypres.

The Head of State absorbed this literature daily, marking in red pencil anything that seemed to him worth reproducing in the national press, to cause confusion and shame among certain officers, ex-associates of Hoffmann, or "Little Fredericks" in the making, who were known to be disgusted— though they didn't show it openly—by the recent suppression of the pointed helmet with full dress uniform in the National Army. These readers must be de-Germanized, and the articles he destined particularly for them were those about the sacking of famous castles, theft of clocks—this had begun in '70— melting down of bells six hundred years old, using cathedrals as latrines, profanation of the host, and shooting-matches by intoxicated captains with Memlings or Rembrandts as targets.

The Head of State looked towards the cloudy heights of the Olmedo Colony—black rocks, between mulberry trees, an occasional naturalized silver fir, light northerly breezes in the mornings—and thought that those bastards up there, in spite of the shouts of "Loooooong live our Cooooountry!" from girls with fair plaits wearing national dress, who received him with bunches of violets when he paid a visit to their chief village, were at heart in sympathy with the men who cut off children's hands in Artois or Champagne, whose cataclysmic landscapes—eroded, defoliated, mutilated by shells—were shown us in the pictures of Georges Scott and Lucien Simon, offered for sale complete with passe-partout, their muddy colours accentuating in a masterly fashion the tragic desolation of village squares, ruined town halls and mediaeval houses reduced to the skeletons of their beams, while like some accusation proffered by the Earth itself, the bare trunk of an ancient oak seemed to speak in the middle of all this desolation through the hundred mouths of its lacerated bark.

Every morning the Head of State stopped reading this painful material to watch from his window as the Little German Train started to ascend the mountain, sometimes braking with furious whistling to drive away a goat capering in the young grass between the rails. And after his usual breakfast of maize tortillas, curds, and meat pancakes, he used to sit at his Welte-Mignon pianola, a present from the Spanish colony of Nueva Córdoba. Pedalling hard and manipulating the regulators so as to extract *Für Elise* from the perforated roll, and the beginning—he never got beyond the beginning—of the *Moonlight Sonata*, he reflected that working this musical machine must be a little like the activity of the engine-driver who was now taking the Little German Train up to the woods, where imported squirrels were frisking, and in the opinion of a trouble-making journalist—an unfair opponent—threatening to cause an epidemic of psittacosis among the country's cattle—already ailing and in a state of decline, it was quite true, since experience showed that the cows of the region suffered from weak legs and narrow haunches and couldn't support the weight on their hindquarters of the stock bulls brought from Charolais to improve the breed, when they mounted them.

"Ah, what a war this is, my President," groaned Doctor Peralta every morning between a cup of very black coffee and the first cigar of the day.

"Terrible, terrible," the Head of State would reply, thinking about the Little German Train: "And how long it's lasting."

But then they heard that those who discussed strategy in the capital over brandy and grilled steak had been celebrating the news, received by cablegram, that *Le Matin* had just published a really sensational headline covering eight columns: *"Cossacks only five days' march from Berlin."*

"So now the Cossacks are the new defenders of Latinity, along with the Sepoys and Senegalese we already had on our side," remarked Peralta slyly.

"Let's hope they get held up on the way!" murmured his friend, thinking that thanks to the expectations and enthusiasms provoked by this amazing war, many people had had their attention diverted to remote events. The Head of State was at last enjoying peace and quiet in the shade of a flowering tree.

10

Many things which may appear to us supremely extravagant and ridiculous are generally accepted and approved by other great nations.

DESCARTES

The Head of State prolonged his stay in Marbella from week to week, carrying out the business of government from a somewhat Pompeian pergola in the middle of a labyrinth of orange trees at the far end of the garden. He took an early-morning ride along the shore on his horse Holofernes, a powerful sorrel with a glistening coat, wild and uncontrollable with most people but hypocritically submissive to a master who brought him a pail of the best English beer in his stable every afternoon, which he always received with delighted whinnying. The President had reasons for feeling contented during these months, for he had never known such a prosperous and happy period for the Nation. This European War—

which really, though it was better not to say so, was turning out a blessing—was raising the prices of sugar, bananas, coffee and gutta-percha to unheard-of heights, swelling the funds in the banks, making fortunes, bringing the country luxuries and refinements which until yesterday had seemed to belong to worldly novels or films centred round the almost mythological figures of Gabrielle Robinne, Pina Menichelli, Francesca Bertini or Lydia Borelli. Surrounded by age-old forests, the capital had itself become a modern forest of scaffolding, wooden beams pointing to the sky, cranes in action, and mechanical scoops, accompanied by a perpetual clanking of pulleys, hammer-blows of iron on steel, pouring of cement, rivetting and percussion, interspersed with shouts between workmen up aloft and workmen on the ground, whistles, sirens, trucks carrying sand and snorting of engines. Shops enlarged their premises overnight, and dawn showed them with new windows where a few wax figures—another novelty— were celebrating their first communion, showing off wedding-dresses, the latest fashions, and even officers' uniforms, well-cut and finished in English gabardine. Toffee-making machines, installed in the entrance to the old Royal Granary, astonished passers-by with the concerted movements of their metal arms, mixing, stretching and compressing white substances streaked with red, and smelling of vanilla and marshmallow. Offices, banks, insurance companies, chain-stores, and brokers proliferated. Theodolites and other surveying instruments transformed flooded regions, waste land and goat pastures, dividing them into a number of marked-out squares, which having been since remote times "The Lazar's small-holding", "Mexican farm" or "Misia Petra's ranch", suddenly adopted the names of "Bagatelle", "West Side" or "Armenonville", and were divided into plots to be selected from a plan but hardly ever built on, since their price increased every time they were bought and sold (sometimes several times in one day) in offices with many Underwood typewriters, gilt ventilators, relief maps, attractive maquettes, and brandy and gin in the safe, with much haggling and discussing between drinks and Havanas, and telephone calls from women—this was quite new—who offered their services by telephone in foreign accents, promising refinements which were refused—and it was the worse for them—by our own too-modest tarts, with whom "the business" had to be performed in the classic manner, with nothing baroque, perverse or fantastic such as went on in other countries. Pianolas had invaded the capital, rolling and unrolling cylinders of *La Madelon, Roses of Picardy, It's a long way to Tipperary* from dawn to midnight. In the bars where cards and dominoes were played, or where Santa Inés rum gave way to White Horse whisky, the only subject of conversation was the profits, due to the war, which had made them forget the war itself, although everyone—whites, cholos, zambos, Indians and those of swarthy complexion—had become Frenchified, pro-tricolor, avengers, cockade-wearers, Joan-of-Arcists and Barrèsians, declaring that we should soon get our own back for the disaster of Sedan, and the storks of Hansi would come back to the steeples of Alsace and Lorraine. At the same time the first skyscraper arose—five stories and an attic—immediately followed by the *Edificio Titán* close by, with eight. And the old city with its two-storey houses was very quickly transformed into an Invisible City. Invisible because, changing from horizontal to vertical, there were no eyes now that could see it and know it. Each architect, engaged in the task of making his buildings higher than those that went up before, thought only of the particular aesthetic qualities of *his* façade, as if it could be seen from a hundred yards off, whereas the streets were made to take only one car at a time—one mule-train, one cart—and were only six or seven yards wide. Thus, with his back to an infinitely tall column, the passer-by tried in vain to admire the elegant decoration lost in the sky among vultures and turkey-buzzards. It was *known* that up aloft there were garlands, cornucopias and caducei, or there even might be a Greek temple perched on the fifth floor with Phidias' horses and everything; but this was only *known*, because those citadels, domes and entablatures existed—city upon city—in a kingdom that could not be seen. And higher still were solitary, unknown, banished statues, of Mercury—on the Chamber of Commerce—or of Minerva,

whose lance attracted August lightning, of charioteers, winged
spirits, Christian saints, isolated from each other and unknown
to men, who yet lorded it over intricate gradations of terraces,
slate-covered roofs, water-tanks, chimneys, lightning-con-
ductors and huts containing lift machinery. Without realizing
it, people were living in unsuspected Ninevehs, vertiginous
Westminsters and flying Trianons, with gargoyles and bronze
figures who would become old without ever having had contact
with the people below, busy among the porticos, arcades and
colonnades which carried the great weight of invisible con-
structions. And as everyone was eager to have what was new,
those who had inhabited colonial mansions for two centuries,
hastily left them and moved into new, modern houses in the
Roman, Chambord or Stanford White style. So the huge
palaces of the old town with their plateresque façades and
coats-of-arms carved in stone were taken over by the rabble,
the poor and diseased—the fictitious blind man with a paid
guide, the drunk whose hands trembled in the mornings, the
wooden-legged accordion-player or the poor paralytic, begging
alms for the love of God. The beautiful rooms were full of
dishevelled women, ragged children, whores and tramps,
living in the fumes from stoves and clothes hung up to dry,
while the patios were given over to boxing, cock-fights and
conjurors with pickpocket partners. Hundreds of Ford cars—
like those in Mack Sennett films—streamed along the badly
paved streets, avoiding the potholes, running on to the pavements, knocking over baskets of fruit, breaking shop windows,
in a mania for speed never before known in these latitudes. It
was all urgency, haste, rush and impatience. In a few months
of war, oil-lamps had been supplanted by electric bulbs,
gourds by bidets, pineapple juice by Coca-Cola, lotto by
roulette, Rocambole by Pearl White, the messenger-boy's
donkey by the telegraphist's bicycle, the mule-cart with its
tassels and bells by a smart Renault, which had to go forward
and reverse ten or twelve times to get round a narrow corner
and enter an alley recently christened "Boulevard", causing a
frenzied flight among the goats which still abounded in some
quarters where the grass growing between the paving-stones

was good. The Ursuline nuns instituted a Grotto of Lourdes with wonderful effects of electric light; the first dance-hall was opened, with a jazz-band from New Orleans; horses and jockeys were brought from Tijuana to race in a gaily-decorated hippodrome made on the site of the swamp, and one morning the old Town, described as "Very Loyal and Very Illustrious" in the deed of its foundation in 1553, awoke to the full realization that it had become a leading twentieth-century capital. The last reptiles vanished—rattlesnakes and elaps—from the building-sites, the goldfinches were silent, and phonographs opened their mouths. And there were bridge championships, fashion-parades, Turkish baths, money-changers and exclusive brothels, admitting no one with darker skin than the Minister for Public Works, who was taken as a yardstick because although not perhaps the black sheep of the Cabinet he was indubitably its brownest sheep. The police exchanged their worn slippers for regulation boots, and their white-gloved hands controlled a traffic whose noise was enriched by klaxons with several rubber bulbs, so that they could play *The Merry Widow Waltz* or the first bars of the National Anthem.

As he watched the metropolis grow and grow, the Head of State was sometimes worried by the changes in the view from the Palace windows. He was himself involved in a real-estate business managed by Doctor Peralta, whose buildings were destroying the panorama for so long part of his life, so that when his attention was suddenly drawn to some alteration in it by the Mayorala Elmira—"just look at that", "look at that"— he started as if at some evil omen. The factory chimneys he had had erected broke up and destroyed a natural scene until recently innocent of the ugly cross-trees of telegraph poles. The Volcano, the Grandfather Volcano, the Tutelary Volcano, abode of the Ancient Gods, symbol and emblem, whose cone figured on the National Coat of Arms, was less a volcano—less even the abode of the Ancient Gods—when on misty mornings its majestic presence seemed to insinuate itself, with the modesty of a humiliated king, a monarch without a court, above the dense clouds of smoke sent up by four tall chimneys from the recently inaugurated Central Electricity Company.

By becoming more vertical and geometric, and by dividing up the verdant background of mountains, hills and distant valleys, the city was shutting the President in. The population was being augmented by an ever-increasing influx of peasants, labourers, day-workers, artisans from the provinces, attracted by the wealth of the Metropolis, all bringing their dependants with them: grandfathers with bilharzia or weak from years of malaria, scrofulous children, sufferers from amoebic dysentery —easy preys to the periodical epidemics of virulent influenza coming from no one knew where—and it was a common sight to see a funeral procession tightening its circle of black clothes and coffins around the Presidential Palace.

"Here comes the Whore!" the Mayorala Elmira would exclaim, when a hearse appeared in the Plaza Mayor on its way to the cemetery.

"Be off!" replied the Head of State, joining the first and little fingers of both hands to ward off the Evil Eye.

"Even Napoleon couldn't lick you," concluded the Mayorala, giving actual existence to someone whose name she took to represent the greatest power God had ever given to a human being, because coming from nothing, born in the manger as one might say, he had finally conquered the whole World—while still remaining a good son and brother, a good friend (even of his laundress, it was said when he became a great man!) and always the lover of fine women, like that one from the Caribbean, who had got hold of him you know where, because mulattos and cholas are born with the Devil between their legs. . . . (There were some men who would throw up everything, disappear and leave home at the summons of Women of Great Power, who held their lamps in the doorway repeating as often as there are beads on a rosary: "Let him come after me like a mad dog. Amen.")

After a great deal of thought the Head of State devoted himself with renewed energy—energy which was diminishing with age in some directions—to the project of a great building, the material symbol in stone of his government: he would give the country a National Capitol.

Once the decision was made, he planned to promote a great

international concourse, open to all architects, so that they could compare ideas, projects and plans. But hardly was the news spread around than the nation's own architects, who had recently formed themselves into a college, protested that there were quite enough of them for such an undertaking. And then began a tiresome process of criticisms, changes, arguments, producing a succession of metamorphoses in the appearance, style and proportions of the future building. First it was a Greek Temple with Doric columns without bases, thirty metres high—a copy of Paestum with the dimensions of the Vatican. But the Head of State thought he remembered that Kaiser Wilhelm, incarnation of Prussian barbarism, was addicted to such Hellenisms, going so far as to possess an Achilleion, reminiscent of the Parthenon, in Corfu. Besides the Greeks had no domes, and a Capitol without a dome is no Capitol at all. Better to look towards eternal Rome, mother of our culture. Therefore our architects quickly substituted Corinthian for Doric (without passing through the Ionic) with a dome rather like that of the Palais de Justice at Brussels. However, the two hemicycles—Chamber and Senate—were too reminiscent of the theatres at Delphi and Epidaurus, and looked rather austere, cold and false when it came to adding the rostrums, whose existence in such a place were a vital democratic necessity. A new national architect, succeeding to two national architects who were already discredited and fallen into disgrace as a result of the intrigues of a great many other national architects, took his inspiration from an English illustration of Shakespeare's *Julius Caesar*, and drew a plan of a hemicycle in the Roman style with columns above, which was for a while approved by the Council of Ministers. But then they remembered that the country was a great producer of mahogany, and that our mahogany, a deep warm red in colour, ought to be copiously used in a work of such size, to face the walls and make panelling, rostrums, benches, doors, presidential throne, etc., in both hemicycles. And since the Romans never used wood in this fashion, a fifth project for the Capitol arose, based on the neo-Gothic style of the Budapest Parliament. But as the Austro-Hungarian empire was at war with Latinity, these plans too were rejected, and someone remembered the genius Herrera and the imposing bulk of the Escorial.

"Not to be thought of," put in the Head of State. "When you say Escorial you say Philip II. And anyone saying Philip II here says: burned Indians, negroes in chains, heroic chiefs tortured, princes on the gridiron, tribunals of the Inquisition. . . ."

Project No. 15 was rejected because in its eagerness to use some national marble recently discovered near Nueva Córdoba, the architect had conceived something too like Milan Cathedral, and such an ecclesiastical flavour would have disgusted the masons and freethinkers and other people whose criticisms carried weight. Project No. 17 was no more nor less than a pretty outrageous copy of the Parisian Opéra.

"Parliament is not a theatre," said the Head of State throwing the plans down on the Council table.

"Sometimes . . ." murmured Doctor Peralta behind him.

At last, after a great deal of cavilling, discussing, considering and reconsidering, Project 31 was accepted as offering the simplest solution: a replica of the Washington Capitol, using national woods and national marbles for the inside—but if the latter should not prove as good as they were thought to be, marbles bought from Carrara would be put in their place, while for the public they would remain "national marbles".

The work began on the day of the Centenary of Independence, with the laying of the First Stone and the obligatory speeches, using all suitable rhetoric fortissimo. But one problem remained: under the dome there ought to be a statue of the Republic. All the nation's sculptors offered to make one. But the Head of State knew that none of them could measure up to such a task.

"What a pity Gérome is dead!" he said, thinking of his gladiators and his retiarius. "There was a man for you!"

"Rodin is alive," observed Doctor Peralta.

"No. Rodin, no . . . A great sculptor—who could doubt it?— when he sticks to reality. But if he fires off a second Balzac, we're completely buggered. If we reject him they'll make fun of us *over there*; and if we accept him we shall have to leave the country."

"You could always ban press comments."

"That would be against my principles. You know that. Bullets and machetes for bastards. But complete liberty of criticism, polemics, discussion and controversy concerning art, literature, schools of poetry, classical philosophy, the enigma of the Universe, the secret of the pyramids, the origin of American Man, the concept of Beauty, and everything else in that line . . . that's culture."

"In Guatemala, our friend Estrada Cabrera founded a cult of Minerva, with a temple and everything."

"A fine enterprise by a great ruler . . ."

". . . who has already been in Power for eighteen years . . ."

". . . for that very reason. But it seems that his statue of Pallas Athene is nothing very wonderful."

In his perplexity the Head of State wrote to Ofelia, who had now returned to Paris, before spending several months on Andalusian ranches, as she had now suddenly become as enthusiastic about bulls, cloaks and *cante jondo* as she had formerly been about Bayreuth or Stratford-on-Avon. Not very fond of writing letters, which revealed her fantastic ideas of spelling, the Infanta simply replied with a cable: ANTOINE BOURDELLE.

"Never heard of him," said Doctor Peralta.

"Nor have I," said the Head of State. "He must be one of her bohemian friends."

His doubts led him to write to the Distinguished Academician for more information. And he received by return of post some photos of reliefs carried out by this artist at the Theatre of the Champs-Elysées in 1913. One was an allegory of music and displeased Peralta outright by two false, confused, distorted figures, who seemed to have been forcibly crushed into a rectangular space: a nymph doubled over her violin in an impossible attempt to use her bow with an arm that passed above her head, and a bestial, twisted satyr, more entomological than Hellene, playing on an enormous pipe, far from suggestive of rustic melody, and much more like part of a 30/30 machine-gun. And with the photos came a number of the *Gazette des Beaux Arts*, where an article by the famous critic Paul Jamot,

underlined in red pencil, said that the sculptor didn't treat his
figures in the archaic style, but with *a coarseness evocative of
Germanic taste* (sic).

"Germanic! Germanic! So this is what Ofelia recommends
us at this moment! It seems to me she's becoming imbecile
from going to so many bullfights. She hasn't a trace of political
sense." Then, suddenly thinking of the phonetic aspect of the
problem: "Besides, he's impossible because of his surname.
Bourdelle. Just think what that sounds like in Spanish."

"I should say so!" said Peralta. "First they'd call him
Booouuurdeye. Until they were told the correct pronunciation!"

"And then, what jokes from my friends. They would simply
be handed them on a plate: the Capitol is a . . . ; the Republic
is a . . . ; my government is a . . . Unthinkable!"

"The best thing we can do is trust ourselves to Fellino,"
suggested Peralta.

And the Italian marble-worker, provider of innumerable
angels, crosses and family vaults for cemeteries, and of very
satisfactory eponymous statues for many of our towns, whether
heroic or religious, warmly recommended a Milanese artist
whose works had won prizes in Florence and Rome, and who
was especially famous for his ideas for monuments, municipal
fountains, civic sanctuaries, equestrian figures and (in general)
every form of official, serious and solemn art, with historically
exact uniforms when necessary, and who treated nudes with
dignity where nudity was needed for some allegory expressed
in a form intelligible to all, neither antiquated nor too modern
in artistic style—for the question of modernism in the plastic
arts was much discussed at that time. Aldo Nardini—that was
the sculptor's name—sent a model which was immediately
approved by the Council of Ministers: in it the Republic was
represented by a huge woman, her stalwart body dressed in
the Greek style, leaning on a spear—symbol of vigilance—with
a noble earnest face, bearing a resemblance to the famous
Juno in the Vatican, and two enormous breasts, one covered,
the other bare—symbols of fecundity and abundance.

"Not a work of genius, but it will please everyone," concluded the Head of State. "Have it carried out."

Several months passed by in executing and casting the statue, with paragraphs in the press about the progress of the work, until one morning a ship from Genoa entered the bay of Puerto Araguato, with the Immense Woman on board. An expectant crowd collected on the quay to witness her arrival. But there was some disappointment on learning that the statue would not emerge complete, already upright, as she would be seen in the Capitol, but would have to be carried out in pieces and put together in her eventual position. However, the sight was well worth watching. The cranes and grappling-irons were raised up, the cables descended into the hold, and all at once in the midst of applause the Head appeared from the shadows and was transported through the air, followed by different pieces of her anatomy. Left Foot, with its corresponding piece of Leg and Drapery—Right Arm, with a piece of the shaft of the spear in her hand; Fertile Belly with the vital axis well grooved in the bronze; Covered Breast, followed by Right Foot and Left Arm, before the ascent of the gigantic Phrygian Cap which was to crown the Republic. But at this moment the twelve o'clock sirens went, the cranes stopped work, and the dockers went to have their dinner, though the crowds didn't disperse. And there was no doubt something big must still remain in the profundities of the ship. At two o'clock the men returned to the job, and amid applause and exclamations, the Bare Breast of the Great Figure rose out of the hold and descended to earth with solemn slowness. Then all the pieces were removed in lorries to a goods train on whose planks and wagons the Giantess was laid, one piece on each wagon, presenting a disconcerting vision of a Form which, although already that of a human body, had its parts displayed in a horizontal series and never achieved a significant totality. First wagon: Phyrgian Cap; Second: Shoulder and Covered Breast; Third: Head; Fourth: Shoulder and Bare Breast; Fifth: Fertile Belly ... And now, in anarchic file, came the thighs, arms, feet shod in sandals something between the Hellenic and the creole, three pieces of spear, with a locomotive in front and a locomotive behind, because the weight was great and the mechanics were afraid this enormous load of bronze

might get stuck on its way up Las Cumbres, where the recent
rains had already caused some landslips on the line.

But the Republic finally arrived at her Capitol, and this
was how, instead of possessing a monument by Bourdelle, the
Nation saw a statue by the Milanese Nardini erected, whose
serene and serious face vanished for ever from public view,
because owing to the excessive height of the figure her head
was lost in the upper part of a dome whose circular colonnade
was visited only when it was cleaned twice a year by workmen
—acrobats of scaffolding, too concerned with keeping the
balance needed for their vertiginous task to be able to stop
and appreciate the merits of a work of art.

11

The Capitol was growing. Its still shapeless white mass, caged
in scaffolding, was rising above the city roofs, sending up
columns, spreading its wings, although its construction was
suddenly delayed by contingencies of wages and cash. Of
course this was not due to the country's economy, for it had
never known better days, but to the fact that the cost of
materials increased from month to month, the price of tools
and machinery, of freight and transport, constantly breaking
the limits of an ever-rising initial estimate—sufficiently encum-
bered, what was more, by the rake-offs promised to many
ministers and high officials of the Commission for the Pro-
motion of Public Decoration, not to mention two cheques, one
considerable and the other more modest, more than once
handed to Doctor Peralta secretly by the Office of Public
Works. All at once work stopped, an arcade remained without
any arches, a porch without a pediment, the chisels of the
engravers of acanthus leaves and astragals were silent, and a
new assignment of credits became necessary, an increase on the
duty on Swedish matches, foreign liquor or profits on horse-
races, to finance the work. And then it happened that in
periods of inactivity the central zone of the capital was trans-

formed into a sort of Roman forum, an esplanade from Baalbek, a terrace from Persepolis, while the moon shone down on this strange chaotic landscape of marbles, half-finished metopes, truncated pillars, blocks of stone between cement and sand—the ruins, the dead remains, of what had never been. And as—though roofless still—the two hemicycles of Chamber and Senate were already rising by stages within this area of expectant building, its empty space was made use of during the pauses in the work by the University's Faculty of Humanities and by the promoter of a skating-rink. Thus, there were nights when one could hear the laments of Ajax, the cries of Oedipus the incestuous parricide in the north hemicycle, used by students as a Theatre of Antique Drama, while on an echoing wooden floor in the southern hemicycle, young women could be seen circling to the strains of Waldteufel's most famous waltz, who rather than renounce fashion for sport had succeeded in fastening their Louis XV heels on to roller-skates. In some intermediate spaces, a travelling Dupuytren Museum might be installed, or a Great Panopticon of the Discovery of America and the Torture of the Indians, an exhibition of animals, the pillar of someone fasting, while up above, on wires fixed to columns without cornices, several tight-rope walkers with pink tights and balancing poles, floodlit as they travelled from capital to capital, passed obliviously over the circulating skaters and the tragedies of Sophocles below, hourly expecting to be expelled by the army of workmen who periodically returned to their abandoned task to continue the almost liturgical elevation of the Civic Temple towards the lantern at the top.

These alternations between building and stoppage were still going on when one morning, with a jubilant air, Doctor Peralta entered the Head of State's private apartments, where the Mayorala Elmira was still in her underclothes:

"A miracle, Señor! A miracle! German submarines have just sunk a North American ship, the *Vigilentia*! All the gringos in the crew went to the bottom! Not one was saved!" (He was laughing.) "Not one, my President! Not one! They were all done for. And although the news isn't official, it's known that this will bring the United States into the war. Yes, really: they'll come into the war!"

And they were both so pleased that without waiting for anything more they took the Hermes case and filled their glasses with Santa Inés. ("So I'm to be treated like dirt, am I?" said the Mayorala, hastily bringing up a tooth-glass.) It was some time since the Head of State had been so delighted, because the European War had become a stationary war of trenches, positions, resistance, and slow struggles to win a height, a copse, the ruins of a fort already ten times ruined, a war of minimal advances and retreats, but with countless dead, and therefore monotonous—in fact: boring. For anyone looking at it from here it lacked interest as a spectacle. People no longer moved little flags over maps of distant lands to mark victories or defeats, because there were no dramatic victories or defeats, and whenever a real battle took place it was always in the same area of the Argonne or Verdun, between places with unknown names, barely a centimetre apart on the 1/1000 maps that were still on display, dusty and ignored, in newspaper offices. Certainly the country was enjoying astonishing prosperity. But the increasing cost of living kept the poor in the same misery as before—breakfast of baked banana, yams at midday, crusts and tapioca after the day's work, with some dried goat's meat or cow dead of foot-and-mouth disease on Sundays and birthdays—in spite of wages appearing to be good. As a result of this state of things, students, intellectuals and professional agitators—that filthy intelligentsia who always destroy one's patience—had gradually combined together to make an opposition movement. And just when he was counting on peace and quiet, the Head of State was surprised by a proliferation of hostile forces invading the city, manifested here, there, where least expected, to trouble his mind and interrupt his sleep. When he thought he had been quite forgotten, the hand of Doctor Luis Leoncio Martínez reappeared in proclamations arriving in envelopes with different postmarks, and denouncing events—this was the serious part of it—only known to a few people connected with the intimate life of the Presidential Palace. It had been discovered too late (that cretin the Chief of Police we waste money on never knew!) that a professor of Modern History at the University had given lectures on the Mexican Revolution, speaking about the strength of its proletariat, peasants' leagues, the Syndicate of Tenant Farmers of Vera Cruz, agrarianism, the socialist government of Carrillo Puerto in Yucatán, and the articles written by the gringo adventurer John Reed—about everything in fact that had ruined, sunk and impoverished the magnificent estates of Don Porfirio, humanist and civilizer, who instead of reposing in a huge national pantheon, was buried, a victim of ingratitude, in a sad corner of the cemetery at Montparnasse. And as a last straw our Secret Service had failed to catch some anarchists, probably from Barcelona, who came out at night like elusive ghosts and chalked the letters R.A.S. on the walls, which appeared to stand for *Revolution of Anarchists and Syndicalists*, sometimes accompanied by phrases like: "Property is theft", and other well-worn formulae only taken seriously in our imitative and backward America.

Now, with this splendid sinking of the *Vigilentia* the United States would come into the war, we should come into the war ourselves, patriotic feelings would be galvanized, and since a state of war necessarily implies a permanent state of emergency, we should round up, to the tune of the National Anthem, the Marseillaise, God Save the King, God Save the Tsar and the Star-Spangled Banner, the most formidable cast of oppositionists, conspirators and suspicious ideologues—all pro-German—that had ever been seen in the country.

Meanwhile the Head of State drank rum on fast days and sent for the Ambassador of the United States to inform him that the Republic would stand beside her Great Sister of the North in these days of trial; then, after holding a rapid Council of Ministers, he urgently summoned the two Chambers, appeared before them, and the text of a Declaration of War against the Central Powers was approved by acclamation, with applause for every "considering that" and "whereas" serving to justify it.

And that same day the war began with an operation as excellently profitable as it was speedy in execution: at exactly five o'clock in the afternoon the military authorities from

Puerto Araguato went on board four German ships—the
Lübeck, the *Grane*, the *Schwert* and the *Cuxhaven*, which were
moored to the quay awaiting orders from their government—
took possession of them and seized their crews. Delighted to
see that the war was over for them, the sailors welcomed the
port authorities with cheers, and marched gaily off to their
place of internment, boisterously greeting passers-by on the
way. One Nietzschean officer who shouted: "We'll die rather
than hand over our ship!" was thrown overboard with an
insult obviously meaning something like "son of a whore" in
the Teuton tongue. And the captives were taken to a farm
surrounded by a lot of land, where they slung their hammocks
from trees and at once began gathering herbs and parasitic
plants. Next morning they used some wood given them by
orders from above to build pretty chalets in the Rhenish style,
while others planted gladioli and rolled the ground to make
tennis-courts. Three weeks later the farm had become a model
estate. There was a library, with the poems of Heinrich Heine
and even of the socialist Dehmel. Of course it lacked women,
but many of them had no need of them, being homosexual
on the whole, and as for the unyielding few, they got permission
to visit the brothel of La Ramona every Friday, under military
escort. And as they were very musical, they made an orchestra
from the instruments they had brought on board ship, and
began to play the lesser works of Haydn, Mendelssohn and
Raff, his *Cavatina* in particular. Sometimes a poisonous reptile,
rattlesnake, coral or mapanare, would join the concert; but it
was always seen in time by the 'cellist, who looked at the
ground more than the other musicians, and the serpent died
at a single blow accurately given on its spine by the stick of
the bow—*col legno* as it is technically called. And the purser of
the *Lübeck* would often sing in his charming tenor voice, well
accompanied by the orchestra:

Winterstürme wichen
dem Wonnemond
in milden lichte
leuchtet der Lenz.

The second action in this war had as its objective the confiscation of the Little German Train—the Head of State directed this operation in person, at the head of the sappers of the Second Tactical Regiment. When H-day dawned, the two terminal stations were occupied—the one above and the one at the bottom—as well as all the intermediate stops, signal boxes and controls of points, etc. And as journeys remained suspended pending a fresh order, the President had the chance to realize an old dream: that of playing with the Little Train to his heart's content, putting Peralta, black in the face with dust, in the coal-tender. Once he'd grasped the mechanism, the engine advanced, reversed, went in and out of the repairing shed, and revolved again and again on the turn-tables; whistled, spouted steam from all its valves and ball-bearings, emitted even more steam, came, went and stopped to take a cargo on board: bundles of sugar-cane, barrels, a basket of squids, pots of areca-nuts, empty cages, a double-bass, hens, and one or two negro drummers. And when the Head of State had mastered the whole technique of stoking the engine, driving, accelerating, keeping up the speed, and braking in such a way as to stop the train with the carriages opposite the platform, the entire Cabinet was invited to take a first trip to the Olmedo Colony, with pies and tamales served in the carriages, and enough champagne to drink the health of the First Mechanic of the Nation. And the President found his artefact so amusing that for several days he quite forgot the European War, and stopped reading the foreign papers regularly brought him by Doctor Peralta—among them a piquant French magazine called *Regiment,* full of nudes amongst uniforms.

Meanwhile, *La Madelon* and *Roses of Picardy* had been succeeded by *Over There,* a tune which invaded the country with astonishing speed. Beginning with the pianolas of Puerto Araguato, it had travelled along the Great Eastern Railway, from gramophone to gramophone, taking possession of pianos in music-schools, pianos in middle-class drawing-rooms, cinema pianos, café pianos, nuns' pianos, tarts' pianos, before reaching its most sonorous expression in the Sunday concerts

in Central Park. *Over There, Over There, Over There* . . .
Huge posters representing a North American soldier charging
an invisible enemy with his bayonet, and shouting "Come on!"
invited the public to buy war loan, and met with such a good
response in the country that a little later Ambassador Ariel
solemnly handed President Woodrow Wilson the sum of a
million dollars, collected in less than twenty-five days. The
cinemas showed documentaries glorifying General Pershing—
the man who had sent a scandalous "punitive expedition" to
Mexico a short while ago. *Over There, Over There, Over There.*
Now, as well as *Over There*, came Sousa's noisy marches with
bass tubas and flourishes on the piccolo. A young officer,
warmly supported by the Government ("War stimulates male
energy," said the Head of State: "War is to man what child-
birth is to woman"), took upon himself the task of raising a
National Legion of Volunteers to go and fight in France—
under his command, of course. Armed warfare was full of
dangers, naturally, but much that was enjoyable went with it.
In proof of this, one need only read an article by Maurice
Barrès, often reprinted in the local press: "Good-humour reigns
in the trenches. Of course on rainy nights it's not like being in
a luxury restaurant. . . . But I know a place where there's a
labyrinth of eight kilometres of very well-kept trenches,
connected by paths called names like the Champs-Elysées or
the Rue Monsieur-le-Prince. I know an underground shelter
where one officer has installed a crimson velvet armchair, and
a table with a vase of roses and old Strasbourg china. The
trenches are furnished with objects found among the ruins of
bombarded villages. Gaiety reigns in the trenches." (sic.) Such
literature was synchronized with pictures of Bengal lancers,
handsome bersaglieri and cossacks—recently become republi-
cans—who were now hurling themselves with fresh energy
against a Germany whose starving population had nothing to
eat but bread made of straw and sawdust; all this, opportunely
reinforced by a portrait of Ofelia dressed as a Red Cross nurse,
looking more creole than ever as she bandaged the forehead
of a wounded Englishman, played a part in raising an
army of two hundred and fifty young men eager to see the

Eiffel Tower, the Moulin Rouge and Maxim's Restaurant. "Now the people *over there* will realize we've got guts," said Peralta.

But there was some disappointment among the public when they heard, weeks later, that as soon as the volunteers from their country arrived *over there* they had been dispersed among different French units, and that the young officer, deprived of the command of his men, had returned in a state of furious indignation, declaring—after taking a close look at the situation—that the Allies would lose this war, even with North American help, because there was nothing to be seen but mismanagement and chaos. But what interested people most was not whether the Allies would win or lose the war, but that it should last as long as possible. Given three, four or five years more war we should become a great nation. From the six o'clock mass to evening rosary, from the bells of daybreak to the ringing of the angelus, everyone was praying for Peace of course, but with the almost universal gesture, difficult for foreigners to understand, of placing their middle fingers on top of their forefingers. When all was said and done, we were not responsible for what was happening in Europe. We weren't guilty at all. The Old Continent had been at fault in setting itself up as an example of wisdom. And if our country was enjoying an unexpected period of progress and plenty today, it was proof that the Almighty—as the Archbishop had said in an eloquent sermon—favoured those who were out of sympathy with empty philosophies leaving dust and ashes in the soul, and with certain social doctrines as wicked as they were corrupt and foreign to our character, but who had known how to safeguard the religious and patriarchal traditions of the Nation. As he said this the prelate made a gesture embracing both the Holy Ghost swinging above his head and the Head of State, who happened to be present in the Cathedral that morning.

The construction of the Capitol was almost complete. Already enclosed between the walls of a palace too narrow to shelter her, the Giantess, the Titaness, the Immense Woman, a combination of Juno, Pomona, Minerva and the Republic, had grown bigger day by day as the building went up around her. Every morning she seemed larger, like those jungle plants that shoot up amazingly during the night, trying to reach a dawn hidden from them by the trees above. As if oppressed, crushed by the surrounding stones, she looked twice as thickset, corpulent and tall—particularly tall—as she did when she had been set up piecemeal in an open space. The cupola had already closed over her head topped by its noble lantern—imitated from the Invalides in Paris—which now that its beacon was lit dominated the city nights, cruelly reducing the Cathedral towers to dwarfish proportions, and interrupting the dialogue they used to carry on with the distant cone of the Tutelary Volcano, according to a poem by one of our great writers of the last century.

The work was nearly finished, but it seemed improbable that the building could be inaugurated, as had been hoped, on the date of the Centenary of Independence which was already fast approaching. On the day when this problem was broached at a stormy meeting of the Cabinet, the Head of State became suddenly enraged and violently dismissed the Minister of Works, threatening the others with exile or prison if the Capitol wasn't finished, painted, gleaming and burnished, complete with gardens, in time for a date that could not be postponed.

And now the work took on Egyptian dimensions. Hundreds of peasants were rounded up with machetes, yoked to carts and drays, lodged in huts and summoned to do alternate shifts of work by bugle-calls; with their help columns and obelisks were erected, gods and warriors, dancers, muses and kings arose, hoplites and horsemen equipped with helmets and breastplates were elevated to the highest friezes. Everything needing polishing was polished, what had to be gilded was gilded, what had to be painted was painted. The work went on at night by the light of spotlights and reflectors. Hammering continued so incessantly that for weeks it was like living in a blacksmith's forge, among drills and anvils, while the last paving-stones were being laid on the steps of the staircase of honour. And one afternoon the Royal Palms entered the city, lying horizontally on lorries and wagons with their leaves sweeping the pavements and raising dust from the streets, to be planted in deep pits filled with black earth, grit and manure. Behind—like Macbeth's forest—appeared small pines, clipped box-trees and arecas, brought from all sorts of places, ready to be transplanted and staked by hundreds of men, waiting watering-can in hand, though it was far from certain, truth to tell, if their leaves would be green in time for the Great Day.

"Any leaves that wither must be painted the night before," said the Head of State. Meanwhile, with their eyes fixed on calendars and watches, impatient and sleepless, the architects and overseers urged on the workers with the shouts and attitudes of slave-drivers, until the building was quite complete, even to the sumptuous final touch of inserting a great diamond from Tiffany in the middle of a star of reddish green marble at the feet of Aldo Nardini's statue, to mark the Zero Point of all the roads of the Republic—the place where, ideally, all the projected means of communication from the furthest limits of the country would meet in the capital.

And at last on the Thursday of the Centenary of Independence, the capital awoke to find itself brilliant and shining, covered in flags, shields, emblems, allegories and cardboard horses representing famous battles. A salvo of a hundred guns went off at dawn, rockets were fired from the roofs, there was a grand military parade and band, many bands, of the regiments of town and provinces, who, when the official procession was over, went on playing all day in the public parks and kiosks at street corners, sending the scores round by messenger—as there were very few copies of some—and choosing mainly national airs and patriotic marches, though they also included some *pièces de résistance* to show what they could do, carefully chosen by the Head of State with the help of the Director of the National Conservatoire. No German music, of course, least of all Wagner who seemed to have been excluded for ever from symphony concerts in Paris after Saint-Saëns had implacably described him as the sinister and abominable incarnation of the German spirit. As to Beethoven, it was best to forget about him for the present—although there were some who maintained that the Germany of his day wasn't the same as Von Hindenburg's, after all. So they marched from square to kiosks, from parks to summer-houses, to the overtures of *Zampa* and *Guillaume Tell*, and to tunes from Massenet's *Scènes Alsaciennes*, Paladilhe's *Patria* and Rubinstein's *Toreador and the Andalusian Girl*—they were short of Russian composers in their repertory—and to Victorin Joncière's *Serenade*—a serenade that dropped its "Hungarian" because we were at war with the Central Powers, just as Berlioz's *Hungarian March*, with its tremendous drumbeats, figured under the simple title of *March*.

A day of general enthusiasm, a day of jugs full of aguardiente, and veal cooking on the grill, free sweet-corn, barrels of beer, toys for poor children, ribbons and bows, choirs singing in the National Pantheon, salves in the churches, dancing in houses and tearooms, alleys and brothels, with every pianola, piano, gramophone, street musician and maraca-player combining full tilt in a general haphazard concert, while waiting for the inauguration ceremony of the Capitol, within whose Large Hemicycle were gathered the entire Government, Heads of the Armed Forces, Diplomatic Corps and an elegant crowd, rigorously filtered, surrounded and observed by a whole legion of agents of our Intelligence Service, who were dressed for the occasion in dinner-jackets too like one another not to look like uniforms. And then the soirée began with all solemnity, pomp and show, epaulettes, gold braid and decorations—the Order of Isabella the Catholic, of Carlos III, of Gustavus Adolphus, the Sovereign Order of the Knights of Malta, Legions of Honour, Honi-soit-qui-mal-y-pense, garters and crosses, and even the exotic insignia of the Dragon of Annam and of the Waterlily and the Arcade, recently granted to our high officials. After listening to the National Anthem, the Head of State walked to the rostrum—he certainly appeared surprisingly confident and in command of himself that afternoon—wearing all the emblems of his high rank. He began his speech slowly as usual, using the theatrical gestures common to a good lawyer and a good orator, sketching an exact and moderate outline of our history from the Conquest to Independence. And those who were ironically expecting his customary verbal flourishes, elaborate epithets and striking vocatives, were surprised to hear him pass from this sober historical narrative to the arid world of statistics, and presenting from the precise viewpoint of an economist, a clear and convincing picture of national prosperity, coinciding as it did—and here his tone became more emotional—with the greatest attempt to destroy Graeco-Latin Culture that had been made in any epoch of human evolution. But that great culture would be saved. Before long, victory for our Spiritual Parents would ensure the permanence of values which, threatened *over there*, would rise again on this side of the Ocean, more splendid than ever. And contemplating, and inviting others to contemplate, this superb building wherein we now were, this crystallization in stone, marble and bronze of the classical orders of Graeco-Latin architecture—Vitruvius, Vignola, Bramante—the Head of State speeded his rhythm and raised his pitch, while his gestures became wider as he suddenly returned to the prolix, ornate and overcharged style that had been so often made fun of by his enemies. And closing an invocation to Her who, as the Guide of all Reason and all Intelligence, must rule over the Republic itself and thus over this recently built Civic Temple, the inspired voice exclaimed: "Oh Archagetis, ideal incarnate in the masterpieces of men of genius, I would rather be the least in your mansion than the first elsewhere! Yes: I will attach myself to the stylobate of your temple; I will forget every discipline except yours; I will be a stylite on your columns and my cell shall be placed upon your architrave. And—something more difficult!—for your sake I will if I can become *intolerant and partial* . . . (The crowd was tense with expectation.) *I shall be unjust to everything that does not concern you; I shall make myself the slave of the last of your sons.* The present inhabitants of the land you gave to Erectheus shall be exalted and flattered by me. I will endeavour to love even their defects, and I will convince myself—oh Hippias!—that they are descendants of the horsemen who are celebrating their eternal festival in the marble of your frieze." (Here he gestured towards the roof.)

The Head of State seemed to have come to the end of his speech. The audience gave him a long standing ovation. But Peralta, sitting in the secretary's place opposite the audience, the better to keep an eye on the Diplomatic Corps, had noticed the French Ambassador nudging the English Ambassador at the name of *Archagetis*. At *stylobate*, the English Ambassador's elbow had nudged the Italian Ambassador in the ribs; from *stylite* to *architrave*, from *Erectheus* to *Hippias* a series of nudges had passed from ambassador to business representative, from councillor to cultural attaché, as far as the lean rib-cage of the Japanese Commercial Attaché, who didn't understand the language and was therefore half asleep. The impact nearly knocked him over, just as in physics the last ball of the apparatus is hurled in the air when the action of a first ball of the same weight communicates its energy to six identical intermediate balls. One or two laughs were stifled behind the many handkerchiefs mopping up non-existent sweat—because it was not a warm night and the winds were from the North, cooled by the snows of the Tutelary Volcano. At this moment the Head of State silenced the audience with a simple gesture and said that he was particularly pleased by this applause, since it was directed at the famous writer Ernest Renan, whose *Prayer on the Acropolis* included the fine paragraph he had just quoted, because it seemed to him to correspond in every way with his profoundest spiritual desires and the solemnity of the occasion.

There was more applause, louder and more prolonged than before—as though some desire for forgiveness lay behind it— during which Peralta left his seat, and going up to the French Ambassador, said to him with sly coarseness:

"*Il vous a bien eu, hein? Pas si con que ça, le vieux!*"

"*Pas si con que ça, en effet,*" replied the other, taken by surprise and suddenly worried by the idea that his thoughtless response might be reported to the Quai d'Orsay, which was in no mood for jokes these days and had had the brilliant ideas of sending Alexis Leger to China and appointing Paul Claudel Minister to Rio de Janeiro, so as to raise the lamentable intellectual level of French representatives in Asia and Latin America.

But this was the signal for the assembly to break up; people abandoned their seats in haste, descended the stairs and made for the doors in an avalanche, pushing with their elbows so as to get as quickly as possible to a gigantic buffet whose tables displayed enormous silver dishes laden with as many good things imported from New York and Paris as could be added to the national delicacies: pheasants decorated with their feathers, truffled quails, sucking pigs stuffed with galantine and pistachios, highly seasoned tamales and turkeys with cranberry sauce, Saint Honoré à la crème and maize cream in glasses, marrons glacés and tamarind pies, national savouries next to black and red caviare piled on to elephants sculptured in ice, the whole spread being surmounted in the middle and at the ends by architectonic cakes made of meringue and almond paste representing the Capitol, without a single column missing, and all the statues and obelisks in marzipan. All this was admired and enjoyed, washed down by wine and liqueurs, brandy and tequila; and fresh bottles of champagne were taken from coolers full of crushed ice tinted pink to enhance their gold-covered corks.

And everyone drank toasts standing round the huge statue of the Republic, while an orchestra, hoisted up inside the cupola, launched into Cuban *danzóns* and creole bambas, interspersed between the *Beautiful Ohio* waltz or the syncopation of *Pretty Baby*. And then fireworks were let off, setting the sky on fire, falling in torrents and cascades of stars and lights on the roofs and terraces of the town.

And at two in the morning—according to the Head of Protocol no official soirée could go on after this hour—Peralta and the Head of State returned to the Palace, exhausted but happy, longing to take off their evening clothes and drink something stronger and more to their taste than what the party provided. The Mayorala Elmira was waiting for them in the presidential apartments, dressed in her petticoat, but with her bosom muffled up against the cold mountain air creeping through the Venetian blinds. And as the Secretary had been as good as his word and brought her some of what had been served at the buffet that night, despite her doubts as to whether she would find it to her liking, the zamba eagerly took them out of their hamper, one by one, with the mistrustful caution of a bomb-disposal expert examining the suspicious contents of an anarchist's case. She found a derogatory definition for them all; the Burgundian snails were "slugs"; the caviare, "buckshot in oil"; the truffles, "chips of charcoal"; the halva, "nougat trying to be like turrón from Jijona".

The President had already drunk a lot and was asking for more; he didn't feel ready for sleep, while Peralta never tired of praising his brilliant use of the quotation from Ernest Renan.

"Don't they say I'm an affected and ridiculous speaker?" remarked the President. "But I'm really sorry our friend the Academician wasn't there. Because he would certainly have fallen into the trap too."

"The thing is that that passage seemed to have been written expressly for the inauguration of our Capitol," said Peralta, "and with such appropriate threats against the bastards of the opposition."

The Head of State was looking out of the window at the confused panorama of scaffolding and building, which would soon be covered with workmen. Far away, the Tutelary Volcano had hardly emerged from its veils of mist in the belated dawn. After drinking a sixth large beer from the neck of the bottle, the Mayorala pulled her camp-bed into the doorway and threw herself down to sleep, as always, with a sawn-off shot-gun in reach of her hand. Peralta, who was rather drunk, drowsed off on the leather sofa, with its wide back and deep cushions, standing opposite the somewhat Renaissance-style fireplace—with Louis XII's porcupine at the top—where for lack of the fire that was never lit, red electric-light bulbs winked among false logs.

"The ceremony was a success, a real success," the Head of State kept repeating, listening to the discreet summons to matins from the Cathedral—the bell had been muted because the neighbours wouldn't get up as early as usual and had asked that it should sound less loudly than before. And he went on pacing round the room, from chair to chair, having a last drink which always turned into a penultimate drink. A man accustomed to short nights and long siestas, whose spartan audiences lasting into the small hours were the torment of his colleagues, he couldn't make up his mind to rest a few hours in his hammock tonight—a long net hammock like the one in Paris—before he took the bath that the Mayorala Elmira would prepare for him as usual, scented with English bath-salts and the water at blood-heat. He was delighted by the Capitol affair. Now photographs of the building would be sent to our embassies and published in the European and Continental papers—paying for the space according to the columns occupied and tariff per centimetre, as he always did when he wanted to control the captions under a picture. Thus the world would hear how greatly increased in importance this town had become, which at the beginning of the century had been hardly more than a village surrounded by wasteland full of snakes, bare hills, thorny scrub, water-tanks breeding mosquitoes, and cattle driven along the main streets with shouts and whistles.

He was happy with such thoughts as these, and hardly had daylight dawned, when he became aware of distant reveilles from the barracks, and the first trams carrying people with baskets, knapsacks and crates to the marketplace, where caged birds were already fidgeting and turtles munching lettuces in their boxes. The Head of State looked at his agenda. Today was free from councils, audiences and other worries. So maybe he would change the order of his habits: he would have a bath first and then a sleep till the middle of the morning. But he lounged in an armchair and ate liqueur chocolates, in no hurry to make up his mind.

"Whatever you like," murmured the Mayorala as if talking in her sleep.

"A bit later, my dear. Don't trouble."

He felt himself possessed of the same strength and sovereignty as the Volcano, which had now emerged from its trammelling clouds and stood revealed among craggy spurs of blue quartz. "A success! . . . a success," he went on repeating to himself. "As for the rest . . ."

A tremendous explosion shook the Palace. All the windows of the façade broke at once; several candelabra fell from ceilings; bottles, vases, ornamental pottery and plates were shattered, and a few pictures came away from the walls. A large high explosive bomb had just gone off in the presidential bathroom, spreading heavy fumes smelling of bitter almonds. Ashy pale from the effort to appear calm, the Head of State looked at his watch: "Half past six . . . my regular bath time . . . Congratulations, gentlemen; but I wasn't there today." And while guards, footmen and maidservants came running with all speed and noise and the Mayorala shouted for more, he added, pointing towards the town: "This is what I get for being too lenient."

12

. . . there is something like a very powerful and clever

deceiver who uses all his skill to keep me

constantly deceived . . .

DESCARTES

Ministers were dragged out of bed by telephone calls from Doctor Peralta—they had been sleeping off the official dinner, prolonged when they got home by large doses of digestive drinks, yellow liqueurs, green benedictines and purple cherry brandy—and summoned to an urgent Council Meeting at 8.30 in the morning, where there would be plenty of coffee-trays to help those who were still drowsy to shake off the effect of their drinks. When they arrived—chewing peppermint, sweating out aspirins and clearing their eyes with lotion—the Mayorala Elmira took them to the President's bathroom, where they were shocked at the sight of broken porcelain, shattered mirrors, debris of bottles and soap-dishes in a pool of eau de Cologne, a bidet with its taps wrenched from their sockets, spouting out uncontrollable fountains of water, and even the ceiling smashed by the explosion.

"Horrible ... Terrifying ... Inconceivable ... And to think how nearly ..."

"I've refrained from going in," declared the Head of State somewhat dramatically, when everyone was seated, "because I'm afraid of my own anger."

There was a long pause, charged with menacing possibilities. Then, in a calmer tone:

"Gentlemen, let us get to work." The Secretary opened the meeting by describing what had happened, the exact time, circumstances, etc. Captain Valverde, Chief of the Judicial Police, had already begun his investigations. Because of the inauguration of the Capitol, the presidential guard had yesterday been transferred to the Great Hemicycle, and it was true that the Palace itself had had insufficient attention, the key posts being left to soldiers who were inexperienced in such duties. However, no one except the domestic, personal and confidential staff had entered the building after the changing of the guard.

"Apart from that," observed the President, "the bomb which exploded here was not one that could have been brought in someone's pocket. It must have been under the bathtub itself for many hours, with its mechanism set to go off at the appointed time. This wasn't the work of some amateur using nitrobenzene, gunpowder or picric acid; the bomb was made by someone who knew his job. The expert says that the smell of bitter almonds, which is still noticeable, is a sign of technical skill."

These were the possible hypotheses: the RAS (Revolution of Anarchists and Syndicalists) who had for months past been scrawling their initials on the walls of the city with invisible hands; or perhaps Doctor Luis Leoncio Martínez's supporters might be more active than was realized—they had been agitating lately with some skill, it must be admitted, and gaining followers in the city and provinces; students, possibly, because students always got mixed up in rioting and bloody-mindedness (and why shouldn't we close the University of

San Lucas this very day?); Russian nihilists ("rubbish", murmured the President); members of Samuel Gompers' American Federation of Labor ("that's absurd") who had recently carried on revolutionary activities in the North of Mexico.

"And then, there's Red Literature," said the Minister of Education.

"That's it: Red Literature," said the others as one man. But the Chief of the Judicial Police saw no relation between that morning's incident and the circulation of books such as are published by the Biblioteca Barbadillo, called *The Pleasures of the Caesars*, which he had been shown recently, containing reproductions of Roman cameos wherein the Emperor Octavian was to be seen laying hands—and how!—on his daughter Julia, while in another Nero appeared doing things he couldn't describe here out of respect for the company.

"That's not what we're talking about; pornography does no harm to anyone, after all," said the Minister for Education. "We mean books on anarchism, socialism, communism, workmen's Internationals, revolution—*Red Books*: that's what they're called everywhere."

"Don't let's digress, gentlemen; don't let's digress," said the Chief of Police, somewhat peevishly. The problem was simpler. As everyone knew, certain printed leaflets were in circulation, full of insults against the Government, and written in an unmistakably creole style—calumnies, of course, but the sort of calumny in common use among some sectors of the opposition. Not nihilist, nor anarcho-syndicalist, nor of the "as the gentleman says, but I don't understand English" description. Our enemies were, quite simply, politicians in disguise, who were trying every way they knew to stir up feelings and overthrow the Government. They've been watching us, they are all around; and now, with last night's business, they have declared open war. And now that it was war, we would reply with war, he said, laying his pistol on the table.

"But if there is to be war, we must know where the enemy is," remarked the President.

"Leave that to me. I know where to begin. I've already

got some names on my list. I'll read them if you like . . ."

"Better not, Captain. I'm quite capable of being too lenient to some. I trust you entirely. Carry on. At once and forcibly. We understand one another."

"A mistake would be disastrous, however," put in Peralta.

"*Errare humanum est*," concluded the Head of State in *Petit Larousse* Latin. And to cheer up his Ministers, who were still looking worn out with anxiety and their late night, he sent for some bottles of cognac: "Just this once," he said, filling a glass.

"You've got every justification," chorused the rest.

The masons and plumbers were beginning to arrive to repair the bathroom, bringing tiles, blow-lamps and tools.

"Anyway, look into this business of Red Literature," said the Head of State to the Captain, but in the tone of someone who doesn't consider the matter of great importance.

"Don't worry, Señor. I have people trained for that sort of thing," replied the other, taking his leave with the praiseworthy haste of someone who is eager to get to work.

"We shall pull in a fine haul of pro-Germans today," said Peralta.

The people of the capital were treated to a strange and unexpected performance at about two in the afternoon that day. It was the hour when employees went back to their offices, the hour of dessert in restaurants, or of drinking under the awnings of cafés—the *Tortoni*, the *Granja* or the *Marquise de Sevigné*—installed as a great novelty in imitation of what one saw in Paris, so the streets were full of people. And in these crowded streets there suddenly appeared, preceded by small cars—Fords, naturally—with their sirens screaming, some Black Marias, like cages on wheels, with fierce-looking policemen standing on the back steps, rifle in hand. It was soon learnt that these sinister vehicles, recently acquired by the Government, were being used as substitutes for the earlier prison cars—"bird-cages" as they were called—hitherto used to pick up drunks, thieves and homosexuals. At the same time, unusual activity was noticed among the city police. Motorcycles going to and fro. Sudden appearances, now here, now there, of detectives, quickly spotted as such by their obvious attempts at "not attracting attention", and dressed in a commerical traveller style mixed with that of Nick Carter, which left no room for doubt. And all the time those sirens went on calling to each other, stridently, disturbingly, from district to district, over the roofs and terraces, causing a panic among the pigeons fluttering between the modern buildings.

"Something's up," people said in surprise. "Something's happening."

And a great deal was happening, a great deal was in fact happening that day, which was becoming more and more overcast, with warm drizzle falling, hour by hour. At half past two in the afternoon the Vice-Chancellor of the University was explaining in a lecture the nominalism and voluntarism of William of Occam, when the police burst into his classroom, and took him and all his pupils prisoners for holding a demonstration. Continuing their task of subjugating the Faculty of Humanities, they carried off eight more professors with kicks and shoves towards the new prison-cars. Tired of hearing him call upon their century-old rights and autonomy, Captain Valverde threw the Chancellor into the fountain in the central court, along with his mortarboard and gown—attributes he had tried to use to gain the 'invaders'' respect.

At three o'clock, under orders from Lieutenant Calvo, the chosen expert, the authorities occupied several bookshops where cheap editions were on sale of such books as *Red Week in Barcelona* (a tract about the anarchist Ferrer), *The Knight of the Red House*, *The Red Lily*, *Red Dawn* (Pío Baroja), *The Red Virgin* (a biography of Louise Michel), *Le Rouge et le Noir*, *The Scarlet Letter* (by Nathaniel Hawthorne)—all examples, according to the expert, of *red literature*, revolutionary propaganda, to a large extent responsible for such incidents as had happened at the Palace last night. The books were thrown into lorries and dispatched on their way to the Rubbish Incinerator, built a short while before on the outskirts of the town.

"Take *Little Red Riding Hood* while you're about it," shouted one of the booksellers, beside himself with rage.

"You're under arrest, you joker," said Lieutenant Calvo, handing him over to one of his agents.

Then—it was about five—they began on private houses: police rained from heaven, ran over roofs, jumped into patios, entered kitchens, broke down doors, crept under beds, searched wardrobes, turned drawers upside down and opened trunks, while women wept, children screamed and old women cursed, a patriarch raged from his wheel-chair, and a consumptive, near to death, declared that the Head of State was the son of a drunk and that his late wife Doña Hermenegilda, so often described as a saint, had worn herself out accommodating the organ of a young officer of hussars, famous for his exceptional proportions.

So night fell, amid confused rumours of arrests, detentions, disappearance of "subversive elements", German spies and pro-German socialists, yet the pulse of the city's normal activities seemed unchanged. The advertisements for Vino Mariani, Gyraldose and Urodonal turned on their lights, bells rang in the cinemas, while—in cafés and bars—people vainly turned the pages of the evening papers, which mentioned everything except what they were looking for. The Black Marias seemed to be taking a rest from their rounds. As it was a Thursday, the Fire Brigade Band played the march called *Sambre et Meuse*, the ballet from *Samson and Delilah* and several bullfight pasodobles in the bandstand in Central Park. The streets in the red light district—San Isidro, la Chayota, el Mangue, Economía and San Juan de Letrán—filled with clients. But on the stroke of eleven there was a sudden, violent invasion of brothels, gambling dens, bars and halls where people danced to violin and guitar. Everyone who couldn't prove that he was a public employee or a soldier was piled into military lorries—sometimes without his clothes—and carried off to the old Central Prison, whose cells, corridors and courtyards were already crammed with people.

And when dawn came, Terror reigned in the city. The arrests continued. The Black Marias went their rounds again. But in spite of the Terror, when the Mayorala Elmira was cleaning the little library of the Council Chamber that afternoon, she found, behind a copy of Cesar Cantú's *Universal History*, a suspicious looking tin of animal crackers, which

turned out to be a crude home-made bomb. It was defused in
time by one of the Palace guards, apprentice to an expert.
"We'll have to tighten the pressure," commented Peralta.

With age and the hardening of his arteries, the Head of
State's eyes—he would never wear spectacles as he didn't need
them for reading—had acquired the strange defect of eliminating the third dimension. He saw things, whether near or
far, as flat images without relief, like the stained glass in
Gothic windows. So every morning, just as if they were figures
in a Gothic window, he looked at the Men of Regulation
Colours—this one in blue and black, the next in white and gold
and the third in a buff-coloured tunic—who told him about
the work they had carried out the day before, their night spent
in police stations and prisons, barracks and cellars extracting
words, names, addresses and information from people who
didn't want to speak. And their accounts of ducking and
racking, hanging and violence, their catalogue of pincers,
truncheons, braziers, and even corn-cobs—these were for
women—called up visions from hagiography, the downfall of
the damned, illustrations of torture, all transferred to a large
stained-glass window opening on to the remote splendour of
the Tutelary Volcano. With a "Thank you, gentlemen," the
first stained glass window broke, eliminating the blues, whites
and yellows of the original image, while in at the other door to
take their place in the second window came the Listening and
Looking men, the Watchers, the Hearers, the Hypocrites, the
masters in maieutics, virtuosos in heuristics, who not only
brought information extracted by skill, snatched in flight, half
understood, of some guilty remark picked up at a diplomatic
reception, a bar counter, in the warmth of a bedroom—they
were everywhere, they entered without being seen, Guests of
Glass one day, Guests of Stone if more acceptable, insinuating,
snooping, often charming—but were in fact Watchers of
the Watchful, Observers of the Cunning, recorders of everything invented, plotted and schemed, even by the collaborators,
familiars and associates of the Head of State himself, thanks to
his Exalted Protection. As he listened to these people of his,
who had their eyes to the keyhole and their curiosity on the

alert, he realized (sometimes with annoyance, sometimes with amusement) what diverse and picturesque transactions were going on behind his back: there was the business of a bridge built over a river that wasn't shown on any map; the business of the Municipal Library without any books; the business of the stud animals from Normandy that had never crossed the ocean; the business of the toys and alphabets for kindergartens that didn't exist; the business of the Peasant Women's Maternity Homes, to which peasant women naturally never went, since for centuries they had been in the habit of giving birth on a broken stool, pulling on a rope hanging from the ceiling with their husband's hat on their head so that they should get a boy; the business of the kilometre stones which were still only painted boards; the business of pornographic films sold in Quaker Oats tins; the business of the Chinese Charade (*"jeux des trente-six bêtes"*, as it was called by Baron Drummond who introduced the Cantonese lottery of numbered animals to America), managed by the brigade of the National Police for the Repression of Illicit Games; the business of *Erectyl*, a Korean liquor containing mandragora root, the "stallion liana" from Santo Domingo, powdered tortoiseshell and extract of Spanish fly; the business of the slot-machines—three bells, or three plums or three cherries gave you the jack-pot —owned by the Chief of the Secret Service; the business of birth certificates *ad perpetuam memoriam* for those "interdits de séjour" and Frenchmen from Cayenne wanting to become our compatriots; the business of consultations with astrologers, fortune-tellers, palmists, card-readers, horoscopes by correspondence, Hindu mystics—forbidden by law—who all had understandings with the Minister of the Interior; the business of the Verascopes of Love, tolerated in fairs and amusement parks, and owned by Captain Valverde; the business of Catalan postcards—less refined than the French, said those in the know—run by Captain Calvo; the business of "Lucky Sheets for Newly-weds" (*"Draps bénis pour jeunes mariés"* [sic]), manufactured in the Marais in Paris and designed for the trousseau of every Christian bride.

Between amusement and annoyance—but more amused than

annoyed—the Head of State contemplated this panorama of swindling and gangsterism every morning, reflecting that the least he could do was reward the fidelity and zeal of those who served him with the currency of folklore. Because he was not, and had never been, a man for small transactions, owner of companies managed by stealth, he was Master of Bread and Fish, of Corn and Herds, of Ice and Springs, of Fluid and the Wheel, beneath a multiple identity of symbols, syndicates, trade names and always anonymous societies immune from failure or setbacks. Thus the Head of State contemplated his early morning windows, but observed that, in spite of the Terror unloosed by the first bomb in the Palace, there was *something*, something that his men had been unable to grasp, something that slipped from their fingers, that neither prison nor torture, nor a state of siege could put a stop to; *something* that was moving in the subsoil, underground, that arose from urban catacombs not previously known to exist; something new in the country, with unpredictable manifestations, mysterious mechanisms, which the President could not explain. It was as if the atmosphere had been changed by the addition of some impalpable pollen or hidden ferment, an elusive, slippery, occult but manifest force, silent although throbbingly alive with a circulation of clandestine leaflets, manifestos, proclamations, pamphlets small enough to go in the pocket sent forth by ghostly printers ("and are you incapable of finding something so difficult to conceal, so noisy, as a printing-press?" the Head of State would shout, on his angrier mornings). These didn't insult him in the creole argot of the tenement house, with its simple-minded puns and jokes as formerly, but described him as *Dictator* (a word that wounded him more than the most obscene epithet or untranslatable nickname, because it was annoyingly current abroad—especially in France) and revealed to the public in plain and cutting language many things about him—actions, business matters, decisions and *eliminations*—that should never have been known.

"But who, who, who publishes these leaflets, libels and infamous calumnies?" the Head of State would cry aloud every morning to his usual stained-glass windows of sweating, twitching faces, distressed by their inability to answer. Those in the regulation colours of blue, white and yellow stammered something or other; the pale Maieutic Brotherhood hinted and contradicted one another, proceeding by elimination although obviously disorientated. They tightened their noose around the printed matter and searched for guilt between the lines. It wasn't the anarchists: they had all been taken; it wasn't Luis Leoncio Martínez's followers, who were all shut up in different prisons; nor was it the timid oppositionists of other factions, who were thoroughly taped and watched, and hadn't the technical means to keep an underground printing-press functioning so continuously and exasperatingly.

And so, by dint of subjecting conjectures and hypotheses to calculation of probabilities, and by joining the loose letters together like the pieces of a jigsaw puzzle, they arrived at the word C—O—M—M—U—N—I—S—M, the last to come to mind.

But the fact was—as the Head of State remarked when he was alone with Peralta—we were a very imaginative people, like all Latin Americans. It was enough for something to travel about the world—whether a fashion, a product, a doctrine, an idea, a style of painting, writing, poetry or of foolish talk—for us to welcome it with enthusiasm. This was just as true of Italian Futurism as it was of the *Juvencia del Abate Soury*; or of theosophy as of dancing marathons; of the philosophy of Krause as of table-turning. And now this exotic, impossible Russian communism, condemned by all honest men ever since the infamous Treaty of Brest-Litovsk, was stretching its tentacles towards America. Luckily this doctrine without a future and so alien to our customs had few supporters—or at least their activities had not been obvious hitherto—but as soon as they thought of it as a possible motive, there rose to the minds of those present the despised figure of a young man called Álvarez or Álvaro or Álvarado—Peralta wasn't sure which—better known as *The Student* ever since he had said in a particularly aggressive speech: "You mustn't think of me as a student, but as any student, *The Student*," and who had played a prominent part in recent university agitations. One informer had heard him talking approvingly of this fellow Lenin who had overthrown Kerensky in Russia and established a regime there in which riches, land, cattle, silver plate and women were all shared.

"Well, you must look for him," said the President. "Maybe we'll get something out of him." But the usual morning stained-glass window at once became a picture of consternation. There was no conceivable way of seizing The Student. And as he had seemed too harmless even to be kept under observation—he was more interested in poetry than politics—the Security Experts couldn't agree about his physical appearance, height, physiognomy or degree of corpulence. Some said he had green eyes, others that they were chestnut; some that he was of athletic build, others that he was weak and sickly; he was twenty-three years old according to the university registers; his mother was dead; his father was a schoolmaster who had been killed in the Nueva Córdoba massacre. He should be in the city, however; but when the police broke into his hideout all they found was a rumpled bed with indications of recent occupation, a half-empty bottle of beer, burned papers, cigar ends, and a book lying on the floor: Volume I of *Das Kapital* by Karl Marx, bought—as could be seen by the shop stamp—in the Atenea bookshop, kept by Valentin Jiménez, now in prison for selling red books.

"That's it!" cried the Head of State when he heard. "The cretins were busy confiscating *Le Rouge et le Noir* and *The Knight of the Red House*, but left the most dangerous books in the shop windows."

And as the Distinguished Academician had sometimes talked to him in Paris about the "Marxist danger", or "Marxist literature", he instructed Peralta ("he's much more intelligent than these bloody detectives, including present company") to bring him all the literature of this type he could find in the city....

Two hours later, a number of volumes were ranged on the table of the presidential study: Marx's *The Class Struggle in France* (*1848–1850*), *Louis Bonaparte's 18 Brumaire* and *The Civil War in France* (*1871*).

"Bah! All that's prehistory," said the Head of State, pushing the books away contemptuously. Marx–Engels: *Critique of the Gotha and Erfürt Programmes.* "This seems to savour of a pamphlet against the European nobility. Because Gotha, as you know, is a sort of annual telephone book of princes, dukes, counts and marquises." Engels: *Ludwig Feuerbach and the end of Classical German philosophy.* . . . "I don't think that's likely to pervert our tram conductors." Marx: *Value, price and profit.* And the President read aloud: "The determination of the values of commodities according to the relative amount of work incorporated in them is totally different from the tautological method of determining values of commodities by the value of the work and the wages." . . . "Do you understand any of it? Nor do I." . . . Marx: *Contribution to the critique of political economy.* He skimmed through the book as far as the appendix, which provoked his hilarity: "With poems in English, poems in Latin and poems in Greek. Let's see if they can indoctrinate the Mayorala Elmira with this." ("You always think I'm stupider than I really am," she said, piqued.) And he laughed again when he picked up another volume: "Ah! Here's the famous *Kapital* . . . Let's have a look:

The first metamorphosis of one commodity, its transformation from a commodity into money, is therefore also invariably the second metamorphosis of some other commodity, the retransformation of the latter from money into a commodity . . . M—C, a purchase, is at the same time C—M, a sale; the concluding metamorphosis of one commodity is the first metamorphosis of another. With regard to our weaver, the life of his commodity ends with the Bible into which he has reconverted his £2. But suppose the seller of the Bible turns the £2 set free by the weaver into brandy, M—C, the concluding phase of C—M—C (linen, money, Bible) is also C—M, the first phase of C—M—C (Bible, money, brandy) . . .

"The only thing I find comprehensible here is the brandy," said the Head of State, in high good humour.

"And what does this whacking great German tome cost?"

"Twenty-two pesos, Señor."

"Then let them sell it, let them sell it; let them go on selling it. There aren't twenty-two people in the whole country who would pay twenty-two pesos for a book as heavy as lead . . . C—M—C, M—C—M . . . I never could get on with equations."

"But look at this, on the other hand," said Peralta, taking a thin pamphlet out of his pocket: *Breeding Rhode Island Red Poultry*.

"What's this got to do with the other?" asked the President. "We've never been able to acclimatize American poultry here. Neither Nat Pinkertons, with feathers on their legs; nor Leghorns, though in the North they lay more eggs than there are days in the year; but here, I don't know why, they shut up their arses and only lay four a week; as for those plump Rhode Island Reds, as soon as they get here they're devoured by lice."

"Open this little book, President. And take a good look," Marx–Engels: *Manifesto of the Communist Party*.

"Ah, hell! this is quite another thing!"

And frowning suspiciously, he read aloud: "A spectre is haunting Europe—the spectre of communism. All the powers of old Europe have entered into a holy alliance to exorcize this spectre: the Pope, Tsar, Metternich and Guizot, French radicals and German police-spies."

There was a silence. Then: "As usual: hieroglyphics or prehistory. The Holy Alliance (wasn't that after the fall of Napoleon?), the Pope who never bothered anyone, Metternich and Guizot (does anyone in this country remember that gentlemen called Metternich and Guizot ever existed?), the Tsar of Russia (which one? Even I can't tell). Prehistory, pure prehistory."

However, when, turning several pages together, he came to the last lines of the pamphlet disguised as a guide to poultry-keeping, he paused deep in thought at a sentence he found there: "In short, the Communists everywhere support every revolutionary movement against the existing social and political order of things."

There was an even longer pause. Then, at last: "The same anarchism as ever: bombs in Paris, bombs in Madrid;

attempts to assassinate kings and queens; anarcho-syndicalism, communism, R.S.A., C—M—C, M—C—M, P.O.S.D.R., and Y.M.C.A. Alphabetic chaos, proliferation of initials, a sign of the decadence of the age. However, this business of breeding Rhode Island Reds. It's ingenious. Order everyone found carrying this avicultural literature to be picked up and imprisoned. And also . . . But—what's going on?"

It was three o'clock in the afternoon. The clapper of the Cathedral bell began its solemn, measured strokes. And as if some gigantic hammer, progenitor of bell-children or children-bells, were striking the first bell created by some enormous liturgical bronze-worker, the sharp but never timid bells of the Hermitage of the Dove replied from up aloft on the snow-covered slopes of the Tutelary Volcano; then their voices were taken up by the soprano of San Vicente of Rio-Frio, the baritone of the Little Sisters of Tarbes, the coloratura of the carillon of the Jesuits, the contralto of San Dionisio, the basso profondo of San Juan de Letrán, the silvery music of the Divine Shepherdess, setting alight a festival of chimes and peals, of calling and ringing, rejoicing and gladness, while from their ropes were hanging, rising and sinking, striding, dancing in the air, bell-ringers and acolytes, agile seminarists and dexterous capuchins, who kicked themselves off the ground and swung themselves aloft again in time to the tumult pouring from the great resonant shafts of the church towers. And the concert spread from North to South, and from East to West, involving the city in a prodigious polyphony of swinging, throbbing and percussion, while factory sirens, motor horns, frying pans hit with spoons, saucepans, tins, everything that could make a noise, resounded, set up a deafening din, above narrow old alleys and wide new asphalt streets. Now railway engines whistled, fire-engine sirens wailed, trams set their copper bells quivering.

"The war is over!" cried the Foreign Secretary, entering without waiting to be announced, and seizing the bottle of Santa Inés, which the Head of State and his secretary had left on the book table, after uncorking it in complete confidence that they were unobserved. "The war is over. Civilization has triumphed over Barbarism, Latinity over Germanism. A victory which is our victory too!"

"Then we're buggered," said the President softly. "Yes, now we're properly buggered."

Children, let out of class, ran shouting and singing out of school. The gay girls of the Calles de La Chayota, Economía or San Isidro rushed into the street wearing Lorraine head-dresses, or black Alsatian bows in their hair. "The war is over . . . the war is over."

Artisans, bricklayers, piano-tuners, pawnbrokers, brakes-men, hawkers of mangoes and tamarinds, maize millers, athletes in picture shirts, ice-cream sellers, organ-grinders with monkeys dressed as Italians, street-cleaners, professors with starched shirt-fronts, sugar-refiners, naturists, theosophists, spiritualists, laboratory workers, homosexuals with carnations in their mouths, students of folk lore, bookish men, gamblers, men in cap and gown, all streamed past shouting as one man: "The war is over! The war is over!"

Newspaper boys appeared crying a special edition with letters 64 points high: "The war is over! The war is over!"

Students, knowing that the police would have the good sense to leave them alone at such a time of rejoicing, ran into the streets in a dense crowd, those from the University of San Lucas carrying a wooden platform on their shoulders, on which a mechanical mule wearing a pointed helmet and with a German flag on its back, kicked into space and was beaten each time by a blow from the sword of a dummy in tricolor and gold, representing Marshal Joffre. And the procession following behind sang:

The Kaiser cuts capers
And Joffre calls the tune.

This animated allegory went round the town to Central Park more than once with their Joffre in red trousers. They stopped in front of the Presidential Palace. Then they followed the Boulevard of the Republic to the upper town, just as the priests of the Divine Shepherdess were bringing out another platform supporting the Virgin in a great glittering cloak, victoriously mounted on a green dragon twisted in its death agony—it had been taken from the altar of Saint George—from whose demonic head hung a cardboard notice bearing the word WAR written in thick indian ink letters. And this time women were singing the old village song:

Santa Maria
Save us from evil
Protect us, Señora
From this terrible devil.

Then the others returned through the Calle del Comercio with their mule and Marshal moved by wires, playing on maracas and firing off rockets:

The Kaiser cuts capers
And Joffre calls the tune.

The retinue of the Divine Shepherdess entered the Calle de los Plateros, and climbed the steps to the Boulevard Auguste Comte:

To kill the Devil
The Virgin seized a blade
On all fours the monster
Lay down in the glade.

"We're done for," said the Head of State watching all this with a far from happy expression.

"But, President, it's the triumph of Reason, the triumph of Descartes."

"Look here, Peralta: this means that the bottom will at once fall out of our market for sugar, bananas, coffee, chewing-gum and gutta percha. The days of the Fat Kine are numbered. And people will say that my rule had nothing to do with the country's prosperity."

The Kaiser cuts capers
And Joffre calls the tune.

"Give orders for a grand official banquet to celebrate the victory of Sainte Geneviève over the Huns, of Joan of Arc over Clausewitz, of the Divine Shepherdess over International Communism. Now the storks can come back from Hansi to the roofs of Colmar, and Déroulède's glorious bugle will sound. Descartes won the war, but we must mop up the mess" . . .

> Santa Maria
> Save us from evil.

. . . "All the same, there is a way of getting a last cut from the conflict. Now, while people still have cash, we'll open a large fund for the Reconstruction of the Devastated Regions of France. Send Ofelia a cable. Tell her to come as soon as possible. We can still make use of her Red Cross nurse's outfit." Indifferent to what was happening in the street, and out of sympathy with the general pandemonium, but a prey to nostalgia and secret anxiety, the Head of State wound up the long-horned gramophone sleeping in a corner of his study and listened to a record of Fortugé's:

> Lorsque la nuit tombe sur Paris
> La belle église de Notre-Dâââââme
> Semble monter au Paradis
> Pour lui conter son état d'âââme.

13

The Campaign to Collect Funds for the Reconstruction of Regions Devastated by the War was a magnificent success; besides procuring marginal benefits as plentiful as they were uncontrollable, it re-established the prestige of the country and its intelligent Government in a Europe too absorbed in the problems of peace to remember small, local exotic events taking place in the now blurred distance of a period before a certain historic August which had turned the world upside down.

In her Red Cross nurse's uniform, Ofelia travelled from city to city, from meeting to meeting, with an exhibition of prints, drawings, posters and eloquent photographs showing scenes of destruction, dead villages, mine craters, severely damaged cathedrals and crosses stretching to the horizon. *"We ask you for schools for the children of these men"* was inscribed on the desolate view of a military cemetery. *"Give me back my home"* was at the feet of a Christ pierced with bullets.

Meanwhile, this exaggerated stimulation of an already inflated prosperity swelled the tide of speculation and extravagance, nor did those whom fortune favoured pay any attention to the gloomy forecasts of some economists—puritan kill-joys whose sibylline calculations were out of tune with the confident tones of those singing the praises of a myth that was renewed every day. For they were living in a fable. Without being aware of it people were taking part in a huge conjuring display, where all values were upset, ideas inverted, appearances changed, roads deviated, and disguise and metamorphosis created a perpetual state of illusion, transformations and topsy-turvydom, through the vertiginous effect of a currency which changed its appearance, weight and value between night and morning without ever leaving the purse—or rather, the bank account—of its owner. Everything was upside-down. The poor lived in Foundation Palaces, dating from the days of Orellana and Pizarro—but now given over to filth and rats—while their masters inhabited houses belonging to no tradition, native, baroque or Jesuitic, but theatrically got up in Mediaeval, Renaissance or Hollywood-Andalusian colour-schemes, and without the smallest connection with the country's history, or else in large buildings aping the Second Empire style of the Boulevard Haussman. The new Central Post Office had a superb Big Ben. The new head Police Station was a Temple from Luxor in eau-de-nil. The country house of the Chancellor of the Exchequer was a pretty miniature Schönbrunn. The President of the Chamber kept his mistress in a little Abbaye de Cluny, swathed in imported ivy. Fortunes were made and lost every night at Basque pelota courts and English grey-hound races. People dined at the Villa d'Este or La Troika (a night club recently opened by the first white Russians arrived here via Constantinople) while only in Chinese eating-houses could one eat the national dishes, now scorned as something connected with rope-soled shoes and ballads sung by the blind—Cantonese kitchen-boys thus becoming conservers of the National Culinary Arts. The musical successes of the day were *Caravan, Egyptland, Japanese Sandman, Chinatown my Chinatown,* and above all *Hindustan,* to be seen on the music-stand of every piano, bound in a cover showing an elephant and a mahout silhouetted in black against a crimson sun. Women who profiteered from the boom didn't know where to go and show off their tiaras, pendants and necklaces, and their dresses from Worth, Doucet and Callot. And by the same token the Head of State remembered his long-cherished but now realizable desire to install an Opera House inside the Opera-City, the Capital of Fiction, and offer his compatriots a spectacle like those to be seen in Buenos Aires and Rio de Janeiro—towns that had always kept their eyes on the arts and refinements of the Old World. Adolfo Bracale was entrusted with the task of giving the National Theatre "the best staging in the world". Impresario of American touring companies, animated by such a passion for lyric drama that he had taken *Simon Boccanegra, Manon* and *Lucia de Lammermoor* to the Chilean nitre works, banana-growers' haciendas, Southern ports and rubber-plantations in Manaos, crossing deserts, travelling up rivers, visiting the West Indian islands great and small with his cast, wardrobe and scenery, he was a man capable of taking the baton if the principal conductor fell ill of malaria, or of putting on *Madame Butterfly* with an orchestra of a piano, seven violins, flute, saxophone, ophicleide, two 'cellos and a double-bass, if nothing better could be found.

So, one fine morning, the train from Puerto Araguato entered the station of the capital bringing antique temples, alchemist's retorts, a Scottish cemetery, several Japanese houses, the Castle of Elsinore, the platform of Sant'Angelo, monasteries, grottoes and dungeons, all folded or rolled in pieces to be put together with expanding forests and fabric cloisters, filling so many cases that two trains were hardly enough to take the lot. And finally, when evening came, a third convoy—that of the ultra-modern dining-car with its menu in French—arrived at the Terminal Station, glittering with celebrities who stepped on to the platform among magnesium flashes and a profusion of flowers, complete with officials, applause according to their fame, and mandoline music by the Italian Colony. Chief among them was the great Enrico Caruso, wearing a double-breasted waistcoat, diamond tie-pin, pale grey hat and platinum cuff-links. Amiable, verbose and cheerful, but bewildered by so much solicitous flattery, he forgot where he was, greeted a lance-corporal as "General", and the Head Porter as "Excellency", ignored the real Minister but embraced a melomaniac who looked like a minister, distributed autographs by the dozen, kissed children and seemed happy in surroundings reminiscent of some small Neapolitan piazza on a day of revelry. The next to appear was Titta Ruffo scowling dramatically, robust of figure, roaring like a lion, and dressed in a light Palm Beach suit; it seemed impossible that a man of such athletic stamp could come to terms with the tormented fragility of Hamlet as displayed on the hoardings, a part he was to play in a few days' time. Now Lucrecia Bori descended from the train, all teeth and coloratura, already assuming the role of Rosina in her Spanish hat and skirt; then Gabriella Bezanzoni, the contralto, with a knife in her garter, her expensive elegance contrasting cruelly with the feebleness of some pale North American ballerinas carrying their ballet-shoes in oil-cloth bags, who got out of the presidential coach behind her. Riccardo Stracciari, wearing kid gloves and the frock-coat of a close relative at an important funeral, replied to journalists' questions in an affected voice. The tall thin Mansueto, looking like a shady schoolmaster, had thought it amusing to disembark with Don Basilio's shovel hat under his arm; and lastly came Nicoletti-Korman, whom we were to see bare-chested, Chaliapinesque and blaspheming in Boito's *Mefistofele*.

The tailors of the capital worked day and night, snipping for all they were worth at cloth for tail coats and piqué waistcoats, while the dressmakers ran from fitting to fitting to put finishing touches or slight alterations to this and that, let out skirts, lower neck-lines, readjust some thin woman's dress to her taste, stretch seams for some fat woman, let out an expectant mother's waistband, modernize and adapt out-of-date fashions in line with the latest models. The chorus was organized from students and members of glee-clubs; the best musicians in the country were united into an orchestra under the direction of an atrociously bad-tempered Bolognese who, without pausing in a passage he was conducting, would shout instructions like: "Sustain that note, you bastard," or "Crotchets, you brute" . . . *"Dolce ma non pederasta"* (this was for the prelude to *La Traviata*), *"Allegro con coglioni"* (this for the overture to *Carmen*), declaring all the time—and in this he imitated his maestro Toscanini— that it was better to live among pimps and prostitutes than with musicians, although as a matter of fact as soon as the rehearsal was over he wrapped his neck in towels and went with them to the *Roma*, a popular and lively bar, to drink several glasses of Santa Inés rum diluted with Fernet Branca.

While waiting for the season to begin, a party was given every night in honour of the singers from the Scala and the Metropolitan, who always declared that they "weren't in voice" before finally singing some romance from Piedigrotta's repertory or else Tosti's *Vorrei morire*. And meanwhile, in spite of hammering, grumbling, oaths, accidents, damage to scenery, trap-doors that failed to work, lost spears, broken accessories, a distaff left behind in Italy, inadequate spotlights, vapours from the underworld that never emerged at the right time, an invasion of rats in the dressing-rooms, dysentery, spring colics, the soprano's allergy to certain flowers, a quarrel between Mansueto and Nicoletti over a mulatto, contracts broken and signed again, the leader of the orchestra punching the second bassoon, an infinite number of complaints, several attacks of lost voice, two boils due to the climate, mosquitoes, stained costumes, tropical rains, one hernia, more losses of voice, bruises and swellings—such an impressive and memorable *Faust* was mounted that its marvellous qualities at once passed into the verses of Gaucho singers, to the amazement of those who hadn't heard it. Afterwards came a magnificent *Carmen* with Bezanzoni and Caruso, although in the smugglers' act, because the pistols had been lost on the journey, the chorus were armed with Winchester rifles, but this was only noticed by the cognoscenti. Then there was a *Barber of Seville* wherein Mansueto's Don Basilio was so truculent and comic that his performance excelled Titta Ruffo's Figaro in brilliance and conception. Maria Barrientos' *Traviata* reduced the audience to a frenzy of delight: the brindisi had to be sung three times, the applause being so great as to prevent carrying on with the score; the great scene between the elder Germont and Violetta produced discreet tears, and at the end so many flowers were thrown on to the stage that when the performers made their bow they trod on a carpet of roses, carnations and tuberoses.

The season continued triumphantly with *La Favorita*, Flotow's *Marta* (one of Caruso's greatest successes), *Hamlet* by Ambroise Thomas, *Rigoletto* and *La Sonnambula*. The Head of State was happy. The opera had transformed the capital. After performances the smart cafés were full of expensively-dressed people, glittering with jewels, and stared at from the street by crowds who were amazed to see here, within reach as it were, a luxurious world hitherto only imagined through the media of romantic novels, films in a millionaire's setting, or the covers of *Vanity Fair* in the magazine kiosks, and to find so many of our own women suddenly taking to fashion and finery in an ambience reminiscent of John Singer Sargent or Jean-Gabriel Domergue.

"We're winning, Peralta; we're winning them round," said the President, looking at the sumptuous auditorium, where nothing was talked about in the intervals except racconto, portamento, fiato, tessitura and arioso.

All went well until the first night of *Tosca*, when something very unusual happened: at the end of the second act when Floria buried her knife in Scarpia's chest, a torrent of applause exploded from the upper seats, and persisted for so long that the orchestra had to stop playing. As nothing had been sung at this moment of the action to justify such enthusiasm, Maria Jeritza didn't know what to do—she was making her début that night—except move the candlesticks to right and left of the corpse of a Titta Ruffo who was as stupefied as she was. Finally a shout from above of: "Death to the sbirros! Down with

Valverde!" gave a meaning to this thunderous applause and caused Tosca to leave the stage, the curtain to descend rapidly and the orchestra to remain dumb with bewilderment, while the police broke in among the gods and arrested everyone who hadn't time to escape down the staircase. Next day Giordano's *Andrea Chénier* was given in a theatre surrounded by troops, and under military occupation by officers in full dress uniform, strategically placed in stalls and galleries. Even so during the Revolutionary Tribunal a cry of "Viva Robespierre!" went up from some situation unknown.

From now on every opera was the occasion for ovations, murmurs, hissing and exclamations which had nothing to do with the quality of the music or aptness of the interpretation. Outlaws, regicides, rebel troubadors and Hernanis were always applauded; informers, governors, Uskoks, stool pigeons and Spolettas were hissed. The Head of State thought it advisable to cancel Giordano's *Siberia*, and now awaited with irritation and impatience the performance of *Aida* which was to close the season. For this, unheard-of scenic effects were projected. The New York firm of Leady had provided the straight trumpets for the triumphal march. Camels and elephants from a recently-arrived circus would figure in the procession, followed by fifty horsemen from the third battalion of Hussars, dressed as Egyptians and carefully made up, unless their natural complexions gave them a sufficiently Nubian or Ethiopian appearance. And no performance ever began so brilliantly as to scenery, production, the action of the chorus and the skill of an orchestra, which had enormously improved during the last few weeks under the direction of an energetic and confident conductor. The clothes and décor were praised; *Ritorna vincitor* was encored as expected, and the second act opened in an atmosphere of tension, anticipation of pleasure and general appreciation of scenery, singers and production as the action approached the concerted paroxysm of the return of Radames. The famous theme of the march was hummed by the entire audience. And the great final scene arrived, with two hundred persons assembled between columns and palm trees, Horus and Anubis and the Nile as background—a Nile picked out with electric lights—when suddenly there was a terrific explosion in the orchestra pit under the footlights, sending cymbals, violin cases, tympani and kettle-drums flying in a sudden cloud of white smoke. A second bomb exploded beneath the double-basses, causing the musicians to clamber on to the stage and try to escape through the pit and boxes, increasing the panic in the audience who rushed helter-skelter towards the exits, jumping over stalls, pushing, screaming, trampling on anyone who fell down in the mad rush, while the flies collapsed on the heads of Pharaoh's guards, priests, archers, captives in chains and soldiers of the third battalion of Hussars as they ran, fought and struggled to get to the doors into the street, among fallen obelisks, sphinxes and broken scenery.

"The Hymn! The Hymn!" yelled the Head of State to the Bolognese conductor, who had remained on the rostrum, pale and vociferating as he tried to control his disbanded orchestra. But as only seven or eight musicians were left, the only response to his cries of "The Hymn! Quick! The Hymn!" came from an almost inaudible wail of four violins, a clarinet, oboe and 'cello.

While the public gathered in the square outside trying to pluck up their courage, and those who had been bruised or kicked (none were really wounded) were carried from the theatre in the arms of the police, the Head of State found out that the explosions had not come from bombs, but large petards emitting noise and smoke.

"The performance must go on," he said to Adolfo Bracale, who had bravely accompanied him on this tour of inspection, followed by the electricians. But it was impossible; the theatre was full of the smell of gunpowder, the scenery was ruined, the parchment of the drums had burst, the double basses were in splinters, the curtain wouldn't come down, several members of the chorus had been hurt in the rush, the horses of the triumphal procession were kicking and biting, and Amonasro had lost his voice. The victim of a nervous crisis, Amneris had shut herself in her dressing-room and was shouting that this was what came from singing in a country of savages. As for Caruso-Radames, he had disappeared. As someone remembered having seen him go out at a back door, they hunted for

him in vain in bars and cafés near the building. Nor had he
returned to his hotel. He might have been hurt, hit, or perhaps
he was lying in a faint in some dark corner. The impresario
was anxiously looking for him when a short circuit left the
theatre without lights.

The Head of State returned to the Palace, followed by his
ministers and generals. His silence at such a time expressed a
rage that went far beyond mere rage. An inner rage, shut in
upon itself, a violent nervous crisis expressed in a terrible fixed
stare, unaware of the faces confronting him, an apocalyptic
stare apparently directed at distant visions in which tempests,
screams and retribution figured. He was in this state of intolerable tension when the telephone rang in the Council chamber.
His Excellency the Italian Minister was calling. He informed
them that Enrico Caruso had been arrested in the street by
a policeman for wearing fancy dress when it was not carnival
time, and women's clothes what was more, and with ochre-
coloured make-up and painted eyes and mouth—such were
the details of the accusation; this made him subject to the
Law of Repression of Scandalous Behaviour and Defence of
Civic Morality, whose article 132 anticipated thirty days'
imprisonment for an attempt on decent living, and unbecoming
behaviour in public, with increased punishment if it was
accompanied by manifest evidence of homosexuality in personal
attire and appearance, which in the present case was plainly
shown by a coiffure of horizontal strands brought down over the
forehead, ornamental rings in the ears, fancy bracelets, and
round the neck several chains adorned with scarabs, amulets,
charms and stones of colours which—according to the police
report—were a sure indication of being "queer".

"This to happen, in a civilized country!" cried the Head of
State, passing from his dramatically silent rage to verbal
explosion, at the same time throwing books, paperweights and
inkpots on to the carpet. But he did what was necessary. And
it was Doctor Peralta who rescued Enrico Caruso from
confinement; the singer arrived, much amused and still dressed
as Radames, saying that it was nothing, and that he and his
Ambassador wished to recommend the policeman who had

arrested him—"a good chap, splendid fellow, only doing his duty"—to the President's indulgence ("he was merely carrying out the law, he had never seen an ancient Egyptian in the streets of the capital") and everything came to an end in the light of dawn with drinks and Havana cigars—long thick cigars such as the singer liked best, whose trade-mark was the blond blue-eyed head of Fonseca.

The Tutelary Volcano emerged from its cold mists, the Mayorala Elmira brought sandwiches and fruit juice, and before he left Adolfo Bracale announced that the opera season would definitely close with Verdi's *Masked Ball* that night—*Aida* was out of the question after the disaster.

"A masked ball is what I shall give those brutes who go planting petards," said the Head of State to Doctor Peralta before going to bed.

And now there began to arise above the city a round building—round as a bull-ring, round as the Coliseum in Rome, round as a circus for contortionists and lion-tamers: it was the Model Prison, based on the most modern ideas of penitentiary construction invented by North American architects, who were masters of that art. Accustomed to the slow progress of stone buildings—the sawing-up of stone provided a lesson in stereotomy, demonstrating theorems with hammer and chisel—and the very long time needed to produce their main bulk and details, the Head of State had now discovered the magic of building in concrete. Gravel and sand rotated in enormous grey iron cocktail-shakers, plates of cement miraculously hardened and tightened over a metal skeleton; the city witnessed the marvel of a building that started by being liquid, a soup full of gravel and pebbles, before it rose with astonishing verticality, placing walls on walls, floors on floors, cornices on cornices, until—in a matter of days—it reached the sky with a flag-staff or a gilt statue with winged ankles. And since the Head of State had fallen in love with the speed of concrete, with the fidelity of concrete and the docility of concrete, he had entrusted concrete with the task of closing the gigantic circle of the Model Prison (on the Hill of La Cruz above the cupola of the Capitol, above the spire of the Sacred Heart) before he started a political operation on a large scale. Day and night, by the light of reflectors when darkness or fog made them necessary, work continued on this exemplary building, whose concentric walls had the euclidean beauty of a series of orbits whose radii grew progressively smaller, enclosing one another, until reaching the axis of a central patio, whence watch could be kept on all the cells and corridors. When the work was finished and nothing was left to do but bring the aluminium bath-tubs, and armchairs with buckles and straps destined for some of the underground rooms (these figured on the plans as "technical annexes"), photographs of this beautiful building were sent to several international reviews of architecture, and it was much praised for its functional qualities, as well as for solving the difficulty of harmonizing something necessarily grim in appearance with the beauty of the surrounding landscape. Here could be seen an evident and perhaps unique attempt to humanize—the aim of architecture being to help man to live—the conceptual and organic vision of a penitentiary establishment, thus making it tolerable to the delinquent who after all (as modern psychologists had shown) was a sick man, an antisocial being, usually the product of his environment and victim of heredity, whose behaviour had been distorted by certain things that were just beginning to be called "complexes", "inhibitions", etc., etc. The days of Venetian prisons and the dungeons of the Inquisition were over, or of the fortresses of Ceuta or Cádiz—so similar to those of La Guayra, Havana or San Juan de Ulúa—or of the penitentiaries named in the classic songs of Bruant. In the matter of imprisonment we had outdistanced Europe—a logical state of things, since as members of the Continent-of-the-Future, we must make a start somewhere.

But while the finishing touches were being put to the Model Prison, the country was falling sick of a crisis; most disappointingly threatening to the fertility of an exceptionally rich if virgin soil, giving fabulous promise of productivity under cultivation, age-old humus, a boundless supply of wood (forests covering an area as large as the whole of Belgium) and rich underground seams of invaluable minerals. We had them all: space, land, fruit, nickel, iron. We were a privileged country in the World of the Future. Such was the report of the Ministry of Agriculture and Public Works. To realize the splendour of our earthly benefits we had only to follow the convincing picture given by statistics, organograms, columns of figures, weekly balance-sheets, expert comments, futuro-logical equations enhanced by the eloquent presence of a well-placed letter from the Greek alphabet. But though these memoranda and bound reports were brought him every day after the unfortunate opera season was over, and considered retrospectively in financial terms, the Head of State realized that as a background to these orchestral preludes and tenor cadenzas, the sugar-supply of the Republic had suffered an alarming drop compared to rubber and slate in world markets. Our sugar was fetching 23 centavos a pound when Nicoletti-Korman, a magnificent devil, was sending up prayers to the Golden Calf. With the North American anthem in the first act of *Madame Butterfly*, it fell to 17.20. It was quoted at 11.35 during *Thaïs*—"*Alexandria, terrible cité*," sang Titta Ruffo. On the disastrous day of *Rigoletto*—and hunchbacks are supposed to bring good luck—it fell to 8.40. The cheating at cards in the fourth act of *Manon* hastened the collapse, which with the catastrophe of *Aïda*, left us at 5.22. And when carnival time came, sugar—far the most important substance in the whole of agricultural Latin America—had slumped, with warehouses full of unsold sacks, to 2.15 centavos a pound.

And suddenly one morning, as if nothing had happened, the recently founded *Banco International* announced that it was suspending payments until further notice. The *Banco Español*, the *Banco Miranon*, the *Banco Comercial y Agricola* and the *Banco de la Construccion* shut down their guichets with a sharp click, while the *Banco Nacional* and the *Clearing House* filled the newspapers with communiqués and information, promises, calls for confidence and calm, in order to stem a panic which had started from small savings-books registering minimal family accounts and ascended to the realms of high finance. The situation was described as "accidental and temporary" in the newspapers, and a Cabinet meeting was called to consider it. The Government asked for calm, confidence and patriotism. No queuing or disturbances. A Moratorium—a word unknown to the public, but whose sound had for some of them a disagreeable relationship with death and wills—was proposed as a certain means of straightening out the confusion in a few weeks; this brought relief to the minds of many, and as it was Carnival time, the Festival of Masks opened in a clamour of processions, Chinese trumpeters and negro drummers, with fancy dress parades including cars decked with much ingenuity, such as the "Venetian Bucentaur", which won a special prize although it had been tremendously difficult to get it as far as the judges' dais, since its prow crowded with female doges dressed in sequins was too high to get under the telephone wires. All this revelry had come at a fortunate time, because it had always been important to the life of the country, and people forgot their troubles and dangers when absorbed in this multitudinous catharsis. At this time funerals were without mourners, telephones without operators, bakers had no flour, and babies at the breast no milk. People were dancing, singing, joining processions, abandoning themselves without regard to discipline or time-tables, commitments or promises, to satisfying the desires they had accumulated during months of repression. A lot of women were naked under their dominoes. Everyone did as they liked under the protection of hood, veil or tawdry mask. People sang and danced in the parks, on terraces roofed with vines; cafés were taken by storm. They fornicated on the upper floors of the National Observatory, under the arches of bridges, in halls decorated with holy images and in suburban shrubberies and even installed themselves in church porches to drink sugar-cane spirit, tequila and aguardiente. These were days when dusk merged into dawn and dawn into dusk, when the traditional fraternities used heron feathers and raffia to polish up their magic chains, diabolical costumes, cardboard sharks, serpents worked by a spring, hawk-men, carnival dragons, grotesques, old figures inherited from Africa or from rituals whose original purpose was lost in aboriginal darkness. What with dancing and paper streamers, competitions, beauty queens, gilt cardboard crowns, giants and monstrous heads, turbans and stilts, a long week went by in pleasure, swaggering, musical rhythms, drunkenness and hang-overs. But suddenly, in the middle of this tumultuous jollity, one or two harlequins with their faces covered in black stockings fired at the police; one or two gypsies from the cast of *Carmen*, who had failed to return the Winchesters borrowed from the smugglers' scene, seized the rifles and revolvers from Santa Barbara barracks and loaded them into Red Cross ambulances; members of the Pompadour processions, dressed in salmon pink, with their wigs pulled down over their eyes, threw a bomb into the police station of the fifth District, setting free more than forty political prisoners. In the police station of the second District, some of our Indians, apparently high on mescal but disguised as Red Indians from North America in imitation of Vitagraph films they had seen, cleared a secret arsenal of its hand-grenades and then disappeared among the crowd; three anarchist leaders were rescued from their cells by false agents of Social Security; a snow-storm of proclamations and mani-festos fell from the spire of the Sacred Heart and the cupola of the Capitol, calling for a revolutionary rising. But now, to the report of rockets and firecrackers from the familiar troupes of clowns, reports with a sharper repercussion were added. The harmless bottles of chloride of ethyl intended to be pushed down the front of women's dresses were replaced by tear gas bombs, an amazing invention being used for the first time by the police; the cavalry charged at random against strolling players and allegoric groups; the screeching of carnival whistles and cardboard trumpets was transformed into the cries of the trampled and wounded, and fancy dress gave way in panic to military uniforms. A whole rainbow of different colours became neutralized into the two-fold range of indigo and buff. A violent presidential decree suspended the carnival there and then, and the Model Prison quickly filled with masks. There were yells and gasps of the dying, tightening of garrottes, dentists' drills boring into sound teeth, beating with sticks and whips, kicking in the balls, men hung up by their heels and wrists or revolving on cartwheels for days on end, naked women pursued through the corridors, thrown to the ground with legs apart and violated, their breasts burned, their flesh penetrated with red hot irons. There were fictitious shootings and real shootings; blood and lead from Mausers spattered the newly built walls, still smelling of mortar; and there were defenestrations, strappados, piercing with nails, and people herded to the Great Olympic stadium where there was more room to machine-gun a crowd together—thus avoiding the loss of time involved in forming shooting-parties; and there were those who were shut in great rectangular boxes filled with cement and the blocks so formed were lined up against one wall of the prison, in such numbers that the neighbours thought they must contain stones for enlarging the building. . . . (And many years passed before it was discovered that each of these blocks contained a body in fancy dress and mask, moulded by the hard material surrounding it—a perfect record of a human anatomy within a solid substance.)

FIVE

... I am, I exist, that is certain. But ...

for how long?

DESCARTES

14

Ay... Bee... Cee... Dee... Ay... The alphabet
resounded strangely, very strangely, in the classrooms of the
North American Methodist Colleges and Augustinian Lycées
now open in our principal cities, arousing serious doubts
concerning the efficiency and modernity—especially the
modernity—of the teaching given to children by the Salesian
fathers and French Marists, the Dominican and Ursuline nuns
or the Little Sisters of Tarbes. Now one could hear: "This is a
pencil, this is a dog, this is a girl," where formerly the classical
declensions of *Rosa, Rosae, Rosa, Rosam* had flourished,
obliterating the memory of the inevitable jokes at Aunt
Jemima's expense, a short while earlier, when they had moved
on to adjectives of the first category with *Nigra, Nigrae, Nigra,
Nigram*. The Cid, Roland, Saint Louis, the Catholic Queen and
Henry IV emigrated from the history books along with sword,
horn, centenarian oak, pawned jewels, chicken stew and all the
rest, to be advantageously replaced by Benjamin Franklin,
with his lightning-conductor and Poor Richard's Almanac;
Washington at Mount Vernon, surrounded by good negroes
whom he treated like members of his family; Jefferson and the
Independence Hall at Philadelphia; Lincoln's Gettysburg
speech; the migration to the West and the dramatic death of
General Custer in the Battle of Little Bighorn against the
barbarian hordes of Sitting Bull. As soon as they were weaned
by their Indian wet-nurses who sang them nursery rhymes and

taught them, like Pythagoras, that it was bad to poke the fire with a knife, children were guided to where the little Mozart lay in the Pantheon of Infant Prodigies, next to Daniel Webster because of his early battle against a malignant growth—which, as it was God's creation, had a right to life just as the slaves in *Uncle Tom's Cabin* had a right to life. Rapidly moving on from *L'Illustration, Lectures pour tous, Collier's* and *The Saturday Evening Post*—with attractive covers by Norman Korwin—they began to tell the truth (bitter truths, maybe, but now it was possible to speak plainly and History was History) about the recent war.

Without *Over There* and General Pershing, France would have been lost. England had fought half-heartedly, without conviction: the "Tommies" belonged to folk-lore, Marble Arch, and tea served in the trenches to turbaned sepoys and Scots with bagpipes. Italy was a country of bad soldiers with cock-feathers in their hats, and only one battle: Caporetto. As for Russia: the monk Rasputin, the Tsarevich, haemophilia, Madame Virúbova, mystical orgies, inspired idiots, *Resurrection*, Yasnaya Polyana, and the unstable, tortured Slav soul, always oscillating between the angelic and infernal abysses, had collectively borne fruit in a deluded reformer—a man of the Kremlin like Ivan the Terrible—the ephemeral Marxist Paraclete, whose days were already counted, weighed, divided by the onslaught of the forces of Denikin, Wrangel, Kolchak and the Franco-British armies of the Baltic, who would quickly achieve the ruin of a system already doomed to disaster. For (as the Evangelists said in a verse of the Bible as emphatic as it is difficult to find among so many pages printed in two columns on India paper) there would always be both rich and poor in the world—and as for the camel and the eye of the needle, we know that a rather low and narrow Door of the Needle existed in Jerusalem, through which intelligent camels could always pass if they bent their knees a little. It had been proved that Europeans were incapable of living in peace, and President Wilson had been obliged to cross the Atlantic to put some order into their affairs. But this would be the last time. We would never again trouble to devote our youthful energies to defend a culture whose axis of gravitation—as it was time to say openly—had been displaced in the direction of America, North America of course, while awaiting the time when we of the South finally succeeded in freeing ourselves from the evil traditions that kept us living in the past. The world had entered the technical age, and Spain had bequeathed us a language incapable of developing a technical vocabulary. The future belonged to Inventors not Humanists. And Spaniards had not invented a thing for centuries. The internal combustion engine, the telephone, electric light, the phonograph, on the other hand . . .

If, by some whim of the All-powerful, Columbus' caravels had crossed with the *Mayflower* and stopped at the island of Manhattan, while the English Puritans had hit on Paraguay, New York would today be rather like Illescas or Castilleja de la Cuesta, whereas Asunción would astonish the whole world with its skyscrapers, Times Square, Brooklyn Bridge and all the rest of it. Europe was the world of the past. A good world in which to float in a gondola, dream among Roman remains, look at stained-glass windows, visit museums and spend pleasant, instructive holidays—but a world whose decadence was being speeded up by an increasing amorality manifest in everything to do with sex, with women who were ready to go to bed with anyone, with those "horrid French customs" brought back by young North American soldiers and sometimes alluded to in a hushed and shocked voice (though the mother of a family ought to know everything) by the chaste "Daughters of the Revolution". The triumph of Latinity—as Latin American papers persisted in calling the European War—had had the most disastrous consequences for Latinity in our countries, by renewing the Quarrel of the Investitures,* and by the multiple influences of the North. Bookshops formerly selling the works of Anatole France and Romain Rolland—nor must the legendary success of Barbusse's *Le Feu* be forgotten—now displayed *The Prisoner of Zenda, Scaramouche, Ben-Hur, Monsieur Beaucaire* and the novels of Elinor Glyn, in gaudy coloured wrappers suggesting that they would appeal to readers who wanted to keep up to date with the latest literary movements. And in

* Between the popes and the emperors (1074–1122), and ending in the separation of spiritual and temporal powers.

contrast to a feeble European cinema without any outstanding
stars—they all seemed to have fallen in battle—the magnificent
artistry of the miracle-working David Griffith, mover of
multitudes and explorer of Time, was showing us images such
as we had never before seen (much more impressive than any
erudite evocation) interpreting the Birth of a Nation, the
Tragedy of Golgotha, the Massacre of Saint Bartholomew, and
even the world of Babylon—although Doctor Peralta, who was
an addict of Mallet's handbooks and Reinach's *Apollo*, declared
that the enormous Elephant-Gods appearing in Griffith's
Babylon had never been seen there, and irreverently described
them as the "visions of a gringo with a hangover".

Aware that she was losing ground in these spheres, France
arranged to send us a short official tour—a three-day convention, while the Head of State was resting at Bellamar from the
disappointments of his operatic venture—including Sarah
Bernhardt, plastered with powder and paint, gravitating on
the axis of her one leg, bewigged like one of Toulouse-Lautrec's
clowns, but still sustained by her desperate determination to
rise superior to her own decline, and declaiming the most
pathetic alexandrines from *Phèdre*, or the dying tirades of an
almost octogenarian Aiglon, in a quavering voice of approaching doom—while having to be carried in someone's arms, lean
on the furniture, sit on a throne, lie prostrate or be conveyed
in King Titurel's litter. Next, to be greeted by the cheerful
indifference of a public enthralled by dazzling young actresses
from Hollywood, Italy sent us Eleanora Duse, fantastically
attired in a braided and frogged hussar's jacket and high black
hat, as one of Heine's grenadiers, bringing with her the ruins
and broken columns of *La Città Morta* by D'Annunzio, an author
the young had suddenly tired of, after years of enthusiasm for
La figlia di Iorio. All this belonged to the past, and as things of the
past do, it seemed to them to smell of funereal flowers. Perhaps
this was why there was an increase in the sales of North
American reviews, or periodicals like the *New York Times*,
whose Sunday magazine provided information about new
music, extraordinary painting and eccentric literary movements
going on in Paris (despite what was said, they seemed to be

having a minor renaissance there). *L'Illustration* and *Lectures pour tous* ignored these developments, or if they alluded to them at all it was only to trounce them in the name of "order, proportion and moderation", so that to find out about these surprising innovations—the poetry of someone called Apollinaire, for instance, who died on the very day of the Armistice—people had to go to New York publications.

"Young people always like newfangled things," said the Head of State. But he didn't know that these verses without rhyme or punctuation, these sonatas full of dissonances, amounted, interestingly enough, to formidable criticisms of our country. One morning, the news spread quickly that the *New York Times'* expert on Latin American affairs had published a long editorial, ruthlessly analysing our financial ruin, alluding to repression by the police and torture, going into the mystery of some disappearances, denouncing assassinations that no one here knew about, and reminding its readers that the Head of State—who was put in the same category as Rosas, Doctor Francia (permanent Dictator of Paraguay), Porfirio Díaz, Estrada Cabrera of Guatemala, and Juan Vicente Gómez of Venezuela, not to mention all the Louis of France and Catherines of Russia—had been nearly twenty years in power.

Orders were given for the issue to be instantly suppressed—there were no copies left on kiosks and bookstalls, except three found by Doctor Peralta on a vegetable stall, whose owner regularly bought this paper to wrap up his cabbages, greens and yams in its 120 pages.

"We ought to ban the paper from coming into the country," said the Secretary, noticing the anger on the Head of State's face as he read it.

"A Yankee paper. A major scandal. They'll soon be dumping the whole of Randolph Hearst's chain on us." There was a pause. "Besides, the printed word slips in everywhere. You can put a political enemy in prison. But you can't stop the circulation of a foreign paper even if it tells lies about your mother. One copy is enough. It arrives by air, is hidden in travellers' brief-cases, diplomatic bags or ladies' petticoats, and passes from hand to hand, across frontiers, rivers and mountain ranges." There was another silence, rather longer than the last. "It was a bad day when I signed the order for English to be taught in schools. Now everyone here can say 'Son of a bitch'." There was a third silence, even longer than the second, broken by Peralta, who had just re-read the editorial:

"It alludes here to Article 39 of the 1910 Constitution." And, quoting by heart, as if it were part of a betrothal ceremony: *"Presidential elections will take place not less than three months before the current six year period has expired."* There was a fourth silence, longer than the third.

"But who the hell told them that we had elections of any description here?" burst out the Head of State suddenly.

"Yes, but the 1910 Constitution says . . ."

"It says what you've said, but it also says that those elections aren't held if the nation happens to be in a state of armed conflict or war declared against a foreign power."

"Exactly. But who are we fighting, except those shits in the interior?"

The Head of State looked at his Secretary with an expression of sly solemnity: "We're still at war with Hungary."

"So we are!"

"I've not signed a peace treaty with Hungary, nor do I intend to at present, because it's in utter chaos. The Ambassador hasn't received his salary for months and has had to pawn his wife's jewels. If his country goes on like that we shall soon see him playing the violin in some gypsy cabaret. It's bloody well all up with them! But we're at war with Hungary. And when there's a war there are no elections. To hold elections now would be to violate the Constitution. Quite simply."

"Ah, my President! There's nobody like you!" said Doctor Peralta, bringing up the Hermes case to celebrate this unforeseen prolongation of the world war. This business about war with Hungary smacked of a marvellous cocktail of cumbias and czardas, bambas and friskas, creole serenades and Liszt Rhapsodies, all dominated by the oneiric voice of the soprano who inhabited the looking-glass of Jules Verne's *Castle in the Carpathians*—just as the Mayorala Elmira was now inhabiting the mirrors of this Audience Chamber, busily looking for wine glasses.

The *New York Times* published three more articles on the country's economic and political situation and these were widely circulated in spite of Peralta's vigilance in buying up all copies of the paper as soon as they arrived at the bookshop, including the American Book Shops. But the fact was that an office as clandestine as it was active—and obviously run by supporters of Doctor Leoncio Martínez—secretly translated the articles, had hundreds of copies made by a machine, and distributed them by post in envelopes of various sizes, very often fraudulently stamped with the trademarks and patent names of well-known industrial and commercial businesses, so that they were circulated like innocent advertisements. Meanwhile our own press, although censored and prevented from broaching the numerous subjects it was thought desirable to suppress, devoted itself with increasing skill—inspired by old supplements of *Le Petit Journal*, and New York tabloids—to exploiting the sensationalism of any horrific incidents or unusual developments. Suddenly the Crime of the Calle Hermosilla or the Trial of the Parricide Sisters filled whole pages with headlines stretching across six columns and lasted for several weeks. And they were a blood-curdling and monstrous procession, making magnificent use of adjectives, subtle euphemisms for the scabrous, sly metaphors for the sexual, osteological nomenclature, terms from legal anthropometry, the language of necrophily and the dissecting-room. There was the case of the Man Buried Alive at Bayarta, the Child Born with the Head of a Cavy, A Troglodyte Village in the Middle of the Twentieth Century, A Doctor's Honour Cleared, The Sextuplets of Puerto Negro, He Killed his Mother without Cause, Sadism in Seaport Taverns must be Suppressed, Savage Shooting Affray at Birthday Party, Old Man Devoured by Ants, Den of Sodomy Discovered, Recrudescence of White Slavery, Woman Quartered at Crossroads—all this sort of stuff being mixed with matters of permanent interest, historical or human content, such as the Queen's Necklace, the death of the Prince Imperial at the hands of Zulus, the drowned continent of Atlantis, the story of Abelard and Heloise, subjected to necessary euphemisms when it came to the action of Canon Fulbert, whom certain blackguards identified—so eager were they not to miss a trick—with the Chief of the Judicial Police.

In the midst of homicides, crimes of passion and unheard-of events, the season of the Nativity came round, and in a strange guise, for it was the first time that it was transformed into Christmas. Charming family traditions were quickly forgotten: no cribs were constructed by sticking together pieces of paper, with manger, Virgin, Saint Joseph, ass, ox and shepherds— more numerous if the house was a richer one—who came to adore the chubby, angelic Child, lying on a bed of guava leaves, which were changed every day to give more fragrance to the scene. Families no longer worked hard at repainting and varnishing the figures of saints from last year, glueing together those that were broken, and fixing the Angel of the Annunciation to his gold wire under the silver star on the ceiling. Strange things happened this year: a forest like that which advanced on Dunsinane marched up to the capital from the Atlantic ports: they were thousands of fir-trees from Canada and the United States, bringing their exotic aroma to the rich quarters of the city, where they were set up and festively decorated with glass balls, garlands of gold tinsel, small twisted candles and paper bells covered with cotton-wool snow. Peculiar deer with branched horns appeared, never seen before in the country and known as "reindeer", pulling sledges laden with parcels. And at the doors of toy-shops stood bearded old men dressed in red, called Santa Claus—or *Santicloses* by the populace. The traditional Nativity of yester-year, of all time, was supplanted in a single day by the Nordic Christmas. This year no parties of revellers singing carols to tambourines went out into the street and called on the neighbours with their normal "Rat-a-plan . . . Who is it? . . . Men of peace", their singers reeling through the streets from all the aguardiente, etc., they had been given as a reward for the happy news that the Messiah had become flesh once again, and was alive among us. These old-fashioned songs were supplanted in respectable houses by musical boxes playing such tunes as *Silent night, holy night,* or *Twinkle, twinkle, little star.*

Alarmed by this sudden transformation of Christmas, priests

(in their Midnight Mass sermons to which few listened) denounced Santa Claus as a heretic invention, an introduction of Saxon customs, which, like decorating a fir tree, could only represent a revival of German paganism—dating from a period when (while we were listening to the divine voices of Ambrosian plainsong and witnessing the splendid ritual of the Sacrament) they were still hairy savages living in forests, just as Julius Caesar had found them, wearing rough horned helmets, drinking mead and worshipping the Holly and the Mistletoe. Besides, no lives of the saints referred to this "Santicló" who brought toys to children *three days before* the Three Magi had done the same thing—as had always happened here. Spanish shopkeepers, whose dolls in Toledan, Valencian and Galician dress, little kitchens with earthenware cooking-pots, and rocking-horses, had still not been unloaded in Puerto Araguato, protested against the unpatriotic competition which had filled their windows ever since December 20 with mechanical objects, Red Indian feather head-dresses, ouija boards to play at spiritualism—I ask you!—and cowboy outfits—Texan hat, sheriff's star, studded belt and two pistols in a fringed case.

Some said that Santicló was really Saint Nicholas. But people who understood hagiography declared that neither Saint Nicholas of Mira, patron saint of Russia, nor Saint Nicholas the Great, the first pope of that name, had had anything to do with selling toys. And someone finally asked ironically in an article overlooked by the censor, if this Santicló in his species of Phrygian cap, dressed all in red, in spite of the white trimmings, might not be a *Red* in the most dangerous sense of the word. However, the journalist and his attempt at a joke came to a bad end, because when Holy Week came round he was still shut up with pimps and sodomites in Gallery 13 of the Model Prison. And if this last Christmas had been strange, Holy Week was stranger still, because instead of evoking the Story of the Cross, the length and breadth of the country witnessed the Story of the Strike.

It all began on Ash Wednesday, in the quietest way imaginable, when some hands in the American Refinery unexpectedly stopped work and refused to accept vouchers exchangeable for goods instead of wages. The movement quickly spread to all sugar-mills. The rural police, the mounted police and the provincial garrisons were all mobilized; but there was nothing they could do against men who were not demonstrating nor rioting, who were not creating a public disturbance, but who remained quietly in the doorways of their houses, refusing to work, and singing to the accompaniment of lutes or guitars:

I'm not cutting cane,
The wind can lay it low,
Or else the women
As they go to and fro.

That strike was defeated. But on Easter Saturday the miners of Nueva Córdoba began one of their own, as a protest against arbitrary dismissal, and this was promptly followed by that of the stevedores of Puerto Araguato and the dockers of Puerto Negro.

Like the rashes of those tropical diseases which break out unexpectedly and redden first one shoulder before moving on to the right thigh and the left hip, the evening before they reach the chest, by way of those parts of the human body where the Cabbalists located the centres of Splendour, Triumph, Love, Justice and Stability, the red eruptions suddenly appeared without warning on the map of the Republic, here, there, in the North, in the South, where the fruit of the cacao was ripening, mounds of coal were steaming, bananas were growing, tobacco plants were coming into leaf or rocks waiting to be blown up with dynamite. Nothing could halt the epidemic; threats and edicts from the authorities, proclamations, troops with machetes or bayonets; people had become aware of the tremendous strength of inertia, folded arms and silent resistance, and when they were herded to their farms and factories with kicks, they went determined to do their work badly, to produce very little, using every trick like causing a mechanical fault, paralysing the cranes or filing through the links in chains, when they didn't throw handfuls of sand into the axle of the principal wheel in the conduit of a pump. It was said that The Student—that same "student" who was beginning to be someone to reckon with, incessantly active though invisible, on the move and ubiquitous, working underground but manifestly, travelling from the plains to the mountains, from the fishing ports to the sawmills of the Torrid Zone—was the instigator and originator of the whole business. And it was obvious now that he wasn't alone in these multiple, combined activities; there were many, many more who adopted his tactics and ingenuity and used the same system.

"They work in *cells*," said Doctor Peralta, trying to explain everything by a term the Head of State didn't fully understand. "As for cells, there's the Model Prison," he replied. "And there aren't enough to take so many." (He tried to laugh.) "I've become the foremost hotelkeeper in the Republic." And he impatiently turned the pages of *Anti-Dühring* and the *Critique of the Gotha and Erfürt Programmes*, which were still lying on the table. "There's nothing here about cells. Nor in the *Manifesto*. The only clear statement is this on the last page but one: '*The communists everywhere support every revolutionary movement against the existing social and political order.*'"

At about this time Doctor Peralta brought the President a strange periodical which had arrived by the ordinary mail. It was a curious publication, the like of which had never been seen in the country: printed on India paper, consisting of eight pages in 16mo, small and light, no bulkier than an ordinary letter. Its title was simply: *Liberation*. Well-produced, however, with four columns to a page but as perfectly legible as a dictionary. This *Number I, year I* began with an editorial severely attacking the regime, without unnecessary adjectives, but as sharp as the crack of a whip and written in clear and concise prose.

"This is something new," murmured the Head of State, finding its contents much more upsetting than the exaggerated and outrageously creole insults commonly fired at him by the supporters of Luis Leoncio Martínez. Afterwards came a full report on the most recent brutalities committed by the police, with the names of the victims and agents. Next a thorough analysis of the recent strikes, drawing practical conclusions from their successes and mistakes. And in the middle pages came the worst of all—a detailed list with dates and numbers, undoubtedly obtained from highly secret documents, of the most private business carried out by the President, his ministers, generals and followers in the last few months.

"There's a Judas among us," cried the Head of State in a furious rage.

"But . . . who published this?" asked Doctor Peralta in a puzzled tone.

"No need to ask. Read the sentence at the end of this number: '*Workers of the world unite!*' "

"Damn it, that's the end of the *Manifesto!*"

"What it means is that this unsigned pamphlet is really signed."

Before ten o'clock it turned out that thousands of people had received this clandestine pamphlet in their morning mail. Typographical experts, summoned to a Cabinet meeting to examine the situation, gave their opinion that it could only have been produced outside the country, judging by the type used, the style of composition and the origin—German apparently— of the India paper, which wasn't available in the city at present. Perhaps the printing-press was in some frontier town. Censorship was therefore imposed on all correspondence from neighbouring countries. But on the following Tuesday, soon after waking up, the Head of State received Number 2 of *Liberation* on his breakfast tray, brought him by the Mayorala Elmira. Internal censorship was next imposed on all distributing offices. But this didn't prevent the appearance of Number 3, without help from the post office—in a wrapper but with no stamp—in the letter-boxes of ministries, public offices, businesses and private houses, not to mention copies passed from pocket to pocket or drawer to drawer, slipped under doors, thrown on to balconies or left on flat roofs and window-sills, by mysterious hands. All the printing presses in the Republic were put under military guard. There was a detective in every newspaper office, and behind every linotype and every machine turning out proofs. But nothing could prevent Numbers 4, 5, 6, and 7 of *Liberation* from appearing. The clandestine printing-press, the ghostly, invisible, silent press, went on working with exasperating efficiency. It was like some Central Laboratory, a gnomes' forge, perhaps here in this quarter of the town, or perhaps in that, further away, but producing without noise or fuss those accursed little 16mo pages, which kept the Head of State awake every night.

It was about now that, during one Cabinet Meeting, the Home Secretary uttered for the first time a threatening and sinister phrase: "Moscow Gold".

"What Moscow Gold, what on earth do you mean by Moscow Gold?" roared the President. "The Bolsheviks haven't any; they're all dropping dead, and you think they have gold to spare for . . ." (He picked up a recent number of *Illustration* from Paris.) "Look. Look at these photos. Mountains of corpses on the shores of the Dnieper and the Volga. Children nothing but bones and eyes. People starving as they did in the year 1000. Cholera. Typhus. Grand Duchesses begging in the streets. Endless, hopeless poverty."

The Minister insisted. All this was quite true. But those Bolsheviks were selling the treasures of Potemkin and Catherine the Great, crowns from the Kremlin, jewels confiscated from princes and boyars, the pictures from the Hermitage, so as to pay for international revolution, the only thing that could save communism from disaster.

"Read, read Kerensky's articles in the North American press." Moscow Gold was no fiction. Moscow Gold was the only thing that could explain the existence of something like *Liberation* in this country (Number 8 had just appeared), with its expensive paper, its presses hidden in some cave or in one of the undiscovered passages which—according to some historians—the Spanish Conquistadors had made underneath what was today the capital of the Republic, to connect three fortresses, now in ruins.

And when, a few nights later, another petard exploded in the Palace—although it did little damage as it had been put in a storeroom full of useless furniture—the Head of State became convinced of the reality of Moscow Gold. The caricatures in *Le Rire* showing a Bear throwing bombs with fuses alight on to the map of Europe, were not foolish fantasies by humorists, nor was the picture of the Red Octopus, stretching its tentacles to every corner of the globe from the onion domes of Saint Basil. One of these tentacles had entered our country.

"We must take emergency measures," murmured Peralta.

"And what is left for us to do?" replied the President, as if suddenly exhausted, suddenly missing the Arc de Triomphe, which if it had stood here instead of this useless Volcano, would have led him under its high vault into the delicious peace, smelling of wine and wood, of Monsieur Musard's *Bois-Charbons*.

In times of agitation and anxiety he used to yearn for the Land of Intelligence, where even in the Metro one could read an alexandrine worthy of Racine:

Le train ne peut partir que les portes fermées . . .

A country where, as the Distinguished Academician (now so far away) would sometimes remark, *Athalie*'s Azarias, reincarnated in the person of the Station Master of the Pigalle Station, might have said, "*en un lieu | souterrain par nos pères creusé*" (*Athalie*, Act 5) as the train set off for the Etoile:

J'en fait devant moi fermer toutes les portes (Act 3).

15

I do not think that fear or terror can be
praiseworthy or useful . . .

DESCARTES

One morning the news went round that a dead and putrefied horse, with a blown-up stomach, had turned up in the city's chief reservoir of drinking-water, and that as a result anyone who had drunk from the taps connected with the Municipal Aqueduct—and it was now eleven o'clock—was threatened with typhus. But when the Minister of Health went in person to investigate the situation, he found that the only thing floating in the famous Almond Basin, pride of national hydraulic engineering, was a black wooden horse with silver hooves: a famous model from the harness-maker's, "The Andalusian Horse", stolen thence during the night by sinister jokers. As soon as calm was restored, a fierce and blazing red fire—too red— broke out in a tobacco warehouse in the suburbs. And when a lot of wailing fire-engines had been mobilized, the firemen found themselves faced with a large flare of Bengal lights, set going in some inexplicable way and bringing their display to an end with a cheerful explosion of rockets. Next day, several newspapers published in all good faith the announcement of the death (with corresponding *requiescat in pace*) of some officials who were actually enjoying the best of health. This was the beginning of a period of mystification, of unpleasant jokes, spreading of rumours to create a climate of disturbance, anxiety, mistrust and uneasiness throughout the country. Skulls were received by post; funeral wreaths arrived at houses where no one had died; the telephone rang in the middle of the night to say that the master of the house, who was away, had died of a heart-attack in a brothel. And there was a flood of anonymous correspondence, sometimes made from letters cut from newspapers, with threats of imprisonment or assault, accusations— nearly always truthful—of homosexuality or adultery, false reports of risings in the provinces, disagreement in the Military High Command, imminent strikes, failure of insurance companies and preparations to ration essential foods. They were pitched in a minor key, promoted gatherings, processions, protests, arguments with the police, and spread false news of profitable exchanges—old casseroles for sewing-machines, tools for Swiss watches, wheel-barrows for bicycles—in shops with a wealthy clientele or a recently-opened American grocery. Workers were advertised for at magnificent wages in factories long since closed down.

"Don't eat meat of animals with foot and mouth disease," warned a handbill circulated at midday. "The National Bank is suspending transactions," announced another at dusk, and next morning people rushed to the guichets. And life went on in the midst of disorder, with incorrect information, street notices altered, crossing of wires, where the telephone from the morgue was mysteriously connected with the Head of State's Office, and the number of a brothel rang the papal nuncio very early in the morning. Someone who ordered a Steinway piano from New York found a decapitated donkey inside it; someone who bought a record of Tito Schipa, a tenor much admired because he sang in Spanish, heard a stream of abuse of the Government as soon as the needle was placed on the disk although it bore the trademark of His Master's Voice. All these escapades, growing more and more audacious, were the work of activists, who started panics in cinemas with explosions of magnesium, carried off tramway rails and cut electric wires—leaving half the town without light, the better to throw stones at the windows of business houses.

There was a whole underground army, mobile, intelligent, full of bright ideas and treachery, operating everywhere to disorganize the structure of society, disconnect administrative arrangements, keep the authorities in a perennial state of shock, and above all to stimulate an increasing climate of alarm. No one trusted anyone any longer. And the police were impotent in spite of their numbers being continually augmented by agents, detectives, informers and spies, and kept on making false moves, without ever catching the people really responsible for this or that incident. Two bombs had exploded in the Palace, although visitors were all searched when they entered the building and all parcels from outside were examined. And since someone had to be accused, yet none of them liked to admit their bewilderment, they tried to find valid reasons for being sure that the promoter of everything, the master-mind behind these fiendish activities and mysterious devices was The Student. But the editorials of *Liberation*—never signed, of course—stated that the strange events disturbing the citizens were not due to communist action:

"We do not make use of jokes and mystifications to further our struggle." And then in a more characteristically Latin American tone: "True revolutionaries don't come from brothels and gambling dives." And next to this as usual was a collection of Marxist ideas printed inside a frame: "Humanity only sets itself problems that can be solved, because if they are carefully studied it is found that the problem only arises where material conditions for solving it exist" (*Introduction to a Critique of Political Economy*).

"I'm beginning to believe," said the President, much disturbed, "that that little bastard is telling the truth. He's got other aims in view. He's deluded. But sincere. He wouldn't waste time telephoning to say I died like Félix Faure last night."

"But the bombs?" said Peralta.

"Yes, the bombs," said the Head of State, once more undecided. "Communists, like anarchists, put bombs anywhere they can. One only has to see the pictures in the international press. All the same . . ."

"The trouble is that people think The Student is responsible for everything that's happening here," remarked the Secretary. "And so he's becoming a sort of myth: something like Robin Hood but who owns Gyges' ring. And our poor population is charmed by such stories."

And he was quite right, for the novels of Ponson du Terrail, and also *Les Misérables*, had had an extremely wide appeal throughout the country, with their characters who changed name, age and appearance and always deceived their pursuers. Gaston Leroux had shown a criminal's powers of mimicry in his often translated and much read *Mystery of the Yellow Room*. So it was against a background of classic rebels, historical outlaws, impossible to catch and always on the side of justice, that the image of The Student was evoked among little groups of farm workers, in tenement-house gatherings, in the *coplas* sung softly in the back rooms of village shops (although in fact these people had very little idea what communism was), as a sort of fighter for reform, defender of the poor, enemy of the rich, scourge of corruption, saver of a nation alienated by capitalism, a descendant of the popular leaders in our wars of independence, whose generous and just deeds lived on in people's memories. The fame of his ubiquity, above all, increased day by day: he was the genius of unpredictable journeys, who made fun of police cordons, customs officers and sentinels, and flew from the mines in the North to the dockyards of la Verónica, from forest to cistus-covered highlands. And the legend of The Student, greatly enriched by stories of laudable deeds, whispered news, and ballads that passed from mouth to mouth, slipped through windows so narrow that it seemed like magic; he ran over the roofs, jumped from terrace to terrace, now disguised as a protestant pastor, now as a Franciscan capuchin, pretended to be blind one day, acted the policeman another—farmhand, miner, muleteer, doctor with his black bag, English tourist, wandering harpist, loader of crates. And while the forces of State Security were hunting for him, clattering about on their motor-cycles and besieging whole suburbs, the hunted man was probably sitting on a seat in Central Park, wearing an old man's wig, a white beard and black spectacles, with his nose buried in the daily paper, while a few of his followers—if they really were his followers—began singing far away among the agaves and prickly pears, the nets and seaweed, the mountain wheatfields and threshing-floors among the clouds, a *copla* very popular in Mexico some years ago:

We farmworkers—or so they say—
Are just a lot of twisters
Because we have no wish to be
The oxen of our masters.

"I don't like myths," said the Head of State, faced with the increasing reality of The Student, whose imaginary—but unknown—profile crossed between the large window in his study and the earthly presence of the Tutelary Volcano every morning. "I don't like myths. Nothing can travel about so far and so fast in this continent as a myth."

"Certainly, that's true," observed the schoolmaster who often emerged in Peralta. "Montezuma was overthrown by the messianic Aztec myth of A-man-with-a-pale-skin-who-was-to-come-from-the-East. The Andes knew the myth of the Inca Paraclete, later incarnate in Tupac Amaru, who put up a good fight against the Spaniards. We had the myths of the Resurrection-of-the-Ancient-Gods, which gained us a Fantastic City in the jungles of Yucatán, when Paris was celebrating the advent of the Century of Science and worshipping the Good Fairy Electricity. There was Auguste Comte's myth in the Brazilian style, with a mystical marriage between Batacada and Positivism. Myth of the gauchos being immune to bullets. Myth of that Haitan—I think he was called Mackandal—who could tranform himself into a butterfly, an iguana, a horse or a dove. Myth of Emiliano Zapata, going up to heaven after his death on a black horse breathing out flames."

"And in Mexico too," observed the President, "our friend Porfirio Díaz was done for by the myth of 'effective suffrage, no re-election', and the awakening of the Eagle and the Serpent, who had both been asleep for rather more than thirty years, luckily for their country. And now, here, everyone believes the Myth of The Student—the virtuous redeemer, spartan and omnipresent. We must deflate the Myth of The Student . . . And our bloody police, trained in the United States, are no fucking use; they don't know how to tie men up and beat and torture them, or drown them in the bath-tub."

But Peralta was already opening the Hermes case to calm his master's rage, when the surprising, unhoped-for and altogether astounding news arrived that The Student had been found in the least likely place, feebly allowed himself to be taken prisoner without resistance or glory at a customs office in the South, where the ingenuous police—but not as ingenuous as all that—had been surprised to find a cane-cutter with uncalloused hands travelling in a cane-cart. The photo of this individual, taken at the time, agreed with one on his student's record of entry to the university. And for almost two hours he had been shut up in a cell in the Model Prison, of course denying that he was The Student—didn't he like *cells*?

"For God's sake don't do him any harm!" exclaimed the Head of State. "A good breakfast with corn griddle cakes, butter, cheeese, black beans, fried eggs, and even a long drink if he wants one. And afterwards bring him to my study. We'll have a man-to-man talk. And I give you my word I have no intention of using my powers against him. That way there will be less resistance."

The Head of State had set his scene very carefully. Dressed

in an austere frock-coat bound with silk—a pinkish grey tie, a decoration in the button-hole—he was sitting with his back to the large plate glass window giving on to the central court-yard of the Palace, with his work table in front of him, so that the light would shine on his victim's face. In the middle of the table was a classical grey blotter bound in embossed leather; an inkpot—a napoleonic eagle on a pedestal of green marble; the obligatory leather cylinder full of well-sharpened pencils; a paper-weight souvenir of Waterloo; a gold paper-knife with the arms of the Republic engraved on the handle, and files— a great many files in ostentatious disarray, with their papers turned out, here, there, as when someone is laboriously going through their documents. And here, on the right of the blotter, as if casually, lay a copy of the manual on breeding Rhode Island Reds in its yellow cover.

Doctor Peralta showed The Student into the room with the utmost courtesy, although the Head of State did not interrupt his apparent checking of numbers and ticking them with his fountain pen. Raising his occupied hand he indicated an arm-chair to the visitor. And after clipping together a few pages he handed them to his secretary:

"There was an error of 320 pesos in the estimate for the viaduct. That won't do. Tell those gentlemen they had better see about getting one of those 'adding machines', as they call them, from the United States."

Peralta left the room and there was a long silence. Corpulent, heavy-shouldered, his stature increased by the regal proportions of the presidential chair, the Head of State gazed at his adversary in some surprise. Where he had thought to find an athletic young man, his muscles hardened by playing fives at the university, with a tense defiant face, as if ready for battle, he was now looking at a thin, frail youth, half-way between adolescence and maturity, his hair rather ruffled, his face pale, but who was certainly confronting him almost without blinking, with very bright eyes, perhaps grey-green, perhaps grey-blue, and who in spite of a somewhat feminine sensibility, expressed the force of character and determination of someone who can act when necessary with the toughness of a convinced believer.

So they both looked at each other, the Master, the Invested, Immovable Ruler, and the Weak, Invisible Utopian, across the trench dividing the generations, seeing each other in flesh and blood for the first time. Their mutual contemplation produced a lamentable effect on both. To the Inferior his Superior was an archetype, an exhibit in a historical museum, a figure created to take the centre of one of those posters (the products of very recent folklore) that illustrate the triad situated in a single body, of Power, Capitalism and the Boss, an image as invariably printed on the retina as were, centuries earlier, those of Turlupin or the Matamoros of the Italian Commedia del Arte. Today's protagonist of revolutionary allegories was this individual sitting in front of him in his frock-coat and striped trousers, with a pearl tie-pin and expensive scent, only lacking the emblem of a shiny top hat and a cigar stuck between his fierce teeth to symbolize—sitting on sacks of dollars which really existed, even if in the vaults of a Swiss bank—the Spirit of the Bourgeoisie.

To the Superior, his Inferior was a character from folklore, whom he was measuring, weighing up and analysing, while conscious of surprise at having to attend to someone so unimportant. The man in front of him was something like a Latin American version of the classical student in Russian novels, full of dreams and theories, more of a nihilist than a politician, proletarian out of sense of duty, who lived in a garret, under-nourished, badly dressed, falling asleep among his books, roused to bitterness by the mediocrity of his existence. They had both had the same origins. But while the Superior, a pragmatist who thoroughly understood his environment, had taken with impatient haste the upward path, which was today bordered with statues and busts of himself, his Inferior had fallen into the trap of a new form of Messianism, whose fatal progress would carry him to the Siberias of the Tropics, to the indignities of Bertillon's tests, or to the denouement—a theme for the articles of journalists in the far future—of disappearing-without-trace, leaving the relatives of this weak, insubstantial figure to take flowers on assumed anniversaries and lay them on aimless tombs, engraved with names, but with the sadness, worse even than that of an occupied coffin, of an empty grave.

And in a silence barely broken by the whistle of a bird frisking among the areca-palms in the patio, there took place a dialogue between voices that never emerged from lips. Each was looking at the other: *He doesn't realize to what extent he's playing a part | he seems more like a provincial poet than anything else | he's absolutely "taken up a position" | one of those who win prizes in Flower Festivals | flashy clothes | suit from "The Quality Shop" | face like a bottom | cheeks like a girl | comes out paler in photos: as he gets older he returns to his origins | hair uncombed, tie crooked, to give himself some style | smells like a tart, with all that Cologne | he needs size, strength to make something of him | there's a repulsive quality in his expression | he thinks he's Masaniello | I thought he was older | I wonder if it's hate or fear he's looking at me with | his hands are trembling: alcohol | he's got a pianist's hands, but he ought to clean his nails | the classical Tyrant | the Archangel we all were once | a vicious, obscene man: it's all in his appearance | the face of a boy who hasn't screwed many women: intellectual lightweight | not even a monster: a petty tyrant giving himself airs | those weak ones are the worst | all this is pure theatre: this way of receiving me, the light on my face, that book on the table | capable of anything: he's got nothing to lose | don't look at me like that, I won't lower my eyes | although he may be brave, he wouldn't resist torture | I wonder if I could stand torture: some people can't | I believe he's afraid | . . . torture . . . | if they put him under a certain amount of pressure | they'll try to get names out of me | why such a long wait? a good fright to start with | his hand's going to the bell: he's going to ring | no: I gave my word | I don't know if I could resist | talk to him first | it's horrible thinking of that, of that, of that . . . | one mustn't make martyrs, one mustn't make martyrs of these people: avoid it if possible | he gave me his word; but his word isn't worth a fuck | everyone knows that He is here now, and that I've given my word | he's going to ring: I shall be handcuffed | others, tougher than this one, have been persuaded | when will he decide to speak? | let him go, and have him followed: he must go somewhere | why doesn't the bugger speak to me? Why can't he open his mouth? | He's sweating! Now I'm sweating and I've no handkerchief, I've no handkerchief; not in that pocket either . . . | He's afraid |*

he's smiling | he wants to suggest something: some beastliness | I'll offer him a drink | I'm sure he's going to offer me a drink | he won't accept it, so as to pride himself on his virtue | if only he'd offer me a drink: I'd feel better | I don't want to risk a refusal | come on, go on, that's it, risk it; it'll be a bottle from that case; everyone knows what's inside it | however, yes: I tell you . . . I repeat . . . *But he doesn't seem to have heard me: that lorry | now it's the tram | I don't understand his expression | I don't think he understood my expression | we've stared at each other quite long enough; now for the book, so that he can see . . .*

The Head of State picked up the book on breeding Rhode Island Red poultry. He opened it and, pushing back his spectacles began to read in a markedly sarcastic tone: "A spectre was haunting Europe: the spectre of Communism."

And the other went on, with even more marked sarcasm: "All the old European powers combined together to pursue this spectre: The Pope and Wilson, Clemenceau and Lloyd George."

"Metternich and Guizot," corrected the President.

"I see you know the classics," said The Student.

"I know more about poultry-breeding. Don't forget I'm a son of the soil. Perhaps that's why . . ." And he stopped, perplexed as to the style he ought to adopt in this dialogue. Ornate language, like that of the *Prayer on the Acropolis*, would never do; a young man of the coming generation would find it ridiculous, nor must he fall into the opposite extreme of the rough vocabulary that coarsened his intimate conversations with Doctor Peralta and the Mayorala Elmira, though giving them a certain jauntiness. He therefore opted for a deliberate, humanistic tone, without the familiar form we always used, a tone which by its remoteness from that world of drink and confidences, immediately created a distance greater than that set by the table separating them. Like an actor very much in command of his gestures and talking between his teeth like Lucien Guitry, he addressed the boy in front of him as if he were a character in a tragedy, about to be overwhelmed by the inscrutable designs of Fate:

"Why do you* detest me so much?"

* *Usted*, the polite form, is used.

His formal manner of speech sufficiently conveyed his verbal strategy to The Student / *he approaches me in the style of Voltaire when he tells us he "had the honour to go off" with an Indian woman in a loin-cloth . . .* /, who replied in the meekest and most peaceable voice that his terrified throat could produce:

"I do not detest you, Señor."

"But actions speak louder than words," said the Powerful One without raising the pitch. "Bombs aren't thrown against the Palace servants. Therefore there is hatred, anger in you."

"Nothing against you, Señor."

"But . . . those bombs?"

"I didn't plant them, Señor. I don't understand anything about explosives."

"Well, it wasn't you,* then? But your followers planted them, your friends and accomplices / *he suddenly thought the word "accomplice" was vulgar and belonged to the vocabulary of police reports* / your co-religionists, your helpers, those on your side." / *careful: I've dropped into flowery language again.*

"We don't plant bombs, Señor."

The Head of State began to grow impatient. The fable of the Wolf and the Lamb was being played out between them.

"But . . . who planted them, then? Who? Will you tell me?"

"Others, not one of us. We've too often seen the failure of anarchists' attempts to change the world. Ravachol and Caserio are just as futile with their deliberate self-immolation as Bakunin and Kropotkin with their doctrines."

"Don't try and come it over me with your pointless discussions and sophistries from the Council of Nicaea / *as if mine were different!* / it all amounts to the same thing in fact. Even supposing you and your friends didn't explode a bomb in my bath, you applauded it."

"On the contrary, Señor. The worst that could happen to us now is that someone should kill *you*. I have a comrade, a practising Catholic—there's nothing to be done about it—who prays and makes vows to the Divine Shepherdess to preserve your precious life for us."

---

* *tu* (familiar form, rectified to *usted*).

The Head of State got to his feet, moved by astonishment and rage mixed.

"My precious existence? You've* got a nerve and no mistake! And nerve is a euphemism." / *Now he's beginning to call me "tu".* /

"We need you, Señor."

The Powerful, Enormous man burst out laughing.

"That's really great! So now I'm a Marxist, communist, Menshevik and revolutionary, and the same mother bore all these, who are all the same and all after the same ends: to be installed in the Kremlin, the Elysée, Buckingham Palace, or sit on this chair (and he thumped the back of the presidential chair), enjoy life, fill one's purse with money, and fuck all the rest. The Tsar's Ambassador who stayed here with us, waiting and hoping that all that business would come to grief, told me that Lenin's wife used to wear the jewels, necklaces and crowns of the Empress Alexandra."

"It's splendid that you think that way, and make up such stories, Señor. It's better we shouldn't understand each other at all than only half understand one another. Those who half understand us fight us more effectively than those who take us for visionaries."

"However, if I were in fact to die tomorrow . . ."

"It would be lamentable for us, Señor. Because a military junta would seize power, and everything would go on just the same or worse under the government of someone like Walter Hoffmann, God rest his soul."

"Well, what *do* you want, then?"

In a slightly raised voice but not speeded up at all, the young man said, "That you should be overthrown *by-a-popular-uprising.*"

"And afterwards? You would come and occupy my place, isn't that certain?"

"I have never desired anything of the sort."

"Have you got a candidate, then?"

"The word *candidate* doesn't figure in our vocabulary, Señor."

The Head of State shrugged his shoulders. "Tarradiddles!

* *tu.*

Because, in fact, someone, someone must take power. There must be a Man, always a Man, at the head of a Government. Look at Lenin in Russia. Ah! I know! Luis Leoncio Martínez, your professor at the University."

"He's a cretin. He can go to Hell with his Puranas, his Camille Flammarion and Leon Tolstoy (and he laughed). 'Return to the Earth' indeed! Whose earth? The United Fruit Company's?"

The Head of State was beginning to be irritated and impatient at the turn taken by the conversation.

"Then you mean to introduce socialism here?"

"We're looking for a way."

"The Russian way?"

"It may not be the same. Here we are in a different latitude. It's both easier and more difficult."

The President was pacing up and down his study and apparently talking to himself:

"Oh boys, boys, boys! If socialism was introduced here, in forty-eight hours you would have North American marines landing at Puerto Araguato."

"It's very probable, Señor."

"And then?" (in a protective, amiable tone) "I envy you.* At your age I thought about the same sort of things. But . . . now? Look here: they burned Joan of Arc at nineteen because if she had reached thirty she would have gone to bed with the King of France, and then she would have got as much by negotiating with the English and not had to die at the stake for it. You've got your idols. Good. I respect them. But don't forget that the gringos are the Romans of America. And you can't do a thing against Rome. And less, with the rabble" (an intimate tone, now). "You can talk to me in absolute confidence as if to an older brother. I have political experience which none of you have. I can explain why some things are possible and others not. All I want to do is understand. Let us understand each other . . . Trust me . . . Tell me . . ."

"I'm not quite mad!" said the young man, suddenly laughing, and beginning to pace the room in the opposite

* *tu.*

direction to his interlocutor, in such a way that when one of them had his back to the fire of imitation logs the other was against the corbel supporting a mirror between two doors, which made the room look larger. Suddenly the President made a gesture of depression, in the style of a good actor:

"One never stops learning lessons in this life. Hearing you talk today I suddenly realized that I'm the First Prisoner of the Nation. Yes. Don't smile. I live here surrounded by ministers, officials, generals and doctors, all bent double with obsequiousness and bowing, who do nothing but hide the truth from me. They only let me see a world of appearances. I live in Plato's cave. You know about Plato's cave? Of course! Stupid of me to ask. . . . And suddenly you arrive, full of faith, impetuosity, fresh blood, and the phrase of the French poet comes alive for me: 'I learn more from a young friend than an old master.' Ah, if I could count on the sincerity of men like you! I should make fewer mistakes! Now listen: you see one eager to take the conversation into a new climate. For instance, look here: I realize that we've been too—what shall I say?—rigorous in dealing with the problems of the university. How would you like it if we considered them now, face to face, and if you left here within an hour with a solution satisfactory to your people? It depends on you: what do you think?"

The young man walked from the fireplace to the mirror:

"Comedian!"

The President was taking irritated strides between the mirror and the fireplace, his former composure rapidly disappearing.

"Look here! If you've read Alfred de Vigny, so have I. Don't try playing the part of Pius VII before Napoleon. Because before you'd said 'Tragedian!' you know what would happen." And he took his Browning out of the left inside pocket of his frock-coat and laid it on the table with the barrel pointing at the young man.

"So the war is to go on?"

"It'll go on, with me—or without me."

"You persist in your utopias, your socialisms, although they've failed everywhere?"

"That's my affair—and a lot more besides."

"The Mexican Revolution was a failure."

"And taught us a lot, for that very reason."

"The Russian Revolution has failed."

"That's not yet been proved."

The Head of State was playing with his pistol, ostentatiously filling and emptying it of its five bullets.

"Kill me and have done with it," said The Student.

"No," said the President, taking up his pistol again. "Not here in the Palace. It would dirty the carpet." There is a silence. The humming-birds are twittering in the patio. Two pairs of eyes avoid each other by looking at the walls. (*How long is this going on? . . . That picture wants straightening . . . A situation with no way out.*) At last, as if it cost him an effort, the President spoke:

"All right. As you don't want to come to an understanding with me, I give you three days to leave the country. Ask Peralta for anything you want. You can go where you like. Paris for instance. I'll give instructions for you to get a month's allowance extra, unconditionally. You won't have to go to our Embassy. Your friends won't be surprised to see you go, because they'll know that you're *finished* as a revolutionary here. . . . No! Wait a moment! Don't be melodramatic! I'm not trying to buy you off: I'm offering you a simple choice." He changed his tone: "I'm not offering you the Paris of women and Maxim's Restaurant, as I would one of our social climbers. I'm offering you the Paris of the Sorbonne, of Bergson, of Paul Rivet, who seems to know a lot about us, and certainly published the other day a magnificent piece of research into a mummy I presented to the Trocadero Palace. The rest is your affair. Salute Racine from me when you visit Saint-Etienne-du-Mont; and Voltaire and Rousseau in the Panthéon. Or if you want to make your Prayer on the Acropolis in the Bolshevik manner, you've got the Mur des Fédérés at Père La Chaise. . . . There's something for all tastes . . . you can choose." (And he repeated "You can choose," several times in an increasingly ambiguous tone of voice.)

"I've got nothing to do in Paris," said The Student, after a marked pause.

"I leave it to you. Stay here, then. But from Tuesday" (the day after tomorrow), "I shall give orders for you to be killed without hesitation, wherever you are found."

"My death would be the worst possible publicity for you."

"My boy, the law of flight is a universally accepted lie. Like saying that a fugitive committed suicide, or that a man hanged himself in his cell because they forgot to take away his shoelaces. And that happens in the most civilized countries, where they have spendid leagues of Human Rights and other equally respectable institutions to safeguard the Liberty and Dignity of the Individual. Ah! And I warn you that anyone who has sheltered you will fall with you, their family and all. Understand?"

"May I go now?"

"Go to hell! And prepare your epitaph: *Here lies one who died because he was stupid.*" The Student got up. The Head of State made a gesture of dismissal, not wanting to risk holding out his hand for fear of a snub.

"You don't know how sorry I am. Such an estimable young man. The worst of it is that I envy you: if I were your age I should be with your lot. But you don't know what it's like governing these countries. You don't know what it's like cultivating the soil with human material that . . ." The Head of State's reflection vanished in an avalanche of broken glass. The mirror, the shelves, pictures and fireplace had come crashing down in a confusion of plaster, broken laths, gilt woodwork, splinters and paper, with a thunderous, ear-splitting noise, which seemed to reverberate in the chest and stomach. The President, very pale, brushing away the powdered plaster that whitened his frock-coat, gazed at the destruction. The Student had fallen on the floor. Now he was feeling himself all over, and looking for blood on his hands. His face, first, because women were important to him.

"Nothing. We've escaped death this time," said the President.

"And did you think I was idiotic enough to throw bombs at myself?" said the other, getting up.

"Yes, I believe you now. But that changes nothing. What I said before; that's all."

The room was filling with people: servants, officials, police, the Mayorala Elmira, the secretaries.

"Go out this way," said the Head of State, taking The Student to a little room next door, decorated in pink with elegantly licentious engravings on the wall and a wide sofa covered in cushions, connected with the street by a spiral staircase, the subject of much gossip in the town:

"Is this how the girls come in?"

"At my age, I can still hold their interest. You've realized that." And putting his hand on the young man's shoulder: "To you I must seem a sort of Caligula, don't I?"

"More like Caligula's horse," replied the other, driven to some unheard-of insolence, before dashing down the stairs with the speed of a squirrel.

The Head of State was so dumbfounded that when Doctor Peralta appeared, all he could say was:

"Open up downstairs. And let him go free."

"They've just brought the first-aid chest, Señor."

"I don't think I need it. I'm quite all right. All right. All right." And he felt his body, from chest to knees, but his fingers found neither pain nor moisture.

16

. . . there is greater honour and safety
in resistance than in flight.

DESCARTES

In March of that year it was necessary to extend the Moratorium, because the result of an official decision not to extend it had been that all those who normally operated it had prolonged, stretched and extended it to the limits of the calendar. Bad faith, trickery and cunning combined with insolvency, all sheltered under the magic, healing and somewhat sepulchral word Moratorium. No one paid for anything. The inhabitants of labourers' quarters and tenements received rent collectors with blows from sticks and stones, and loosed the dogs at them to drive the message home. Merchants from the Canary Islands, Syrian pedlars and dealers on credit were accused of being anarchists by housewives sure that the police were close at hand, should they insist on presenting a long-due account for lace or lingerie. Things were bought on credit and pawned the same day, cash taken from here to stop a deficiency there, and people had recourse to bullies and money-lenders, were perpetually shuffling papers, or attaching signatures and bribes to the margin of denunciations, and lived by expedients and miracles, by lotteries and borrowing, while there were so many dud cheques in circulation that even those who still had a reputation for wealth had to pay cash for everything. The result of all this was that the new town decreased—that is the word: *decreased*—as rapidly as it had increased. What had been large grew smaller, flatter, contracted, as if returning to the clay of its foundations. Suddenly exuding poverty, the city's ambitious skyscrapers—now more like fog-scrapers than sky-scrapers—looked smaller as their topmost storeys were deserted, abandoned by companies that had gone bust, and made opaque and gloomy by stains of damp, the sadness of dirty windows, loneliness of statues grown leprous in a few weeks. Unpainted, uncared-for, these buildings combined to make a sort of urban grisaille which degraded, crippled and decomposed the modern part of the town, swathing it in the decay of what had already been old at the beginning of the century. The porches of the Stock Exchange, half asleep and almost deserted, had been transformed into a market for the sale of singing birds, parrots and turtles, with stalls of salad vegetables and sweet corn, workshops for cobblers and knife-grinders, sellers of prayers and amulets and booths where one could consult healers using mountain herbs. ("For you with sugar in your blood, an infusion of purple basil is good; for you, for your asthma, cigars of double bell-flower; for you, for the discharge from your member, coconut milk with hollands; and for you, neighbour, for delayed monthly, balsam tea with two leaves of lentisk, applied here—excuse me—between your legs. . . .")

"The merchants of the temple," sighed the Head of State, in biblical mood.

"In spite of the Treaty of Versailles, things are going badly in Europe," said Doctor Peralta by way of consolation, dreaming of another good long, enjoyable war, perhaps nearer than people thought. "With his Fourteen Points, Wilson has annoyed everyone."

Countless notices of clearance sales and liquidations sang the requiem of business firms. Abandoned by their contractors, buildings which had not passed the stage of their milk teeth (with incipient walls not yet as high as a man) were to be seen everywhere, ruins of the unborn, presences of what had never existed, permanent beginnings, with roofless drawing-rooms, staircases leading nowhere, involuntarily Pompeian columns, while vast urbanizations and building-lots in the outskirts had been reconquered by the plants descending from the mountains—plants returning to the capital with their bells and festive plumes; and behind them shrubs, and behind the shrubs trees and tree ferns, all the seedling vegetation of Quick Advance and Quick Growth, shading the small stones among which exiled snakes were now returning to spawn. Meanwhile, the hills surrounding the city had been overspread with a rash of shacks made of corrugated iron, tarred cloth, packing-cases, or newspapers pasted together, supported on wooden props, and placed on such impossibly steep slopes that the early spring rains were tilting their floors and tumbling whole families into the river bed. These were the Squalor-towns, the Hunger-towns, the Shanty-towns, from which every night the spectator could contemplate the paradisal view of the town with all its lights—shops selling silver and cut glass, specialist philatelists, and wine-shops with their vintage bottles, where there were still people who planned tombolas in aid of the Preservation of Colonial Churches, or elected a beauty queen to represent us (creole, but not too dark-skinned) in the International Contest of Coral Gables, whence came the waltz *On Miami Shore*, now all the rage.

That year the sugar-mills had closed down earlier than usual. Left to their fate, the wounds in the trunks of the rubber trees in the southern jungles healed over. There were more strikes in the North, rioting in the sawmills of Ciudad Urrutia, bloody clashes between miners and the army in Nueva Córdoba. Several armed bands, under hitherto unknown ringleaders, roamed the mountains of the South, burning farms, sacking warehouses, attacking barracks, and for two or three days taking possession of villages where they made the mayor, merchants and notables dance to their tune, firing at the ground to increase their animation. The authorities of some provinces were powerless against the rebels, who—as had been observed more than once in the history of the country—awoke from their meek, resigned slumber of thirty years' duration, to pass suddenly, when least expected, to a violence thought by our sociologists to be foreign to the congenital good nature so characteristic of the national temperament. Peasants suffering from malaria and bilharzia, sandal-shod, and hollow-eyed with disease, now rode on wretched flea-bitten nags, covered with sores and spavins, against the magnificent shining Kentucky-bred horses of the Rural Police. There were battles between catapults and Mausers, or the knives and goads of farmhands against well-sharpened regulation machetes. In the bigger villages they fought with tiles, bricks, stones, and sometimes dynamite, against bullets.

All these events kept the Head of State confined within an island, an island with look-out posts and windows, many gates and a symmetrical arrangement of palm trees which was the Presidential Palace—where he received so many confused, contradictory, false or true reports, optimistic or tinged with gloom, that it was impossible to gather a clear, general and chronological picture of what was happening. Anyone wanting to minimize the severity of a defeat denied its importance and spoke of a meeting between bandits and cattle-rustlers, when they had really clashed with a strong popular force; anyone wanting to justify his impotence exaggerated the size of the hostile forces; anyone wanting to conceal his complete lack of information side-tracked the facts.

"You remind me of those European generals," said the Head of State angrily, "who having lost a battle, speak of 'strategic

withdrawal' or 'straightening the line', elegant ways of admitting that they've received a thorough thrashing."

And governors and garrison-commanders fell from grace, as
did leaders in uniform or in Panama hats; so that there was a
continual shuffle and reshuffle of dismissals, replacements,
substitutions, responsibility taken away and given back again,
unwelcome tasks entrusted to those who preferred to remain at
home, renunciations exacted by telegram, summonses to
ex-colleagues out of a job, patriotic speeches and exhortations to
national concord. And the island of the Palace became more
isolated day by day, with its ever closer concentration of
Government servants, who felt themselves protected and
defended, as it were, between these walls of good Colonial
masonry, against hostile forces which like a swell caused by
distant hurricanes (for their course was just as unpredictable)
pounded against sentry-boxes, loop-holes and parapets, where
the bluish metal of long weapons gleamed at all hours of the
day. And there were sand-bags—a precaution that is never
unnecessary—on the flat roofs of the building. There was a
smell of criminal assault in the air. A door suddenly banging
in the wind, the brutal starting up of a motor-bicycle, a flash
of lightning from a dry sky, without the warning of rain—as so
often happened during these months—produced a sudden scare,
and the Mayorala Elmira's "don't be so stupid!" echoed
through the vastness of the well-guarded corridors like the
repeated leitmotiv in a Wagnerian opera.

"Be tough with them, President, be tough. You must be
tougher," said Peralta when some unpleasant incident occurred
to darken a new day. But the worst of it was that, though he
might have been tough previously, it had now become difficult,
because beside the island of the Palace another island—
extremely close yet inaccessible—had sprung up in the city:
a yellow island, overcharged with mouldings and ornament—
Californian plateresque in style—in the shape of a block almost
next door, which grew and grew steadily. In it were to be found
the cool shadows of the Hotel Cleveland, the Grocery smelling
of maple syrup, the half-asleep Clearing House, Sloppy Joe's
Bar and various curio and souvenir shops, which for lack of

local handicrafts—our people were very musical but deficient in plastic feeling—sold ponchos from Oaxaca, Cuban rattles, shrunken heads, half nutshells containing fleas dressed for weddings and funerals, gaudy buttons and other things not produced in the region, as well as bogus archaeological finds. And the centre of this island was the American Club—where, according to reliable information—as well as poker parties, meetings of Daughters of the Revolution, sessions of Masons wearing Turkish fezes, celebrations of Independence Day, Thanksgiving, July 4th and Halloween—with fire-crackers and children carrying illuminated pumpkins—serious discussions took place about the national crisis, disorder and bankruptcy, reaching the incredible conclusion that, for lack of anyone better, the Man needed at this moment—their last hope as it were—might well be Luis Leoncio Martínez, defeated at Nueva Córdoba it was true, but suddenly and astonishingly approved by the North American Department of State.

"Although it was all very hush-hush, Ariel knows that he spent several days in Washington," commented Peralta, "which only shows yet once again that in politics no enemy is ever dead."

The Head of State reflected out loud: "And those were the people, *those*, whose interests I always made a point of defending; *they* got anything they wanted out of me, and now they accuse me of everything that has gone wrong in the country. They won't admit that the crisis is nothing to do with us: it's general, it's universal. Let them take a look at Europe, where all they've done is turn the map upside down, ruin currencies, create artificial nationalities—chaos, I tell you, absolute chaos. And now they're trying to interfere in our troubles by means of this idiotic professor."

"They think a change—it's the everlasting Myth of Change—will straighten out our problems. Perhaps they think we're moth-eaten, a bit *vieux-jeu*," groaned Peralta, while the President was revolving in his mind an idea that had for several days perturbed him:

"What an imbecile I was not to polish off The Student when I had him in front of me as plain as I see you now. And with my Browning on the table. A mere gesture. And for the benefit of the public; *he tried to attack me and I defended myself.* The Mayorala Elmira could have fired a shot at the right-hand shoulder of my frock-coat suspended from a coat-hanger, and I would have put it on afterwards. And a good photo of the young man stretched on the carpet, the unfortunate victim of my legitimate instinct of self-preservation. Plain as a pikestaff. All clear. And the first applause would have come from the American Club."

"It wouldn't have improved the situation at all."

"But The Student is still here: he hasn't gone. Our police are just as unable to get him today as they were yesterday. And he's still publishing his pamphlets on India paper."

"Principally read by the members of the American Club. Because the public it's intended for are almost illiterate. His ideas are too complicated for our people in sandals and overalls."

"They don't understand our young man's ideas, but they believe in him."

"Bah! In an abstract way. He's someone-who-will-put-things-to-rights. The Myth of Change again! But he's lacking flesh and blood, an image, palpability. For our peasants, Saint Speed (unknown to the calendar of saints) has more solidarity and is someone they can turn to when they want something, just as they pray to a picture printed in Paris, showing the Miracle-worker, unknown to the Church, brandishing a sword with the word *Hodie,** only they pronounce it *Jode,*† engraved in the steel."

"And you think Leoncio has more popular appeal than The Student?"

"Not at all. But it's just because the gringos are afraid of The Student—and especially of the ideas he represents—that they support the man from Nueva Córdoba. They care very little about the individual. But he's come to personify a type of *Democracy* that they invoke every time they want to change something in Latin America."

"A matter of vocabulary."

* today.   † fuck.

"Everyone has their own; they talk about Defender of Democracy, we about Defender of the Established Order."

The Head of State began thinking aloud again: "Perhaps we could twang the string of national honour: the unforgivable interference of Yankees in the interior affairs of our country. Our people loathe gringos."

"Our people do—yes; but our bourgeoisie always gets along with them. To our wealthy people Gringo is a synonym for Order, Technique and Progress. Those sons of the family who aren't educated by the Jesuits of Belén are at Cornell or Troy, if not West Point. We're being invaded—and you know it—by Methodists, Baptists, Jehovah's Witnesses and Christian Scientists. North American Bibles are part of the furniture of our rich houses, like Mary Pickford's photo in a silver frame rubber-stamped with her familiar 'Sincerely yours'."

"We're losing all our character: we've got too far away from our Mother Spain."

"We shan't do any good by bemoaning that. You've got plenty of guts and I've fought bulls myself in better days. Generals like Ataúlfo Galván and Walter Hoffmann were the real danger, with some of the army behind them. At least we haven't got to keep our eye on the barracks."

"That's true enough: I can count on the army. Without the smallest doubt."

"And the Yankees know that, President; that's one thing the Yankees know."

Just then music from stringed instruments struck up from behind the flamboyant trees in Central Park, slow, sweet and smoothly bowed.

"There they go!" cried the Head of State. "Elmirita says they're bringing a coffin. Shut that window, Peralta."

And the Secretary shut the window, suddenly shocked by this contact with the every-day Business of Death, the only thriving business, managed in these times of crisis by clever men, connoisseurs of a safe clientèle moved by ancestral and scatalogical emotions towards that Sleep-which-has-no-Awakening. Throughout the country, by a fusion of traditions wherein Extremadurans—our first Conquistador had come from Cáceres, like Pizarro—had combined with Indians, funeral ceremonies were complicated, ostentatious and prolonged. When someone died in a village, the neighbours invaded the house and turned the funeral wake into a collective activity with widespread repercussions, a gathering of men in doorways, patios and on pavements against a dramatic background of weeping, wailing and fainting women; and the whole night was punctuated by servings of black coffee, cups of chocolate, strong wine and brandy, with much histrionic and emotional embracing, speeches and lamenting round the coffin, and exaggerated reconciliations between relations who had been at daggers drawn and passed years without meeting, before coming together on this solemn occasion. Afterwards came mourning, half-mourning, quarter-mourning, and then permanent mourning, which in the case of a good-looking widow was observed until she married again. And this continued in the important modern capital, although the scenario was somewhat transformed. The corpses were no longer laid out and the wakes held in private houses, but in undertakers' establishments, which were becoming more numerous all the time—with a growing population, more deaths—and competing with one another in the sumptuous innovations they offered their clients. And, little by little, these funerals had multiplied in the middle of the town, spreading a taint of affliction around the Presidential Palace—with constant coming and going of coffins and flowers, movements of angels and crosses, horses draped in black, hearses with glass sides, arrival by night of stiff corpses wrapped in green sheets . . .

But the most extraordinary of all these establishments had just been set up nearby, next to the Ministry of the Interior and the dyeworks: this was an imitation of the *Deuil en vingt-quatre heures* to be seen in Paris behind the Madeleine, at the corner of the Rue Tronchet. The speciality of "Eternity" was that the families could choose a style of furnishing, decoration and ambience in which to receive condolences at the foot of the coffin. There was a Colonial Room, an Imperial Room, a Spanish Renaissance Room, a Louis XV Room, an Escorial Room, a Gothic Room, a Byzantine Room, an Egyptian Room, a Rustic Room, a Masonic Room, a Spiritualist Room, a Rosicrucian Room, all with seats, emblems, ornaments and symbols adjusted to the character of the funeral chapel. And if the users wished, they could benefit from a great innovation introduced from the United States: the wake could be accompanied by noble and serene music, devoid of contrasts in loudness or tempo—although not at all funereal—performed by quartets or small string orchestras with harmonium, perfumed with incense and hidden behind a trellis of evergreens or a hedge of wreaths on trestles. Their repertory was drawn from the *Méditation* from *Thaïs*, *Le cygne* by Saint-Saëns, Massenet's *Elégie*, Schubert's *Ave Maria*, as well as Gounod's, played and played again tirelessly from the arrival of the urn until its departure to the cemetery. When these melodies came creeping into the Palace in the small hours, the Head of State, exasperated at hearing the same tune over and over again, repeated a hundred times—and louder when there were no cars circulating in Central Park—ordered all the windows to be shut, though he went on suffering torments from the themes reverberating inside his head. And he could only get to sleep again with the help of the Santa Inés rum in the Hermes case, which was always placed on the night-table at the head of his hammock.

And since *that* had been going on for weeks and weeks, there came a morning when he felt deafened—but deafened by the silence, the unaccustomed silence. The windows had been opened early that morning by the Mayorala Elmira, but the light breeze coming into his room smelling of the verdurous dawn did not bring with it the *Elégie*, *Le cygne*, the *Méditation* nor the *Ave Marias*.

"Something strange is happening," he thought. And something strange, very strange indeed, was in fact happening: something never before seen or remembered—even by the oldest inhabitants with the longest memories. The capital was starting the day—that day—in silence, a silence that was not merely funereal, a silence of other eras, a silence of distant dawns, a silence of the days when goats grazed in the main streets of the town; a silence broken only by far-off a donkey's bray, the cough of someone with bronchitis, the wail of a child.

No buses went by. There was no tinkling from trams. Milk-floats weren't going their rounds. And what was stranger still, early businesses like the bakers and cafés hadn't opened their doors, and the shops still had their metal shutters down. The total absence of street cries—no "hot churros" nor "tamarinds for the liver", nor "fresh oysters from Chichiriviche", nor "good tamales", nor the fruit seller's bugle—seemed to announce events of extreme gravity, with that sense of contraction, that fearful expectation, latent and undefined, which is often felt—although the warning is never listened to—on the eve of great earthquakes or volcanic eruptions. (The trees in the Paricutín region *were afraid*, turned grey with silent terror, many weeks before the slow, inexorable advance of lava had bubbled with a dull sound round their roots.)

"But—what's happening? What is all this?" asked the Head of State, seeing Doctor Peralta enter his room followed by Ministers and military officers, unceremoniously violating his privacy and over-riding protocol:

"General strike, Señor President."

"General strike? General strike?" he asked (asked himself, rather) as if stunned, not hearing what they said, nor what he said himself.

"General strike. Or, if you prefer: a *general standstill*. Every-thing is shut. No one has gone to work."

"And public servants?"

"There are no buses, trams or trains."

"And there's not a soul in the streets," said the Mayorala Elmira, making her way between alpaca suits and military uniforms. The Head of State went on to the balcony. The Palace dogs, led by the remains of the police force, were pissing round the fountain in the park. But dogs had no souls. They weren't people. And that undertaker's establishment without music. . . .

He turned back to the others in the room with a face of thunder: "A general strike, is there? And you knew nothing about it?" The others began talking incoherently, tying themselves up in explanations, clarifications and excuses—"you remember I advised you," "you remember that at the last Council meeting, I . . ." but they never succeeded in producing a single convincing argument. Hitherto, real strikes had only been seen in the interior of the Republic—in Nueva Córdoba and the ports; calls for a standstill had had no more serious consequences here; it was true that during these last days papers and clandestine leaflets had been distributed; moreover it was The Student who had predicted strikes of farm workers, porters, road-men and so forth, and everyone knew that merchants, shop-workers and members of the middle classes had never listened to The Student's instructions and calls to action; men employed on regular work didn't feel that *Proletarians of the Whole World* referred to them, because they never thought of themselves as proletarians; "and I was away from the capital, and I had to take my family to Bellamar and I couldn't imagine it, all the same my daughter told me . . ." (*we don't care a fuck what your daughter told you*); besides, never, never, never in the history of the Continent had a strike of white-collar workers been seen; that sort of hooliganism was confined to disreputable characters, so we didn't pay attention to all the rumours; my daughter told me that the nuns of Tarbes . . . (*stop bothering us with your daughter*); I always said that that campaign of rumours, false epidemics, the wooden horse in the aqueduct, threats of death, skulls sent through the post, in fact I always said that . . .

"And now we're on the subject of deaths," said Peralta, interrupting the confused sound of voices all talking together, "the Mayorala has just told me something most unexpected, most unusual: all the undertakers' staff has joined the movement. Not only the musicians of 'Eternity', but those who lay out the corpses, the drivers of hearses, grave-diggers and sextons. Families have to keep watch at home over anyone who died last night, because no one will come and take charge of them."

"People who died last night didn't at least join the strike," said the Head of State, suddenly calming down. "What's more, we'll give them some company so that they shan't be bored in the Next World. They deserve a reward." There was an expectant silence. "Let's talk briefly and to the point. Ask Elmira to bring some coffee."

At about ten in the morning vehicles began driving rapidly through the streets—fire-engines and motor-cycles with side-cars, manned by police who yelled through leather megaphones and aluminium speaking-trumpets, such as are used at sporting contests, to tell any tradesmen with ears to hear that anyone failing to open his shop before two o'clock, either with or without his workers, would be deprived of his licence and punished by fines and imprisonment; and that anyone of foreign origin—however long ago he might have been naturalized—would be expelled from the country. These warnings were repeated again and again until the Cathedral clock struck twelve:

"At least the bell-ringer isn't on strike," observed the President.

"That's because an electric machine has been installed," explained Peralta, very quickly repenting of saying what might be interpreted as a joke. "We must wait."

The Mayorala brought bottles of cognac and earthenware jugs of hollands, and Romeo and Juliet Havanas and Henry Clays.

At least once every half hour the Head of State took out his watch to see whether an hour had passed. One o'clock. Two. A coffin emerged from "Eternity" carried on the shoulders of black-clad men—obviously members of the family—who set off on foot towards the cemetery. And at three the same silence as before reigned throughout the capital. Only a few Cantonese traders had opened their shops selling fans, screens and ivory goods, for fear of being sent back to China, which was now in the hands of the Kuo-Ming-Tang and the War Lords.

Suddenly the President broke the long wait by saying curtly and firmly to the Commander-in-Chief of the Army: "Machine-gun the closed shops." A click of the heels, and a salute.

A quarter of an hour later the first fusillade was heard, bullets against metal shutters, corrugated iron, signboards and shop windows. Never had such a frivolous war been waged. Never had the infantry enjoyed themselves so much as on this moving shooting-range, where without aiming, merely firing bullets in strips, they were bound to hit some target—a splendid battle with no danger of reply from enemy bullets. It was a massacre of wax people—wax brides with wax orange-blossom; gentlemen in frock-coats with wigs on their wax skulls; amazons playing golf and tennis, with very pale wax complexions; a maid, dressed in the French style and made of less pale wax; the footman, like our Sylvestre in Paris, but of darker wax than the maid-servant; an acolyte, a mace-bearer, a jockey, all represented by a shade of wax suitable to their occupations—and, of course, the Virgins and Saints, brought from the Saint Sulpice district, in their robes of polychrome plaster, with haloes and other attributes, offered for sale by traders in missals and articles of devotion. As well as the 30/30s, the army fired off their Mausers and even some old Lebel rifles, brought from the back regions of the Arsenal. And in this great battle-against-things, shop-windows disintegrated, dinner-services set out as wedding-presents were sent flying, bottles of scent, Dresden and Murano vases and porcelain were splintered to bits, earthenware casseroles, flagons and pitchers broken, and bottles of sparkling wine liberated so much energy as they exploded that they broke the bottles next to them. For several hours the attack on toys went on, firing on babies' bottles, fusillade of Buster Brown and Mutt and Jeff, defenestration of puppets, massacre of Swiss cuckoo-clocks, and a second decapitation of Saint Dionysius, who saw the head he was already carrying in his hands fall to the ground struck in the middle of the cheek by a large-bore bullet.

But in spite of all this activity and travail, night fell over the city without public illumination or spot-lighting in parks, and with bulbs in the advertisements and street-lamps unlit—only a few gas-jets still remained, and the lamps carried by watchmen in the poorer quarters—even the moon was waning and overcast with clouds. It was a long, interminable night, a night of gloom weighing on a paralysed, silent town, a town abandoned to senseless firing—a few intermittent bursts of which could still be heard here and there. During these hours of waiting, of not knowing what the morning would bring, people realized that certain silences, silences not leading to any sound of voice or meaningful phrase, could be more agonizing than the clamour of a prophet or the delirium of an inspired diviner.

However, there were many houses, silent houses with the blinds drawn, ministers' or generals' houses, houses belonging to those in Power or wearing soutanes, there were attics, rooms beyond the patio, where someone would go by with a lantern or an oil-lamp, or candles held high, to conceal things, take jewels out of trunks, lock boxes, dust suit-cases, sew bank-notes (especially dollars) inside the linings, lapels and skirts of suits, coats and capes, in preparation for some possibly necessary flight. In the morning the children would be sent to the Atlantic beaches (*they were anaemic*; *medical prescription*); many families would disperse into the provinces or towns of the interior (*sick grandmother; grandfather of ninety-seven*), or had gone to their ancestral homes (*my sister had a miscarriage; the other is queer in the head*), while they waited to see what was going to happen. Meanwhile, in kitchens whose only light came from cigars outlining a face with every puff, the men of the family, smoking more as they felt more conscious of danger, gathered round bottles of rum and whisky, groping for them in the dark to refill their glasses gropingly, and discussing the situation. A dull, infectious, increasing panic filled all the shadows and was brooded over in a thousand different ways, until the sweat of fear broke out on temples and napes of necks. . . .

The Great and Little Bears and other constellations were fading in the grey dawn, and still there was silence in the capital. The whole country was plunged in silence. The machine-gun fusillade had been useless. Slowly the sun invaded the streets, striking small flashes of light from the broken glass covering the pavements. And now, as a last straw, the Chief of Police found out that his men were panic-stricken. They hadn't seemed so timid and surly-looking when called upon to fight their way up streets, or assault barricades, during some clash between infantry and horsemen, or when marching shoulder to shoulder against a mob armed with sticks, belaying-pins, metal pipes or even fire-arms (generally old pistols, sporting rifles or antique muskets); what terrified them was this silence, the solitude all round them, the emptiness of streets leading to the lower slopes of the surrounding mountains, where there wasn't a single passer-by as far as the eye could see. They would have been less afraid of an attack from an angry crowd than of solitary, isolated shots; these separate, single, carefully-considered shots, taking careful aim, from a roof or a terrace, might leave a man stretched on the asphalt with a hole bored through his temple or brow as cleanly and surely as if drilled by a saddler's bit. The troops were in barracks; the infantry bivouacked in the patios and the sentries smoked in their sentry-boxes. And there was nothing. Silence. A silence broken occasionally—very seldom—by the clamour of a motor-cycle (they were always of the brand called *Indian*) accelerating as the terrified rider made his way to the Palace with some disagreeable, laconic and confidential message. There, some of them lying exhausted in armchairs or on divans, and those too soaked in liquor to drink more keeping awake with the help of tobacco and coffee, were the high officials and dignitaries of the nation, waxen-faced, their necks sweating, their coats off, and braces dangling. In the middle of this general collapse, the Head of State was waiting, tense, motion-less, dignified and frowning; he was waiting for the Mayorala Elmira who had muffled herself in a lacy shawl and gone out to get some hot news, walking about in the streets, listening at doors, peering through shut windows, getting information from some unlikely passer-by—such as a drunk female crony and collector of gossip, tremulous with aguardiente. But now she came back, after having walked a long way, and not heard anything of interest. Or rather, yes: one thing only. On all the walls and palings of the city, thousands of mysterious hands had written in pale chalk—white, blue or pink—a single phrase, always the same: "Get out! Get out!"

After a brief pause the President rang a hand-bell, as though in a parliamentary session. The others got up from where they were resting, straightening their ties, doing up buttons and smoothing their hair in an attempt to regain a little composure.

"Excuse me—your fly," said Elmira to the Minister of Communications, who had left it undone.

"Gentlemen," said the Head of State. And there followed a

good speech, dramatic but free from emotion or eloquence, a straightforward commentary on the Mayorala's narrative. If his compatriots thought it necessary for him to resign, if his most faithful colleagues (and he begged them to answer simply, frankly and with equanimity) shared this judgement, he was determined to hand over the power immediately to whomever was thought best fitted to assume it. "I await your reply, gentlemen." But the gentlemen did not reply. And after a few minutes of stupor and agonized consideration of the facts, they were left with the fear, overpowering fear, insuperable Blue Funk caused by the people's war-cry. Suddenly, looking at each other, they were all thinking that the permanence, the rigour and above all the Full Acceptance of Responsibility, the Full Acceptance of Guilt, of the Man who was awaiting the sound of their voices with growing impatience, was the only thing that could save them from the menace now haunting them. If the anger of the populace were unloosed, if the masses rushed into the streets, they would look for an abscess to lance, an object on which to rain their blows, a scape-goat, a Head to raise aloft on the point of a pike, while the rest of them might perhaps take different escape routes and manage to get away somehow or other. Otherwise, the general fury would reach them all equally, and for lack of the Body now standing before them their bodies would end up, dragged along, quartered, unidentifiable in the city drains—unless they had been hung up to a telegraph post with infamous placards pinned to their chests.

At last the President of the Senate spoke up and said what they all wanted him to say: That after so many sacrifices for the good of the nation (here came a list of some of them), at a time when our country was threatened by dissolving forces (here came imprecations against all socialists, communists, international crooks, The Student and his paper, the professor of Nueva Córdoba and the party he created yesterday and gave the pedantic name of Alpha-Omega—"he's the worst bugger of the lot" remarked Peralta, and was immediately silenced by a gesture of annoyance from his listener), in these critical hours they were asking a supreme proof of self-sacrifice, etc., etc., on the part of the Head of State, because if in so serious a moment of peril he abandoned us, and deprived us of the help of his lucidity and political sense (here came mention of his other qualities and virtues) our friendless country could only groan, like our Lord on the Cross: *"Eloi, Eloi, lama sabachtani."*

The President, who had been listening to all this with bent head and chin on his breast, now flung his arms apart and straightened his whole body:

"Gentlemen, let us set to work. The Council is open." There was long applause and each man took his place at the long table running down the middle of the room next door, which was hung with Gobelins.

At three o'clock that day a great many telephones began ringing. At first there were a few only, intermittent and at intervals. Then more numerous, with louder voices, impatiently shouting. A host of telephones. A vast chorus of telephones. A world of telephones. And calls from patio to patio, voices running along roofs and terraces, crossing gaps, flying from corner to corner. And windows began opening. And doors began opening. And someone leans out, gesticulating. And ten lean out, gesticulating. And people run out into the streets; and some embrace and others laugh, some run, meet, gather in groups, inflate their chests, form into a procession, and another procession, and more processions appear at the entries to streets, come down from the hills and up from the depths of valleys, and coalesce into a crowd, an enormous crowd, shouting: "Long live Liberty!"

Now everyone knows and is telling his neighbour: the Head of State has just died. Of a heart attack say some. But no; he was assassinated by conspirators. No, not that either: he was shot by a sergeant affiliated to Alpha-Omega. No, that wasn't right either: someone really in the know said that he was killed by The Student, with the same Belgian pistol the Man always had on his desk, and that he emptied the whole lot of bullets— some said it contained six, others eight—into his body. One of the Palace servants had seen the whole thing, and he said . . . But he's dead, all right. He's dead. That is the great, beautiful, joyful, tremendous cause for jubilation. And it seems that they are taking the Corpse—the enormous Corpse—through the streets. The people living in San José district saw it being dragged along by a lorry, with the skull bumping on the paving-stones. Now everyone must go to the centre of the town, singing in chorus the National Anthem, the Liberator's Anthem, the Marseillaise and the Internationale, which unexpectedly came to mind.

But at this moment the armoured cars of the 4th Motorized Division appear, and open fire on the crowd. The men of the Palace garrison fire all together from behind the cover given by the wide banisters of the upper terrace and sandbags brought days before. Grenades fall from the Telephone tower, leaving screaming gaps in the crowds holding a meeting below. Dozens of machine-guns poke out from corners. Closing the avenues, police and soldiers are now advancing at a slow measured tread in close files, letting off their rifles at every three paces. The now terrified people are running, fleeing, leaving bodies and more bodies and yet more bodies on the pavements, throwing down flags and placards, trying to get inside houses by forcing shut doors, or jump into interior patios or lift the lids of sewers. And still the troops advance, slowly, very slowly, firing all the time, trampling on the wounded lying on the ground, or finishing off with bayonets or butt ends of their rifles any who clutch at their boots and leggings. And at last, after the crowd has been reduced and dispersed, the streets are once again deserted. The fire brigades come out to put out a few fires. Here and there are heard the long vicious, insistent sirens of ambulances. When night falls all the streets are patrolled by the army. And everyone—all those who had sung so many hymns and given cheers for this and that—had to face an appalling truth. The Head of State had assassinated himself; he had spread abroad the news of his death, so that crowds should throng the streets and be shot down with supreme ease.

And now, sitting on the presidential chair with all his supporters round him, he was celebrating the victory.

"You'll see they'll open all the shops tomorrow and stop making such bloody nuisances of themselves."

Outside, the chorus of sirens was still going on.

"Bring some champagne, Elmira. The best: from that cupboard; you know where it is . . ."

An occasional single rifle-shot could be heard, far away, and sounding feebler than the weapons of the army.

"There are still one or two fools left," said the President. "Gentlemen, once again, we have won."

So much had happened during the day, and public buildings were so deserted that nobody noticed one very strange thing: the sudden disappearance—by theft of course—of the Diamond from the Capitol; yes, of that enormous Tiffany diamond set in the heart of a star at the feet of the gigantic statue of the Republic, and marking the Zero Point—of convergence and departure—of all the large roads in the country.

SIX

*. . . if the contest is too unequal, it is better to choose
honourable resignation or abandon the game rather
than expose oneself to certain death.*

DESCARTES

17

When I remember that day, it seems to me that I lived
through some sort of improbable carnival, whose hours were
fuller, more crowded than whole years—a confusion of images,
descent into hell, mobs, aimless shouting, figures revolving,
masks, metamorphoses, mutations, din, substitution of one
thing by another, everything upside down, owls hooting at
midday, sunshine in shadow, appearance of harpies, lambs
biting, roars of the meek, fury of weaklings; uproar where
yesterday there was only whispering; and faces that have
stopped looking, and receding backs, and a decor suddenly
changed by the scene-shifters of tragedies hatched in secret,
grown in shadow, born in my proximity, although, deafened
as I was by other choirs, I would not have heard the sound of
real choirs—choirs with few singers, but those few possessing the
voices of Great Singers. . . .

And so, I "opened my heart" to you—as they say here—
with the help of the wine of that triumphant night; at dawn,
after everyone left, I added a bottle of Armagnac, as we sat
there alone watching the peaks of the Tutelary Volcano turn
blue; *we must have a sort of Chamonix up there, and a skating rink—
skiing is marvellous exercise—and a cable railway to get there, as they
do in Switzerland*; two swings of the hammock and it was three
in the afternoon; thus, as an adolescent, you opened your eyes

in the operating theatre after being relieved of an appendix full of seeds—they said at the time that the appendicitis had been caused by eating guavas, whose pips accumulated in that useless organ, left over from the prehistoric days when men were *vêtus de peaux de bêtes*, like those painted by Cormon, and fed on roots and stones of fruits; so you emerged from the chloroform dream, and that male nurse with the white cap and stethoscope round his neck was leaning over you: *have they taken it out already?*; but the nurse is Peralta in male nurse's clothes—*why?*—; and behind him—to my surprise—is Mr Enoch Crowder, in his round spectacles, with his old puritan's face, but now instead of his frock-coat, he has come dressed in tennis clothes, *here, to the Palace?*, striped flannel trousers, with YALE in red letters on his sweater and his racket in his hand; the United States Ambassador coming into your room like this, without asking for an interview, without a top-hat or a stiff collar; *they aren't trying to annoy you, you idiot; I'm high on aguardiente, remember*; a half-turn, a swing of the hammock and leave me in peace to sleep; but now some words seem to be coming from a long way off, and swelling, getting louder as they approach, talking to me about a battleship; the *Minnesota* is in Puerto Araguato; a great big ship it is too, with its metal tower and its guns turning and taking aim by electricity, and by some strange chance navigating six miles off our coast for several weeks; they tell me (I'm understanding more and more) that they are going to land marines, that they are already landing; *coffee, damn it, coffee! where is the Mayorala?*; the marines, here; that's what they did in Veracruz; what they did in Haiti, hunting down the niggers; and in Nicaragua and in many other places, with bayonets ready for zambos and Latins; intervention, perhaps, as in Cuba with that General Wood, who was a worse thief than the mother who bore him; landing, intervention, General Pershing's "punitive" expedition, the man of *Over There* and *The Star-spangled Banner* in the exhausted Europe of '17, who was made fun of and harassed in Sonora by a few guerrillas with cartridge-belts round their chests; I'm laughing, but it isn't a joke—oh no; Mr Enoch Crowder has come here like this, in tennis clothes, racket and all, because he's

spent two days without once leaving the Country Club,
deliberating in conference with the live wires of the Bank,
Trade and Industry; and it's these sons of bitches who are
asking for the *Minnesota* to come here with her filthy marines;
but the Army, our Army, won't allow such an affront to our
national honour; only the Army happens to have revolted at
the present moment; soldiers have deserted their sentry-boxes
and machine-gun posts, saying that that business yesterday
wasn't their fault; that they only fired because they were
ordered to by their sergeants and lieutenants; and the sergeants
and lieutenants have rebelled against their captains and
generals, who have dug themselves in to the tall building of the
Hotel Waldorf, and go from the bar to the roof and from the
roof to the bar, hoping that the marines will arrive and relieve
them from being besieged by the crowd—the huge crowd
yelling round the building and clamouring for their heads;
the Palace garrison has disappeared; not even a door-keeper
is left, nor a servant, nor a waiter; don't ask for your Ministers;
no one knows where your Ministers are; *the telephone*: the
telephones aren't working; *don't ask for coffee: much better have a
glass of aguardiente,* says Peralta (but why the hell is he dressed
as a male nurse, with that stethoscope, and that thermometer
in the pocket of his overall?); *don't ask for coffee, the Mayorala's
got other things to do*; but yes, now that I consider the question
more thoroughly I agree with the captains and generals; let
the marines land, let them land: we'll arrange about that
afterwards—we'll negotiate, we'll talk—but for the moment,
order, order is what we need. . . .

"*You're crazy*," says the male nurse: "*what these people of the
Bank and Business, and also this Gentleman here, all want, is for you
to go to hell; they've had enough; you've been playing the devil with
their patience for more than twenty years; they don't like you; no one
likes you; if you're still alive it's because everyone thinks you're with
the others in the Waldorf; they can't believe you could possibly be such
a fool as to stay here alone, without companions or guards; it hasn't
entered anyone's head; but when they do find out . . . I don't like to
think what'll happen! . . . So let's bugger off. But—at once!*"

I begin to understand. I get up. I hunt for my slippers.

"*But, fuck it all, I've not resigned! I'm the President!*"

"*You think so?*", says the male nurse. "*Luis Leoncio is already in Nueva Córdoba. A procession of cars has gone to fetch him.*"

"*That cretin, with his Alpha-Omega?*"

"*He's the only man who can clear up the situation,*" says the tennis-player.

"*But . . .*"

"*For the present we're backing him.*"

"*So you're dropping me?*"

"*Our Department of State knows what it's doing.*"

"*How can they take that professor seriously, a man who . . .*"

The tennis-player was showing signs of impatience: "*I've not come here to argue, but to face facts. Doctor Luis Leoncio has the support of the active forces in this country. A lot of young people with democratic ideals are supporting him.*"

"*I see: Belén, the Methodist colleges and the Statue of Liberty.*"

"*Don't waste any more time, damn it: finish dressing!*"

"*Doctor Luis Leoncio has ideas, a plan,*" says the tennis-player.

"*So has The Student,*" I say.

"*But that's a very different matter,*" says the tennis-player, passing his racket from one hand to another.

"*You must know that it was really The Student who did you in,*" says the male nurse. "*The bombs, those macabre jokes and false rumours all came from Alpha-Omega. But the general strike was The Student's doing. A splendid piece of work, by the way. I wouldn't have thought him capable of it.*"

"*And are you going to tell me that all the tradesmen who refused to open their shops were Bolsheviks?*"

"*It was precisely because they were afraid of the Bolsheviks that they didn't open their shops. By joining the stoppage they were protecting their goods. And now they will lay them at the feet of the Caudillo of Nueva Córdoba, defender of order and prosperity, who will try and tame The Student—or something of the sort—and give some legality to his party. Because now there'll be political parties in the country.*"

"*The business men are managing things intelligently,*" said the tennis-player; "*wise men.*"

Coming to my senses, I suddenly say that there's still time to do something: make peace with Hungary, which now has a stable government, restore constitutional guarantees, create a Ministry of Employment, remove press censorship, create a coalition cabinet until the forthcoming elections, to be supervised by a mixed commission, if that seemed suitable.

"*Stop talking rubbish,*" says the male nurse. "*We've come to the crunch now. If we don't clear out quickly, the crowd will soon be here, and you can imagine what that means. They loathe your guts!*"

At that moment a strange figure loomed up in the passage leading to the patio; it was Aunt Jemima, Walter Hoffmann's grandmother, quietly making her way towards the main staircase, carrying on her head, as if it were a coffin, the grandfather clock from the dining-room. "I've been in love with it for years," she said as she passed. Behind her came several shady characters—obviously her great-great-grandsons, carrying trays of silver, decanters and table ornaments taken from the sideboards. This struck me as a final warning:

"*I shall take refuge in the United States Embassy.*"

"*Out of the question!*" says the tennis-player. "*There'd be a riot in front of the building. Demonstrations. Violence. An impossible situation. The only thing I can do is give you shelter in our consulate at Puerto Araguato. There you will be protected by our marines. My government consents to that.*"

"*You'll take me in your car . . .*"

"*I'm sorry, but I can't expose myself to being fired at on the way. The Morejón woodcutters don't understand diplomatic car-plates. And there are said to be armed bands in El Bajío.*"

"*It's only that there are no trains . . . the strike,*" I say, in a voice that trembles because of saliva that refuses to be swallowed.

"*That's not my fault,*" says the tennis-player. Peralta points to his clothes, his cap and stethoscope:

"*I've got an ambulance downstairs. There are no tolls on the road to the Olmedo Colony. And those Germans don't care a fuck for our politics.*"

"*Good luck, Señor President,*" says the tennis-player.

"*Son of a bitch,*" I say under my breath. But he hears me and says in the manner of a comic clergyman:

"*Rahab, the woman of Jericho, was a bitch. And today she's reckoned among our Lord's ancestresses. Try reading the Bible on*

*your way, Señor. It's a most comforting book and full of information.
There's a lot about overturned thrones in it.*" And he picked up his
racket, one of those—I remember—that are carried in a
trapezoid wooden frame, with four screws holding down the
rim of the racket, and took himself off without more ado
(I think he said, "*So long*"), and as casually as if he were
returning to the American Club, with its deep arm-chairs,
Bourbon on the rocks, ticker-tape and central heating.

"*Son of a bitch,*" I say, and say again and again, because I have
no worse insults in my limited English vocabulary. Now I look
towards the gleaming peak of the Tutelary Volcano, no longer
white but a pale orange from the approach of dusk. And I
can't help my expression being saddened by the tender melancholy of departure. But now the Mayorala arrives, eccentrically
attired as a Nazarene Penitent, in a purple tunic, yellow sash,
sandals, a *rebozo* to match the tunic, and carrying a bundle of
clothes.

"She's coming with us," says Peralta. And she explains with
her special combination of mimicry and onomatopeia: "Everyone knows that when I was (gesture of pouting out her breasts
and rounding her hips) . . . you me (a faint whistle, and one
forefinger making a cross with the other) and although I'm
not the same (hands re-modelling a face that was now a little
coarsened) you and I still go on (now she joins her forefingers
and rubs one against the other). And with them being so mad
at me, if they caught me (a whistle accompanied by a hand
clapped to her forehead, and her head falling on her left
shoulder with the mouth open). So that's why I . . ." (loud
whistle and arms imitating the movements of someone running).

"Besides, the Nazarene dress is a splendid idea," says
Peralta. And suddenly I come to myself and remember the
most important thing of all:

"Money! Fuck! Money!"

The Mayorala shows me her bundle of clothes. "The cash is
in here." I open it, to make sure. Yes. Between petticoats and
blouses, there are the 200,000 dollars of my private reserve, in
four bundles of fifty notes each, with portraits of Washington
on them of course.

And now everything seems to speed up. Peralta is running; the Mayorala is running. A trunk appears. Without thinking clearly what I'm doing I start putting things in it. Too many things. The blotting-paper from my writing-table, several medals and decorations, the book of our eleven Constitutions, a photo of Ofelia with Gabriele D'Annunzio, that toy—a lizard made of rope—given me by my mother, that beautiful edition of *Les femmes savantes*, containing the lines which, at this moment of crisis, come absurdly to my memory, enlivened by a glass of rum: "*Guenille si l'on veut, ma guenille m'est chère.*"

"Don't put any more rubbish in the trunk," shouts the Mayorala.

"Two shirts, one pair of pants, that's enough," shouts Peralta.

"Two ties and three vests," shouts the Mayorala.

"And now put this waterproof cape right over yourself. Like the poor when they're ill and go to hospital," says Peralta.

"But quickly, for God's sake, quickly!" yells the Mayorala, her voice echoing through the vastness of the Deserted Palace. And they wrap my head in bandages and strips of sticking-plaster. A little ketchup to look as if I'd bled. And I go downstairs. The first time in more than twenty years that I don't hear cries of "Attention!", that no one is there to salute me. Palomo, the porter's dog, comes and licks your sweaty hands. You'd like to take him with you.

"*Out of the question. No one has ever seen a dog in an ambulance.*"

And you lie on the stretcher for urgent cases, under the smell of macintosh, disguised as a wounded man—carnival is still going on, terrifying carnival, an apocalyptic transformation scene—and during the vicissitudes of the journey, you live through the hazards of the road you are travelling. Out through the back gate of the Palace—former entrance for horse-drawn carriages. Turn to the right. Drive over asphalt. Calle Beltrán: a short stretch of cobblestones. Left: smoothness of asphalt. Calle de los Plateros. Peralta in the driving-seat—a bogus nurse-chauffeur of the Emergency Service—sets the siren going. I'm terrified, thinking we must be attracting attention: but no; it's exactly what we aren't doing. No one looks at the face of the man driving a wailing ambulance. They look at the siren; what's more, anyone who can help by doing so tries to clear the road. Right: more asphalt: the Boulevard del Brasil with its cafés—the *Paris,* the *Tortoni,* the *Delmonico*—sure to be shut because of the strike. Then we drive on and on: there seems to be no traffic on the roads. Peralta doesn't stop at crossroads. And there's a huge rut; there at the corner of the Gallo—the Ministry of Works gave sixty thousand pesos for it to be filled in and the drain put right, but it was never done. I know where we are, and suddenly, for that very reason I feel afraid, terribly afraid. My flesh tightens over my bones; my thighs are trembling; my breathing has become irregular. Why are we driving so slowly? I know why. And now the male nurse with the stethoscope and smoked glasses is braking—his white cap is well pulled down right over his brows. There is a silence which opens my bladder—I can do nothing to stop it.

"*Excuse me: I've got a seriously wounded man here.*" Another silence, worse than the first. And then the Mayorala's voice: "*Please, Captain, let us by. Don't stop us, for his mamma's sake . . . My brother . . . A bullet . . . In front of the Palace.*"

The soldier's voice: "*Did they shoot your cunt of a mother too?*"

"*They shot her . . .* (whistle) *bang! . . . From the balcony. . . . Now* (a long blood-curdling whistle on a downward note) *. . . they're dragging her away. . . . And leaving bits of brains . . .* (a loud slap) *. . . at every corner.*"

Soldier: "*Thank God for that!*"

Peralta: "*May we please go by, Captain?*"

"*Go on!*"

And now the streets are of trodden earth. I seem to feel all through my body the ambulance wheels heeling over, falling, rising, staggering, between pot-holes full of water, whose stench of decay reaches me in my moving cell in spite of the wafts of chloroform pervading it.

"*I ought to have thought about that.*" A little beyond the Italian villas with their nacreous domes, cornucopias, box-hedges and vine arbors—miniature gardens of Aranjuez or Chantilly—we reach the suburbs of the Cerros, Yaguas and Favelas; villages made of cardboard, dung, and tin cans, with paper walls, the tins rusty, cut up with scissors to cover the roofs—dwellings, if they deserve the name, which are ruined, knocked down and demolished by the rains every year, leaving the children paddling about like pigs, in puddles and mud.

"*I should have thought about that. A plan to build houses for poor families. There would still be time . . .*"

The Mayorala's voice: "*The road's clear.*" And the ambulance begins to climb, creaking, bumping, bouncing, turning, twisting but always climbing. I recognize the corners on the road. I know we have already reached the farm of El Rengo, from the smell of the brushwood fire burning esparto grass, something forbidden by law; now we are coming to the Little Spanish Castles, because there is the sound of a plank bridge beneath us. The zone of pine forests is beginning. Our road is edged with mulberry trees, whose shade attracts so many poisonous snakes.

I am so exhausted from fighting my terror that I fall asleep.

I open my eyes. We have passed in front of the Germans' Lutheran Church. I take off my bandages and sticking-plaster. The ambulance doors open and I descend into the square with an air of calm dignity. But although a few people are about, no one looks at me. The Woglindes, Wellgundes and Flosshildes go on with their milking. Too many curtains are drawn across windows. I expect human smiles and all I see is braces drawn tight over backs, and backsides with broad buttocks in leather breeches. Peralta talks to the Pastor:

"The mechanics are on strike. So do what you like. We shan't interfere."

Followed by the Mayorala who has just finished tying up my badly-fastened suitcase with her sash, we go to the little brick station with its weathercock, and imitation stork's nest occupied by a marbled bird lifting up a lobster-red foot. The Little Train is put away in its little hangar. There's enough coal in the tender. And the burnished engine, polished and shining like something just out of a luxury shoe-shop, soon starts puffing out smoke. It is as if I could feel its impatient, vibrating life in the levers throbbing under my hands. All the houses in the Olmedo Colony have shut themselves into a darkness whose aim is to ignore me. I let in the steam: the connecting-rods begin to move. And the Little German Train enters the curving track cut in the flank of the mountain. We pass the pines—leaving their scent behind—and descend steep slopes covered with cactus and agave, where the spikes of the asphodels are buzzing with bees and quivering in the sea breeze; then, from small to large, from grassy filaments to plumes, come the reeds, bamboos, shady banana-trees, with their red fruit tasting of poverty; and then the ochre patches of bare earth—I don't see them, but guess at them from familiarity with the deep ruts in them—before arriving at the sandy plain, where we advance in a straight line as fast as possible, without signals or lights or level-crossing gates, until we stop in the tiny terminus of Puerto Araguato with a tremendous bump owing to tardy braking.

Several marines—white leggings and sweat shirts, rum-drinkers' eyes—are drawn up on the two platforms. I discover that they have already occupied the power-station, the vital points, bars and brothels of the town, after pissing on the Monument to the Heroes of Independence as they passed it. The North American Consul comes up to me, wearing creased trousers and a cowboy shirt of the sort that has little air-holes in the armpits.

"Here I am; I've got the auto outside." And he drives us in a Pathfinder creaking in every joint to the building diplomatically representing his country: a wooden house, with columns and pediment, in a strictly Jeffersonian style, and a North American eagle with a shield on its breast displayed on the balcony.

"You've given me a fat lot of trouble," says the Consul, taking us to the kitchen. "I've got orders to put you on one of our cargo-boats arriving here tomorrow, and send you to Nassau. If you're hungry, there are some packets of cornflakes, tins of Campbell's soup, and pork and beans. There's whisky in that cupboard. Help yourself, Mister President, because we know that if you don't get your booze you very soon go round the bend."

"A little more respect, please," I say in a stern tone.

"We're all equals here," says the Consul, going into an office full of bills and papers.

"The Hermes case, Peralta: I prefer our own."

The walls of the kitchen were decorated with cuttings from *Shadowland* and *Motion Pictures*: Theda Bara in *Cleopatra*: Nazimova in *Salomé*; Dempsey knocking out Georges Carpentier; a scene from *Male and Female* with Thomas Meigham and Gloria Swanson; Babe Ruth hitting a home-run under the welcoming—almost presbyterian—eyes of an umpire dressed in dark blue.

We've eaten something, and are now sitting in the reception-waiting-room-living-room of the house, Peralta the Mayorala and I. After the tension of the last days, and the paroxysms of anxiety of the last few hours, I feel almost serene. My muscles relax. I begin fanning myself with a palm-leaf, rocking myself in what the gringos call a "rocking-chair", and we call, I've no idea why, a Viennese chair—I've never noticed any furniture of this description in Vienna. I look at my secretary:

"For the present, we must concentrate on saving our skins. *Guenille si l'on veut, ma guenille m'est chère.* Now, the sea, Bermuda. And afterwards, Paris. In the end we'll get a bit of rest."

"Yes," replies Peralta.

"Our morning walks. Monsieur Musard's *Bois-Charbons*. *Auxglaces*, the Rue Sainte-Apolline, the Chabanais."

"Yes," replies Peralta.

"Happiness prevails, I see," I say.

"Yes," replies Peralta with a gesture of displeasure and boredom.

"When one's luck is out, even dogs piss on one," says the Mayorala, with her usual philosophy, expressed in proverbs and sayings. And she flings herself down to sleep on a raffia ottoman. Close to the gramophone horn, on an antique corner-cupboard, lies an old Bible, used by the Consul when some sailor who had lost his papers in a drinking-bout could only lay valid claim to having been born in Baltimore or Charleston by swearing with one hand on the Scriptures. Knowing the habits of the members of certain North American sects at moments of crisis, I shut my eyes, opened the book at random and after describing three circles with the forefinger of my right hand, I let it fall on a page: *"Deliver me out of the mire, and let me not sink; let me be delivered from them that hate me, and out of the deep waters. Let not the waterflood overflow me; neither let the deep swallow me up, and let not the pit shut her mouth on me."* (Psalm 69) I tried again: *"Cast me not off in the time of old age; forsake me not when my strength faileth. For mine enemies speak against me; and they that lay wait for my soul take counsel together."* (Psalm 71) A third time (Jeremiah 12): *"I have forsaken mine house, I have left mine heritage."* "Fuck the book!" I exclaimed, shutting it so violently that a cloud of dust came out of the binding. And I lounged in the Viennese chair, which was ornamented with a blue ribbon passed through the holes in the wicker-work, and fell into a drowsy state not far from actual sleep. Confused noises. Reality becomes blurred and transformed into incoherent images. I'm asleep.

But I can't have slept long because very soon—I think—a hand shook the rocking-chair violently to waken me.

"Peralta," I said, "Peralta."

"No use calling him," said the Consul. "He's just decamped."

"It's true," said the Mayorala.

And I learned, in a state of such astonishment that I couldn't take in everything I was being told, that dozens of automobiles displaying the greenish-white emblems of Alpha-Omega were driving round the town, and that one of them—which appeared to be a grey Chevrolet—had come to fetch my Secretary.

"They'll kill him!" I cried.

"I don't think so."

"But—this is insane! Didn't he resist? He was armed!"

The Consul looked at me sarcastically.

"They were some charming young men wearing greenish-white armlets and a badge—*Alpha* in silvery metal—on their lapels. They embraced Doctor Peralta, who seemed very pleased, and set off for the capital laughing and joking."

"And Peralta didn't explain anything? Didn't he leave me any message?"

"Yes: that I was to tell you he was sorry, but his Country came first."

"It's true!" shouted the Mayorala, seeing my stupefied expression, as if it was necessary to shout or I wouldn't understand.

"*Tu quoque, fili mi . . .*"

"What *tu quoque*, and what the hell," said the gringo. "He was doing the dirty on you, that's all. You don't need Latin to see that. It's just politics, and happens everywhere,"

"I thought the bastard was a traitor," muttered the Mayorala. "My aunt Candelaria, who knows a lot, saw it in the snails and by breathing into a plate of flour. And now I'm beginning to believe that those bombs that went off in the Palace were brought by him in that French case of flasks. It was the only thing that wasn't searched at the door."

And there was the Hermes case, open, with its ten bottle-tops in two rows of five. We took out the pigskin-covered flasks. That smell—it seems to me, but I'm not sure—is bitter almonds: the same smell left by the explosion.

"Maybe, maybe not," said the Consul. "It's pretty like the smell of old leather which has had a lot of rum spilled on it."

"The snails don't lie," murmured the Mayorala.

"Maybe yes, maybe not," repeated the Yankee.

Burdened by an enormous feeling of sadness, as of a father spat on, or a beaten cuckold, or King Lear thrown out by his daughters, I hugged my dear Elmira: "You're the only one I've got left."

"Better look out of the window," said the Consul, "but be careful you're not seen."

18

. . . it sometimes happens that after listening to a
speech whose meaning we have perfectly understood,
we cannot say in what language it was uttered.

DESCARTES

Outside, beyond the guard of eight marines with rifles sloped
from hip to shoulder, a slow and silent procession of people
were passing and repassing, but always looking towards the
house. They knew I was there, and they went on walking
round and round, like students on a Sunday walk, hoping that
I would look out of a window, open a door, or make my
presence shown somehow or other.

"In the capital, they're looting the Ministers' houses,
hunting out police and informers, carrying off spies, burning
secret archives. The people have opened the prisons and set
free all political prisoners."

"The end of the world," said the Mayorala, looking panic-
stricken.

"And when will they get me?" I said, with a forced smile.

"I don't think they'll jump over the wall," said the Yankee.
"And they won't do that because The Student—the chap who
started the strike—has distributed an intelligent manifesto to
the public. Read that . . ."

But my hands were trembling too much, and my spectacles
were misted with sweat.

"Better tell me."

"Well, to sum it up: he says they mustn't provoke our
soldiers (no throwing stones or bottles, nor even insulting
them); they mustn't attack our diplomatic representatives, nor
our compatriots; in fact, nothing that could justify a major
military action on our part. Up till now, there's been no

intervention, only a *landing*. Question of subtle differences of
meaning—*nuances* as the French say. And The Student under-
stands nuances. He says that the pleasure of hanging you from
a telegraph pole isn't worth the risk of an *intervention*, which
might very well turn into *occupation*."

"As in Haiti," I said.

"Exactly. That's what The Student doesn't want. He's
intelligent, that boy!"

And I was thinking of the vertiginous transformation of
roles that had taken place in the course of a few hours in the
scenario of the revolt. Now it was The Student who had in a
flash become the custodian of my threatened existence. And,
while still remaining hidden, without replying to the calls
from Alpha-Omega, who offered him guarantees and invited
him to collaborate in the National Coalition Government
which Luis Leoncio Martínez was setting up in the Palace,
with the advice of Enoch Crowder and the help of those of the
military leaders not implicated in the shooting of the day
before yesterday, and one or two sergeants promoted to
colonels, he remained faithful to his underground work as
Invisible Man, and could still with one word control those who
had collected in front of the Eagle-with-a-shield-on-its-Breast,
and were beginning—by ones, twos and threes—to join their
voices in a chorus of insults.

"So long as they don't go further than shouting," says the
Consul. But I'm beginning to be afraid that they will in fact
go further than shouting. And I suddenly see myself in a
looking-glass covered in fly-shit, supported on a rickety bracket
and covering one wall of the office; I'm a pitiful sight; the
dressing-gown I was wearing when I left the Palace is filthy;
my shirt from New and Lingwood in London is filthy and
crumpled from so much coming and going, all the starch of its
collar melted by the sweat of fear; my pearl-grey tie, very
suitable to the Head of State, is stained with the saliva that has
trickled from my mouth during my recent sleep. And my
striped trousers, suddenly detached from a stomach dwindled
in size in the last few hours, are slipping down over my hips,
giving me the look of the funny man in an English music hall.

And the Mayorala is replying with tremendously obscene gestures, illustrating a large repertory of internal imprecations, to those people shouting outside. And all at once I'm terrified. "Why don't you take me on board the *Minnesota*?" I entreat.

"You're just talking big," says the Yankee, in an unexpectedly joking tone, very unsuitable (truth to tell) to a diplomatic official. "I'm merely a simple Consul, who believes he's doing the correct thing in giving you shelter. If tomorrow it suits my people to say I've made a mistake, I shall accept that I've made a mistake, inform the press that I've made a mistake and say I'm sorry I made a mistake; then they'll send me somewhere else, and no one will be any the wiser. On board the *Minnesota*, on the other hand, you would be the official protégé of our Great American Democracy" (he made a comic military salute), "which can't at a moment like this figure publicly as protecting the 'Butcher of Nueva Córdoba', who has once more been appearing from coast to coast in Randolph Hearst's chain of periodicals, along with Monsieur Garcin's photos and everything that cooked your goose when they appeared in Paris. Besides, we don't know how long the *Minnesota* will remain in these waters. Maybe a week; maybe a month; maybe years: just look at Haiti, where from *landing* to *intervention* and from *intervention* to *occupation*—*des nuances, des nuances, des nuances toujours*—one thing followed another. Don't get into a stew. Keep calm. I'll have you out of danger by tomorrow. Besides, I can't do anything else: I'm carrying out instructions."

I'm feeling swindled, made fun of, tricked.

"And I've always got on so well with all of you. You're indebted to me for so many favours!"

The Consul is smiling behind his tortoiseshell-rimmed spectacles: "And without that, how do you suppose you'd have kept in power so long? Favours indeed? Now we shall receive them from the professor of theosophy."

"And why not from The Student while we're about it?" I said, to mortify him.

"That's difficult to bring off. He's a new species of man even within his species. A lot of his sort are appearing on the continent, although your generals and doctors try to ignore them."

"They loathe you North Americans."

"That can't be helped: our Bibles and their *Kapital* are hopelessly incompatible."

The row outside intensified. The Mayorala multiplied her dumb-show gestures in response to those who were insulting me. It would be easy enough to break through the guard of marines; easy enough to jump over the wall . . .

"Anyhow, I should be better off on board the *Minnesota*," I insisted.

"I don't think so," said the Yankee. And speaking between little hiccoughs of suppressed laughter he said:

"You've forgotten Amendment Eighteen to the North American Constitution. Ever since 1919—I'm quoting from memory—'the manufacture and consumption (I said: *consumption*) of all forms of alcoholic drink in the entire territory of the United States is forbidden'. The *Minnesota* is an integral part, in juridical and military terms, of the United States. All right for a man who drinks only ginger ale and Coca-Cola. But one doesn't wake up with trembling hands on drinks like those . . ."

"But aren't we on United States territory here too?" I said, pointing to the case left by Peralta, so it happened, just beneath an orographic and hydrographic map of the country.

"I can't prevent an invalid from bringing his medicines along. And as I've been *taken in*, over this whole affair, I can very well believe that this is chest mixture or Scott's Emulsion. On the *Minnesota* they'd throw *that* into the sea, in strict observance of Amendment Eighteen of our Constitution—although left to himself the captain might be more of a drunk than the mother who bore him."

"They seem to be going away," said the Mayorala, with her nose glued to the shutters. I looked out: as if impelled by some event, people were making off in groups towards the Customs house, where some sort of movement of lorries and goods' trucks was going on.

"*The strike is over*," I announced, deepening my voice without noticing it. "*The situation has been normalized.*"

"*There is order throughout the country,*" said the Consul, imitating me in a comic manner. And regaining his good humour: "Come to Captain Nemo's cabin. You'll be better off there."

And letting me out of the house by a passage at the back, he took me to a long outhouse with its doors hanging from the hinges, and shut in by the water of the bay, which reached under cover as far as the extremity of a floor of wooden planks, smelling of the green slime of winkles, clams in shadow, stranded jellyfish and rotting seaweed: with that penetrating odour of fermenting sourness, of sex and moss, dried fish-scales, amber and saturated wood which is the smell of the sea at its work of destruction—a smell reminiscent of that of a wine-press sleeping under its floor of grapes and nightly distilling its after-taste of must. This was the boathouse where had been kept, only a short while ago, the elegant, light, pointed boats of the members of a Yacht Club that had come down in the world through the collapse of my currency. The boats themselves had vanished and what in fact remained—the Consul's remarks had prepared me for this—indefinably reminded me by their Victorian style, like a copper-plate engraving, a *ciné Lumière* and a junk shop at the same time, of the illustrations to *Twenty Thousand Leagues under the Sea* in the Hetzel edition, with its title stamped in gilt on raspberry-coloured boards. Old arm-chairs, furniture suitable to Mr Pickwick, with hunting-horns hanging on the walls; etchings so encroached upon by funguses and saltpetre that their subject had disappeared beneath fungus and saltpetre, and fungus and saltpetre had become the only subject. And, looking at these unexpected objects filling the place—feeling somewhat strengthened personally by the unhoped-for disappearance of the people who had been insulting me a few minutes ago, and my legs cured of their trembling by the drinks I had swallowed—I am surprised by the value certain elements in my surroundings have suddenly acquired, by the new significance objects now possess, and by the way time is lengthened and expanded by immediate danger of death. An hour suddenly seems to last for two hours; each movement becomes a member of a hierarchy of successive movements, as in a military exercise; the sun moves more slowly or more quickly; a vast space yawns between ten o'clock and eleven; night is so far away that its arrival might perhaps be indefinitely delayed; the advance of an insect over the cover of that book acquires enormous importance; the spiders' webs spread themselves out into works of art from the Sistine Chapel; the indifference of the seagulls, busy over their fishing as usual on a day like this, seems to me nothing short of indecent; the bell tolling once more from the hermitage in the mountains sounds disrespectful; I am deafened by the dripping of a tap, with its obsessional "never more, never more, never more". Yet, at the same time, this fantastic capacity to give sustained, acute, excessive attention to the appearances of things, to what is revealed, or grows bigger without changing shape, is as if contemplation were equivalent to clutching something, to saying: "I see, therefore I am". And since "I see" will have greater significance when I do see more, I am establishing the permanence of existence both within and outside myself.

Now the Consul is showing me a rare collection of root-sculptures, sculpture-roots, root-forms, root-objects—baroque roots or roots that are austere in their smoothness; complicated, intricate or nobly geometrical; at times dancing, at times static, or totemic, or sexual, something between an animal and a theorem, a play of knots, a play of asymmetry, now alive, now fossilized—which the Yankee tells me he has collected on numerous expeditions along the shores of the Continent. Roots torn up from remote soil, dragged along, cast up, and again transported by rivers in spate; roots sculptured by the water, hurled about, knocked over, polished, burnished, silvered, denuded of their silver, until from so many journeys, falls, collisions with rocks, battles with other pieces of wood on the move, they have finally lost their vegetable morphology, become separated from the tree-mother, the genealogical tree, and acquired breast-like roundnesses, polyhedric arms, boars' heads or idols' faces, teeth, claws, tentacles, penises and crowns, or are intimately connected in obscene imbrications, before being stranded, after a journey lasting centuries, on some beach forgotten by maps. That huge mandragora with its fierce thorns had been found by the Consul at the mouth of the Bio-Bio, close to the jagged rocks of Con-Con, rocking in a hammock of black waters. That other mandragora, contorted and acrobatic, with its fungus-hat and bulging eyes—rather like the "root of life" which certain Asiatic peoples put in flasks of aguardiente—had been found near Tucupita in the estuary of the Orinoco. Others came from the island of Nervis, from Aruba, from the rocks like basalt menhirs that rise amid thunderous marine gorges near Valparaiso. And it was enough to mention the name of a port to the collector for him to pass from the root found there to the invocation, evocation, presentation of images brought to life by the syllables making up its name, or the proliferative activity of the letters—so he said—a process such as was foreshadowed in the Hebrew Cabbala. And merely by pronouncing the word Valparaiso there were plateaux of jurel-fish lying on seaweed, a display of fruit in the church porch, the windows of inns showing the whole counter covered in apocalyptic spider-crabs from Tierra del Fuego; and there were the German beer-shops in the main street, where reddish-black sausages spotted with bacon-fat lay beside warm strudels powdered with sugar; and there were the enormous public lifts, tirelessly moving parallel to each other, with orchestras of blind men playing polkas in the tunnels by which you reached them; and there were the pawnshops, with a broad-buckled belt, a reliquary made of shells, a scalpel with a jagged edge, a negro figure from Easter Island, slippers embroidered with *Souv* (for the left foot) and *Enir* (for the right) which, when put endways on to the passer-by, illustrated with amazing eloquence Kant's Paradox of the Looking-glass.

This other root—known as Leap-frog—looking like a terrified flying lemur because it is running in the uttermost panic without moving, recalls Rio de Janeiro. The Itamaraty district, amongst municipal buildings crowded with acromegalic statues (always one and a half times or two and three quarters times as large as the real figure of the hero or important figure they are supposed to immortalize) has shops full of embalmed animals: boas gazing through glass marbles, armadillos, ounces, herons, monkeys, and even dusty, saddled horses, which appear to be standing waiting on their green wooden pedestals for a rider who never arrives—who is dead perhaps and has long been lying under a flamboyant Portuguese tomb. This other root, a sort of gnome whose stomach-head swings between feeble limbs—he is called "Humpty-Dumpty"—comes from Port-au-Prince, where in the district of La Frontière between taverns built of planks and musty Voodoo charms, naked negresses lie in woven hammocks awaiting their visitors with supreme haughtiness, as if lost in their own thoughts, far away, and unconsciously imitating with a hand lying softly open over their stiff pubic curls the gesture of Manet's *Olympia*.

Next the Consul shows me "Erasmus of Rotterdam", a Veracruzan root in the style of Holbein and looking very much like a pensive humanist; "Pichrochole" and "Ragamuffin", bamboo roots, with the aggressive appearance of German mercenaries, and bristling with nails; "Chimera", with a long beak and battlemented crest; "Kikimora", dishevelled and spurred, and those three shoots from a single stem known as the "Pieds-Nickelés" (familiar to me because I had subscribed for years to the Parisian paper *L'Epatant*—a fact not generally known); and a little further back a Romanesque monstrosity of a Cuban mangrove, called the "Spanish Heretic", next to the liana ballerina "Anna Pavlova"; and the "Cyclops", who, with his red stone buried in his forehead, seems to be watching over a wild world arranged on brackets, wherein live the "Hydra of Larna", "Rackham's Witch", riding on a broomstick which is part of herself, "The Silent Woman", seemingly cut from basalt of vegetable origin and (without direct allusion to feminine forms) a figure of curves and turgidity, of superimposed roundnesses, of flexions and hollows, arousing unambiguous recollections in the hands raised to feel them.

The truth was that because of the eccentricity of his culture and his understanding of languages—unusual in a North American—the Consul was beginning to figure as a dream element in the real daytime nightmare now being experienced by eyes that were all too wide open—as I descended into the depths of terror with the help of alcohol; although I had hardly emerged from the vapour of one or two drinks when the sweat of anxiety broke out on the nape of my neck, my forehead, in my grey hairs, over a ground-bass of hammering heart-beats so violent that I thought they were in the armchair where I was sitting. And now the Yankee is sitting in front of a harmonium in the corner, pulling out three stops, pressing down the pedals, and he begins playing something bearing a relation to the music that invaded my country many years ago, although it's more angular and full of contrasts and accents of course than such tunes as *Whispering*, or *Three o'clock in the morning*, so often heard recently in the capital. With his fingers still restlessly moving, marking time with his head and releasing the notes with the casual automatism of popular music:

"I'm a southerner . . . New Orleans. White enough to pass as a white man, although my hair—well, my hair would be too frizzy if it weren't for the pomades they make to deal with that. (*B flat*, damn you!) I've 'crossed the line' as we say there, although in *sentimental* matters, as you might call them, I only get on well with darkies. That way I take after my great-uncle Gottschalk, a musician—you wouldn't know him—who though preferred to Chopin by Théophile Gautier, adored by the same Lamartinian and philharmonic nymphs who went to bed with Franz Liszt, celebrated in Europe, favoured by royalty, friend of the Queen of Spain, ten times decorated—yet suddenly left all this (public, palaces, coaches, lackeys) to respond to the imperious, urgent call of negresses and mulattos waiting in the Tropics to reclaim from him what was theirs by temporary right of conquest. And he followed them to Cuba, Puerto Rico, all the Antilles, rejuvenated, adventurous, liberated from protocol and honours, restored to the billing and cooing of early days, to his adolescent appetite, finally going to die in Brazil, where the Sacred Places of his peregrination also abounded—and how! '*Et les servantes de ta mère, grandes filles luisantes, remuaient leurs jambes chaudes près de toi qui tremblait . . . sa bouche avait le goût des pommes-roses, dans la rivière, avant midi.*'" (I don't know who wrote what he had just recited, but I do remember, yes, I remember that when my daughter Ofelia was learning the piano she played some charming creole dances by that same Moreau Gottschalk, and that I was told how he once let loose on Havana a symphony he had written, including thunderous African drums among its instruments.)

The Consul goes on: "He was a friend, a very great friend of the amazing W. C. Handy, who wrote this *Memphis Blues* I'm playing now." From there he passes to the *St Louis Blues* by the same Handy, which has the effect of rousing the Mayorala and starting her off dancing—and probably very well, because she suits her steps and swaggering movements magnificently to the rhythms of music quite new to her.

"It's that they've got it in their blood," says the southerner. I look at his hands moving over the keys: it's a sort of dialogue —sometimes a battle—opposition and agreement between the female hand (the right) and the male hand (the left) which combine, complement one another, respond, but in a synchronization that is situated both within and outside the rhythm. The Mayorala, as though under the spell of a novelty that she is absorbing through her skin, sits herself down on the harmonium stool making sexy, enveloping and brazen movements with her shoulders, with one buttock unsupported because there isn't room for both in the space left by the Consul. He forgets his keys and presses his face to Elmira's neck, while she laughs as though being tickled, letting herself be sniffed with the delight of a Christian penetrating the perfumed ambit left by a censer.

Guidé par ton odeur vers de charmants climats
Je vois un port rempli de voilures et de mâts

comes from the Consul.

"Leave Baudelaire alone!" I cry, jealous at this incursion into my own territory, first ploughed and tilled by me more than twenty years ago, and always yielding to my desires ever since, and which now that I had lost everything was all that I had left, the only plot ruled over by me in a country that was mine yesterday, mine from North to South, from Ocean to Ocean, and now reduced to a wretched shed made of rotten planks, filled with dead roots, a beggarly landing-stage, where I must wait for tomorrow's launch—how far away, remote, unattainable that *tomorrow* seemed!—fated to be smuggled out

of here like contraband goods, like a dead man's coffin in a
rich hospital, from here where I had been the master of men,
destinies and property. Hauling her up by one arm, I drag
the Mayorala from where her sexual behaviour is exceeding
what is admissible, and push her into an armchair in the
corner of the room.

"That's better," says the gringo laughing, "because *that* is
what sunk me in my career." This word *career*—diplomacy
presumably—in the other man's mouth, in view of who he is
and where he is, is associated in my mind with the epithet of
"great nonsense" given by Don Quixote to a chivalrous
romance badly represented by the figures in an altarpiece.
For every Latin American of my generation, a *career* is a
sinecure involving little work and much pleasure, in embassies
surrounded by scenes from grand opera, Italian marbles and
the lights of Versailles, with violins on the platform, waltzers
in braided uniforms and low-cut dresses, solemn ushers,
chamberlains in knee-breeches, intrigues, soirées, love affairs,
alcoves, romance, the manners of the Marqués de Bradomín
and the wit of Talleyrand, prodigies of tact and "savoir vivre",
much too remote generally from the notions of our own people
who never succeeded in absorbing the rules of etiquette, and
who—through not asking, and not taking advice—committed
errors such as (it happened in my Palace) arranging for the
Rondo alla turca to be played when Abdul-Amid's Ambassador
was presenting his credentials, or Huerta's *Hymn of Riego* for one
of Alfonso XIII's Ministers.

"Everything went well with me," went on the southerner,
"until they found out in Paris that I went too often to a
Martiniquan dance-hall in the Rue Blomet. Since then, I have
only filled brilliant posts in North American diplomacy.
Consul in Aracajú, in Antigua, in Guanta, in Mollendo, in
Jacmel, and even in Manta, opposite the beaches of which
sharks appear at noon every day with a punctuality only
comparable to that of the Apostles in Strasbourg cathedral.
And now I am here, which is the devil's own hide-out. And
it's because they knew" (he was looking at the Mayorala)
"that I . . . well, you and I understand one another." He

played an arpeggio. "If I were to show myself as I now am at my birthplace I should be lynched by the cowled members of the Ku-Klux-Klan; chaps with white souls, and white robes, with that peculiar whiteness, very much ours, which was also Benjamin Franklin's, according to whom the negro was 'the animal who ate most and produced least'; the whiteness of Mount Vernon, where a slave-owner used to philosophize about the equality of men before God; the whiteness of our Capitol, the temple where the hymn of the Gettysburg Address is sung—'government of the people, by the people and for the people'—with a chorus of negro street-sweepers, boot-blacks, ash-can emptiers and lavatory attendants; whiteness of our most illustrious White House, where the roundabout of uniforms, frock-coats and top-hats is organized, which in this Latin America of ours, brings thieves and sons of bitches to the fore—present company not excepted—with each turn of the handle."

I remarked to the Consul that the epithet Son of a Bitch was rather strong in tone for someone who barely forty-eight hours ago was Head of the State of a free and sovereign nation, which, as to heroic antecedents, great men, history, etc., etc.

"If my tongue was loosened, it was the fault of Santa Inés," said the Consul, filling my glass. "I had no desire to be offensive. Besides . . ."

"Look, look!" said the Mayorala in a tone that boded no good, inviting us by gestures to go close to a small window with broken panes giving on to the bay.

"Yes," said the gringo, "something is going on there on the wharf." He opened the exit hatches of the—hitherto non-existent—racing launches. Over there, towards the end of the quay used by sugar-boats, something strange was undoubtedly happening. A crowd had collected round one or two lorries—the same they had seen a little time ago, which were loaded with enormous objects, upright or horizontal, a bazaar of shapes laid crossways and in disorder, which . . .

"Take the binoculars," said the Consul to me. I looked. Singing and dancing tipsily, people were lowering from lorries and throwing into the sea with roars of laughter and shouts, busts and heads and statues of me, which had years ago been officially set up in schools, colleges, town halls, public offices, town and village squares, or one-horse dumps, where they had often kept company with some Lourdes Grotto or rusticized niche full of candles and tapers always kept lit in honour of our Divine Shepherdess. And there were marble figures, the work of local sculptors or pupils of the School of Fine Arts; and there were bronze busts, cast in Italy in the same foundry where Aldo Nardini's gigantic Republic had seen the light; standing statues—the full figure—in tail-coat with crosses and ribbon in relief, as General of the armies (with such an exaggerated kepi that my enemies used to say there was "a peak in advance and a peak in retreat"), and as Doctor Honoris Causa of the University of San Lucas (this had been in 1909) in gown and cap with a tassel falling over the left shoulder, as a Roman patrician, as a tribune making some sort of signal with his arm (inspired to some extent by the statue of Gambetta in Paris), as a thoughtful paterfamilias; a stern Mentor, as Cincinnatus crowned with laurels—now all these were lying prostrate, carried on stretchers, loaded on to carts and barrows, drawn by oxen, dragged along and thrown into the water, one after another, with crowbars and the rhythmic shoving of men and women together: "one . . . two . . . threeeee." Finally my equestrian statue appeared—the one I used to see every day from the Palace balconies—lying on a railway truck, but now without its rider, because the rider had been torn down on the night of my flight, leaving only the bronze horse. And the Horse, hoisted to an erect position by a crane and deprived of Him who used to control his bit from above, rose for a moment in one final heroic rearing movement before plunging into a sheet of foam.

"*Memento homo,*" I said, leaving the rest unsaid, because the classical phrase had suddenly been supplanted in my mind by the recollection of a cruel joke The Student had made at my expense.

"Don't make fun of the text of the Requiem," said the Consul. "Now those statues of yours are resting at the bottom of the sea; they'll turn green with saltpetre, corals will cling to them, and sand cover them. And in the year 2500 or 3000 a dredger's scoop will come across them and bring them to light again. And people will ask, in the tone of Arvers' sonnet: 'And who was this man?' and very likely no one will be able to answer. It will happen just as it did to the Roman sculptures of the worst period that one sees in so many museums: all that's known about them is that they represent *A Gladiator*, *A Patrician* or *A Centurion*. The names are lost. In your case they'll say: 'Bust, or statue, of *A Dictator*. There have been so many and there still will be in this hemisphere that his name isn't important.'" (He picked up a book lying on a table.) "Do you figure in *Pequeño Larousse?* No? ... Well then, that's the end of you."

And that afternoon I wept. I wept because a dictionary— "*Je sême à tout vent*"—was unaware of my existence.

SEVEN

And deciding not to seek more knowledge than what I
could find in myself . . .

DESCARTES

19

Seignorial and harmonious, solidly established within the circle of architectural blocks that surrounded the triumphal square—as if armoured against some attack from outside by a thick patina, growing darker every year, and variegated by mouldings and reliefs—the house in the Rue de Tilsitt received him in the lap of her porch protected by high black grilles, just as a mountain inn receives the alpinist who has lost his way and knocks at the door after a hallucinatory journey between avalanches and precipices. It was five o'clock in the morning. Using his private key so as not to wake Sylvestre, the Head of State entered the hall and turned on the light. Behind him came the Mayorala, who had been shivering and coughing all the way from the Gare Saint-Lazare, in spite of the moth-eaten fur-lined coat she had bought in Bermuda; she complained of fainting-fits, a cold on her chest and aching bones, and asked for rum, a bed and some balsam of Tolu.

"Give her whatever Santa Inés is left and take her up the back stairs to one of the rooms in the attic," said the *Ex* (he called himself the *Ex* now, with irritable irony) to the Cholo Mendoza, who arrived with the luggage. Alone at last, he looked round, noticing changes in decoration and furniture. Where he had expected to find the mahogany table with Chinese vases on it, the marble flower in whose corolla visiting-cards used to be left, the water-nymph swathed in her hair who had as long as he could remember stood in front of crimson velvet hangings covered in daggers and swords, he now found himself faced by the nudity of walls painted a pale colour and with no decoration beside a few plaster arabesques, which with much thought might be seen as a very stylized representation of curving waves. As for the furniture, there was a long bench with cushions of a fiery colour which was perhaps the shade known as "tango", and standing on narrow pedestals were glass spheres, prisms, and rhombs, enclosing electric light bulbs.

"It's not ugly; but what was here before was more distinguished-looking, more in keeping with the house," reflected the *Ex*.

He went up to the first floor, delightedly sniffing the aroma of the polished walnut stairs, whose very permanence helped to annihilate the long, infinitely long time that had passed. The pale yellow light of the rising sun was already beginning to appear through the drawing-room curtains. The President went to one of the windows and parted the brocade to look out into the Place de la Concorde. There, as magnificent and regal as ever, stood the Arc de Triomphe, with its open-mouthed Marseillaise, its vociferous Tyrtaeus in armour, and the old warrior in a helmet, followed by the boy hero with his little balls exposed to view. There, for all time, was represented the genius of Cartesian France, the only country capable of having created the anti-Cartesian world, imagined, given life, raised up and then broken by an improbable Corsican, a portentous foreigner, sexually bewitched by a mulatto from Martinique, who had lost his general's hat in a Muscovite fire, after his armies, diluted with Poles and Mamelukes, had been thrashed by the guerilla troops of the Cura Merino and the indomitable Juan Martín. But behind the man looking at this monument were some pictures which might have represented the spirit of Cartesian France more completely. He turned on the light and went up to them. And what met his eyes was so unexpected, so absurd and so inconceivable that he sank into a chair, stupefied but trying to understand.

Instead of Jean-Paul Laurens' Merovingian Saint Radegonde with her pilgrims from Jerusalem, there now stood three

persons, if persons they could be called, their perfectly flat
anatomy reduced to geometric planes, whose faces—assuming
they were faces—were covered with masks. One of them wore
a monk's hood and carried a musical score in his hand; the
middle one, in a clown's hat, was blowing on something like a
clarinet; the third, in harlequin checks, had a mandoline or
guitar or lute, or heaven knows what, slung round his middle.
And these three persons—if they really were persons—were
there, motionless and grotesque, like creatures in a nightmare,
gazing out—if that was what they were doing—with the air of
people who are annoyed by the presence of an intruder.
"What are you doing here?" they seemed to be saying. "What
are you doing here?"

But this wasn't all: on the other wall instead of Elstir's
delicate seascape there was something indescribable: a con-
junction of lines—horizontal, vertical and diagonal, in the
colours of earth and sand—on which had been stuck a piece cut
out of a newspaper (*Le Matin*), which the *Ex* tried to remove
with his thumbnail, but without success, as the varnish resisted
his efforts. Opposite, where Dumont's *Cardinals at Supper* used
to hang, there was now something completely meaningless,
which might perhaps be a pattern-book of Ripolin paints,
because it consisted of white, red and green rectangles and
circles, edged with thick black outlines. To the side, the place
of Chocarne-Moreau's *Little Chimney-sweep* had been taken by a
kind of crooked, hunch-backed, bandy Eiffel Tower, apparently
broken down the middle by a titanic sledge-hammer fallen
from the sky. Over there, between the two doors, some women
—women?—whose legs and arms were made of something like
sections of central-heating tubing. Where I had placed Bérard's
Fashionable Reception, with its marvels of lace, décolletages and
figures silhouetted against the light, I was faced with an indescribable galimatias which, to crown all, displayed in clear
round letters the title: *Cacodylate Eye*. And there on a revolving
pedestal of green marble, stood a marble form, a formless
form, without discernible meaning or purpose, with one
ball—two—in its lower part, and a longer object above,
which—forgive me the shocking idea—could only be taken

for a not very realistic representation, much exaggerated in its proportions—and obscene of course—of what every virile male has where he has to have it.

"But what the hell is all this?"

"It's modern art, Señor President," murmured the Cholo Mendoza softly; he had just left the Mayorala upstairs, wrapped in blankets, prostrate under a feather eiderdown.

And now the *Ex* hurried from room to room, finding everywhere the same pictorial transmutations, the same disasters: crazy, absurd, esoteric pictures, without any historical or legendary significance, without subject or message, dishes of fruit that weren't dishes of fruit, houses looking like polyhedrons, faces with a set-square for a nose, women with their tits out of place—one up, one down—or with one pupil on their temple, and further on, so confused that it looked as if they must be fornicating, two fractured anatomies entangled in their own outlines, Lesbian perhaps, although to paint two people doing *that* (and he had a good collection of pornographic plates locked away) one needed skill in draughtsmanship, knowledge of perspective, and art in portraying entwined limbs, which these failed artists known as "modern" were very far from possessing, because they were incapable of drawing a nude perfectly, of planting a young Spartan in Thermopylae, of making a horse cantering that looked at all like a horse, of decorating—one may as well say at once—the ceilings of the Paris Opera House or of creating the illusion of a battle with Detaille's epic brio.

"I shall give orders for all this filth to be taken down!" cried the master of the house, suddenly becoming the Master of the House and seizing hold of the picture of the *Cacodylate Eye.*

"What d'you think of it?" said Ofelia, who had just come into the room dressed in a dark blue tailor-made, her hair rather wild, her mascara smudged, and very obviously under the influence of drink.

"My dear girl!" said the Head of State, crushing her in his arms so suddenly and fondly that his voice ended in a sob. "My girl! My own flesh and blood!"

"Darling little papa!" she said, weeping also.

"So sexy and so lovely!"

"And you, so strong and splendid!"

"Come and sit beside me . . . I've got so much to talk to you about . . . I've so much to tell you . . ."

"It's only that . . ." And over Ofelia's shoulder, on which an orchid smelling of tobacco had finally finished fading, the *Ex* saw appearing, like the grotesque figures in a Flemish kermess, dishevelled, painted faces, faces that had been up all night and were certainly drunk.

"Some friends of mine . . . they shut the dance hall where we were having supper . . . We've come to go on with the party." People, more people; unbuttoned, ungainly, slovenly people; rude, disrespectful, impudent people; people who made themselves at home—more than at home: as if in a brothel— sitting on the floor, fetching bottles from the pantry, rolling back the carpet so as to be able to dance on the waxed wooden boards, regardless of the harm they might do. Women with their skirts above their knees, with their hair in a fringe which was the mark of a whore *over there*; young pederasts, with check shirts that looked as if made out of cook's aprons. And now the gramophone: "*Yes, we have no bananas*" (he had already endured this horror on board the boat throughout the whole Atlantic crossing), "*we have no bananas today*". Ofelia was laughing with her friends, went away, turned, took records from the book-case, came back with more drink, filled glasses, wound up the gramophone, and as the *Ex* sat himself down resignedly on a divan, there was a dialogue of truncated scrappy sentences, never answered, and remarks that were left incompletely expressed between turns round the room: Ofelia hadn't gone to the Gare Saint-Lazare because the marconigram announcing his arrival had arrived yesterday afternoon when she was at a vernissage; from there they'd gone to celebrate and it wasn't till now that she was given it by the concierge, who had only just got up: "But now we'll really be happy; you mustn't go back to that country of savages." (*St Louis Blues* was starting on the gramophone, bringing painful memories: it was what the Consul had played that afternoon. . . .)

"Listen: I've brought the Mayorala."

"And where is she?"

"Asleep upstairs."

"Frankly, I wouldn't have brought her,"

"She was the only person who didn't betray me *over there* . . . why, even Peralta!"

"I always felt in my bones that he was a skunk."

"Worse than that: a pocket Machiavelli."

"Not that even: but Machiavelli's pocket perhaps." (Again: *Yes, we have no bananas.*) "I wouldn't have brought the Mayorala: I can't imagine her in Paris: she'll be one more responsibility."

"We must talk about that, we've got lots to talk about."

"Tomorrow, tomorrow, tomorrow."

"But it already is *tomorrow*—it's day already." (*St Louis Blues* again.)

"I say, are you going to leave all that filthy rubbish on the walls?"

"Oh, don't be such a back number, my old darling; this is the art of today; you'll soon get used to it."

"And what about my Jean-Paul Laurens, my *Wolf of Gubbio*, my seascapes?"

"I sold them at the Hotel Drouot; of course I only got a miserable sum for the lot: people aren't interested in that stuff now."

"Damn it all! You might have asked me first!"

"How could I ask you when the papers kept saying at the time that they'd shot you? I got the news at the Seville Feria." (*Yes, we have no bananas* once more.)

"And when they told you did you cry much?"

"I cried and cried and cried."

"Of course you wore a black mantilla."

"Wait, I must wind up the gramophone." ("*Yes, we have no* . . ." rose in pitch from the depths where it had descended.)

"I say, are these people going to stay much longer?"

"If they want to stay, I won't chuck them out."

"It's just that we've so much to talk about."

"Tomorrow, tomorrow, tomorrow . . ."

"But it's tomorrow already."

"If you're tired, why not go and have a sleep?" (A new record: *Je cherche après Titine, Titine, oh! ma Titine*: another obsessional tune from the boat.)

Now Ofelia left him alone on the divan and began dancing wildly with an Englishman with curly hair, whom she introduced to me as she passed, but without letting go of him, as Lord—I forget his name—whom she'd met in Capri and who—so I was told by the Cholo Mendoza, now sitting beside me—had got into a scrape with the French police for using schoolboys from the Lycée Jeanson-de-Sailly in artistic scenic productions of one of Virgil's *Bucolics*, yes, the one about Alexis, the shepherd boy; I know it, I know it. The *Ex* looked at his daughter and at all the others with growing irritation: those two women dancing together cheek to cheek. And those two men clutching each other round the waist. And that other short-haired female kissing the skinny blonde in a yellow shawl. And those stupid incomprehensible paintings on the walls. And that obscene white sculpture, the marble phallus, surrounded by bottles of whisky with a horse on the label—white, too, but which had at least come to signify sterling worth. His face turned suddenly red in an access of rage—Mendoza recognized the symptoms—he crossed the room, lifted the sound-box of the gramophone, threw several records on the floor and stamped them to pieces.

"Clear all this drunken rubbish out of here!" he shouted. Standing protectively in front of the astonished few who remained, it was now Ofelia's turn to look at her father with growing anger, like the chief of a tribe, measuring the strength of the adversary before attacking. The "darling little papa" was growing before her eyes—growing, blowing himself out, turning into a giant, breaking the walls with his hands and raising the roof with his shoulders. If he regained his old authority, and if she let him dominate her, order her about and make decisions in a house where she had dispensed with his presence very pleasantly for several years; if she didn't humble his pride, and check his impulsive behaviour, he would end up just as much of a tyrant *here* as he had been *there*—for he was accustomed to be a tyrant always.

"If you don't like my friends," she said, adopting the dry cold tone which he had sometimes been afraid of, "if you don't like my friends, take your bags and go to the Crillon or the Ritz. They have good rooms. Room service and an elegant atmosphere."

"Sodom and Gomorrah!" yelled the Head of State.

"That's why they got rid of you; for talking drivel," said Ofelia.

"And who is this?" asked all the others.

"*Mon père, le Président,*" said Ofelia, suddenly solemn, as if to mitigate the brutality of her earlier remarks.

"*Vive le Président! Vive le Président!*" they all shouted together, while one imitated a clown's foolish antics, and sang the Marseillaise.

"Go to bed, papa."

The sunlight shone through the drawing-room curtains in spite of the electric light still on in the room. Morning had begun for the whole city.

"Let's go to *Bois-Charbons,*" said the *Ex* to the Cholo Mendoza.

"Bye-bye!" said Ofelia, and while the two men went down the great staircase, the others leant over the balustrade with masks on their faces, singing to the music of *Malbrough*:

L'vieux con s'en va-t-en guerre
Mironton, mironton, mirontaine.
L'vieux con s'en va-t-en guerre
Et n'en reviendra pas!

"*Alors . . . on a eu des malheurs, mon bon Monsieur?*" said Musard, looking more than ever like the moustachioed leader of the Arc de Triomphe, when he saw us arrive. (It was clear he had come across my portrait in some newspaper recently.)

"*Oh! Vous savez—les révolutions . . .*" I said.

"*Les révolutions, ça tourne toujours mal,*" said the wine-merchant, taking out a bottle. "*Voyez ce qui s'est passé en France avec Louis XVI.*" (I thought of the frontispiece of Michelet's *La Convention* in Nelson's edition, with Citizen Capet on the scaffold, very dignified, with his shirt open at the neck as if he were consulting an otolaryngologist.)

"*Ce sera pour la prochaine fois,*" I said, raising my hand to my neck. Possibly realizing, rather late in the day, that his reference to Louis XVI had been slightly unfortunate, Monsieur Musard tried to mend matters:

"*Les révolutions, vous savez . . . Il paraît que sous l'Ancien Régime on était bien mieux. Ce sont nos quarante Rois qui ont fait la grandeur de la France.*"

"This chap has been reading *Action Française,*" said the Cholo Mendoza.

"He's treating us to a bit of Barrèsism," I said.

"*Le Beaujolais nouveau est arrivé.*" said Monsieur Musard, filling three glasses. "*C'est la maison qui régale.*"

I drank my wine with delight. From the back of the humble café came a pleasant smell of resinous wood, such as was sold in little bundles fastened with wire, to light coal fires with. There on the shelves, as if no time had passed, their shapes and labels unchanged, stood the bottles of Suze, Picon, Raphaël and Dubonnet.

"What are you going to live on now?" I asked the Cholo. "You're not an ambassador any more."

"A man who thinks ahead is worth two. I've got more than enough money."

"Where did you get it from?"

"Thanks to me the population of our country has 30,000 new citizens, who don't figure in the census or know what our map looks like; forged passports and cards of citizenship for them. . . . Poor people without any country. Victims of the war. White Russians. Expatriates. *Heimatlos.* I was doing good. Besides, the transactions went through the diplomatic bag. I wouldn't have been the only one. I'm no saint. Other people use it for worse things." (He made the gesture of someone sniffing.) "*That business* is a great temptation, because now it brings in a lot. But it's dangerous. However, with the passports, I keep a duplicate of the Embassy stamps and seals. So the shop stays open . . . discreetly, of course."

"Excellent: our compatriots deserve nothing better" (a sigh).

"Oh well! it's difficult to serve one's country, old man!"

We returned to the Rue de Tilsitt. As I went in, out came a new porter, a war casualty probably, because his left cuff was fastened with a safety-pin to the shoulder of his blue jacket, and he wore a badge on his lapel. I had to explain that I was the master of the house, before he let me pass, with theatrically embarrassed excuses. The drawing-room curtains were still drawn. Several of last night's revellers were asleep on the divan, in armchairs or on cushions scattered on the carpet. Stepping over their bodies—some of them interlaced or piled in heaps—I at last reached my bedroom. I took my hammock out of the cupboard and hung it to the two rings put there for it. On the Arc de Triomphe, Rude's Marseillaise was singing, as yesterday, as always.

But if the Marseillaise was still there, with her vociferous leader and the boy-hero between sabres and palm-trees, to me Paris seemed deserted. I realized that this very afternoon when, after a long sleep, I tried to make a list of what could be rescued of my life in this city. Reynaldo Hahn didn't answer the telephone. Perhaps he'd gone to live in the suburbs. "*Abonné absent*", said a female voice from the Exchange. The Distinguished Academician, always so understanding, to whom I wanted to confide my sadness and disappointments and whose advice I wanted to ask about—possibly—writing my Memoirs, had died months ago in his flat on the Quai Voltaire, the victim of an incurable disease, after a mystical crisis which created a considerable stir in Catholic circles and caused him to spend whole days praying in the cold church of Saint-Roch, associated for me with a novel by Balzac I read as an adolescent in Surgidero de la Verónica. (I don't know why churches connected with Bossuet or Fénelon—in style I mean—like Saint-Roch, Saint Sulpice or the chapel at Versailles, fail to inspire me with devotion. To get the feel of a Christian church, I need it to be shadowy, enveloping, full of relics and marvellous images of decapitated saints, blood, sores, tears and sweat, lifelike wounds, jungles of tapers, silver limbs and gold viscera on the altar for ex-votos.) I knew that after Gabriele D'Annunzio had got caught in Fiume, he had retired—so they said—now a prince—so they said—to his Italian house, where with his back against a wall of rock he could see the prow of a battleship, raised up there in memory of some brave deed or other. I learned that Ofelia had told the truth and that Elstir's paintings had fallen out of public favour: his delicious seascapes could still be found in the less successful galleries, mixed up among any pictures containing waves, boats, sand and foam that appealed to those who had made fortunes out of the War. Embittered by the fall in the price of his work, Elstir had retired angrily to his studio at Balbec, where he tried to achieve some sort of "modernity", which distorted but added nothing to his individual style, giving a sense of uneasy effort, as little appreciated by his admirers of yesterday as by those who were today following new currents. In music something similar was happening: nobody played Vinteuil's work any more—least of all his Sonata— except schoolgirls, who put away his music in a drawer, after their piano-lessons, and devoted themselves to the strange subtleties of *La cathédrale engloutie* or the *Pavane pour une infante défunte*, unless they were indulging themselves with the vulgarities of Zez Confrey's *Kitten-on-the-Keys*. And the young, those "in the know"—of what?—the snobs, amazed by the Russian music brought over by Diaghilev, treated the fine maestro Juan Cristóbal as a "vieille barbe", and disowned him just as they used to disown *Rhinegold*. And worse, inconceivable things had happened: Anatole France, who could well have remained in the world of Thaïs and Jérôme Coignard, had irrelevantly declared himself a socialist at the last moment, proclaiming the necessity of a "universal revolution", including America—no less!—and giving large sums of money to that abominable periodical *L'Humanité*. Things were going very badly for others: the Comte de Argencourt, Belgian chargé d'affaires, formerly a ceremonious, stiff diplomatist in the grand style, had been seen by the Cholo Mendoza a few days earlier, opposite the puppet theatre in the Champs-Elysées, in a state of utter collapse, imbecile, with the face and expression of a smiling beggar, apparently about to stretch out his hand for alms. . . .

During these days, I didn't dare telephone Madame Verdurin, now a princess by marriage. I was afraid a princess —or someone with the presumptions of one—would scorn a man who was, after all, only a Latin-American president thrown out of his palace. And I thought bitterly of the deplorable end of Estrada Cabrera; of many dictators dragged through the streets of their capitals; of those expelled and humiliated, like Porfirio Díaz, or of those who had gone to ground here in France, after a long stretch of power, like Guzmán Blanco; of Rosas of Argentina, whose daughter, tired of playing the part of unselfish virgin, or magnanimous intercessor against the cruelty of her terrible father, suddenly revealed herself as she really was at heart, and abandoned her stern parent when she got the chance, leaving him to die in melancholy solitude in the grey town of Southampton—he, who had owned boundless pampas, rivers of silver, moons such as are only seen there, suns rising every day above horizons he had ruled over since he was in breeches, and watched the heads of his enemies go by, hawked as "good, cheap water-melons" in the carts of his rejoicing followers.

The days passed, and I hardly saw Ofelia, who was always involved in fun and games. The Mayorala, curled up into a ball under her feather eiderdown, refused to be attended by a French doctor and suffered the high fever of pleurisy without accepting any remedy but Santa Inés rum and balsam of Tolu—since none of the sort of herbal concoctions which performed miracles *over there* were to be had *here*. And I resumed my walks about Paris with the Cholo Mendoza, going from Notre-Dame de Lorette to the Chope Danton, from an Avenue du Bois which hadn't been there before to Monsieur Musard's *Bois-Charbons*, without experiencing a single quiver of the city life, the air, the atmosphere that my nose and my memory sought in vain. The smell of petrol had taken the place of the country aroma formerly everywhere, knowing no frontiers, belonging as much to the capital as to a hamlet—of horse dung. In the early morning one no longer heard the cries of the old-clothes man, the seller of watercress and birdseed, nor the rustic pipe of the scissors-grinder. In the purlieus of the Place des Ternes, makers of porous jugs from Badajoz no longer arrived after a very long journey, with their donkeys decorated in the Extramaduran style. The only place which seemed permanent and unchanged was *Aux glaces* at 25 rue Saint-Apolline, where (among scagliola or mosaic tables, coloured glass windows, floral transfers on the long backs of leather settees, a pianola with a loud tone, two waiters in white aprons with bottles on tray-covered trolleys— like those on the Raphaël labels) women were waiting for me, who in spite of the passage of years, difference in generations, changes in personnel, a new hair-do, a certain delicate restraint now being preferred to the opulence of the end of the century, restored me to the early chapters of my history, with its first pleasures and a thousand rejuvenating memories, and far-off events, whence—as in other continental countries—everything had been transformed, turned upside down and perverted by the accelerated changes in ways of life. Languages had been mixed together, values degraded, adolescents corrupted, patriarchs insulted, palaces profaned, and the Just expelled. . . .

Here, at *Aux glaces*, I found the only permanence that had always existed—despite larger breasts or smaller breasts—here as *over there*, I found presence and uniqueness, dialectic of irreplaceable forms, a common language of universal understanding. In the irreversible Time of the flesh, it was possible to pass, according to period, from the style of Bouguereau to that of a medieval Eve, from the décolletage of Boldini to the décolletage of Tintoretto, or, inversely, from Rubens' multitudinous buttocks and bellies to the fragile, ambiguous appearance of a nymph by Puvis de Chavannes; aesthetic fashions, variants and fluctuations of taste all passed, lengthening silhouettes, playing with proportions, amplifying—while in other departments of life, too, fashions were subject to perennial changes—yet never altering the fundamental reality of a nude. Here, looking at what I am looking at, I feel I am witnessing the Arrest of Time, somewhere outside the present epoch, maybe in the days of sun clocks or sand clocks, and therefore liberated from everything that binds me to the dates of my own history. I am less aware of being unseated from my bronze horses, thrown down from my pedestals; less of an exiled ruler, or actor in decline, and more identified with my own *ego*, still possessing eyes for looking, and impulses arising from the depths of a vitality that is deliciously stimulated by something worth looking at—riches definitely preferable (*I feel* therefore I am) to those of a fictitious existence in the stupid ubiquity of a hundred statues in municipal parks, patios and town halls.

When such serious reflections beset me in a place where I hadn't come for that purpose, and I took in the disparity between thought and situation, I burst out laughing, and made a remark to the Cholo Mendoza which never failed to delight him: "Anything but 'To be or not to be' in a whorehouse." "That is the question," he replied (for he too fancied himself as well-read), making signs to an ample Leda, who knew she had been chosen beforehand, and so was awaiting her time without impatience, drinking some aperitif flavoured with aniseed at the next table, and counting on a client who had said nothing to her, but was worth waiting for, because foreigners were generous clients and knew how to appreciate professional conscientiousness in work of every kind.

20

Suddenly cured of her fever and pains, the Mayorala had arisen from beneath her eiderdown, clamouring to know where she could find a church in which to carry out her promise of dedicating prayers and candles to the Virgin.

"Church, church," she cried to the concierge, who was amazed to be approached by someone wearing three petticoats, one on top of another, for fear of the dew produced by the unusually early summer sunshine.

"Church, church," she repeated, crossing herself, joining her hands in a gesture of prayer, and displaying a rosary of silver beads. The concierge, possibly understanding, signed to her to go "there, turn left, turn right, and go straight on a little way". And the Mayorala, life now restored to the strong calves of her legs, had walked, walked, walked, until she came to an enormous church—it must be a church, although there was no cross on it, because it had somewhat religious-looking sculptures, such as Mignel Estatua used to make, at the top of a façade with many columns—whence came organ music, murmured prayers, and where a priest was saying things she didn't understand, but an altar is an altar everywhere, the holy images had a familiar air and the smell of incense left no room for doubt.

Her prayers said, she bought candles with some French money the Head of State had given her when they arrived at Cherbourg ("in case you get lost when you want to pee"), descended a few steps and stopped in a very pretty flower market—although these carnations didn't have so much scent as the ones *over there*—stopping afterwards in amazement in front of a shop-window where a solitary and magnificent mango was offered for sale, reclining on a bed of fine cotton-wool. *There,* mangoes were sold in barrows decorated with palm leaves "five for half a peso", and here it was lying in a box, like the gems displayed in French jewellers' shops in her country. The Mayorala boldly entered the store. From table to table, from counter to counter she went in delighted surprise; the yucca reached out brown arms to her as if calling her attention; green bananas were turning greener before her eyes, the rough peel of yams was developing pale blotches on its redness—more like coral than a subterranean fruit. And further on she found the intense black of beans, the liturgical white of custard-apples. And by means of her language of gestures and onomatopoeia, making signs, using her fingers, exclaiming, and grunting assent or negation, she had secured five of these, three of the others, ten of those, eight from this sack, fifteen from the box, and put the lot in one of the wide baskets sold there—which basket she proceeded to put on her head when the time came to pay, to the great astonishment of the cashier: "*Vous voulez un taxi, Mademoiselle?*" She understood not a word. She left the shop and took her bearings. On her way here the sun had been in her face. The sun hadn't yet got overhead and she wasn't hungry: therefore it must be ten or half past. So, to retrace her steps, she must walk with her shadow in front of her. The trouble was that these bloody streets turned, twisted and changed direction, and her shadow —getting smaller all the time—crossed over from right to left and refused to remain in the desired position. Then she saw so many strange things to distract her: that café full of Americans —you could tell them by their clothes; the toyshop with a blue dwarf in it; that enormous column with a tiny man on the top—a liberator obviously; that park full of statues with a grille. Here, with the trees on the left, her shadow came back to its proper place. She walked and walked, till she came to a vast square where there was a stone standing, like those in some of the cemeteries *over there*, but much bigger—and however had they managed to stand it upright? Now came an avenue, with some goats pulling little carriages. There were stalls of sweets and toffees. And now the basket was beginning to weigh more than she'd bargained for, but suddenly—when the sun was directly overhead—she saw far off at the top of the road that enormous, heavy, but life-saving monument, called the Arc de Triomphe or What-Have-You. She walked faster. Home at last. She wanted to go straight to the kitchen, but just then she was struck by a sharp pain in the back. And her fever returned. She left the basket in a corner of the room, took a glass of rum beaten up with balsam of Tolu and went back under her eiderdown, complaining bitterly of these countries with climates cold enough to skin one alive.

And at about half past eleven next day, Ofelia was woken by unusually loud voices. The maid came in, looking and sounding upset: "*Mademoiselle, pardonnez-moi, mais . . .*" The cook wanted to see her; to see her immediately, she insisted. There she was. Furious. And she came in, dishevelled—very like a Fury, in fact—telling everyone whether half asleep or not, who would listen, that this was impossible, it was intolerable, and she wouldn't stay another day in the house, she'd hand back her apron. And she suited the action to the words, taking it off and handing it over with an angry expression, looking like some venerable master mason returning his leather apron. It was intolerable: a short while ago a woman had come down

from the attic, wearing three skirts, gesticulating, dark-skinned
—*"une peau de boudin, Mademoiselle"*; she had taken possession
of her world of pots and pans, and set about cooking extraordinary things—*"des mangeailles de sauvage, Mademoiselle"*—
dirtying everything, spilling oil, throwing corn-cobs into
corners, contaminating the casseroles with mixtures of pimen-
toes and cocoa, using a carpenter's plane to slice plantains,
cramming handfuls of fritters into brown paper. And after
preparing this unspeakable pigswill, and leaving the kitchen
poisoned with greasy vapours and the stink of frying, she had
carried off trays and soup bowls to the little room that used to
belong to Sylvestre, which out of respect for the memory of
that exemplary servant, had remained exactly as he left it
before he went away and died gloriously in battle on the
plateau of Craonne, with the croix de guerre on his breast and
his photo published in *L'Illustration* because of his heroic
behaviour in the face of the enemy.

Beginning to understand the situation, Ofelia returned her
apron to the cook, wrapped herself in a dressing-gown, and
went up to the attic.

The Head of State and the Cholo Mendoza, their shirts
undone, hairy and unshaven—and looking as if they had
hangovers—were sitting at a long table, which was really a
door taken off its hinges and placed on two chairs. On several
trays and dishes, as if in some low restaurant in the tropics, were
laid out green avocado pears, red chillis, ochre and chocolate
sauces from which emerged breasts and joints of turkey, frosted
over with grated onion. In a row on the carving-board there
were little maize cakes and omelettes seasoned with chillis,
next to yellow tamales, wrapped in hot moist leaves and exuding
aromas suggestive of a country fiesta. There were ripe fried
bananas, plantains cut in fine slices by the carpenter's plane
(those that had been crushed in handfuls). And yam fritters and
coconut cakes browned in the oven, and a punch bowl where,
in a mixture of tequila and Spanish cider such as was drunk
at weddings *over there*, there floated pine kernels, green lemons,
mint and orange blossom.

"Care to join us?" asked the Cholo Mendoza.

"And who prepared all this?" asked Ofelia, still stupefied by her sudden awakening and the cook's protestations.

"Elmirita, servant of God and your honour," replied the mulatto, bowing with her legs crossed as girls are taught to do in French Dominican colleges.

Ofelia had been about to overturn the improvised table and put an end to the junketings. But now a maize tamale on the end of a fork approached her eyes and descended to her mouth. When it was opposite her nose, a sudden inner emotion, coming from a long way off, a fluttering in her entrails, weakened her knees and made her sit down on a chair. She bit into it, and all at once her body grew younger by thirty years. In white socks, and with her hair in curling-papers, she was in the patio with the millstones and the tamarind tree. And from the tree dangled cinnamon-coloured parchment pods full of dark pulp, with a forgotten bitter-sweetness which made her mouth water. And there came back to her too the smell of fermented guavas—ambiguously combining pears and rasp-berries—from behind the fence where Jongolojongo the pig, with his long bristles and long snout, was grunting and rootling among broken tiles and rusty old tins. And the smells from the kitchen full of pots, vases, jugs, and black pottery, whence came the sounds of chewing, of the slow tread of boots on wet earth, of the pestle falling as rhythmically as a pendulum on the milky fragrant foaming mass of maize pulp. And Mayflower the cow, who had just calved, was calling to her little one to relieve her udders, and outside a street-seller was crying molasses for sale; and the bell from the hermitage among the medlar and cherry-trees; and this maize here (I'm seven years old, and already I look at myself in the mirror every morning to see if I've grown breasts in the night) entering my body at every pore. I'm seven years old:

Santa Maria,
Save us from evil
Protect us, Señora
From this terrible devil

And then everyone sang:

To kill the devil
The Virgin seized a blade
On all fours the monster
Lay down in a glade.

"*Des mangeailles de sauvages,*" said the cook, standing in the doorway with her arms akimbo.

"To hell with Brillat-Savarin!" cried Ofelia, her cheeks blazing from the cider mixed with tequila and pineapple-juice, tasting this and that, plunging her spoon in the avocado salad, and dipping a turkey joint into chilli sauce. And suddenly seized by an unexpected impulse of affection, she sat on her father's knees and kissed his cheeks, where once again she recaptured the smell of tobacco, aguardiente, French lotion (with some hint of mint, liquorice and Mimi Pinson powder) —but less old, more virile, almost young—in a marvellous rediscovery of time past. For the first time since the days of the Craonne plateau, they played the gramophone that had remained silent ever since Sylvestre's heroic death. They heard, in tones that grew deeper or almost died away when the mechanism ran down, several tunes collected by the Cholo Mendoza: Lerdo de Tejado's *Faisan*, *Alma campera*, *El Tamborito*, and Milonguita, flower of luxury and pleasure, men did you wrong and now you would give anything for a cotton dress; and listen to the story the old gravedigger told me one day: it was a lover whose sweetness cruel fate stole away; and goodbye lads, my lifelong friends; and every night he went to the cemetery to see the corpse of his beloved, and crowned her skull with orange blossom and covered her horrible mouth with kisses; and goodbye lads, my lifelong friends of happy days; and the day that you love me will be sunnier than June, with music by Beethoven singing from every flower; and again and again and again those happy festive days, and goodbye and goodbye, light of my nights, sang the soldier underneath the window. . . .

By now Elmirita and Ofelia had their arms round each other and were singing a duet, skilfully keeping to intervals of thirds and sixths, which the Cholo accompanied with opportunely onomatopoeic flourishes on an imaginary guitar.

And when night fell, what with drinking, singing and titbits of tomato and chilli sauce, the Head of State decided to instal himself finally in Sylvestre's rooms, entering and leaving by the back staircase: "I shall be more independent like that." Then Ofelia, down below, could go on having her parties of young people and live among those horrible pictures which so frayed his nerves—quite apart from the fact that he didn't understand them and never would. And the Mayorala would go on living here in the room next door, to keep him company and look after him. The Infanta agreed: Elmirita was a splendid girl, most unselfish and good, "Much more respectable and honourable than many of the friends of Madame What's-her-name, with her musical evenings, who doesn't want to clap eyes on you now that she's become a princess." But the zamba must be dressed differently. And Ofelia ran to her wardrobe to find her some clothes she no longer wore. Although full of praise for their quality, the Mayorala eyed them a little suspiciously: this one was cut so low as to be brazen; the slit skirt of the other seemed to her immodest. When she saw the lapels of a suit tailored by Redfern: "I don't wear men's clothes." To a black ensemble by Paquin she said, "Yes, perhaps it would do for a funeral." In the end she happily accepted a model of Paul Poiret's, partly inspired by Léon Bakst's designs for *Schéhérazade*, which reminded her of the flowered skirts and blouses of her own people. And that night they finally consecrated the new dwelling by fixing two rings in the walls, knotting cords to them and hanging up the woven hammock for the Head of State to sleep in—"I beg your pardon: the *Ex*," corrected the Patriarch, enjoying his first swing in it.

The Mayorala soon became familiar with a large region of Paris centred round the Arc de Triomphe and with the river as its extreme frontier—a river she never crossed, because people who did a lot of ironing and cooking were in danger of catching a chill if they crossed a bridge. She had come across a church in the Place where a bronze horseman, a very good poet who had been a friend of the Emperor Pedro of Brazil—so the Cholo Mendoza had explained—seemed plunged in endless thought, and behind the church of a Saint Honoré of somewhere or other was a superb fish-market where they sold octopuses, prawns, and quahogs fairly like those she used to get *over there*, as well as clams identical with the ones from the beaches of la Verónica, which came out of the sand as though drawn by a magnet whenever they found out that a woman eager for a man had sat down on them. In a shop close by, earthenware pots and casseroles were sold, and by stealing bricks from a house being built—she carried them two at a time in the oilskin bag she used for lemons, garlic and parsley—she had transformed the stove in the attic into a creole range, feeding it with wood brought, tied up in wire, from Monsieur Musard's *Bois-Charbons*, where she went very often these days, having become much addicted to Muscadet and sweet Gaillac —wines which she used to say "toned up her system".

And she began to live there, under the slate roof, in a latitude and at times belonging to another region and another epoch.

The early morning was filled with the aroma of strong coffee, filtered through a woollen stocking and sweetened with cane syrup which the zamba got near the Madeleine; she could always find her way there without getting lost because she had proved that by going under the Arc de Triomphe exactly in the middle she could see the Standing Stone a long way off, and having reached it she turned left and found the building with many columns where she had given thanks for her recovery. Then followed a short rest on her hammock with a glass of aguardiente and a Romeo and Juliet cigar, and later still a cry of "Come along in" announced the appearance, on two broad mahogany tables supported on carpenter's trestles, of a country breakfast of eggs in peppery sauce, fried black beans, maize tortillas, pork, and white cheese pounded together in a mortar and served in any leaf available—so long as it was green—for lack of a banana leaf. After that came her morning siesta, interrupted when she was half asleep about eleven, by the Cholo Mendoza, bringing the daily newspapers. But these papers hadn't seen the light in the small hours in Parisian printing-presses. They were papers from overseas, had travelled a long way and were concerned with other things than current events. *Le Figaro, Le Journal* and *Le Petit Parisien* never came up to this floor; they had been gradually supplanted by *El Mercurio, El Mundo* and *Ultimas Noticias* from *over there*, or even by *El Faro* from Nueva Córdoba or *El Centinela* from Puerto Araguato. The Head of State was beginning to forget the names of politicians *over here*, and he cared very little what was happening in Europe—although the recent assassination of Matteotti had stimulated his admiration for Italian fascism, and that great man Mussolini who was going to put an end to international communism—he was only interested in what might be happening *over there*.

(Hailed as restorer and custodian of Liberty, after a triumphal entry riding on a black horse—but without boots, and in the white drill-suit he had always worn in the university—Luis Leoncio had climbed the stairs of the Presidential Palace he had described in a recent manifesto as an "Augean stable" with the majestic step of an archon, his expression stern, his gestures few, and looking coldly—with some vague threat in his retinas—at those who were overreaching themselves to congratulate him on his triumph. Much had been hoped of the Man who—after making a roll of public employees, thanks to a prompt North American loan—had undertaken in a monkish, frugal manner, the enormous task of examining the national problems. For weeks and weeks he shut himself up in his study, silent and remote, poring over estimates, statistics and political documents, preferring to get help from technical books, encyclopedias, reports and memoranda, rather than consult experts trained to go into these questions in detail, and analyse a whole, in the Cartesian manner, into parts whose multiplicity was obscuring the vision of the whole itself. They awaited the results of his toil with unction and eager impatience. People walked through Central Park almost on tiptoe every evening, talking in low voices and pointing to the window where lights would be burning until the small hours, and behind which Something Important was being worked out. Everyone was waiting for the Wise Man of

Nueva Córdoba to speak. It couldn't be long now. And at last he did speak, before an immense crowd gathered in the Olympic Stadium. And his speech was a torrential onslaught—without pause to take breath—as if a dictionary were unbound, let loose, with pages in confusion, words in revolt, a tumult of concepts and ideas, accelerated impact of figures, images and abstractions in a vertiginous flood of words launched to the four winds, and moving from Morgan's Bank to Plato's Republic, from the Logos to foot-and-mouth disease, from General Motors to Ramakrishna, coming at last to the conclusion—or at least some understood it thus—that from the Mystic Marriage between the Eagle and the Condor, and as a result of the fertilization of our inexhaustible soil by foreign investment, our America would be transformed by the vigorous Technology that would come to us from the North (and we were on the threshold of a century which would be the Century of Technology for our Young Continent), by the light of our own innate spirituality, a synthesis would be born between the Vedanta, the Popol-Vuh and the parables of Christ-the-first-socialist, the only true socialist, nothing to do with Moscow Gold or the Red Peril, or an exhausted, dying Europe, without sap or talent—and it would be as well for us to break finally with its useless teaching—whose hopeless decadence had been proclaimed not long ago by the German philosopher Oswald Spengler. The start of this new Era, in which the thesis-antithesis of North-South was complemented by the telluric and the scientific, would be manifested in the creation of a New Humanity, the Alpha-Omega, the party of Hope, expressing the *sturm-und-drang*, the political pulse of new generations, marking the end of Dictatorships in this Continent, and establishing a true and authentic Democracy, where there would be freedom of syndical action, provided that it did not break the necessary harmony between Capital and Labour; the need for an opposition must be recognized, provided that it was a *co-operative opposition* (critical, yes, but always *constructive*); the right to strike was accepted, provided that the strikes didn't paralyse private enterprise or public services; and, finally, the Communist Party would be legalized, since it in fact existed in our country, provided that it did not obstruct the functioning of institutions nor stimulate class war.

And by the time the orator brought his speech to an end with "Long live our Country!" he had uttered so many "buts", "howevers", "neverthelesses", "despite the sayings" and "provided thats", that his hearers were left with the impression that time had stood still, independently of the ticking of clocks, and that when the Austere Doctor stepped down from the rostrum he left behind him a total mental emptiness—blank brains, and an agnostic trance in his listeners.

And in the ensuing months all was dismay and confusion. The Provisional President—not so provisional after all—could never come to any decision. Every suggestion made by his colleagues, every measure to be applied at once, seemed to him "premature", "inopportune", "hasty", because "we weren't ready", "it wasn't yet time for that", "the masses weren't mature enough", etc. And after a few months scepticism and shrugging of shoulders became the order of the day, and living for the day's pleasure, and renewed interest in lottery tickets and guitars and maracas on the part of those who had been too optimistic, while at the same time there was talk of "Discontent in the Army".

"A Military Coup on the way," prophesied the Head of State. "It wouldn't be anything new. As the proverb says: 'one stripe more on a tiger makes very little difference'."

"But now they say that it's the *young officers* who are involved," remarked the Cholo.

"Sub-machine guns instead of machetes," said the former holder of Power. "It's all the same."

But there was something new in the air: *Liberation*, now a legal newspaper, appeared every morning and contained eight pages—in spite of which, from time to time it would be unexpectedly suppressed by officious members of Alpha-Omega, who overturned crates, dispersed the galley-proofs and beat up the lino-typists. People who couldn't possibly be suspected of communist affiliation were working together on the paper at the time, and signing their names at the foot of their articles. The music publishing house of Francis Salabert

in Paris had received an order for a thousand copies of the
Internationale, which was now being sung *over there* in a
Spanish translation, recently published in Mexico by Diego
Rivera in a review called *El Machete*.)

And so the months passed, February papers being read in
April, and those of October in December, while past events
were talked of more and more and vanished individuals came
to life. A Yesterday, unmistakably *yesterday* though present
today, was living among us in flesh and blood that was in
process of losing its fleshly nature, because it was obvious that
the usually tall, strapping figure of the *Ex* was beginning to
deteriorate, as it was also obvious that the passage of time was
progressively speeding up, diminishing and narrowing the
space between one Christmas and the next, between one
military review of July 14 and the next military review of
July 14, so that the huge flag fluttering beneath the Arc de
Triomphe appeared to have been there ever since the last
occasion. Chestnuts bloomed, chestnuts dropped their flowers,
chestnuts bloomed again, as pages from the calendar were
thrown into the waste-paper basket, and Monsieur le Président's
tailor came again and again to the Rue de Tilsitt to alter his
clothes to fit a dwindling anatomy, growing thinner day by day.
His watch-chain retreated visibly over a less prominent waistcoat, while his shoulders, formerly held up with inflexible
rigidity, were now drooping over collar-bones relieved of
the extra flesh on his thorax—as the Mayorala noticed when at
bath time she rubbed her President's chest with sponge and
loofah. And since this progressive loss of flesh alarmed her
and she didn't believe in medicine in bottles such as was sold
here, she had dictated—stammered rather—a letter to the
Cholo Mendoza, arranging that a certain Balbina, from the
village of Palmar de Siquire where there was no post office,
should send her a parcel of healing herbs—to travel by donkey,
mule, bicycle, 'bus, several trains, two boats and another
train, and be picked up today by Elmira at the Parcels Office
in the Rue Etienne Marcel. Her Ex-President and Ex-
Ambassador went with her because a great many forms had to
be filled in and signed, and all this was for people who could

read and write—and in French, which made it far worse.

With the package wrapped in a scarf, and all three wearing thick overcoats because it was a cold day, though the sun shone brightly from a cloudless sky, Elmira had her first sight of the towers of Notre Dame. When she heard it was the Cathedral of Paris she insisted on going there to light a candle to the Virgin. She stopped still in amazement in front of the building:

"What I say is: we ought to do things like this in our country to attract tourists." The figures on the tympanum and lintels reminded her of the sculptures of Miguel Estatua, her fellow-countryman from Nueva Córdoba.

"The zamba isn't being foolish," remarked the *Ex* who hadn't hitherto noticed the stylistic resemblance between the two, especially in the devils' faces, the rearing horse, the horned demons, and all the infernal zoology of the Last Judgement. There followed an awestruck Penetration into the Nave—the nave alight with the whole gamut of colour from its windows, the figures of the visitors making dark silhouettes against this brilliance, slight forms in this mid-afternoon of fictitious spring. They sat down to rest between the two rose windows in the transept. At the other end of the row of seats, a young man in a long overcoat and warm muffler was gazing at everything with deep and careful attention.

"A worshipper," said the Mayorala.

"An aesthete," said Mendoza.

"A student from the Beaux Arts," said the Head of State. And in a low voice, to entertain the zamba, he began telling her, like a grandfather to his grandchild, true stories of things he had seen here: the archdeacon who was enamoured of a gypsy who used to make a white nanny-goat dance to a tambourine (Elmira had seen gypsies like that when she was a child, but they had made a bear dance); and the story of the itinerant poet who egged on some beggars to attack the church ("When there's rioting churches always get damaged," said Elmira, remembering a case which it would have been better to forget); and the story of a hunch-backed bell-ringer, who was also in love with the gypsy ("hunch-backs are very amorous, and women notice this, but only want to touch the hump because it brings good luck"); and the story of two skeletons which seemed to be embracing and perhaps were those of Esmeralda and the bell-ringer ("such cases have been seen, so the old village sexton used to tell in his song; we've got a record of it"). But now the organ began blaring out a sudden outburst of music. They couldn't hear each other speak.

"Let's go," said the *Ex*, thinking of the delicious Alsace wine they served at the café on the corner, where it would certainly be warmer than here.

But the "worshipper"—as Elmira had called him—was still sitting in his seat at the far end of the row, absorbed in dazzled contemplation. It was his first encounter with Gothic architecture. And the Gothic arches and stained-glass windows rising on both sides of him were an unsuspected revelation to him; beside this all other architecture seemed to him primitive, rooted in the earth, chthonic, even when it was expressed in terms conforming to the principles of Proportion, the Golden Rules. This building, soaring upwards in exaltation of verticality, seemed to him to make even the pediments of the Parthenon dwindle, for they were merely a living, exalted version of the sloping roof of the archaic dwelling, and its fluted column was a transcendent, glorified form of the roof-tree— four tree-trunks, six or eight—which supported the lintels and cedarwood beams of the rustic doorways of peasants. In Greek and Roman times this original relationship with the telluric and vegetal was lost. From the hut of Eumeus the swineherd to the temple of Phidias, the way was clear and open, through a series of successive stylizations. Here, on the other hand, architecture had become a matter of invention, ideas, pure creation, materials had achieved unheard-of lightness—as if stone was weightless—with a nervature owing nothing to the structure of trees—and with the characteristic suns of the prodigious rose windows: Northern Sun, Southern Sun. The contemplator in the transept was caught between these two suns, the fiery red of the sunset and the grave, mystical blue symphony of the North window. On the North window the Mother occupied the centre of a temporal court—to receive

Intercession as it were—of prophets, kings, judges and patriarchs. On the South—in the blood of sacrifice—the Sun ruled
over an ecclesiastical court of apostles, confessors, martyrs,
wise virgins and foolish virgins. The entire mystery of birth,
death, the eternal renaissance of life and the changing seasons
was to be found in the straight, imaginary and invisible line
stretched between the two central circles of those immense
sources of light, openings in a structural magnificat rising from
the ground, as if suspended weightlessly from its bells and
gargoyles. From the shadows, the organ pipes suddenly broke out
into triumphal fanfares.

An atheist because his inner questionings did not seek for
replies on religious soil; a disbeliever because disbelief was
natural to his generation, and the way had been prepared by
the scientific spirit that came before; an enemy of the politics
and compromise which so often, in his world, took the Church
into the camp of his adversaries, and in the name of faith
maintained a false order which was self-destructive, the
contemplator of the Sun Windows was nevertheless responsive
to the dynamic quality of the Gospels, and recognized that
their texts had, at one time, had the merit of causing a
resounding devaluation of all the totems and inexorable
spirits, dark presences and zodiacal threats, of oracles, sub-
missions to the ides of March and inevitable fate. But if some
new self-awareness—putting the drama of life *within* instead of
outside himself—had induced man to analyse the values
which led him into primitive terrors, he had developed into
an erring giant, tyrannized over by others like himself, who had
become faithless to their first vows, and had created new
totems, new destinies, temples without altars and irreligious
cults which it was necessary to destroy. Perhaps the days were
close at hand when the trumpets of the Apocalypse would
sound, but this time it would not be by the angels of the Last
Judgement but by those appearing before it. It was time to
decide upon the protocols of the future and to plan a Tribunal
of Redistribution.

The young man looked at his watch. Four o'clock. The
train. He sank himself again into the total beauty of his

surroundings, now that it was time to return to his own. "I don't feel needed where everything is so perfect," he thought, as he left Notre Dame by the centre door—the door of the Resurrection of the Dead. There was still time to drink some of the excellent Alsatian wine to be had in the café where he had left his suitcase in the care of a waiter. He crossed the road and went into the bistro without noticing that three people—a woman and two men—sitting on a bench at the back, were staring at him in amazement. Paying for his drink, The Student returned to the street and hailed a taxi.

"*A la garra del Norte, please.*"

His appointment was in the station buffet, where several delegates for the First World Conference against Colonial and Imperialist Politics were already gathered; it was to open next day, February 10, at Brussels, with Barbusse as president. Among them was the Cuban, Julio Antonio Mella, whom he had met a few hours before, in company with Jawaharlal Nehru, delegate for the National Hindu Congress.

"The train has come in already," said someone, pointing to platform 8. The three picked up their shabby cases and got into a second-class carriage. The Indian was sitting in a corner by the window studying some papers, while Mella was showing interest in the political situation of our country.

"We've just got rid of a dictator," said The Student. "But the struggle goes on, because our enemies are the same as before. The curtain has gone down on the first act, and very long it was. Now we're in the middle of the second, which in spite of new scenery and lighting, is very like the first."

"We're just starting on what you've been through," said Mella. And he told him about the dictator recently in power in Cuba, whom he had defeated by means of a stubborn, prolonged and successful hunger-strike in prison, forcing his enemy to give him his liberty and then leaving for Mexico, where the fight was still going on. . . .

Gerardo Machado was much like our Head of State in physical appearance, political behaviour and methods, but he was different because, being quite uncultured, he didn't build temples to Minerva like Estrada Cabrera (almost his contemporary) nor was he a francophile, as so many dictators and "educated tyrants" of the Continent had been. To him, Supreme Wisdom was to be found in the North: "I'm an imperialist," he declared, looking enthusiastically towards Washington. "I'm not an intellectual, but I am a patriot." However, he showed unconscious humour when he informed the public one day in his newspapers that he was "studying the tragedies of Aeschylus".

"He's a good candidate to join the clan of the Atrides," said The Student.

"From what one can see he already belongs to the family," said Mella.

"He'll soon give orders for confiscation of *red books*," said The Student.

"He's done it already," said the Cuban.

"One goes down here and another goes up there," said The Student.

"And that's a sight we've been seeing repeated for the last hundred years."

"Until the public gets tired of seeing the same thing."

"We must hope for the best."

Opening their leather wallets—both Mexican, with the Aztec calendar embossed on the outside—they exchanged the scripts of their reports and articles, to read on the journey. In his corner, Nehru, with several papers on his knees, seemed to be absorbed in his own thoughts, hidden behind wide open eyes. There was a long silence. The train reached the frontier in the night—the twofold night—of the coal-mines.

"Cool, cool," said Nehru, leaving the others uncertain whether he meant to say "cool" or "coal"—but it was indeed cold in this second-class carriage, excessively cold for these men from hot climates. And the Indian went on sleeping with his eyes open until the train got to Brussels.

21

*. . . those madmen try to make people believe they are
kings, but they are only poor men who dress their
nakedness in gold and purple.*

DESCARTES

"Exiled . . ."
"Banished . . ."
"Or fled . . ."
"Escaped . . ."
"On the run . . ."
"What I know is that he was in a church," remarked the
Mayorala. "And communists don't go to church, not even
in Holy Week." And they started on their conjectures again:
"Exiled . . ."
"Banished . . ."
"Escaped . . ."
"Repentant perhaps . . ."
"Converted . . ."
"A spiritual crisis . . ."
"Had a fight with his friends . . ."
And for days and days nothing else was talked about in the
Rue de Tilsitt, while they waited for the newspapers from
over there—February numbers in April—to arrive on their
specially slow cargo-boats, in tight rolls of seven numbers with
a picture of the Tutelary Volcano on the stamps. Because of
course the papers published here said nothing at all about
The Student, an individual of no interest to them. And at last
they received news, thanks to a copy of *El Faro* of Nueva
Córdoba arriving in May, about the World Conference at
Brussels, where the "National League of Mexican Countrymen" and the "Anti-Imperialist League of the Americas"

(which had affiliations in our country) had both been represented.

"That explains it all," said the Cholo Mendoza.

"What foolishness," murmured the *Ex*. "Imperialism is stronger than ever. That's why the man of the moment in Europe is Benito Mussolini."

And the chestnuts bloomed again, and conversations on the usual topics went on in the attic. They talked at enormous length, under the slate roof, about "the old days". The most trivial events, contemplated in perspective and seen from a distance, acquired significance, greater charm, strangeness or transcendence. "Do you remember? Do you remember?" became a sacramental—almost daily—formula, evoking dead people and dead things which were explained by the often secret mechanisms of a resurrected past, taken out of its distant context and brought to these latitudes. All at once, refreshing his crowded memory, the patriarch began revealing the hitherto concealed background to certain strange events or tiny circumstances, which gave the clue to what might before have caused baffled questioning and a flavour of mystery. As a fakir or conjuror, grown old and retired from the stage, may enjoy revealing the technique of his tricks and miracles, the *Ex* remembered the business of issuing money without security, in order to boost the national finances; the gaming-houses set up by the Government, where marked cards were used (there was a North American press which manufactured them with such subtle indications on their backs that only experts could understand them), and where the stakes had to be made in dollars, pounds sterling, or—to get hidden reserves of cash out of people's houses—in old gold coins or silver Mexican pesos. Then there was the affair of the Diamond in the Capitol, that octagonal diamond of incomparable brilliance, officially bought and solemnly inserted in the floor at the foot of the statue of the Republic, to mark the Zero Point where all the roads of the Nation met—a gem that was so expertly stolen one night that, according to the daily papers, the theft could only be attributed to some international gang, unless they were anarchists or communists who were very proficient in such tasks. Elmira laughed when she heard this story: "He sent me there (she pointed to the Patriarch): I put my friend Juliana up to occupying the night-watchman, while I (gesture) with a chisel you can buy in the ironmonger's at Monserrate, and a hammer that I had hidden between my tits, lifted out the diamond and carried it to the Palace in my mouth. My word! I could hardly breathe! And afterwards, what a hullabaloo! But . . . how we laughed! How we laughed!" And now her laughter was echoed by the Head of State's laughter, as he waved his hand towards a drawer in the cupboard:

"I've got it there. It brings me good luck. Besides, it's what the anarchists call *restitution*. And I too have a right to restitution."

"Bravo, my President!"

"My *Ex*, my dear boy; my *Ex*!"

The months passed while chestnuts were replaced by strawberries, and strawberries by chestnuts, leafy trees by bare trees, green leaves by rust-red leaves, and the Patriarch, all the time growing less interested in outside events, was gradually reducing, limiting and closing in the ambit of his existence. That Christmas was celebrated in the attic, with our carols, with drum and tambourine, Christmas dinner of sucking-pig, with lettuce and radish salad, red wine, and Spanish turrón— as we used to celebrate it *over there*. And seeing the cloth spread and the table laid, the Head of State began talking about Napoleon, who was rising in his estimation every year; but tonight he was not remembering Jena, Austerlitz or Wagram, but was enjoying something he had read in a book: that Bonaparte and Josephine used to eat at Malmaison—he a Corsican, and she from Martinique—in our fashion, just as Elmirita arranged things: all the dishes spread out together, some cold, some hot, in reach of each person's spoon and fork, without all that passing to and fro of dishes which went on in the houses of *nouveaux riches*, trying to behave like real princesses —and I know what I'm talking about!—with long waits and delays and rows of dishes which take your appetite away and scour your stomach with so much useless ceremony. Here you could take the bottle and fill your glass without someone muttering the date in your ear—as if the date was so important, when what one wanted above all in a wine was *cheerfulness*, which was nothing to do with a few years more or less.

And when the Head of State was in this happy condition, he sometimes glanced towards the Arc de Triomphe, and declaimed in a deep voice the famous tirade of Flambeau in l'Aiglon: "*Nous qui marchions fourbus, blessés, crottés, malades*", reciting with brio the last verse—a pretty revolting one, it must be said—where we are offered the blood of a dead horse to drink. But the Cholo Mendoza noticed that as time passed more and more gaps appeared in the *Ex's* recitations: some alexandrines never got beyond eight syllables; Spain and Austria were erased from the poetical map; the sabres, tinder-boxes, shakos, soldiers' songs, roasted crows, flags and bugles, remembered by Napoleon's veteran on the march, were all reduced to a rhymed medley in the reciter's memory, on the pharmaceutical model of:

Nous qui pour notre toux n'ayant pas de jujube,
Prenions des bains de pied d'un jour dans le Danube.

And the Cholo Mendoza ended by thinking that if this last rhyme remained alive in the Head of State's memory, it was because jujubes for the throat were first cousins to the liquorice pastilles he was so addicted to. And perhaps this mnemonic element was necessary, because it was clear that the mental mechanisms of someone who had plotted, calculated and schemed throughout his very long career, were beginning to become disorganized. On rainy days, for example, after announcing that nothing would induce him to go out, he was impelled by the absurd need to visit a distant bookshop and buy a work by Fustel de Coulanges or the twenty volumes of Thiers' *History of the Consulate and Empire*—which he never even glanced inside when he returned, wet and with a cold in the head, from his useless expedition. Always fond of opera, he took it into his head to put on evening dress and go and hear some sort of a *Manon* at the Opéra Comique, but was bewildered because he didn't see Mephistopheles in the act in Saint-Sulpice. The action of *Carmen* got entangled in his mind with that of the *Barbiere*, because they both took place in Seville; and he muddled up the end of *Traviata* with that of *La Bohème*, because in both the heroine died in the arms of her lover.

In his conversation, too, he often made mistakes, such as saying that Plutarch's history was written in Latin, or that the virus of Spanish influenza was called the Peloponnese. Soon he began dictating a leader on the political situation in our country, but stopped astonished, when well into his discourse, because he realized he had nowhere to publish it. Talking for talking's sake, he appointed and sacked Ministers, planned and decorated imaginary public buildings, and ended by laughing at himself when he returned to reality in front of a bottle of Monsieur Musard's Beaujolais Nouveau. He had a surprising passion for visiting museums. He went to the Carnavalet to look at the toy guillotines. In the Louvre, in front of David's *Coronation*, he observed disconcerting parallels between Letitia Bonaparte and Colonel Hoffmann's Aunt Jemima. He visited the Musée Grévin to see if perhaps (one never knew) he might find a wax figure of himself in one of the rooms. And the Cholo began to be alarmed by the Patriarch's eccentricities one May 5, when he awoke with the fixed intention—luckily half-effaced at noon by news from the homeland—of sending an enormous sheaf of flowers to the Invalides, because it was the anniversary of Napoleon's death on Saint Helena. Yet a certain majesty, a certain strength, gave dignity and style to the person of the old dictator. The dignity and style of despots who have come down in the world; of those whose will has for years and years been law in some part of the globe. It was enough for him to lie down in his hammock for that hammock to turn into a Throne again. When he was swinging in it, with his legs over the edge—now this way, now that, by pulling the cord that controlled it—he became a giant, a horizontal immortal ignored by *Pequeño Larousse*. And then he would talk about *his* armies, *his* generals, *his* campaigns, like the one—do you remember? against the traitor Ataúlfo Galván—and do you remember that night?—but no; it wasn't you—in the thunderstorm in the Cave of the Mummies.

And one morning he woke early talking of it, and suddenly

wanted to visit the museum in the Trocadero. And he went
with the Cholo to that gloomy palace, built in a style com-
pounded of Saragossa, Moorish and the Baron de Haussmann,
with its graceless arcades and false minarets; the custodian was
dozing with his jacket unbuttoned in front of a huge Easter
Island head. (The Patriarch's mind can't have been functioning
very well that morning as he asked the name of the sculptor
of that object.) And they set off through the galleries, each
longer than the last, each containing more canoes, totem birds,
idols bristling with nails, dead gods of dead religions, dusty
Eskimoes, Tibetan horns, and drums piled up in corners—
broken drums, with loose cords, worm-eaten parchment, now
silenced for ever, after having presided at scenes of revelry, or
sounded appeals for rain or calls to revolution.

And thus, going from bone sewing-needles to the ritual
masks of the New Hebrides, from negro amulets to gold
breastplates, from Chaman rattles to stone axes, the Head of
State arrived at what he was looking for: that rectangular
glass case in the middle of the room, mounted on a wooden
base, where that mummy—"I've spoken to you about it so
often"—was eternally sitting: the mummy found in the cave
on the night of the thunderstorm.

A ruinous piece of human architecture, consisting of bones
wrapped in shreds of material, its skin dry, full of holes, worm-
eaten, supporting a skull bound with an embroidered fillet, a
skull whose hollow eyes were endowed with a terrifying
expression; whose hollow nose looked angry in spite of its
absence, and with an enormous mouth battlemented with
yellow teeth, as if immobilized for ever in a silent howl at the
pain in the crossed shin-bones, to which there still adhered rope-
soled shoes a thousand years old, yet seeming new because of
the permanence of their red, black and yellow threads.

And here this thing was still sitting—as it had been *over
there*—only a few paces from Rude's Marseillaise, like some
gigantic fleshless foetus that had gone through all the stages
of growth, maturity, decrepitude and death, a thing that
hardly could be called a thing, a ruined skeleton looking out
through two hollow sockets beneath a repulsive mass of dark

hair that fell in tattered locks on either side of the dried-up cheeks. And this exhumed king, judge, priest or general, was looking out angrily across countless centuries at those who had violated his grave.

He seemed to be looking at me, at me alone, as if to start a conversation, and I said something like: "Don't complain, you bastard, because I took you out of your mud and turned you into a person . . . into a per . . ." Uneasiness, vertigo, collapse. Voices. People arriving . . . And I find myself in my hammock, where the Cholo and the Mayorala have put me to bed. But my legs refuse to obey me. Here they are, where they ought to be, they are mine and yet they are alien to me, because they remain inert and refuse to move. The doctor: Doctor Fournier, much aged. His Legion of Honour. I remember. I lift my fore-fingers to my ears to show him that I can hear and understand.

"It's nothing to worry about," he says, taking a hypodermic syringe out of his bag. And the faces of Ofelia and Elmirita are going round and round my hammock, appearing, coming together, talking, and I'm asleep and I wake up. Again—or has he been here all the time?—here is Doctor Fournier with his hypodermic. And I'm awake. And I feel fine. I think of Monsieur Musard's *Bois-Charbons*. But they say no. Not yet. Very soon. But I can't be so well—although I feel pretty good when they rock me in the hammock—because Ofelia and Elmirita have filled my room with pictures of Virgins. There they are, in rows on the wall, surrounding me, watching over my sleep, present as soon as I open my eyes, the Virgin of Guadalupe, the Virgin del Cobre, the Virgin of Chiquinquirá, the Virgin of Regla, the Virgin of the Coromotos, the Virgin of the Valle, the Virgin of Altagracia, the Paraguayan Virgin of Câácupe, and three or four different pictures of the Divine Shepherdess of my own country, and naval Virgins and military Virgins, Virgins with White faces, Indian Virgins, Black Virgins, virgins of all of us, Ineffable Intercessors, Señoras of help in all trouble, disaster, plague, helplessness or misfortune—all are here with me, covered in gold, silver and sequins, beneath flights of doves, the brightness of the Milky Way and the Music of the Spheres.

"God with me and I with Him," I murmur, remembering a simple prayer I learned as a child. . . .

Convalescence. Elmirita brings me a meal of our own sort—pancake, tamale, stuffed pastries, double egg-flip, custard powdered with cinnamon, the only things that seem to me to taste of anything. I'm beginning to walk fairly well, though now I need a stick. The doctor tells me that soon, perhaps tomorrow, he will let me take a short walk. Perhaps go and sit on a seat in the Avenue du Bois, near the beds of gladioli. Watch the dogs from the great houses romping on the lawns, under the vigilant eyes of the servants of the great houses. Then I'll go in a taxi—my body demands it—to the *Bois-Charbons*. And I suddenly think that it's some time, a long time, since I made love. The last time—when?—was with Elmirita. Now all I ask of her is that she lift her skirts a little— a thing she does with innocent simplicity. It does me good to contemplate, now and again, that firm flesh, well-shadowed with hair, deep, generous: here is transcendent goodness. She has changed very little since the days of my triumphant maturity, and looking at her, I feel a renewal of desire to carry on this brute of a life. Because I'm not beaten yet, no. I take my daily walk now. A little further from the house every day. And one day, I don't know why, I think of the cemetery of Montparnasse where my double, Porfirio Díaz, is buried. (From here I can see through the window the house where his minister Limantour lived.) So we go to the cemetery—the Cholo, Elmira and I—where also lies Maupassant, whose stories are so much read and imitated in our countries. We buy some flowers near Joffin's marble works. And we are taken in tow by the porter, dressed in navy blue like the custodian of the Trocadero.

"Cette tombe est très demandée" (sic).

We pass in front of Baudelaire, whom they buried next to General Aupick—a sinister joke. And now we are with Don Porfirio. A sort of Gothic chapel has been raised above his remains—either a dwarf church or a huge dog-kennel, grey, ogival—where, in an altar under the dedication to the Ineffable One of Tepeac, is a marble ark containing a small quantity of

Mexican earth. And this mediaeval tomb, dated 1915, is presided over by the secular and mythical Eagle and Serpent of Anáhuac.

I think about death. About Baudelaire, so close, although I can't remember those lines of his—my memory is failing badly—which speak of old bones and a deep grave for a body more than dead, dead among the dead. When my time comes, I would like them to bury me here. I tried to make some macabre joke, suitable to our surroundings, to show the others that I wasn't afraid of Death. But nothing occurred to me. We returned to the Rue de Tilsitt in silence. And that evening I lost the use of my legs again. And cramp in my left arm. And those sudden cold sweats in the nape of my neck and on my forehead. And that painful bar across my chest at times, but seeming much more as if it was on my flesh—outside—than beneath it. Doctor Fournier wants them to put me to bed. He says a hammock isn't a bed; that it's folklore, belonging to Indians and Fenimore Cooper. The bloody conceit of these people. They would like to put me in a Louis XIII bedroom, so that I can suffocate under a canopy, or in one of those beds like those at Malmaison, which were so narrow and short that I wondered how Napoleon and Josephine could ever make love in them. In the end they left me to rock in my hammock, which moulds itself to the weight of my body—my body that now seems to be full of buckshot. I go to sleep. When I wake the Cholo tells me that Ofelia and Elmirita have gone to the Sacré Coeur to make vows for my speedy—"and certain"—he added, recovery. Early in the morning they dressed themselves as penitents—or *promesas*, as they say *over there*—in violet dresses, with sandals, but no hat or scarf in spite of the rain, with an orange cord round the waist, and they went up the hill to Montmartre, prostrating themselves on the seats of the funicular, before going on their knees, tapers in hand, up the stairs to the chief altar of the church. I go back to sleep. (When they came out of the sanctuary at Montmartre, the Mayorala insisted on putting some flowers at the feet of a saint on the right, who was alone and unprotected and must be very full of compassion, because he had been put in a place apart, very visible, chained to his post, reliving his martyrdom. She kneels on the wet asphalt . . . She prays . . . But Ofelia brutally forces her to get up, and drags her away from her devotions after reading the inscription at the saint's feet: "To the Chevalier de la Barre, executed at the age of 19 years, on July 1, 1766, for failing to salute a procession." Elmirita doesn't understand how a monument to a heretic can be put up so close to a church. Ofelia decides it would be too tiring to enter into explanations which the zamba would in any case not understand, because to her the word "free-thinker" savours of an anarchist sect or something of the sort.)

I wake up. And Ofelia is leaning over me, in her penitent's dress, and Elmirita in hers, but pouting out her breasts in an automatic gesture very typical of her, forgetting the garment she is wearing. And now a new figure, a nun of Saint Vincent de Paul—but a real one this time—who injects my right arm with a needle. Her headdress is starched, her collar is starched, her apron is starched; her blue dress, the blue of washed-out indigo, reminds me of the North American overalls worn by all the workmen in my country. Candles, such as they've lit in front of the Virgins in my room; candles, just lit and beginning to sweat their wax; little red candles of altar lamps, floating in a cup of oil. Candles that will soon be put round me. I see it in those faces, yellow in the light of so many candles, leaning over my hammock and looking at me with forced smiles, while a pharmaceutical smell pervades everything. I sleep. I wake. There are times when I wake and don't know whether it's day or night. An effort. To my right I hear ticking. What time is it? Quarter past six. Perhaps not. Perhaps it's quarter past seven. More likely. Quarter past eight. This alarm clock would be a marvel of Swiss watch-making but its hands are so slim that one can hardly see them. Quarter past nine. That's not right either. My spectacles. Quarter past ten. That's it. I think so, because—as I notice now—daylight is shining on the pieces of stuff the Mayorala has fixed up to muffle the light which pours into this attic from the skylight in the roof. I think about death, as I do whenever I wake. But I'm not afraid of death. I shall accept it bravely, although I've realized

for some time that death is neither a struggle nor conflict—
mere literature—but a surrender of arms, acceptance of defeat,
dreamlike desire to outwit pain that is always possible, always
menacing, with its accompaniment of hypodermic needles, its
Saint Sebastian martyrdom—the body pierced again and
again—the smell of drugs in the nostrils, dry saliva and the
sinister arrival of cylinders of oxygen, heralding the end as
certainly as the oils of extreme unction. All I ask is to sleep
without physical suffering—although it annoys me to think
of the gang of bastards *over there* who will rejoice to hear of my
death. Anyway, if I want to figure in History I must utter some
phrase when the end comes. A phrase. I remember reading one
in the pink pages of *Petit Larousse*: *"Acta est fabula."*

"What did he say?" asked the Cholo Mendoza.

"Something about a fable," said Ofelia. "Aesop? La
Fontaine? Samaniego?"

"He also spoke of a certificate."

"That's easy to understand," said the Mayorala. "He
didn't want to be buried without a death certificate. Cata-
lepsy . . ." (That was the greatest fear of all country people
over there.) "In my village they buried a man as dead, and as
he wasn't dead he woke in his coffin, and he managed to break
the lid but he could only get one hand through the earth. . . .
And there was another case in la Verónica."

It was Sunday. Ofelia closed her father's eyes and covered
him with a sheet which fell to the ground on both sides of the
hammock like the tablecloth at a feast. Then she opened the
drawer containing the Diamond from the Capitol.

"I'll keep it; it'll be safe. When they've re-established order
in our unfortunate country, and the revolutionaries and
communists can't get hold of this jewel, I'll go myself and
solemnly return it to its proper place at the foot of the Statue
of the Republic."

Meanwhile, until this was possible, the diamond was dropped
into the Infanta's handbag, and there, among powder and
lipsticks it marked the Zero point where all the roads in her
distant country met. But now, Ofelia seemed to be in a hurry:

"The Cholo will see to the matter of the certificate. I don't understand anything about it. And don't announce his death until tomorrow. It's the Day of the Drags today. I must go and get dressed."

And soon there was an unusual noise of horses' hooves and wheels in front of the main gate of the house. Elmirita looked out of the window: there was something like a coach there, with a roof and windows, drawn by four horses, and people perched inside, very like the mule-drawn bus which, when she was a small child and there were no trains, made the journey from Nueva Córdoba to Palmar de Siquire.

"How old-fashioned these people are," thought the zamba. And she saw Ofelia go out in a bright dress, open a white sunshade and climb into the carriage. Whips were cracked and the horses trotted off amidst a great noise of laughter and jollity. One candle in a silver candlestick was burning on each side of the hammock where the body of the Head of State was resting. The nun from Saint Vincent de Paul was saying the rosary. Outside the little balls of the boy-hero were turning gold in the sun.

"What indecency!" said Elmirita, shutting the window before proceeding to dress the dead man, whose corpse would be laid out downstairs in the Great Drawing-room. On the back of a chair hung the last tail-coat he had ordered to be made on the eve of his illness: it was too big now for his thin body. But that would make it easier to get him into it—with the wide crimson band, which had been for so many long years the symbol of his Investiture and Power.

*The creeper grows no higher than
the trees that support it.*

DESCARTES. *Discourse on Method*

1972

22

Grey with heavy rain, not a little snow and years of neglect, the small pantheon with two doric columns still stood in the cemetery of Montparnasse, not far from the tomb of Porfirio Díaz, and close to those of Baudelaire and General Aupick. Anyone gazing into the interior through the black grille protecting a door with glass panes set in gold-coloured metal, would see a simple altar on which stood an image of the Divine Shepherdess—a copy of the image worshipped in her Sanctuary at Nueva Córdoba. At her feet, under a mystic garland of roses and cherubs was a marble ark supported on four jaguars, in which a little of the Earth of the Sacred Soil of the Homeland was kept.

What perhaps some people didn't know was that Ofelia, thinking that the Earth is all one and that the earth of the Earth is earth of the Earth everywhere—*memento homo, quia pulvis est et in pulverem reverteris*—had collected this sacred earth, guarded in perpetuity by the four symbolic jaguars, from a flower-bed in the Luxembourg gardens.

Havana—Paris.   1971–1973

A Note About the Author

Alejo Carpentier y Valmont was born in Havana, Cuba, in 1904. After primary and secondary schooling and a brief time at the University of Havana as a student of architecture, he became a journalist and radio station director. A musicologist as well, he has written a study of Afro-Cuban music and taught the history of music, and his *Invocations* have been set to music by Darius Milhaud. He has also held several positions in the Cuban government, both at home and in the diplomatic corps, and is currently a high-ranking official of the Cuban embassy in Paris.

He is the author of several novels, including *The Lost Steps*, his most famous book, and *The Kingdom of This World*, *Explosion in a Cathedral*, and a collection of stories, *War of Time*. Carpentier has been nominated several times for the Nobel Prize.

A Note on the Type

This book was set on the Monotype in Baskerville
No. 353, a recutting of a type face originally
designed by John Baskerville (1706–75). Baskerville,
a writing master in Birmingham, England, began
experimenting about 1750 with type design
and punch cutting. His first book, set throughout
in his new types, was a Virgil in royal quarto,
published in 1757, and it was followed by other
famous editions from his press. Baskerville's types,
which are distinctive and elegant in design, were a
forerunner of what we know today as the
"modern" group of type faces.

Composed by The Camelot Press Limited, Southampton, Great Britain
Printed and Bound by The Book Press, Brattleboro, Vermont